THE
MAN
FROM
BERLIN

THE
MAN
FROM
BERLIN

A GREGOR REINHARDT NOVEL

LUKE McCALLIN

NO EXIT PRESS

First published in the UK in 2014
by No Exit Press, an imprint of
Oldcastle Books Ltd,
PO Box 394, Harpenden,
Herts, AL5 1XJ, UK

noexit.co.uk
@noexitpress

© 2014 Luke McCallin

ISBN
978-1-84344-547-0 (Print)
978-1-84344-548-7 (Epub)
978-1-84344-549-4 (Kindle)
978-1-84344-550-0 (Pdf)

8 10 9

Typeset in 11pt Minion Pro
by Avocet Typeset, Somerton, Somerset TA11 6RT
Printed in Denmark by Nørhaven, Viborg

*For my wife, Barbara, and
my children, Liliane and Julien.*

*Thank you for sharing this journey with me,
and supporting me all the way.*

With all my love.

ACKNOWLEDGMENTS

I would always read acknowledgments in books, and dream of one day writing my own, and what I would say! What I would say is a big thank you to all those who have helped and supported me over the years since I first dreamt – literally – this story and woke to fumble around for a pen and a piece of paper to jot down the ideas and impressions for what became this novel. I would like to thank in particular those who read all or part of the novel and gave me comments and advice. To my wife, Barbara; my parents, John and Margaret; my sisters, Ellie, Cassie and Amy; to my friends Ben Negus, Mat Buczek, Matt Cousins, Jean Verheyden, Mike Flynn, Severine Rey, Chris Sherrill, Stephanie Naman, Jason Lim, Rick Baker, and Chelsea Starling – thank you all for taking the time to read and critique the drafts, and for helping and encouraging me.

Many thanks as well to my father-in-law, Henri Vacquin, who got the whole plot before anyone else did: I hope one day he'll be able to read this in French! Special thanks go to Chelsea for her work on my website – lukemccallin.com – and for her constant encouragement and advice. Check out her own work at chelseastarling.com. To Ryan Christie and Tamara Davies at Geneva Fitness – thank you for keeping me fit and healthy these past couple of years! To the folks at the Algonkian Pitch Conference – to Michael Neff and his staff – thanks for the opportunity of letting me pitch the novel straight to editors. This book would not have been possible without that.

Many, many thanks as well go to Charles Salzburg for leading the pitch discussions at the Algonkian, and then reading the finished manuscript and putting me in touch with my agent, Peter Rubie, at Fine Print Literary Management. And, of course, thanks to Tom Colgan at Berkley, for listening to my pitch, and to my editor, Amanda Ng, for her patience and attention to detail.

Notes on pronunciation

c	'ts' as in *hats*
č	'ch' as in *starch*
ć	'tch' as in *hatch*
Dj	'dg' as in *fridge*
Dž	'dg' as in *hedge*
J	'y' as in *you*
Lj	'ly' as in *million*
Nj	'nj' as in *new*
Š	'sh' as in *shut*
ž	'zh' as in *measure*

Comparative Chart of SS, German Army, and British Army ranks

WAFFEN SS	WEHRMACHT	BRITISH ARMY
Reichsführer-SS	–	–
–	Generalfeldmarschall	Field Marshal
SS-Oberstgruppenführer	Generaloberst	General
SS-Obergruppenführer	General	Lieutenant General
SS-Gruppenführer	Generalleutnant	Major General
SS-Brigadeführer	Generalmajor	Brigadier
SS-Oberführer	–	–
SS-Standartenführer	Oberst	Colonel
SS-Obersturmbannführer	Oberstleutnant	Lieutenant Colonel
SS-Sturmbannführer	Major	Major
SS-Hauptsturmführer	Hauptmann	Captain
SS-Obersturmführer	Oberleutnant	Lieutenant
SS-Untersturmführer	Leutnant	Second Lieutenant
SS-Sturmscharführer	Hauptfeldwebel	Regimental Sergeant Major
SS-Stabsscharführer	Stabsfeldwebel	Sergeant Major
SS-Hauptscharführer	Oberfeldwebel	–
SS-Oberscharführer	Feldwebel	Staff Sergeant
SS-Scharführer	Unterfeldwebel	Sergeant
SS-Unterscharführer	Unteroffizier	Corporal
SS-Rottenführer	Stabsgefreiter	Lance Corporal
–	Obergefreiter	–
–	Gefreiter	–
SS-Sturmmann	Oberschütze	Private
SS-Oberschütze	Schütze	Private
SS-Schütze	Gemeiner, Landser	Private

Part One

1

Reinhardt shuddered awake, again, clawing himself up from that dream, that nightmare of a winter field, the indolent drift of smoke and mist along the hummocked ground, the staccato line of the condemned and the children's screams. He rolled his feet to the floor, sitting slumped on the side of the bed with his head in his hands, and listened to the calls to prayer sounding in ones and twos from the minarets as the sun rose across the Miljačka valley. Eyes glazed with fatigue, an ache in his head and an acid churn in his belly, he watched without seeing the crawl of light across his room, his mind still floundering to escape the clutches of his dream. He jerked as he smelled smoke, an acrid sting of memory, and blinked it back. Only a memory, but another sign of the inside leaking out more and more into his waking world. He wondered if he was going mad.

With trembling hands he lit a cigarette. His head swivelled to the side as he drew deeply, then tilted back as he exhaled through puffed cheeks, his eyes closed, the hangover beginning to bite. The smoke swelled up above him, rising, dissipating. Reinhardt watched it for a moment then let his head sag over his fingers, curled like a cage around the cigarette. Gingerly, he ran a fingertip across his temple, feeling the dull bruise beneath the skin where, more and more, the weight of his pistol was the last thing he felt at night.

Someone knocked at the door, and he froze, startled out of

the fog of his thoughts. The knocking came again, and his
name, muffled through the door. He put a hand on the bedside
table and pushed himself quietly to his feet, but his arm felt
numb and heavy from where he had slept on it, and it slipped,
slid, and bumped the pistol, which clattered and clinked against
the bottles and glasses.

Reinhardt stared guiltily across the room in the sudden
silence. The knocking came again, louder. He put out his
cigarette, gritting the stub into a whisper of ash; put a hand out
to the wall to steady himself as his left knee gave its usual
twitch; and began to shuffle down the side of the bed. He rested
both hands on either side of the door frame, breathed deeply,
and rolled his head on his neck, feeling the ache skitter around
inside his skull like a steel ball in a bowl, and ran a finger across
the bruise at his temple. Another deep breath, and he threw the
latch back on the door and flung it open.

A soldier stood in the hallway outside, a fist raised to hammer
the door again. Steely eyes regarded him from under the rim of
a field cap, a sergeant's insignia on his broad shoulders. For a
moment there was silence, and Reinhardt realised he must
make quite a sight, his hair tangled, shirt twisted out of his
trousers, and his feet in socks.

'Captain Reinhardt?'

Reinhardt looked at him through the spreading ache behind
his eyes, half recognising him. 'I think you bloody well know
who I am.'

The man put his heels together and saluted. 'Sergeant
Claussen, sir. I have orders for you to report to Major Freilinger
immediately.' The man was built like a boulder, short and squat
with his uniform stretched taut over his chest and belly.

Reinhardt stared at the sergeant. 'To Major Freilinger?' he
croaked. He coughed, swallowed, and tried again. 'Freilinger?
What does he want?'

'There has been a murder, sir,' said Claussen.

'Murder?' Reinhardt put his hand behind his neck and
rubbed it, turning his head from side to side. He thought he saw

Claussen's eyes stray to the mark he was sure was on his temple, and he straightened up. 'What's that got to do with us? This city still has a police force, doesn't it?'

'Major Freilinger instructed me to tell you that one of the victims is a fellow military intelligence Abwehr officer. Lieutenant Hendel.'

'Stefan Hendel? Freilinger said he was Abwehr?' Claussen nodded. 'Very well. Give me ten minutes.'

'Yes, sir. Ten minutes.' Claussen was an experienced NCO. The four green stripes of a master sergeant on his arm were proof of that, and a good NCO knew how to frame a statement to an officer so it sounded like an order. Reinhardt flushed again at the picture he must make, picked up his towel and toiletry bag, and stalked out of his room down the corridor to the bathroom.

He bent over one of the sinks as he felt the churning in his stomach come heaving up. He retched, his head beginning to pound as he doubled over but, as so often, nothing came up, only a sickly rasp of bile, like the viscous residue of his life and work. His stomach calmed, eventually, and he shivered as he stayed bent over the sink, the hammering in his head turning into a dull ache that squatted in the top of his skull.

He rested his head in his hands, eyes pressed into the heels of his palms. Another night and he had hardly slept, and what sleep he managed gave him no rest. Another night spent in the cells under the prison, facing prisoners of war across bare rooms under caustic lights. Another night spent piecing together the puzzles these men represented, pulling together information and intelligence from a dozen other interrogations from the nights and days before them, here and elsewhere. Norwegians, Frenchmen, Englishmen, Australians, Arabs... now Yugoslavs. Partisans. They had all come and gone in front of him since this war started.

The pipes shuddered and coughed a spray of water into the cracked porcelain of the basin. He swallowed a couple of aspirin, drank as much water as he could, then carefully shaved, looking through his reflection. He rinsed off and only then allowed himself to look in the mirror. Not quite as bad as he felt, he saw. Dark blue eyes like pits, cheeks gaunt above the tight line of his mouth, the close-cut cap of his brown hair greying at his temples. An average face. One that would go unnoticed in a group of three men, as his old police instructor used to joke.

He wet his tousled hair, combed it, splashed cologne on his face and water in his armpits, and he was done. He looked in the mirror a last time, wiping away the steam to stare at himself.

'As good as it gets,' he muttered, pulling out the light and walking back to his room. Reinhardt shut the door in Claussen's face, let his trousers puddle around his feet, then peeled off his shirt and let his underpants and socks join the heap on the floor. Outside, the call of the muezzins faded away across the valley that held the town of Sarajevo cradled in its slopes. As if needing to fill the silence, the bells of St. Anthony's, up behind the barracks, began to toll.

Outside came the squeal of the trams at Vijećnica as they went around the corner at the city hall. He twisted his shoulders into his braces, sat to pull on his boots, pausing a moment to stare at the picture of his dead wife in its silver frame on the bedside table, tracing a fall of hair with a fingernail along the glass.

Reinhardt placed the picture gently into a drawer and wound his watch. It was just a cheap Phenix, but winding it always made him think of the watch he had left behind in Berlin with Meissner, for safekeeping. A pocket watch, heavy, old fashioned, a British-made Williamson hunter with an inscription on its silver casing, and the memory of his finding it as vivid as ever.

He shrugged into his jacket, medals and metal clinking dully, closing each button with a firm movement as he stared at the window, thinking of nothing except the day to come and how to get through it. A step at a time, he knew. One after the other. Head down, back bent, eyes no more than two steps ahead, step after step until the day was done. He cinched a wide leather belt around his waist and took his cap from a hook on the wall and his pistol from the tabletop, sliding the gun into the holster with a dull rasp of metal on leather. Looking in the small mirror behind the door he adjusted the fit of his cap, then stuffed a pack of Atikahs and some matches into the pocket of his jacket and opened the front door.

'All right, let's go,' he said, as he locked his door. Claussen straightened, his eyes flicking to the Iron Cross pinned to the left breast of Reinhardt's tunic and back to Reinhardt's face. He saw the change come across Claussen's eyes as a decorated captain in the Abwehr came out of the room a half-drunk, half-dressed man had gone into.

Claussen led the way downstairs and into the cobbled length of the central courtyard of the Bistrik barracks, built by the Austrians at the start of their occupation of Bosnia at the end of the nineteenth century. They walked to a slope-nosed *kübelwagen* where a soldier was smoking a cigarette. He stubbed it out and saluted Reinhardt, his eyes looking up and over the captain's left shoulder. 'Corporal Hueber reporting, Captain,' he snapped. He was tall and raw-boned, cheeks flecked with acne.

'Hueber is our Serbo-Croat specialist,' said Claussen as he opened the *kübelwagen*'s door for Reinhardt. 'Major Freilinger said to bring a translator, just in case our Croat friends decide to forget their German.'

'At ease, Corporal,' said Reinhardt. 'You speak the language?' Reinhardt had picked up something of the language in his two tours in Yugoslavia. More than enough to follow the gist of conversations, order drinks, and scan the headlines of what passed for newspapers. He shook a cigarette from his pack and put it in his mouth.

'Yes, sir. My mother's family was from Zagreb.'

'Carry on, then,' he said, settling into the car. The other two climbed in, and Claussen engaged first with a grind and steered them past the sentries in their striped pillboxes and into the street. Reinhardt wedged his shoulders against the rim of the door and put his arm along the central bar behind the front seats, his hand resting on the empty weapons racks. Remembering the cigarette in his mouth, he lit it, drew deeply, exhaled, then after a moment's consideration offered cigarettes to Claussen and Hueber.

Claussen drove over the Latin Bridge to Kvaternik Street, the old Austrian Appelquai, then followed the trams down to Vijećnica. They travelled past the jumbled Oriental warren of Bentbaša with its uneven cobbled streets and Ottoman houses with white walls and red roofs, and back through the city, past Baščaršija with its cafés dotted around its cobbled sweep. The air was cool this early in the morning, underlaid with the smell of coal and wood smoke, but the clear skies promised another scorcher of a day. Up at the top of Vratnik hill, beyond the jumble of roofs and minarets, the white walls of the old Ottoman fortress stared blankly down on the city.

'What more did Freilinger tell you?' asked Reinhardt as Claussen sped up again down King Aleksander Street. The city's latest masters, the Independent State of Croatia – the NDH – had renamed it Ante Pavelić Street after their version of the Führer, but everyone, even those in charge, still called it Aleksander. At a crossroads, Ustaše policemen – Croatian fascists in black uniforms with rifles strapped across their backs – were pulling down Communist Party posters that must have been put up overnight. The walls on both sides of the road were covered in scraps of white paper where dozens more had been pulled down. More Ustaše stood guard over a group of men kneeling on the pavement with their hands on their heads. Two bodies lay in the street.

Claussen squinted around the cigarette smoke spiralling up into his eyes and slowed to bump the car over a bad patch of road. 'The major only said the murders had occurred at an address in Ilidža.'

'Ilidža?' said Reinhardt. 'That's a bugger of a drive. And I need something to eat.' He scanned the road ahead and motioned for Claussen to pull over while he jumped out and bought *kifla* off a trader in baggy black trousers and a red waistcoat pushing a handcart. The man kept his head down, his eyes sliding over him and past, as if around an absence, but Reinhardt was used to that now.

The bread was warm, soft, and salty-sweet as he chewed and watched the city go by. Down past the gutted ruin of the Sephardic synagogue, past the yellow arches of the city market, past the Imperial façades of Marijin Dvor and the old State House where the general staff had its offices, past the tobacco factory, the white exterior of the National Museum, and the long stretch of wall that hid the Kosevo Polje barracks, and then they were leaving the main part of Sarajevo behind and driving almost due west, the Miljačka valley opening out to north and south.

There was space here you never seemed to find in the city's hunched streets. Orchards and fields running away from the road in long rectangles, the rolling countryside speckled with the four-sided roofs of traditional houses. The old Austrian road was dotted with horse carts, donkey carts, sheep and goats, tradesmen, farmers, women in twos and threes wearing long veils who turned away as the car went past. At the other end was the spa resort of Ilidža, nestled at the foot of the forested swell of Mount Igman, a sort of smaller, cleaner, more spacious counterweight to the city that lay behind them all squeezed in and jumbled up the slopes of the mountains that pinched off the eastern end of the valley.

The drive was a fairly long one, and despite the best efforts of the engineers, the road was not standing up well to the constant pounding of the military traffic along it. Claussen was forever slowing, braking, and swerving around ruts and potholes, but the drive gave Reinhardt time to think, time to recover from his binge, and time to start feeling ashamed of himself. He found his fingers again brushing over the spot on his head to which he had put the pistol, his mind opening again to the emptiness he struggled each night to encompass. With an effort, he tamped down on it, pushed it away, but it was becoming harder not to let the depression and despair he felt at night overwhelm him during the day. Again, he caught Claussen looking at him out of the corner of his eye, and he clenched his right fist tight and held it on his leg.

He tried to think instead about the victim, Hendel. In Sarajevo for three months or so. Prior to that with the Abwehr in Belgrade. He did internal army security and before that was in technical work – radios, cameras and such. Spoke the language fairly well, Reinhardt recalled. Liked the ladies and got out on the town whenever he was off duty. That was pretty much all he knew about him. He could not talk to either of the men with him in the car about anything Hendel might have been working on, so he put his head back and closed his eyes.

He must have dozed off to the vibration of the car because Claussen woke him up as they arrived in Ilidža. Reinhardt's mouth felt thick, but the few minutes' sleep he had snatched seemed to have refreshed him. Claussen turned left at the crossroads in front of the Hotel Igman, another of the Austrians' neo-Moorish constructions, and continued south. Past the twin Austria and Hungary hotels, staring at each other across the round sweep of their lawn where an old gardener in a white fez watched them go by. Several staff cars were parked on the drive in front of the Austria, big, shiny vehicles with pennants at the front and motorcycle escorts. Just after the hotels, Claussen turned onto the beginning of the long alley that led up to the source of the Bosna River. The alley was bounded on both sides by rows of platane trees and by large, elegant villas standing on swaths of lawn. Ahead, on the left, several cars were pulled over between the trees or on the shoulder. A policeman approached as they drew up.

'Tell him we're here to see Major Freilinger,' said Reinhardt to Hueber. The corporal leaned forward in his seat and spoke to the policeman who saluted and motioned them forward. Claussen pulled over behind a Mercedes with Army plates. Beyond that was a pair of local police Volkswagens and an ambulance with a driver behind the wheel.

'I'll go in and find Freilinger,' said Reinhardt to Claussen. 'Take Hueber and see if you can find the chief uniform in charge here, or the unit that responded first. See what they know.'

'Sir,' said Claussen. 'On me, Corporal.' Reinhardt walked over to the gate in the wrought-iron fence that surrounded the house. Built in the Austrian Imperial style, it had cream-coloured walls and two floors above the ground floor. A garage was built on one side of the house, its doors open and a white sports car just inside. A motorbike and sidecar with German Army plates was parked against the wall to the right of the front door, where a policeman stood guard. He was clearly unsure whether to let him in or not, so Reinhardt fixed him with his eyes and nodded to him as he went past and into the house, ignoring him but with his back suddenly tensed, as if for a blow.

Forcing himself to unwind, he stood for a moment with the light breaking to either side of his shadow. The hallway was dim after the clear day outside and he gave his eyes a moment to adjust, removing his cap as he did so. A staircase curved upstairs at the end of the hall, and doors opened off the hallway to the left and right. Framed photographs hung on the walls. From somewhere towards the back of the house, he heard the clink of china and a woman crying.

The wooden stairs creaked solidly under his weight as he went up towards the sound of voices. He breathed deep just before he reached the top and felt it, a gag that pinched the back of his throat as he caught the smell of putrefaction. Breathing slowly, Reinhardt tucked his cap under his arm and walked up the last few stairs.

The stairway opened into a living room, sumptuously furnished, a sofa and armchairs in warm brown leather gathered under a chandelier of washed blue glass. There was a low coffee table, with a bottle of French brandy and two tumblers, atop an Oriental-looking carpet. Two doors led off from the room, to the left and right. Directly in front, cabinets and tables in dark wood lined the walls beneath and between tall windows, and a clock kept soft time on the marble mantelpiece below a huge mirror in a worked gold frame. A portrait photograph of a man in a black uniform stood next to the clock, with a black band running laterally across the bottom right corner.

More Oriental carpets were laid out in other parts of the room, some of them rumpled, stained with the alcohol that had run from the bottles smashed across the floor from where they had fallen out of the drinks cabinet, itself lying facedown in shards of glass. A lamp on the floor, pokers strewn around the fireplace. One of the leather chairs askew, out of line with the others. And everywhere, lingering underneath it all, incongruous in this setting of refined luxury, was the smell of death.

Hendel's body lay just to the right of the stairs, against the wall, with its torso slumped partly upright. A spray of blood and something darker had dribbled and dried down the wall above his head. He had been shot just below the nose, and from the burn marks around the wound the gun had been placed against his skin. Reinhardt's right hand began to rise again of its own volition towards his temple and to the mark his own pistol had made there, but he covered it with a move to adjust the tuck of his cap under his other arm.

There was another smear of blood on the wall next to the door to the left. Freilinger was standing by that door with a big man in a dark but ill-fitting suit, both of them looking into the room beyond, which seemed to be brightly lit. Freilinger turned and saw Reinhardt standing by the hallway door. The major's bullet head of close grey hair almost glowed in the strong light. As Freilinger's eyes met his, Reinhardt suppressed a flinch at the sudden smell of smoke, there and gone just as fast. Swallowing, and looking left and right, Reinhardt walked across the living room, the parquet squeaking under his steps. His feet crunched on glass. Looking down, he saw a crescent of broken bottle with a Hennessy label, gold on black, like a piece of flotsam on the parquet floor.

Freilinger and the other man stepped away from the door, motioning Reinhardt over to the fireplace between the two tall windows. Glancing left, Reinhardt looked into a bedroom, saw part of a huge four-poster bed hung with silk, dark wood floors. He turned back to the two men, came to attention.

'Reinhardt reporting as ordered, Major.'

'This is Chief Inspector Putković, of the Sarajevo police. We have a problem, Reinhardt,' said Freilinger, getting straight to the point as always. Freilinger had always maintained some distance between himself and Reinhardt, despite the common connection they had in Meissner, going back to the first war. 'A double homicide, and one of the victims an army officer. Not only that, but an officer in military intelligence.' He spoke quietly, his voice underlaid by a low, hoarse rasp, the legacy of a British gas attack in the first war. Speaking was painful for him. 'This causes some jurisdictional problems, as you can well imagine, but I think the inspector and I have been able to come to a suitable arrangement.'

The inspector in question did not look like he felt a suitable arrangement had been reached at all. The man was big, in the way so many men in the Balkans seemed to be. Lots of fat on large bones. A taut paunch sagged over his belt, and his fists were like hams, the knuckles indented in the flesh. A porcine face, flat eyes that looked like anvils. He smelled of sweat and alcohol. 'There is no need for German involvement. My men can handle this.' His German was good, although heavily accented. He spoke to Freilinger, but his eyes bored into Reinhardt. 'We are professionals.'

'Quite frankly, I don't care, and I'm getting tired of saying it,' rasped Freilinger. Putković's face went florid with his anger. 'There are agreements and protocols for this sort of thing. I don't care who the dead girl is. A German officer is dead. The two seem to me quite obviously to be linked together, however much you might not want them to be. You'll work with Captain Reinhardt, who, I will remind you, has nearly twenty years as a detective in the Berlin Kriminalpolizei. Homicide and organised crime.' He paused for breath but raised a hand to forestall the next protest from the Croat. 'You will extend him every courtesy required. If you still wish to debate this, tell your commander to take it up with the general. Otherwise, we're done.'

Putković's jaws clenched. He stuck out his jaw, nodded, and then started for the stairs, clattering down them and hollering something to someone on the way out. Freilinger breathed out, shaking his head and putting his hand on the mantel of the fireplace. 'God, what a bore.' He looked up at Reinhardt. Freilinger was a small man, wiry, with piercing blue eyes. His skin was leathery and creased from a lifetime of soldiering. 'This is no picnic I've landed you in, Reinhardt.'

'No, sir.'

'What do you have going at the moment?'

'Third round of interrogations of the Partisan officers captured after Operation Weiss.'

'Still?'

'It's the way I work, sir,' wishing, as always, he did not sound so defensive about it.

Freilinger stared down at the carpet. 'Very well,' he said. 'Hand them over to the camp authorities.'

'Sir, I'm not finished with them.'

'You are now. You won't have time for them anyway.' Freilinger lifted his eyes, flicked them around the room. 'The reason I want you on this is Hendel was one of ours, and we keep this investigation close. I'm having Weninger and Maier go over his files, see if anything pops out that would link him to the dead girl.' He paused as he took a small tin of French mints from his pocket, which he swore were the only thing that helped his throat, and popped one in his mouth. It was, as far as Reinhardt knew, the only habit or vice he had. 'The dead girl is Marija Vukić.' Reinhardt's eyes widened. 'You've heard of her?'

'Marija Vukić? Yes, I have. I even met her once.'

'Sort of a cross between Leni Riefenstahl and Marika Roekk?' Reinhardt shrugged, nodded. 'A filmmaker. A journalist. Well connected. And with a film star's looks?' Reinhardt nodded again, remembering the one time he had met her, and the impression she had made on him. 'The Croats want whoever did this to her for themselves. I'm not sure they're too bothered about Hendel, but if they can find a way to embarrass us with his death, they'll probably try. They already have their list of usual suspects. I don't doubt they'll be breaking bones down at police headquarters fairly soon.'

'I can perfectly understand the Croats' preoccupation with finding the killer. Are you saying we're in competition for suspects?'

'Possibly. Possibly not. Maybe Hendel was killed after Vukić. But on the bright side, Putković has agreed to have Hendel examined by the police pathologist. It'll save us time. We'll know more then.'

'Yes, sir.' Reinhardt nodded, feeling a sudden sense of trepidation. In the hollow at the base of his spine he began to sweat. 'Sir, shouldn't the Feldgendarmerie have this one?'

Freilinger stared at Reinhardt, his chin moving as he rolled the mint around inside his mouth. 'I'll make sure the military police know you are leading this investigation, and that they give you whatever assistance you require. They've got enough on their plate with Operation Schwarz coming up, I would think. All eyes and effort's going to be on that, on prising the Partisans down from out of their mountains and smashing them once and for all. And, like I said, Hendel was one of ours. We'll take care of it.' He paused, his fingers rubbing his throat. Thumb on one side, forefinger on the other. 'I don't know who the police'll give you to work with, but try to be civil, and try to be quick.' A swallow, the mint clicking against his teeth. 'No one's pretending the "Independent" in NDH means anything anymore. Especially now that just about every soldier they ever had that was worth anything is dead at Stalingrad.' If he noticed Reinhardt's discomfort at the mention of that city, he did not show it. 'Relations are tense. Let's see if we can't keep these on an even keel.'

'I'll do my best, sir.' Freilinger nodded. 'One thing, sir. You do know that I haven't attended a crime scene in over four years?'

The major looked back at him, his blue eyes like chips of glass, and a sudden flare, like a fire, deep within them, and again there was the smell of smoke in his nose. 'That will be all, Reinhardt. I've assigned Claussen to you. He's Abwehr, so you can talk freely with him. He's also ex-police. He's a resourceful man, and even if he does not look that way now you'll appreciate having a friendly face around. Report to me at the end of the day.'

'Do I wait for Putković's man before starting?' The major walked to the window over the alley. Heated words were being exchanged out there.

'I'm guessing Putković's man is being briefed now.' Reinhardt looked down at the big detective talking loudly with a handful of policemen, one in a suit. Putković emphasised whatever points he was making by slapping one fist into the palm of the other. Even from up here, Reinhardt could hear the meaty thud they made. There was a space around the man the others would not, or could not, enter. Not surprising, given the animal ferocity the man gave off. Freilinger shook his head. 'Get going. Let them catch up.'

With that, he was gone. Standing alone, Reinhardt put his hands on the mantel and breathed deeply. He hung his head down between his arms, feeling the strain in the back of his neck. His headache was still there, heavy along the base of his skull. He looked at the portrait. A father? An uncle? A quick breath, and he stepped into the bedroom.

2

A middle-aged man, very thin and white, sprawled in a chair in a corner, polishing his glasses on his tie. He blinked owlishly at Reinhardt and said something in Serbo-Croat. 'German,' replied Reinhardt in German. The man put his glasses on, spotted Reinhardt, and half raised himself from the chair.

'Sorry,' he said, sitting back down. 'Dr Begović.' He appraised Reinhardt with an openness strangely refreshing from someone in a city where most people would not meet your eyes, and those who did always seemed to find something wrong with you. 'Forgive me for not getting up, but I've been here for hours now.' He scratched the corner of his mouth. 'You're the one they've been arguing about, eh?'

'It would seem,' replied Reinhardt, distantly. He mentally pushed the doctor aside and remained in the doorway. The bed was a big four-poster, directly in front of the door. A black dress made a crumpled ring on the floor at the end. There was a dresser with an oval mirror and upholstered stool against the wall to his left. Closed curtains ate the daylight along the wall to the right, but the light in the room was still very bright. There were two little tables on the end of the bed nearest him, on which rested two lamps, which were lit. Lights fitted into the wall to either side of the door were also lit, and the head of the bed was a big mirror. He saw himself reflected in the doorway and saw another big mirror hanging on the wall to his right.

His nose caught a subtle hint of fragrance, something expensive, under the heavy smell of blood, and the smell of death, which was much stronger here. The red stain on the door frame, a smear of blood across a panel of light switches, caught his eye. He saw another, a footprint, a third, a smear on the door of what he saw was the bathroom across to his left, as though a hand had reached for balance and slipped and slid. He breathed deeply, and Begović looked from him to the body on the bed.

'Not pretty, is it?' he said, with an ironic twist to his mouth.

Reinhardt's heart began beating faster. He took a couple of steps closer to the bed and looked down at what was on it. 'No, it's not. So. Why don't you tell me what we have here?' he asked, with a nonchalance he did not feel.

Begović took off his thick-framed glasses and rubbed his watery eyes with the heel of his hand. Putting them back on, he blinked furiously, peered at Reinhardt, sniffed, then looked down at a notebook he pulled from a pocket. 'What we have is a dead female, aged twenty-five to thirty years, deceased from approximately eighteen stab wounds to the stomach, upper chest and upper arms. In addition, there are signs of severe beating, strangulation marks around the neck, hair missing. There is blood and tissue under the fingernails, bruising on the knuckles, so she fought back. What little good it did her.'

Reinhardt nodded, listening to Begović reel off the horror that had happened to this woman. It did not do justice to what he saw laid out on the bed in front of him. Reinhardt remembered Marija Vukić as a stunning woman, statuesque, blond, a woman of grace and elegance. She still was, despite what the beating had done to her face, and the knife to the rest of her. Her eyes still kept a clarity of blue behind the veil that death had drawn over them. Her long blond hair still retained a sheen of gold despite its lying in matted disarray across sheets sodden red with her blood. Her skin, though, was ghostly white, the wounds the knife had left crusted and raw edged. Her limbs were long and straight, her legs gorgeous in black stockings, a garter belt around her narrow waist. She lay on the bed as if at rest, head on the pillow, arms at her sides, her legs drawn straight and together. The remains of a silk negligee, shredded and soaked in blood, lay rumpled about her torso.

As he ran his eyes over her, over what had been done to her, Reinhardt felt a peculiar sensation, a sort of fulfilment of an almost-forgotten imagining of what she might look like unclothed. Whatever it was, it felt wrong, but he recalled dancing with her, just the one dance, feeling her pressed lightly against him, her breast against his arm, her thigh against his.

'Your German is very good, Doctor. Murder weapon?'

'Thank you. Medical studies in Berlin in the thirties. A knife. A big one. Very sharp. Something like a kitchen knife, or a bayonet.'

'Has it been found?'

'Not that I'm aware of.'

'Time of death?'

'At a guess, I'd say sometime late on Saturday night.'

'Did you look at the other body?'

'Briefly. I was told to concentrate on this one. But I'd have said he died about the same time.'

'Has forensics had a look at her, yet?'

Begović snorted. '*Forensics?!* Seriously? In *this* town? This isn't Berlin, my friend, and we aren't the Kripo.'

'Right,' Reinhardt breathed. What the doctor said would have been true of the Kriminalpolizei about ten years ago, but not anymore. He raised the dead woman's arm by placing his wrists above and below hers so as to avoid leaving his own prints and saw the telltale marks of lividity underneath and on what he could see of her back. Reinhardt bent her arm, and it moved fairly well. Rigor mortis had come and was mostly gone. Begović was probably right with his guess, but they would need the pathologist to be sure.

The sound of someone taking the stairs two by two came from the other room. There was a pause as the person reached the top, and then the sound of the parquet as he came over to the bedroom. Reinhardt turned as the man in the suit he had seen from the window entered the room. Another tall man, but without Putković's weight. He had longish brown hair, and dark, flat eyes. He glanced over the room and at the two of them standing there. His mouth firmed, and he stepped inside the room. 'You are Reinhardt?' he said. 'I am Inspector Andro Padelin. From the Sarajevo police. My chief informs me we are to work together?'

'That's correct.' Reinhardt stepped over to shake his hand. Not a small man himself, Reinhardt felt his hand enveloped in the other's fist and squeezed, relatively hard. All the while Padelin looked at him with those dead eyes. It was he who let go, with a slight push, and the faintest of glances up and down, from Reinhardt's boots to his greying hair. 'Have you been briefed?' Padelin nodded. 'The doctor here was just giving me some insight into the wounds the woman sustained.'

Padelin turned those heavy eyes on the doctor, who did not seem perturbed. Probably because he had his glasses off again to polish them. 'Yes. Well, it would have been courteous to wait.'

'Shall we hear what he has to say, then?' asked Reinhardt. Padelin nodded, slow and heavy, like a cat sunning itself. 'Doctor, if you please?'

Begović cleared his throat. 'Well, for what it's worth, whoever did it was probably left-handed. Probably. That's from the pattern of the wounds. The stab wounds go from her right to her left. The slashing wounds from her left to her right. And she received nearly all her wounds here, in this room and on the bed.'

'Slashing and stabbing...' said Reinhardt, quietly. 'What does that tell you, Doctor?'

The coroner stared at her arm where it sagged stiffly over the side of the bed, the palm and fingers dark with blood. 'I would guess from the depth of the wounds that whoever did it was not very strong. But from the spread of the wounds, the killer was slashing and stabbing wildly, maybe in a great hurry, or was deranged, or had strong reason to hate her. Maybe a combination of all.'

Still staring at the body, Reinhardt shook an Atikah from his pack and put it in his mouth, before offering the pack to Begović and Padelin. The detective refused with a shake of the head, while Begović pounced eagerly on his cigarette, rolling it delicately between his fingers before letting Reinhardt light it. The flare from his match woke answering glints in Vukić's eyes, and the memory of dancing with her under a spreading chandelier came to him again. A Christmas dance, just a few months ago, for the officers of the garrison, the city caked in snow and ice. She had smiled and laughed, joked and cajoled, given as good as she got with the banter, posed for photographs, danced with them, then left, all light and movement, and a scent that glittered. A smell of tobacco tangled with the iron scent of the woman's blood, clamouring across the memory of that evening. Reinhardt swallowed and took a little round tin from his hip pocket, into which he tapped his ash.

'He beat her, then stabbed her?'

'Could be,' said Begović, around a deep drag. He tore a page from his notebook and crumpled it in his hand to serve as an ashtray.

Reinhardt stared at her. At the rumpled sheets. A champagne glass with a thick smudging of fingerprints stood on a bedside table. On the other side of the bed, on a similar table, was an ashtray with a number of stubbed ends. 'Was there sex?' As he moved slightly, the surface of the table caught the light. A ring mark, faint and almost faded.

'Dressed like that?' Begović quipped. 'I would certainly hope so.' Padelin snarled something at him in Serbo-Croat. Begović sat up a bit straighter in the chair and answered back, but Padelin cut him off. Begović sighed and switched back to German. 'I don't know. I can't tell. The pathologist will know, soon enough.'

'You said most of the wounds she got here on the bed. Where did it start? The stabbings, I mean.' Reinhardt got down on his hands and knees to peer under the bed, squinting around the curl of smoke that drifted across his eyes.

Begović stared down at Reinhardt's back and pointed unnecessarily with his notebook to the foot of the bed. 'There, I think. A spray of blood across the bed hangings. Find something under the bed?' Padelin knelt to see what Reinhardt had seen. He straightened up.

'And is a forensics team coming?' Reinhardt asked Padelin.

'Yes.'

Reinhardt studiously made a point of not looking at Begović, himself engrossed in watching the tip of his cigarette burn. 'Make sure they know there's a bottle and a glass, probably not the woman's, under the bed.' He looked around the room, at the drawn curtains and the lights. 'Do you know whether the room was lit like this when the police arrived?' he asked Padelin.

'I can ask the maid.'

'Please do,' said Reinhardt. 'Are you nearly finished?' he asked Begović.

'Yes. Why do you think it's not the woman's?' asked Begović.

Reinhardt pointed at the glass on the table. 'She lived here. Stands to reason she'd use the side of the bed nearest the bathroom.'

Begović nodded, his mouth making an O. 'Well, I'm all done, unless you gentlemen need something else?'

Reinhardt looked at Padelin questioningly. The big detective shook his head. 'Wait downstairs, please, Doctor.'

'Shall we have a look in the bathroom?' asked Reinhardt, as the doctor left. He dropped his cigarette stub into his little tin and pocketed it, letting Padelin go first, watching. The detective walked right in, standing in the middle of the room. Reinhardt paused in the doorway. It was lavishly equipped, with a huge white bath, gold taps, an ornate showerhead. Tiles in a repeating blue-and-gold motif ran around the room at waist height, and a mirror in a mosaic frame that looked Spanish hung over the sink. Toothbrush, toothpaste, French cosmetics on the white enamel sink. Towels and brushes on a set of tall wrought-iron shelves, from which hung a black silk dressing gown. And luxury of luxuries, a toilet with a shiny wooden seat.

Casting an eye around the room, Reinhardt spotted the blood marks on the wall on either side of the toilet, and a bloody towel wadded up and thrown into a corner. Large as the room was, Padelin filled the space with his bulk, watching Reinhardt with those dead, catlike eyes. Reinhardt peered into the toilet, but it was empty. Blood marks on either side of the sink, as if someone with blood on their hands had leaned on it for balance or support. He stared around the room once more, trying to imagine what had happened and what he might be missing. Putting his tongue between his teeth, he sighed, turned and walked out, back into the bedroom.

Padelin joined him there. 'The maid is waiting to be questioned,' he said, quietly. His German was slow and ponderous.

Reinhardt nodded. 'I need to have a look at the other body first.'

'You do that,' said Padelin, in a tone that implied Hendel was all Reinhardt's. 'I will see what she has to say.'

3

Hendel had been poster-boy good-looking. Chiselled features, blue eyes, blond hair. The works. Looking up at the wall, Reinhardt could see where Hendel's head had struck it, traced the long smear of blood the body's sliding fall had left before it came to rest there, shoulders slumped across the skirting board, one ankle crossed beneath the other. Hendel was in uniform, but whoever had shot him had emptied his pockets and removed his rank insignia, hoping, Reinhardt guessed, to delay identification. It would have worked, if one of the Feldgendarmes who responded to the call had not recognised him.

For once, Reinhardt thanked Hendel's habit of staying out late with the ladies and the number of times the Feldgendarmerie must have fingered him stumbling back to barracks late and drunk. He lifted Hendel's leg by the boot. As with Vukić, the rigor mortis was almost gone. He could not have died much more than a day ago. Definitely about the same time as her.

Reinhardt walked across the living room and entered a study. To his left, a tall window looked out on the garden. Against one wall was a large, heavy-looking table, the wood worn smooth and rich with age, but he did not pay much attention to it because above it, and arranged haphazardly all over the wall, were photographs in black frames. In most of them, Marija Vukić stared or laughed or pouted out at him with an intensity that made his stomach suddenly clench, remembering how they had talked at that dance. Not for long, mostly about Reinhardt's time in the first war, but for as long as he had talked she had listened with a particular intensity, blue eyes boring into his.

Marija in flying gear, posing next to the wing of an old biplane. Marija with her hair flying about her face as she looked down from the railing of a ship, an elderly man at her side. Marija swathed in robes and turban on a camel, two Africans either side of her. Marija at a table filled with people, the glare from the flash reflected in the glasses of champagne in front of them. Pictures of Berlin, Paris, Trafalgar Square almost blotted out by a flock of pigeons caught in the moment of lifting off. Places in Africa, in Asia. Pictures of people, Germans, French couples on café terraces, families picnicking on lawns, Japanese in traditional dress, Africans, soldiers.

Lots of pictures of soldiers. A man in an old Austrian Imperial Army uniform leaning on a rifle in a trench with his feet in water. A mutilated soldier slumped against a brick wall, outstretched hand holding a begging bowl. A picture of an officer on horseback. Columns of infantry, Germans, with slung rifles, blond hair blowing in the breeze. Reinhardt swallowed in a suddenly dry throat, eyes drawn back and caught by that soldier with his head down, begging. *There but for the grace of God*, he thought…

From downstairs came the sudden sound of a man shouting. Faint, beneath it, a woman crying. Frowning in distaste, Reinhardt looked away from the begging soldier and found himself staring at a picture of the Führer. Whoever had taken it had shot him through a crowd of uniforms, black sleeves, and swastikas, some with the Ustaše armbands, and all the faces were looking one way with expressions of anticipation and delight, but *he* was looking straight at the camera, away from everyone else, face utterly expressionless. Reinhardt shivered suddenly, turned his head away.

Down the other wall were shelves filled with books and objects, floor to ceiling. Reinhardt cast a cursory eye over them as he walked slowly over to the other door, which was closed. Taking a handkerchief from his pocket, he opened it slowly, pushing the door open onto darkness, a faint suggestion of surfaces and cabinets appearing out of the gloom, and a smell of chemicals that peaked and faded, as if it had just been waiting for the door to be opened. Peering around the door, he found the light switch, flicked it on. It was a darkroom, and it had been ransacked. Photos blanketed the floor, cabinet doors were open, a drawer lay on the floor. Bottles of fluid, brushes, clips, and string stood or lay strewn across work surfaces. A pair of scissors lay in an empty enamel sink.

'Shit,' muttered Reinhardt. He took a step into the room, knelt, and looked down at the photos scattered across the floor. Soldiers again, most of them. Modern photos, and recent as well, if he was any judge of uniforms. He brushed aside a photo to reveal one of what looked like Afrika Korps soldiers, men swathed in scarves and dust riding atop tanks in column and, for a moment, he was back there with them under that baking sun. Another one, Marija with goggles drawn down around her throat with a man in uniform, a minaret needling the sky behind them, a swath of sea the backdrop to it all. Frowning, Reinhardt leaned closer, then smiled in admiration. The man was Rommel, peaked cap, leather coat, binoculars and all, just as in the pictures. There were steps behind him, and Claussen came to a stop in the doorway.

'Sir?'

'A moment, Sergeant.' Reinhardt straightened and ran his eyes around the room, over the jumble of pictures and paraphernalia that littered the surfaces. There was a cupboard under the sink with its door ajar, and something metallic glittered back at him. Stepping carefully, he reached out and pulled the door open wider. A couple of film cases, round tins of various sizes, stood haphazardly in a curved rack that was otherwise empty. The tins had been opened, and the beginning of each roll of film had been unwound, then put back. He reached in and took the end of the nearest roll between his fingertips and turned and lifted it to the light. He passed the strand of film through his fingers but it was blank. The rest of the rack, where there was space for a couple of dozen tins, was empty. He nodded to Claussen.

'The uniforms told us the neighbour might have seen something.'

'Anything else?'

'Not really, sir, and I was free with the smokes. Hueber did most of the talking, but they're being pretty close-lipped. Especially after that big fellow gave them a right beasting before he left.'

'Yes, I saw that.'

Reinhardt looked around the room again. He doubted he would be back so whatever he needed to take in terms of impressions or conclusions from the murder scene, he needed them now. Taking a deep breath, he turned back into the study, looking down its length, running his eyes over the books in a half dozen languages, objects that looked like they had been collected in a dozen countries.

'Bloody hell, sir,' came Claussen's voice from the darkroom. 'There's pictures of her here with about every general in the Wehrmacht. Guderian. Hoth. There's one here with Kesselring. One with Goering…' Claussen's voice trailed off into muttered remarks.

Taking his handkerchief from his pocket again, Reinhardt opened the desk drawers one by one but saw no sign of anything that looked like an address book. Straightening, he looked back at the bookcase. On a bottom shelf, next to the door, he spotted a gap, books missing. Squatting, he ran his eyes over them. They were all of differing sizes and textures, but each one was carefully annotated along the spine with dates. He opened one or two at random. They were journals, or diaries. They went back a long way, until 1917, the later years covered by two, even three books. The writing was wide and childish in the earlier ones, closer and neater, denser, in the later ones. Pursing his mouth he stared at where the journals for 1942 and 1943 once were. Looking around, he noticed how much it resembled a man's room, rather than a woman's.

Claussen was standing not far away, seemingly absorbed in the picture of the begging soldier. Reinhardt straightened up. 'Sergeant?' he said softly.

Claussen turned and looked at him, then back at the picture. 'You know, for a moment, I thought that it looked like a friend,' he said softly. 'Boeckel. Poor sod got most of himself blown off at Naroch.' The sergeant shook his head, and Reinhardt left him to it, running his eyes over the room one last time and walking back into the living room.

Standing in the centre of the room he looked around, turning slowly, trying to imagine what had happened. There were two glasses on the coffee table. There was a fight. Someone kills the soldier. Takes Vukić into the bedroom, rapes her, beats her. Stabs her to death. No. That did not feel right. Besides, there were the champagne glasses in the bedroom. Vukić and whoever was with her, they took their time, had fun about it. So what went wrong? And why was Hendel shot, when Vukić was stabbed? He looked from the bedroom to Hendel's body, the study, the ransacked darkroom. Back to the bodies, where Hendel lay sprawled across the floor, and Vukić, seemingly at rest on her bed.

Someone was looking for something, came the thought. Searching the study, the darkroom. But they heard a noise… He shook his head. It felt elusive, too light. Not enough evidence.

He turned as Claussen came into the room. 'I'm going to go and find my new partner. Inspector Padelin.'

'He'll be the one giving the maid hell, would he?' quipped Claussen. As they arrived at the stairs, Reinhardt paused, looking up as the sound of voices drew him down.

'Sergeant, have a quick look up there. Don't touch anything. Just see what's there.'

The kitchen was as well appointed as the bathroom upstairs. On a chair in a corner, with Padelin looming over her, sat an elderly lady in a neat black uniform and a cleanly pressed and starched apron. Her hair was grey, tied up behind her head in a bun. She swallowed a sniff as he came into the kitchen and rose quickly to her feet, did a little curtsy. Reinhardt watched her the whole time, saw the fear shoved back in watery little eyes at the sight of him, but the urge he once had to reach out and calm people like her was long gone, quashed deep inside him. It only ever confused them anyway; people did not expect sympathy and understanding from people like him, not anymore.

He looked questioningly at Padelin, who looked down impassively at the maid. She shook her head, not able to look up at him and whispered something into a crumpled handkerchief.

'She has told me what she knows.'

'I look forward to hearing it,' said Reinhardt. He glanced around the kitchen again. It was neat, tidy, smelling of polish and a faint smell of spices. The only thing drawing his eye was a padlock hanging from a tall cupboard door by the stairs. 'Just ask her one thing, if you would. Does she know where her mistress kept an address book?' Padelin rapid-fired a question at the maid, who peered at him over the ripple of her knuckles. She looked at Reinhardt as she replied, gesturing upstairs. She sniffed as Padelin answered for her, her eyes flickering back and forth between the two of them, hands clenched hard around her handkerchief.

'Upstairs in the study. A red leather book.'

'It would seem it's gone.'

As the two of them went out into the hallway, Claussen came downstairs. Padelin looked hard at him, and then at Reinhardt. 'Who is this?'

'This is Sergeant Claussen. He is assisting me.' Claussen nodded cordially at Padelin.

'What were you doing up there?'

'Checking the top floor. There's nothing there, sir,' he said to Reinhardt. 'All the rooms have been closed up for a while. Sheets over the furniture. It hasn't been cleaned in a while. My boots left marks in the dust, and mine were the only tracks up there.'

Padelin said nothing, only stared at Claussen. Claussen, unfazed, stared back. 'And the ground floor, Inspector? What do we have down here?'

The detective turned his eyes slowly from Claussen. 'Downstairs was the father's apartments. The parents were divorced, said the maid. Father and daughter lived here. But he was killed last year by Četniks, and the maid said these rooms have not been used since then.' He turned and went back outside.

Reinhardt and Claussen exchanged glances. 'Sergeant, quickly, go upstairs and have a look at the bodies. Just look at them. I'll ask you later what you think.' Claussen nodded, and then Reinhardt followed Padelin out, holding back when the detective began talking to three uniformed policemen. Hueber was hovering nearby, and Reinhardt motioned to him to listen to what was being said while he went back over to their car.

Padelin gave a flurry of orders to his men, then came over to Reinhardt's car. Reinhardt offered him a cigarette, which he again refused. Lighting his own, he waited for the detective to tell him what the maid had said.

'The last time the maid saw Vukić was Saturday morning. She was asked to prepare food and drinks for Vukić and a guest. A man. She does not know who the man was, but she's positive it wasn't to be your officer. Hendel, she knew. This other one, she didn't.' Reinhardt took a deep pull on his cigarette and nodded for him to continue. 'She has Sunday off. She came in this morning, found the bodies, and called the police. According to her, when Vukić wasn't travelling, she kept a busy social agenda. Lots of parties and outings. People coming and going.'

'Very good. So we need to find some of these friends. Talk to them. See what they know.'

Padelin grunted assent, those eyes flat, far back in his head. 'That is for us, I think.'

Reinhardt pursed his mouth and stared at the ground. Not much to go on, his new partner already playing jurisdiction games, and they were the best part of two days behind the killer, or killers. He raised his head. 'There is something I heard about a witness who might have seen something on the night of the murder?'

Padelin blinked slowly and nodded. 'Hofler. The old lady across the alley. She saw a car on Saturday night.'

'Hofler? A German? I'd like to talk to her. Coming?'

4

The two of them headed over the narrow road and away from Vukić's house. The houses up here were beautiful, set in large lawns, with all the space the city lacked. 'Who lives up here?' Reinhardt asked, as they walked.

Padelin glanced around as he spoke. 'Only the rich live out here. Bankers. Lawyers. Businessmen.'

'And how did Vukić come by the house she was in?'

'The maid said it was her grandfather's.'

Reinhardt nodded. 'And the father? What happened to him? The Serbs got him?'

Padelin's strides were heavy, his arms hanging almost unmoving from his wide shoulders. 'Yes. The father was a senior Ustaše official,' he said, referring to the governing political party in the NDH. The Ustaše were fascists, and quite incredibly brutal about it, to the extent that their excesses sometimes even turned the stomachs of their German allies, and had thrown up two main resistance movements in Bosnia: the Četniks, Serb nationalists and royalists led by a former colonel in the Yugoslav Army called Mihailović, and the more formidable Partisans, who were Communists and, far more worryingly, multiethnic, led by a man known only as 'Tito'. 'Četniks killed him in an ambush in Herzegovina, down near Gacko.' He turned at a house a couple of hundred metres up from Vukić's, with a high, pointed roof and walls of red brick. Reinhardt finished his cigarette and tossed the butt onto the road as Padelin rang the doorbell and heard a dog bark somewhere inside. A maid dressed in a neat, black uniform with a white lace apron answered the door. She ushered them in and asked them to wait a moment in the hallway while she announced them. She whispered down the hall and vanished into the main living room. A shrill, imperious sounding voice rang out in Austrian-accented German.

'But of *course*! *Show* them in, show the brave officers in!'

The maid reappeared at the entrance to the living room, and beckoned them forward. They paused at the door while she took Reinhardt's hat, and even Padelin seemed somewhat overwhelmed by the sheer volume of lace and frills in the living room, such that it took them a moment to spot Frau Hofler, sitting with her back regally straight in an armchair with ornate wooden arms. She wore a flowing dress of a creamy colour and fabric that fell and pooled around her feet and looked like it might have been fashionable in Vienna in the last century. A small dog sat upon her lap, a pink bow tying its hair back above beady black eyes. Hofler sat with the light behind her, grey hair forming a halo around her head. A heavy smell of perfume and talcum powder deadened the still air.

'*Officers!*' she gushed as they came in, her eyes lingering on Reinhardt. She wore heavy red lipstick that split in a smile to reveal teeth far too white and even to be real on a person of her age. She held out a frail-looking hand, a ring on each finger. '*Do* come in,' she said, fluttering her hand like a piece of paper caught in a breeze. The two moved into the room, walking carefully around small tables and display stands that held a profusion of porcelain figurines. 'Sit down. Sit down there. *There*, on the sofa.' Padelin inched his bulk onto a wickerwork sofa strewn with cushions. It groaned under his weight, shifting and squeaking. Padelin looked straight at the old lady, his face carefully blank. Reinhardt hid a smile and took a chair to the left of Frau Hofler. She looked between the two of them, a broad smile deepening the wrinkles around twinkling eyes.

'Well!' she exclaimed, beaming proprietorially at them.

'*What* can I do to help two such fine-looking servants, one of our dear Fatherland, and the other of our dear Poglavnik? But *no*!' she said, holding up her hand as if to stop any questions. 'My manners.' She put her chin down, eyes up, then called out in a ringing voice, 'Gordana! *Gordanaaaa!* Ah, *there* you are, child. I was calling you for an age. Bring some of the coffee you just made, for the two officers. And perhaps a little something stronger on the side,' she added, with a conspiratorial wink at Padelin. Reinhardt hid another smile, the old woman already figuring Padelin for the burly, honest policeman not averse to the odd tipple. 'Chop-chop, dear,' said Hofler as she dismissed the maid. The lapdog glared at Reinhardt with its round, wet eyes while Hofler smiled genially at them.

'You are Austrian, Frau Hofler?' said Padelin, filling the silence.

'From Vienna. My husband is the general manager at the tobacco factory,' she replied.

'And have you been here long?'

'My *dear*, sometimes it feels like forever. *Not* that there's anything wrong with the city, or the wonderful country,' she hastened to add, bringing Reinhardt into her confidence with wide eyes. 'But, it's not *Vienna*. You understand, of *course*, Captain.'

'Quite,' said Reinhardt.

'Do you know Vienna, Captain?'

'I do. I lived there for a year. In 1938.'

'Ah, *what* a year,' enthused Hofler. 'A *great* year.' Reinhardt only smiled. That year, for him, for Carolin, had been anything but great.

'Frau Hofler,' said Padelin, clearing his throat and pulling out a notebook. 'We are investigating the murder of Miss Vukić, who was your neighbour, and were wondering if we might ask you a few questions about the statement you gave earlier?'

A lace handkerchief appeared suddenly in Hofler's hand, and she dabbed delicately at the corner of one eye. 'Yes. Yes, the poor child. Please, ask me *anything*,' she said with a decisive sigh, drawing herself up even straighter.

'You told the police you saw a strange car on Saturday night. Please can you tell us more?'

Frau Hofler sighed again and stroked the back of the little dog, which thumped its tail once, then put its head down. 'I was walking my little Foxi as I often do at night, as I'm something of a late sleeper. It was around nine o'clock at night. I can't be more exact, I'm sorry. And then, as we were approaching poor Miss Vukić's house, Foxi began getting all *restless*, like he never usually does. I wondered what was happening, and then I smelled this *horrible* smell, terribly acrid, and I saw smoke coming from a car parked just in front of Miss Vukić's. *Well*, Foxi was growling – he's *terribly* sensitive to smells, you know – and I picked him up before he began making a fuss and walked by the car. I looked in and saw a man inside smoking a cigarette, and *that* was what was making the smell. And *such* a smell! When I came back, perhaps half an hour later, he was just driving away. He came past me and *honestly* I could *still* smell that beastly smoke.'

'Can you describe the man, Frau Hofler?' asked Padelin, pencil poised over his pad.

'I'm sorry, I don't think so. It was *dark*, you see. But he was wearing a cap. Like a chauffeur's cap.' Reinhardt and Padelin exchanged a glance, and the detective made to ask another question, but the maid arrived with a silver tray, which she set down next to Frau Hofler. The old lady held up an imperious hand. 'One moment, Inspector.' Padelin set his pencil down on his notebook, clearly holding his temper in. Reinhardt watched him carefully. Brauer, Reinhardt's company sergeant during the first war, and then later his partner on the Berlin detective force, had had an explosive temper on him, a temper that had terrified Reinhardt as a young lieutenant new to his regiment. Like Brauer, Padelin was flushing at the back of his neck, a thin crease of white skin showing along the line of his collar. Never a good sign with Brauer; Reinhardt wondered how Padelin would control himself. Hofler shooed the maid away, insisting on serving her gallant officers herself.

'Frau Hofler…' Padelin tried to continue.

'How is the coffee?' She beamed at him, stroking her little dog.

'Very good.' Hofler gave a coquettish smile and sat straighter. 'Can you tell me anything more about the car, perhaps? What colour, or what make?'

'Oh dear, I don't *think* so. It was dark.' She pursed her lips in thought. 'It was big. Long. I *suppose* it was a dark colour.' She fluttered her eyelids and smiled. 'I'm *so* sorry. I'm not terribly helpful, am I?' she said, turning to Reinhardt. She smiled at him, a tight pull of her mouth.

'Not at all, Frau Hofler,' said Reinhardt, who had been thinking about her description of the cigarettes this man had smoked and wondering why it sparked a memory. 'You are being most helpful.' He exchanged a glance with Padelin. 'Now. Just think. Close your eyes, try to see the car. Can you see anything? Anything at all?'

The old lady put her head back with her eyes closed. For a long moment she stayed that way. 'You know, it does seem to me it was an *official* sort of car. The sort that important people drive.'

Reinhardt gestured to Padelin to continue. 'So that means that it might have had a special licence plate, or a badge on the door, or a flag at the front?' said Padelin.

Frau Hofler stayed with her eyes closed, the dramatic effect somewhat spoiled by the beady-eyed little dog that had begun to drool on her skirts. 'A flag. Yeesssss… I *do* believe there was perhaps a flag, at the front.' She opened her eyes and gave that coquettish little smile again. 'Why, *Inspector*, how clever and persistent of you.'

Padelin smiled back, a little tight around the eyes. 'Can you describe the flag?'

'No, I'm afraid not. I can't really remember whether it was unfurled or not, and in any case, there was no wind.'

'Could you see if anyone else was in the car? Maybe in the back?'

'No. No, really, I can't tell you.'

'Thank you, Frau Hofler,' said Padelin, putting down his cup and raising his eyebrows at Reinhardt. The captain leaned forward in his chair.

'You've been most helpful, indeed. Just a few more questions. What can you tell me of Miss Vukić?'

Hofler's mouth firmed a little, and she ran a hand down the dog's back. 'Well, she was often away. Her job, you know. I did not know her that well. In fact, I would say I did not know her at all. I saw her from time to time, and we would exchange greetings, but that was it, really.' Reinhardt stayed silent, and she looked from him to Padelin and back. Her mouth firmed again. 'Well, I suppose it does no harm to say it, but I did not approve of her coming home at all hours, really quite, *quite* drunk, and that *singing*.'

'Singing?' said Reinhardt.

'Yes, *singing*! The most *appalling* songs. The kind that one imagines the commonest sort of labourer might sing.'

'Or soldiers?' said Reinhardt, quietly.

'*Exactly!*' said Frau Hofler. 'Like the sort a common soldier would sing.'

'Did you ever see her in anyone's company? With a man? Perhaps a soldier?'

Hofler frowned, lips pursing as she leaned back, eyes flickering between them. 'Well,' she sighed. 'There were often men at her house, yes.'

'Do you recall any in particular?'

'No, I'm sorry. I do not.'

'How about if we were to show you a photograph?'

'Yes,' the old lady said. 'Yes, that might help.'

Reinhardt glanced at Padelin. 'Someone will show you some pictures, of men you might have seen her with. You will maybe recognise one of them,' said the detective, a peculiar emphasis on his words.

Reinhardt placed his cup and saucer on the table, exchanging a glance with Padelin. 'Well, Frau Hofler, you have been most helpful. If you think of anything, be sure to let us know.'

'Yes, most helpful,' said Padelin, placing a calling card on the table. 'You can contact me at that number.'

'Oh, I will, officers,' smiled Frau Hofler, looking somewhat relieved. 'Gordana! *Gordanaaaa!*' The little dog jumped and barked. 'Ah, there you are, child, don't make me call for so long. Show the officers out.'

Making their bows, they followed the maid to the front door. As she opened it, Padelin put a hand out to stop her. Reinhardt kept walking and paused on the step. '*Koliko dugo ste radili ovdje?*' Padelin asked in a low voice. When the questions were simple, Reinhardt could follow the language.

She kept her eyes down, but that was normal. 'I've been here four years with Frau Hofler.'

'What can you tell me about Miss Vukić?'

'Nothing, sir. I never talked to her.' Padelin said nothing, only kept his eyes on her. After a moment, the maid glanced up, then down and away. 'Honestly, sir,' she whispered.

'*Dobro,*' said Padelin. 'That's it for the car,' he said to Reinhardt, switching back to his German. 'Not much.'

Reinhardt nodded his head in agreement. 'This place. Ilidža. Who lived here before? Serbs? Croats?'

Padelin looked at him, his eyes flat and heavy. 'Serbs. Mostly.'

'Now?'

'Croats. Some Muslims.'

'Is there a Catholic church here?'

'No,' frowned Padelin. 'Time now to get back to town, I think. I have to inform the mother.'

'Mind if I join you?' Reinhardt did not wait for an answer but walked on back down the path. After a moment, he felt Padelin's heavy tread following. He held the gate open for him, noting the flush at the back of his neck as he passed. 'Would you like to sit with us on the way back? Give us a chance to talk, share notes?' Padelin thought a moment, then nodded.

'Let me give instructions to my men.' He walked faster, turning back down towards Vukić's house. As he passed the ambulance, Reinhardt saw Begović sitting on a rock with his coat off, face raised to the sun and with his eyes screwed tightly shut.

'You're still here, then?'

Begović fumbled his glasses back on. 'Until the pathologist and forensics boys arrive, yes,' he said with a straight face.

Reinhardt could not help smiling back. He liked this little man, with his ironic sense of humour and apparent disregard for authority. 'Thank you, Doctor, for your help.'

'My pleasure. And I'm actually just waiting for my driver.'

'These might make the wait a bit more bearable.' He took out his cigarettes, shook a couple out for himself, and offered the rest to Begović. The doctor's eyes lit up as he climbed to his feet.

'Well, thanks very much indeed.' He leaned his head forward as Reinhardt offered a match. He lit the cigarette and watched Begović draw deeply.

Reinhardt put his head to the bright wash of the sky, then looked up and down the long, tree-lined alley. 'They tell me there used to be horses and carriages here. That you could take a ride up to the park.'

'Up to Vrelo Bosne. That's right,' said Begović, as he exhaled a long stream of smoke. 'In the old days. The good old days, one might even say.' He watched Reinhardt as he said it, his expression bland and his eyes blank. It was not as if those few words were incendiary in and of themselves, but you never could tell these days what was meant by what, or who was listening.

Reinhardt looked back at him, his expression and eyes equally devoid of any feeling. 'I went there, once. When I first came here. Very pretty.'

Begović's eyes narrowed, and he gestured at Reinhardt with his cigarette. 'You know, I've seen you before.' Reinhardt raised his eyebrows. 'At the prison. I'm there, sometimes. On call.'

'I'm sorry. I don't recall seeing you.'

'Word gets around. You used to be a policeman?'

'I'm an officer in the Abwehr, now, Doctor. That's all that counts.'

'If you say so,' shrugged Begović, agreeably.

He did say so, although there were times the past would not leave him be. Long before the prisoners of this war were paraded before him, it had been the murderers and gangsters of Berlin's streets and back alleys, back before things spiralled out of control. But that was another life, and one he thought of seldom, even if it still left him a small corner of himself to hang on to.

'Captain,' said Begović, looking intently at him, his eyes suddenly focused, all trace of levity gone from his voice. 'Be careful with them, with Padelin and his like. Don't forget that first and foremost they are Ustaše.'

Reinhardt glanced sideways at the doctor. 'Meaning?'

'Meaning they're interested in three things. Being Croat. Being Catholic. And being unpleasant to anyone who isn't one of the first two.'

'Risky words, Doctor,' said Reinhardt.

'But true,' said Begović, quietly.

'But true,' said Reinhardt, after a moment. He blinked away a flash of memory, of a Serb village the Ustaše had destroyed. Black-faced corpses hanging from the bowed arcs of branches, the bodies swirling slowly to a rhythm the living could not know. He frowned, feeling guilty all of a sudden.

Begović blew smoke at the sky. 'I'd give you good odds that before the end of the day, they'll be trying to pin this on Senka, or whichever Partisan is flavour of the month.'

'*Senka?* "The Shadow"? This is a bit beneath him, isn't it?'

'Is it? The elusive Shadow,' mused Begović, 'coming and going as he pleases, tying the Gestapo in knots, leaving the Ustaše looking like fools.'

'Well,' said Reinhardt, 'I wouldn't overestimate Senka's importance.' He said it straight, but it felt like a bluff, and a weak one. As a military intelligence officer he knew better.

'Ahh, Captain,' replied Begović, his eyes closed to the sky

and a little singsong cadence in his voice. 'Every secret stolen, every train delayed, every patrol ambushed… They say it lights a fire in the people's hearts. Who wouldn't open their doors to him? Lift a hand to help him? Or walk up into the hills in search of the Partisans. And you wouldn't overestimate his importance… ?' He turned his face down and around, his eyes blinking away the light. 'Anyway, he isn't supposed to exist. Is she?' Begović said, with a grin that slid naturally into a smile as he threaded his heavy glasses back on. A car pulled up next to the police cordon and tooted its horn. 'Ah, there's Goran,' said Begović, as the driver got out and waved. The doctor threw his jacket over his shoulder. 'It was a pleasure meeting you, Captain Reinhardt.'

Reinhardt walked back to the *kübelwagen*, his feet shuffling aimlessly in the gravel and dirt at the road's shoulder and feeling somehow like a fraud. He mulled the doctor's words over as he watched his car turn around, seeing the driver's bearded face peering over Begović's shoulder. He walked slowly back down the alley with his hands scrunched deep in his pockets, morose. It was a truly lovely spot here: the green wave of the mountains behind, the open plain in front, and the alley of platanes arrowing straight up to the Bosna's source.

That time he had gone there, he had taken off his boots and rolled up his trousers to dip his feet in the water. It had been icy cold, soothing. There had been soldiers everywhere: Germans, Italians, Croatians, even a few Bulgarians. But he had not been able to shake off the eyes he felt watched only him. Women from behind their veils, children scudding in their wake. Men from behind their moustaches, big fingers curled around little cups of coffee. Waiters with towels folded over their arms and round silver trays in their hands. He had dried his feet on the grass, rolled down his trousers, and left, and had never been back.

Moving suddenly, he began casting around, looking at the ground, looking up at Vukić's house, and Hofler's. A car, she had said. It would have been parked around about… there. Between those two trees, there was space for a car to wait. He began walking slowly, looking at the ground, unaware of the two policemen who watched him curiously. Up, then down, then up again. He leaned closer. Maybe something. Maybe nothing. Sometimes you get lucky.

There.

There was a crunch of feet behind him. He knelt down, picked something up with his handkerchief, and turned around. Padelin was standing behind him, and his men were climbing into their cars, all but the guard on the door. 'I am ready. If we shall go now?'

'Look at this,' Reinhardt said. 'Claussen, you too.' The three of them looked at what he had found. It was a hollow tube of what looked like cardboard, about the length of a finger, squeezed flat at both ends. Reinhardt raised it and sniffed, and wrinkled his nose at the acrid odour it gave off. Padelin sniffed; Claussen just looked at it.

'Papirosa,' Claussen said. 'About the cheapest cigarette you can get.'

Reinhardt nodded, remembering. 'The Russians used to smoke them in the trenches. The smell was so bad, we could smell them across no-man's-land.'

'We captured a stock of it, once,' said Claussen. 'After Kowel. We smoked it until we were sick.'

Padelin stood impassively throughout this impromptu reminiscence as Claussen began walking backwards, searching the ground. Reinhardt smiled up at the detective. 'This is what the old lady smelled,' he said. 'Do you have something we can put this in?' Padelin turned and snapped something at one of his policemen, who came running up with a small paper envelope. Reinhardt slipped the papirosa in and flapped his handkerchief before folding it up.

'Here,' said Claussen. 'Here's another one.'

'I'll take that. You never know,' he said, wrapping it in his handkerchief, and climbed into the back of the car with the detective. Claussen and Hueber got in front, and they began the journey back into town. It was just coming up to eleven o'clock.

5

It was very warm now, the sun smouldering like a hot stone in a sky washed almost white, and Reinhardt was thankful for the *kübelwagen*'s open top and the breeze through his hair as Claussen swung back through Ilidža and onto the main road back into the city. The road was busier, and they fell in with a military convoy moving east. Their pace slowed, the air fouled by the fumes of the trucks ahead. Claussen began to fidget and curse behind the wheel, swinging the car out to try to overtake, but after a while he gave up. Too many trucks, not enough room.

'If you like, we can stop just ahead,' said Padelin. 'There is one small village that has sometimes good coffee.' Claussen looked at Reinhardt in the mirror, raised his eyebrows. Reinhardt nodded and realised he was hungry. Padelin leaned forward and pointed to the right, where a small road left the main one. A pair of Feldgendarmes were on traffic duty there, but they let them pass when they showed their identification. The *kübelwagen* bumped along the dirt road, chased by a three-legged dog for a while through the centre of a small village of white houses. Padelin stopped them outside a small café next to a sluggish stream. A couple of tables sat in the shade of an overhanging roof.

Climbing out, Reinhardt could still see and hear the road and the convoy that ran down it. Padelin went inside while Reinhardt took off his cap and sat at one of the tables. Claussen and Hueber took another. There seemed to be no one in the street, or the village, other than the dog that now lay panting under the *kübelwagen*. He could feel the eyes, though. Padelin came back out and sat next to him, draping his jacket over the other chair. A waiter followed him out with glasses of water.

'There is *burek* and tomatoes,' said Padelin, as he downed his glass and gestured for another.

Reinhardt took his glass a bit slower, putting his elbows on the table. 'So, tell me now, what is it about Marija Vukić?'

Padelin sipped from his new glass of water and licked his lips. His eyes narrowed as he looked out into the sunlight. 'She was like a movie star. Very famous for us. Her, and her father – Vjeko Vukić – they were with the Party from the beginning, when no one knew us, no one wanted to be with us. She studied filmmaking in Italy and in Berlin.'

'She travelled a lot?' The food arrived. The *burek* was minced and fried meat rolled in pastry, served with glasses of yogurt. Few things were better, Reinhardt had found during his time in Yugoslavia, than *burek* for a hangover. Padelin took his apart in his big fingers, shoveling it piece by piece into his mouth.

'I think yes, she did. Even before the war. I always would read her reports in the papers and see her films.' Reinhardt saw it in his eyes, the echo of a teenage crush. 'She would get in trouble, sometimes, with the authorities before the war. About the need for a Croatian state, and freedom from the Serbs. It never stopped her from saying or writing what she wanted, though.

'She would do this, how do you call it… they show films, give books and magazines. Welfare work?' Reinhardt nodded. 'Right. She would organise films, and interviews with even the lowest soldiers. She would distribute magazines and newspapers, and the mail if it was there, she would give it to the soldiers. If you were lucky, you got a kiss. You can imagine, she was very, very popular with the soldiers.'

'Well, I never got one,' said Reinhardt.

Padelin went still in his chair. 'You met her?'

'Even danced with her. At Christmas. She was invited to a party for the officers.'

Padelin turned back to his food. '*Picku materinu*,' he muttered. He glanced up at Reinhardt. 'Means you were lucky.'

'I suppose I was,' Reinhardt agreed. That memory came again, the intense conversation, her blue eyes boring into his as he talked of the trenches.

'Me too, I met her,' said Padelin. He was staring up at the hills. 'I was her police escort. Once in Mostar, and once here. She was very kind.'

Reinhardt could imagine the effect a woman like Vukić would have on someone like Padelin. 'She was born here?' Padelin nodded again around a mouthful of *burek*. 'And you?'

'No, I am from Mostar.'

'So she was Ustaše? A member of the Party?'

'Yes. You know what the Party says about women? It is the same as you Nazis. The woman, she is to look after the house, produce sons for the motherland.' He said this without any trace of irony. 'It was hard for her, to be a woman in that world. She must have needed to be tough to survive. Maybe is why she went to the difficult places. To the Eastern Front. To Norway. To the desert. On a U-boat. She did humanitarian work. With the Red Cross. And with some of the other humanitarian organisations. She was... how do you say it?' he asked, reaching for his glass. 'About the rules, and the... the...'

'The exception that proves the rule?'

Padelin nodded in his slow way as he drank his yogurt. 'That's it. She was the exception that proves the rules.'

'What was she doing here?'

The detective sat back in his chair and ran a hand around the back of his neck. 'She had just finished making a film about army operations in eastern Bosnia, and doing this welfare work with the Croatian Army soldiers and the Ustaše. She was up by Višegrad.'

'How do you know all this?'

'There was an interview with her in the newspaper two, three days ago,' Padelin replied, complacently.

'So we should speak to her crew, then?'

'It is being arranged. Probably only for tomorrow, though.'

'Speaking of filming and photography, did you see her darkroom? It had been turned upside down. Vandalised,' he explained, seeing Padelin's frown at the words. 'I think there may be material missing from there. Photographs. Maybe some film.'

Padelin grunted. 'Interesting,' he said, sounding anything but.

'What about the bodies? Anything strike you?' Padelin frowned. 'Anything interesting occur to you?' Reinhardt clarified.

'It was ugly.'

Reinhardt nodded noncommittally. 'So, what are your impressions? Who did it?' he asked, biting down on his growing frustration with this man.

Padelin yawned, hugely, and scratched his chin. 'Me? Partisans, Communists, Jews, Serbs, take your pick. She liked none of them, and none of them liked her. She lived alone. She was an easy target. You know, she was offered a police guard, several times, but she said no.'

Reinhardt pinched the base of his nose. 'You know, Padelin, in my experience you don't usually have to look far in murder cases to find who did it. More often than not, it's someone the victim knew. Someone in their entourage. Their family, even.'

The detective heard him out with those heavy-lidded eyes of his. 'You think I don't know that?'

'Of course not,' said Reinhardt. Too quickly, he thought. 'I'm just saying that before you head off rounding up suspected Partisan sympathisers, let's work through this methodically first.'

'Well, maybe we can do both,' replied Padelin. He twined his big fingers together, working them against each other. 'But it seems self-evident to me, as it should to you as a former detective, that there is an innate criminal nature that some people have. Some races also have it. The Jews. The Serbs. Gypsies. They cannot help themselves, and they will commit crimes.'

Reinhardt had not heard anything like this in years, not since the Nazis took over the Berlin police academy and began teaching this sort of rubbish.

'I should tell you,' Padelin continued, 'Zagreb is already demanding results.' He looked directly at Reinhardt, who raised his eyebrows questioningly. 'I have explained. Vukić, she was popular, and she was connected. Her friends in Zagreb, they want this solved quickly. And efficiently.'

Reinhardt sat back, and nodded slowly. 'You're saying what?'

'Putković told me the governor is calling already the chief of police. The chief wants results, so he can tell the governor, and the governor can tell Zagreb.'

Reinhardt found himself thinking back to his last, dark days in Berlin's Kripo when police work ceased to be distinct from politics. 'I am not sure the German authorities will be happy having the investigation into Hendel's death treated as a political matter.'

Padelin blinked. 'Our priority is Vukić.' Reinhardt took a long, slow breath. It looked like Freilinger was right. The Croats were interested only in her. 'Convoy is gone,' Padelin said suddenly. 'We should get going, maybe.' Reinhardt pulled his wallet from his pocket, but Padelin stopped him. 'I paid already,' he said as he swung on his jacket.

'Thank you,' said Reinhardt, as they walked out from under the shade into the blare of the sun. The dog looked at them reproachfully as Hueber shooed it away. Reinhardt felt the *kübelwagen*'s engine shudder into life behind him as he sat back in his seat. Claussen accelerated back onto the road, not a moment too soon, as another convoy was visible to the west as they turned. The road ahead was clear, though, and the trip back to the city passed in relative silence.

As they approached Marijin Dvor, Reinhardt's eyes were drawn towards the cathedral on the left, standing tall and white in the sun. He watched it a moment, then turned in his seat. 'Where does the mother live?'

'In Bistrik. Not so far from your barracks.'

'Very well. Claussen, take us back to the barracks, please. The inspector and I will continue from there.'

As they sped down Kvaternik, swerving around a tram, Reinhardt felt his gaze drawn to the ruin of the Ashkenazi synagogue on the other bank, sacked on the second day of the German occupation back in April 1941, its four towers like blackened chimneys. At Ćumurija Bridge, where Gavrilo Princip had assassinated the archduke in June 1914, Claussen crossed the river and turned left and up to the barracks. Claussen stopped the car across from the main entrance and left the engine running as he and Hueber got out. Reinhardt motioned to Padelin to get in the front as he as well stepped out of the car.

'Hueber, you're dismissed, with my thanks. Claussen, you are assigned to me, according to Major Freilinger. I need you to find where Hendel was quartered and start going through his things. See what you can find. Anything that linked her to him.'

'What, other than she was a bit good-looking, and he liked to chase skirts?'

Reinhardt chewed his lower lip and shook his head. 'Just a gut feeling, but he wasn't her type. No doubt he'd have gone for her if he could.'

'So something else was on offer?'

'She was a journalist, as well as a filmmaker. Maybe she was onto something, needed to tell someone about it.'

'Well. I wonder what it could have been to have Hendel out there at the time he was.' Reinhardt motioned for him to go on. 'The doctor said the time of death was sometime late Saturday night. If Hendel wasn't out there in the expectation of getting into bed with her, then what was he doing there at that time?'

'Something to think about. And the maid knew him. He'd been there before. Listen, get onto the Feldgendarmerie traffic boys, too. See what their records are for late Saturday night, early Sunday morning. Arrange a time for me to see them.' He paused, wondering if he should say more about the Feldgendarmerie, then thought better of it. 'I'll look for you later, all right? So.' He turned to Padelin. 'Where are we going?'

'Above the train station. Right up the hill.'

Reinhardt took the car around the back of the barracks, then gunned it up the steep road that climbed almost straight up the hill, his left knee twitching as he struggled with the pedals. He swerved around a porter in wide black trousers going up the hill, bent double under a load he carried high up on his shoulders. There was something peculiarly Oriental about him, about his trade, Reinhardt thought. The man looked up from under his brows, his skin dark and leathery, every bit the swarthy Turk of a hundred stories and postcards of this place. What did such a man think of life, he wondered. What could any man think who bore such loads and looked at little more than cobblestones all day long?

The road curved around a spur of Mount Trebević, nearly all of the city visible down the hill to the right. Padelin pointed, and Reinhardt swung the car across the road and parked next to a large house in yellow brick, with a small front garden. Padelin showed his identity card to the elderly maid who answered their ring, and Reinhardt watched the fear bloom in her eyes as she held the door open for them. They were shown into a living room, in the middle of which stood a woman dressed in black. It was clear she was Marija's mother, such that Reinhardt was taken aback momentarily at the resemblance, at what Marija would have grown into. The looks were the same, as was the clear, flawless skin. Only her hair was a shiny ash blond, worn long over her shoulders. She stood with a calm intensity, clearly braced for bad news, her blue eyes flickering from Reinhardt to Padelin and back again.

Padelin spoke to her gently. Reinhardt heard Marija's name and guessed he was giving her the bad news, because her mouth formed a wordless O, a gasp coming from the maid as she stood by the door. Vukić searched blindly behind her with her hand for the chair. Everyone moved at once, Reinhardt reaching her first and helping her sit down. Her eyes sought and held his, and she spoke to him but he could not answer her. It was

Padelin, surprisingly gently, who did. The tears came then, welling up and rolling down her cheeks. He talked to her for a moment and Reinhardt heard the words for *German* and *officer*. Vukić nodded behind a lace handkerchief that she held with trembling hands.

'Yes, of course. Of course,' she whispered. 'We can talk in German. Please, just give me a moment.' The maid left the room. Reinhardt heard her start to sob as water ran from a tap, and he incongruously found himself thanking the Austrians for having occupied this place and teaching everyone German. The sounds of crockery being arranged underlaid Vukić's quiet tears as she wept into her handkerchief. Reinhardt and Padelin exchanged glances, Padelin looking desperately uncomfortable. Reinhardt looked around the room, which was decorated in what he took to be an old style, all heavy wood and furniture it would have taken two strong men to shift, and Art Deco vases and glasswork. Every flat surface, it seemed, was covered in white lace cloths. A grand piano stood in a corner next to a double door looking out over a small flower garden. Arranged all over its top surface were photographs, portraits mostly. Vjeko Vukić's photo, hard mouth and harder eyes, stared back at him from several of them, including the same one that he had seen in Marija's apartment with the mourning band along the bottom. None of the pictures he could see were of Marija.

After a moment, Vukić looked up from her crying. 'My manners, I do apologise. I am Suzana Vukić. Please sit down.' She rose to her feet. 'If you will excuse me for a moment.' She glided out of the room. Reinhardt heard her going upstairs, and a door closed. A clock ticked heavily in the still air of the room, redolent with the scent of flowers in a silver vase. The maid came in with a tray with a pot and cups, her eyes red-rimmed and puffy. She put the tray down with a soft metal clatter and left as Vukić returned. She had combed her hair and washed her face. She motioned to the two officers to stay seated and sat in her chair, drawing her legs sideways and together, her back straight. 'Now,' she swallowed, dabbing delicately at her nose. 'How can I help you?'

'Mrs Vukić, when was the last time you saw your daughter?' asked Padelin.

She drew a deep breath, nodding to herself. 'It was last week. Last Tuesday.'

'How did she seem to you?'

'As normal. Very excited about everything. And nothing.'

'No signs of unusual behaviour? She mentioned nothing that might have been troubling her?'

'Nothing,' replied Vukić. She blew her nose elegantly into her handkerchief.

'Nothing to do with men? With money? At her work?' Vukić shook her head to all of it. 'Can you tell us what she did, exactly?'

'She was a filmmaker. And a photographer.' Her German was slow, precise. She went over to an elegant escritoire of dark, varnished wood with brass handles and came back with a folder tied up with a ribbon. She spread a collection of clippings, photos, postcards, letters, and other memorabilia onto the table and fingered through it. She found one in particular, a certificate of completed training with the Propaganda Ministry in Berlin. Propaganda Kompagnien. One of Goebbels's little stormtroopers, thought Reinhardt, and a woman. Well, well, well. He put it back as Vukić showed him another page, handwritten in an elegant, old-fashioned script, probably hers. It listed all of Marija's assignments, and the dates she was away. Poland 1939, France and the Netherlands 1940, the Balkans and Greece 1941, USSR twice, in 1941 and again in 1942, North Africa 1942, Italy. Everywhere, it seemed.

The door to the room creaked open and an old dog wandered in. It sniffed aimlessly at Reinhardt's leg before flopping to the floor at Vukić's feet. Vukić stroked its head, then leaned forward in her chair. 'Will you take something to drink? I have coffee that was a present from Marija from her last trip to North Africa.' She offered him a cup of coffee, thick and black, flavoured with cardamom. Reinhardt lifted his cup to his lips, remembering the last time he had tasted something like it, in Benghazi, in a café overlooking the sea with the water like a sheet of molten metal beneath him. She poured for Padelin, but he only put his cup briefly to his lips, putting it down almost untouched. 'Yes, a photographer. A good one, too. She worked with Leni. Leni Riefenstahl,' she added, unnecessarily. A first flicker of an emotion other than grief roused itself in her face and there was pride in her voice 'She travelled with the troops. She followed the Croat soldiers to Russia. I have all her letters and cards. Perhaps you might want to look at them.'

'That might be useful,' said Reinhardt. 'Mrs Vukić, I saw her apartment and the collection of photographs. I understand that she travelled extensively with the military, but did she travel with anyone in particular?'

'Oh, yes. Always with the general staff.'

'There were at least two men at Marija's house that night.' Vukić's mouth firmed, and she dipped her head to sip from her cup. 'One of them was found dead at the scene. A blond man. Blue eyes. A soldier, perhaps thirty to thirty-five years old. Do you know who that might be?'

'She used to see a Major Bruno Gord, in the propaganda companies. I never met him, though. Then again,' she said, quietly, 'it might not be him.'

There was an awkward silence. Padelin indicated with his eyes for Reinhardt to go ahead. The big policeman shifted in his chair as Reinhardt cleared his throat. 'What do you mean, Mrs Vukić?'

Vukić's eyes rose from her cup, first to Padelin, then to Reinhardt, blinking as if surprised to find him there. She held his gaze for a long moment, then sighed. 'I mean that Marija liked men. Men with power, authority. She liked older men. She had a lot of them. I could not… did not try… to keep track of them. I cannot say I liked her behaviour. But… Marija was strong-willed. What I liked and wanted stopped being important to her a long time ago. I mean, she lived by herself, out there in Ilidža, instead of here with me. How many good

Bosnian girls do that to their mothers? She always said she was a "modern" girl. She wanted her own place. Her father indulged her.' Just for a moment her eyes strayed to the photos on the piano. 'He always did. He gave her his father's house, the one in Ilidža. And when we divorced, he moved out there with her.'

She looked at the two of them. 'Understand, I love her.' Her voice hitched as she caught herself, swallowed, and then it seemed that a conscious refusal to talk of her love for her daughter in the past crept over her face. 'But she was complicated. She could be close at times. She was distant more often.' She looked far away. 'Especially since Vjeko – my husband – passed away. Distant. But always dutiful,' she said, her hand passing over the folder and its letters, cards, and snapshots from faraway countries. 'She was her father's daughter. More than she was ever mine.'

Reinhardt, who knew something of complicated family relationships, especially with children, said nothing. He felt a stab of embarrassment for Vukić but screwed it down tight. Vukić seemed to realise she might have said too much of the wrong thing and breathed in deeply, her back straightening. Padelin cleared his throat, but she had not finished talking.

'You know, lots of people liked Marija. Lots of people liked being with her. But I also think there were people who did not like her. What she was. What she did.' She looked directly at Reinhardt as she talked. 'You know, she was not afraid to say what some said was the truth about our situation – that is, the situation of Croats – before the war. But she was not afraid to say some things about women, and what some could and should say about what women did with their lives.'

Reinhardt thought Padelin looked uncomfortable with this, although whether it was the extra detail about an icon he had admired from afar or the talk about disloyalty towards the Party was not clear. He made a valiant effort to bring the conversation back to the case. 'Mrs Vukić, what can you tell us about the guests your daughter had?'

'Nothing,' she said, shortly. 'I don't know who she might

have entertained. But just be sure,' she said, again focusing on Reinhardt, 'just be sure that when you look for whoever did this, you look close to home, not just far from it. Those who would hold her highest are those who would drop her furthest.' She sat back, an expression of satisfaction on her face.

Padelin looked even more uncomfortable with that, to the extent that Reinhardt stepped in for him. 'What do these friends of hers do?'

'I'm afraid I really don't know.' Her eyes were far away again, the shock catching up with her. There seemed to be little more they could do here, now. Reinhardt leaned forward to place his saucer on the table and froze as Vukić began talking again.

'My husband called her feisty,' she said, in little more than a whisper. 'Independent-minded. Very political. Very... involved with the Party. And she liked having a good time. Parties. Dancing. Drinking. Smoking. The men.' Her cup rattled slightly in her hand, but she did not seem to notice.

'Mrs Vukić,' said Padelin. 'Did your daughter have any addictions?'

Vukić seemed to rouse herself. 'No. Heavens, no,' she gushed, a mother roused to automatic defence of a child. If that was what it was, it faded fast, the sudden show of spirit falling back into the increasing emptiness in her eyes. 'She knew how to separate business from pleasure. Another thing my husband taught her. No, no addictions. Her work, perhaps. And the Party.' She sipped from her cup, and the silence grew. The two policemen exchanged looks, and Padelin put his hands on the arms of his chair but stopped, again. 'You know, if I'm honest, I should say I don't know. I don't know anything about the details of her life. I know she worked hard. And she liked to have a good time when she was not working.'

Reinhardt felt an echo of her grief deep inside, the memories of Carolin and Friedrich stirring and shifting. One dead, one as good as dead. He watched her, this woman struggling with herself, her feelings. He felt a stir of admiration for her, for her elegance and composure in the face of her grief. He knew what awaited her, what awaited those left behind by their loved ones, but he showed nothing. It was not difficult anymore, to show little or nothing in the face of another's pain, but there was still a little part of him that reminded him it was not always that way, and he was not always like this.

Reinhardt nodded at Padelin that he was finished. For all his imposing appearance, the inspector could be, it seemed, a gentle man. He put his card down on the table. 'Mrs Vukić, you will need to identify the body. When you are feeling better, please call me at that number, and we will arrange for you to come in.' Padelin nodded to Reinhardt that he had finished his questions, and the two of them rose to their feet. Vukić stayed sitting, looking small and fallen in on herself. 'Please accept our condolences. Do not get up. We will see ourselves out.' They left her there in the middle of her perfumed living room with its ticking clock and the old dog wheezing at her feet.

6

Reinhardt left Padelin in front of police headquarters, the big detective tight-lipped and taciturn on the drive back down from Vukić's mother's house. Getting out, Padelin suggested they meet the next morning, giving him enough time to track down any members of Vukić's production team in the city, and Reinhardt time to start following up on the German side of the investigation. He barely gave Reinhardt time to agree before he was turning away, walking stiffly up into the building.

It was going on three o'clock anyway and those of the city's inhabitants who had jobs mostly worked a seven-to-three-o'clock shift. Reinhardt could feel Sarajevo entering that early-evening phase of relaxation when people downed their tools and came out to visit friends or went for coffee in the old town. He drove the *kübelwagen* back around Kvaternik Street for what seemed the umpteenth time that day. As he had said to Padelin, you often had that feeling with this city, of going around and around in circles.

Sarajevo was a grim place, sometimes. Crammed in between its mountains, hemmed in between the Ustaše on one side and the Germans on the other, it always seemed to find a way to push the weight of the war to one side, at least once a day. More and more with each passing day, Reinhardt found himself waiting for that time, when even someone like himself, even someone who wore the uniform he wore, could simply sit and watch and listen and be around people who made an effort to put their cares aside.

Turning left off Kvaternik, he drove up a narrow street that dead-ended in a guard post. Showing his identification to the soldiers on duty, he parked the car in front of the building the Abwehr used in Sarajevo. Inside, he asked the duty officer for an appointment with Freilinger, only to be told the major was out and not expected back that day, but instructions had been left for Reinhardt to prepare him a report on the day's events. Sighing, Reinhardt sat at his desk and picked up a note from Claussen that told him he had arranged an appointment with the Feldgendarmerie traffic commander for four o'clock.

He leaned back in his chair, lit his last Atikah, blew smoke at the ceiling, stared at the paper, then closed his eyes and wondered whether he would be able to avoid running into Becker at the Feldgendarmerie. He sat in silence for what seemed quite some time, running over the day in his mind. Feeling his way along it, around it. As he did with the prisoners he interrogated in the rooms beneath the prison. Feeling along the hard edges men brought with them, searching for the breach, the chink that would let him in. Letting silence do the work. The wearying rote of routine, long pauses as each question sinks in, the prisoner's mind asking itself a dozen more to his one, his hold on his story weakening from minute to minute, hour to hour. Except, more and more, Reinhardt had found himself sinking into his own silence, his questions falling stillborn, chased into the emptiness between men by memories of a child's scream, the sluggish drift of smoke, the swivel and hunch of rifles into shoulders. Flashes of his nightmares. The inside seeping up into the waking world.

The prisoner in front of him finished his cigarette, stubbed it out. His eyes flicked up at Reinhardt, away, back. The silence was working on him. The hands now empty, nothing to do with them. Nothing to fill them. The air now empty between him and Reinhardt. Space needing to be filled, and

*there were only words to fill them. No one here understood
the value of silence anymore. The burden of words dropped
into emptiness.*

*'Why'd you take so long?' the translator whispered,
words strained as he held back a yawn. 'Just beat him.'*

'Like the others do?'

His eyes flared open as he smelled smoke, and he jerked
upright in his seat. He did not feel like writing; he needed to
move, so he went looking for Weninger and Maier, the two
Abwehr officers Freilinger had put to searching Hendel's material,
and found Maier. The Abwehr was subdivided into *abteilungen*
– offices. Reinhardt ran Abteilung II J. The official designation
was moral sabotage. In reality, it meant interrogations of captured
enemy soldiers, particularly officers. It was not dissimilar to his
police work in Berlin before the war, interrogating suspected
criminals. Hendel had been Abteilung III H, internal army
security. Before that, he had worked in the unit responsible for
document forgery and technical espionage. Hendel had not been
in Sarajevo long, only about three months. Most of what he had
been working on, according to Maier as he sifted through
Hendel's admittedly poor paperwork, dealt with following up on
rumours about a secret line of communication between the
Partisans and German forces. And that the British were now up
in the hills with the Partisans.

'The British?' said Reinhardt. He thought back over the last
interrogations. One of them had been a Partisan lieutenant. He
had mentioned nothing about there being any British, but then
captured Partisans rarely said much. 'With the Partisans? Not
the Četniks? Last I heard, Mihailović still had a British liaison
group.'

'So did we all think the British were with the Četniks?' Maier
wore small pince-nez and still affected the airs and graces of the
university lecturer he once was. 'And we even release signal
traffic overestimating the Četniks and the damage their actions
are causing. You know that, because some of the stuff we release

is through our agents. That way we're pretty sure the Brits pick it up. The last thing we want is the Tommies changing sides, but in the long run, who can know? Those bloody British. Playing both sides, I'm sure of it. These Partisans – I don't know, I think they could really hurt us, you know? I mean, just look at what we've got for allies. The Croats, they're useless without us, and those Ustaše are just berserk. The Italians are getting all squirrelly about getting home to defend against any Allied attack there – and let's face it, they were useless anyway...'

Reinhardt leafed through a few of the files on Hendel's desk in a desultory fashion as he listened to Maier, and eventually he left him to it. The man was right about one thing. The politics of wartime Bosnia were byzantine in the extreme, a kaleidoscope of shifting frontlines as Germans, Italians, Croatians, Ustaše, and Četniks fought the Partisans. A veteran of the first war, Reinhardt was no stranger to war or suffering, and his mind shied away from what he had heard of the Eastern Front, but he had himself never seen or experienced anything like what he had been exposed to here in Bosnia. The slaughter of civilians, the reprisals, the villages and towns razed to the ground, the summary execution of prisoners, the almost medieval barbarity...

Returning to his office, he arrived at the same time as Claussen. 'How was the mother?' the sergeant asked.

'Much as you'd expect,' Reinhardt said. He rummaged in the drawer of his desk, coming up with an old packet of Bosnian cigarettes. The tobacco was stale, but it served its purpose. 'I found out Vukić was in the propaganda companies, though. Although she seemed to do a fair bit of her work herself. The mother mentioned a Bruno Gord. A major in the propaganda companies. We'll need to see him.' His office overlooked Ferhadija Street, itself running parallel to King Aleksander Street through the heart of the city. He watched the ebb and flow of people along it for a moment. 'Did you have a look at Hendel's place?'

Claussen nodded. 'Nothing much, sir. I talked to a couple of the men he bunked with, at the main barracks in Kosevo Polje. One of them linked him definitely to Vukić. Said he must've met her about a month ago. There was a picture of her in his room. A roommate seemed to think he would meet her sometimes at a club in town…' He paused, leafing through a notebook. 'Some place called Ragusa.'

'We'll have a look at it.' Reinhardt looked at the sergeant, considering. 'What did you notice about the bodies, then? Back at the house.'

'The woman. Vukić.' Reinhardt nodded at him to continue. 'She didn't drop dead like that. Like she was just lying down. Whoever killed her…' He trailed off.

'Remorse?' asked Reinhardt.

'Something like that, to lay her out like he did.'

'And he couldn't have cared less about Hendel,' said Reinhardt. Claussen nodded. 'Unless there were two of them,' Reinhardt continued. 'Or the same murderer, but two very different reactions.' He sighed. 'Keep that in mind. For now, shall we go and see what the chain dogs have?'

Back down into the *kübelwagen*, and Reinhardt let Claussen drive again. The sergeant had learned the intricacies of Sarajevo's little side streets and alleys and the one-way system much better than he ever had. Claussen weaved and dodged his way back to the Marijin Dvor intersection, then sped down to Vrbanja, where the Feldgendarmerie had their main headquarters. In the commandant's office a young lieutenant, dressed in a uniform that was regulation ironed and starched, directed them to a Captain Kessler, in charge of Feldgendarmerie traffic. Kessler was a tall young officer who came around from behind his desk to greet them. His gorget – the crescent-shaped piece of metal that hung around his neck and was the source of the Feldgendarmerie's less-than-flattering nickname of 'chain dogs' – was polished to a brilliant shine.

'Captain Reinhardt, yes? I received your request for information.' He turned to a table standing against one wall, two blue folders precisely arrayed upon it. 'However, I have been ordered to have you report to my superior officer, Major Becker, before releasing any official information.' Kessler's face and voice were carefully neutral, and Reinhardt could not tell whether the Feldgendarme thought those orders excessive. Reinhardt breathed in slowly and deeply through teeth that he clenched, carefully. Bureaucracy, it seemed, had caught up with him. It was almost inevitable that Becker would too. 'I can take you to him now, if that is convenient.'

'Very convenient, Captain,' replied Reinhardt. They followed Kessler back to the office where they had started. The captain vanished through a side door, while the lieutenant invited Reinhardt to take a seat. Claussen stood at ease against one of the walls.

Reinhardt ran his eyes over the notices. Traffic regulations, more orders of the day, punishment lists, the list of men gone missing or wanted for desertion. He took the seat the lieutenant had offered, stretched his legs out, and crossed his feet, wriggling his toes in his boots. He felt a sudden tiredness creeping up on him, a stiffness to his neck that presaged another headache. From the corner of his eye, he felt the prim little eyes of the lieutenant disapproving of his slouching. Right then, Reinhardt could not have cared less and he just wished for a moment to close his eyes. He did the next best thing and stared into space, out the window, and tried to let his mind empty of everything but the case. He failed as he thumped up against the impending meeting with Becker. If there was one thing Reinhardt hated and Becker excelled at, it was bureaucratic politics.

'Captain Reinhardt?'

He opened his eyes and looked up. An orderly was standing in front of him. 'Major Becker's compliments, sir. If you would come with me?' Reinhardt motioned to Claussen to stay put and followed the orderly past the lieutenant's snooty gaze and down a hallway into an office that could have been the same as Kessler's in its layout. Kessler stood to one side of a desk behind which sat a major of the Feldgendarmerie with flat grey eyes, dark red hair parted over his right eye as if with a ruler, and wearing a pair of little steel spectacles. Trays of paperwork ran along the edge of the desk nearest the door. The major held a pen poised over a form as Reinhardt came to attention and saluted. He blinked, motioned Reinhardt to take a seat, and turned back to his paper. His pen darted like a bird pecking for grains, once, twice, a flourish of a signature and he handed the paper to the orderly. Becker removed his glasses and folded them, holding the ends of the frames in his hands, and looked at Reinhardt. The orderly stood to attention to Becker's right, just behind him. 'You have requested information regarding traffic movements to and from Ilidža, correct?' asked the major.

'That's correct,' replied Reinhardt.

The Feldgendarme looked at him, up and then down. 'What for, if I may ask?'

'You may.' Reinhardt watched the blood rise to the major's face, the clench of his jaw, and saw the glaze come over the orderly's face as he wished himself away from this clash of officers, and was that the ghost of a smile on Kessler's face… ? Reinhardt wondered if they knew of the history between the two of them, history that went back to Berlin when they were in Kripo together. 'I am investigating the murder of a serving officer in the Abwehr,' he said, judging he had left it just long enough. 'The officer was found dead at the house of a Croatian journalist in Ilidža. I have reason to believe he went out there late on Saturday night. I would like to examine the traffic records for any indication of his killer's movements.'

'Who has assigned you to this investigation?'

'Major Freilinger. Abwehr.'

Becker nodded. 'I see.' He frowned. It was a frown for show, the sort a lawyer would use in court. Or a parent, knowing a child had been disobedient but wanting to play through the pantomime of question-and-answer to its end. Becker was playing to an audience. He always did when he could. 'This city has a police force, no? Why are they not investigating this case?'

'Major Freilinger implemented the standard protocol with

the Sarajevo police that in the event of a criminal investigation involving German intelligence personnel, we would have the lead or equal role in the inquiries.'

Reinhardt could see Becker debating with himself whether to make things personal, but the bureaucrat won. He unfolded his glasses and put them back on. 'I see,' he repeated. 'I am aware of the protocols. I am also surprised. I find the police in Sarajevo to be a thoroughly professional force. We work closely with them.'

'As you say, sir,' replied Reinhardt. Such a painfully transparent man, he thought, not even needing to guess the next question. Interesting, though, that Becker would play the bureaucratic card like this. Normally, he would string things out, play word games, try to humiliate Reinhardt. Usually, he would manage to bring up the disparity in their ranks now as opposed to back in Kripo, when Reinhardt outranked him.

'Indeed. But if Major Freilinger has activated the protocols, would not such an investigation be better conducted by the Feldgendarmerie?'

'Sir, that is a question I respectfully suggest that you address to Major Freilinger.'

'I intend to. Or rather, I shall wait until he, or someone, explains to me why the Feldgendarmerie should merely assist, and not lead.' He took a folder from his in tray and folded his hands atop it. 'There are rules. Procedures to be adhered to. I should like to see some formal request to this unit before I release any information. When I have seen a written request, I will be more than happy to provide whatever assistance I can. Please be so kind as to inform Major Freilinger of that.'

'Sir, I was made to understand by Major Freilinger that the Feldgendarmerie had been consulted on the handling of this investigation and it would be left in the hands of the Abwehr.'

'I have seen nothing to that effect. Until I do, your involvement in a murder investigation is an anomaly to me.'

Reinhardt sat still, clamping down around the anger that he always felt in the face of such bureaucracy. 'There is no way that you might see fit to assist me pending such a notification?'

'None.' Becker's nostrils quivered and narrowed, and his mouth straightened. As if he were clamping it shut around what he really wanted to say. Or holding back a smile.

'Sir, I must respectfully point out to you that time is of the essence in such an inquiry. The longer –'

'I am a policeman, Captain,' Becker said, coldly, but his eyes glittered brightly, daring Reinhardt to contradict him. 'I also am someone who believes no good ever came of bending rules.' His eyes glittered even brighter. 'And now, if you will excuse me,' he said as he opened the folder and pulled a sheet of paper towards him. 'Orderly, please see Captain Reinhardt on his way.'

7

The orderly came back to sudden life, moving back past Reinhardt to hold the door open for him. Good survival instincts, observed Reinhardt, sourly, although he was sure the man had heard every word and stored it away for gossip in the NCOs' mess. Reinhardt saluted and left, pulling Claussen in his wake as he went back outside to the *kübelwagen*. Reinhardt slumped against the side and held his hand out to Claussen. 'Give me a cigarette, would you?'

Claussen shook a Mokri into his fingers. 'No luck with those lists, then?' asked the sergeant after a moment.

'Nothing gets past you, Sergeant, does it?' Reinhardt quipped, then shook his head at the self-serving tone of his irony. Claussen just stood there, imperturbable. '"Written authorisation" and all that crap. Freilinger said he would clear our way with the Feldgendarmerie. Maybe he has, but it hasn't filtered down to Becker yet.'

'There's a bit of history there, isn't there?'

Reinhardt frowned at Claussen. 'What?'

'You and the major.'

Reinhardt knew of Becker before he met him. The night they finally met, he and Brauer had followed him across the nighttime city, the air sodden and chill, back up to the same second-floor apartment. They paused, listening at the door to the low mutter of voices. Moving carefully, Reinhardt tried the handle. The door was unlocked, and he pushed it open and stepped quickly inside.

Two men sat at a table across the room looking at papers. Official-looking documents, with photographs and stamps and seals all half spilled out of a leather satchel. Passports. IDs. One of the men was Becker, thin red hair and little steel spectacles. The second was a bulky man, elderly, a fringe of grey hair seemingly painted onto his brick of a skull. Two more men, big and heavy, sat off to one side, counting piles of money. All of them went still as Reinhardt and Brauer stepped quietly inside.

The two big men began to get to their feet until Brauer pulled a Bergmann submachine gun out from under his coat. 'Let's all just sit still, shall we?' he said, quietly. Its stubby little barrel pointed at the two men, who sat down slowly. 'Hands where I can see them, gents.'

Reinhardt said nothing, only locked eyes with Becker. 'Do I know you?' Becker asked, after a moment.

'You were a useless detective in the Kripo post in Wilhelmshaven,' Reinhardt said, watching Becker flush, then go pale. 'You transferred into Gestapo in 1934. Apparently, you were too useless even for them, and they dumped you back in Kripo here. You're keeping company with Hannes Lemke, Gestapo border control in Bremerhaven,' he said, looking at the man sitting with him, 'and two crooks from the Hamburg mob. Missing are Walter Fischer from the Foreign Ministry, and Gerhard Cordt, from the Gestapo property seizure division. Stop me if I'm wrong, or going too fast.'

The silence was thick, tense. Becker's eyes flashed back and forth between him and Brauer, back to him, to the other men. Becker swallowed, a little smile flickering across his face. 'Go on.'

'You're ripping off people trying to get out of Germany. Jews, mostly. But not exclusively. Fischer provides papers. Lemke facilitates exits, Cordt disposes of properties. You *invest the proceeds with the Hamburg mob, who also provide a little muscle when needed. With me so far?'*

'You have evidence, of course?' asked Becker.

'Other than what's in front of me?'

'This?' Lemke said. 'This is… material… seized…' He trailed off, looked desperately at Becker.

Reinhardt ignored him, looking at Becker. 'I'm not sure where you fit in… ?'

Becker's mouth moved, and then he smiled again, as if he knew a particular secret was out. 'Me? I suppose I'm a talent scout. You might say my forte's organisation. And persuasion.'

'Yes, I've proof,' said Reinhardt to Becker. 'But more to the point, it's who you know more than what you know, these days. Wouldn't you agree?'

Becker nodded. He took off his glasses, tilting his head down and to the right, keeping Reinhardt in sight, considering the implications that Reinhardt's contacts would outweigh his.

'Everyone's got to make a living, I suppose,' he said, eventually.

'The truth is I need your scam.' Becker smiled, and the others seemed to relax, tension draining out of the lines of their shoulders. This was what they had been expecting. 'Make it a good one, Becker. Nice and honest.'

'Four hundred marks.' Becker grinned.

'So you pay.' Reinhardt put a piece of paper on the table, ignoring the protestations from Lemke, watching Becker. 'You can keep your scam going. For as long as you can manage it. You charge the price you just mentioned. I'll be checking. But whoever I send you, you take out for free. Consider it as reinvesting back into the business.'

'You're fucking crazy,' hissed Lemke.

'If you renege, I'll expose you,' said Reinhardt, ignoring him. 'If you roll this scam up within six months, I'll expose

*you. If you harm a hair on the heads of anyone, especially
those I send, I'll kill you.'*

Becker wormed his glasses back on, picked up the paper.
'Isidor and Hilda Rosen,' he read.

Reinhardt nodded. 'They're next. And that's it. I'll be in
touch. And I'll be watching. A pleasant evening, gentlemen.'

'I'll find you,' snarled Lemke. Becker only looked at him,
eyes steady behind his glasses.

Reinhardt walked out, Brauer stepping backwards,
keeping the Bergmann trained on them. They walked
quickly back downstairs and out, over to another street to
the car where another of his men was waiting. He slumped
in the back, lighting a cigarette with a hand that suddenly
trembled.

'Christ,' breathed Brauer, removing the Bergmann's
magazine as the car sped away. He craned his head back
around from the front. 'How long do you give 'em?'

'Before they find us? Not long. I'm not worried about
that. It's what we know, against what they can do...' He
closed his eyes. He felt light-headed, giddy, like he used to
feel after action in the old days, like he used to feel back in
the trenches. Truth was, he had no idea how long he could
ride that particular tiger. But it felt like the first decent
thing he had done in a long time.

Reinhardt took a long draw on the cigarette, then nodded.
'We were both in Kripo. I was a chief inspector, and he worked
Gestapo liaison, among other things. He was a bad officer.' Very
bad. Corruption. Brutality. Incompetence. Becker was so bad,
even the Nazis did not know what to do with him, but he was
connected. And clever, although cunning was more the word.
Always managing to get away with it, until the day when he
messed up one case too many – including one that involved the
death of the daughter of a Party official who had Goering's ear,
and Becker was gone. Reinhardt had happily forgotten him,
until the day he arrived in Sarajevo and found him here, second

in command of the city's Feldgendarmerie detachment.

'What now?'

Reinhardt screwed his eyes shut, rubbed his forehead, and exhaled long and loud. 'Christ, I don't know.'

'Maybe he does.'

'What?' Claussen was staring across the parking area towards where Kessler was coming out of Feldgendarmerie headquarters. The captain looked at them across the yard a moment as he put his cap on his head, then turned away down the side of the building, over to a row of parked vehicles. Reinhardt exchanged a quick look with Claussen, then straightened up, dropping his cigarette and screwing it into the ground with his boot, and went walking after Kessler.

The Feldgendarme was checking out a vehicle as Reinhardt came up. He looked expressionlessly at him, signed off the form, and returned it to a waiting NCO. 'I am sorry it has to be so formal between us,' he said.

'Likewise.'

'Look,' said Kessler, after a moment. 'I cannot give you the files, but I have seen them. There really is not much in them that I think can be of interest to you.'

'That is kind of you, Captain,' Reinhardt replied. 'I would need to come to that conclusion myself, though.'

The two of them were silent a moment. Reinhardt waited, hoping Kessler would feel the silence as an urge to say something more. 'Becker is a stickler for the rules, it's true,' Kessler said, finally. 'What he's really afraid of is that the records will show the killer went right through our controls, and the Feldgendarmerie are culpable in some way. And he may be right. We certainly had our hands full over the weekend.'

'Why's that?' Reinhardt asked, rubbing at his right eye, and then clenching his fist as his finger stole treacherously towards his temple and the imagined mark of his pistol's muzzle.

Kessler cleared his throat, a slight frown creasing his forehead. 'Because of the planning conference. At the spa, in Ilidža.'

Reinhardt remembered suddenly the staff cars parked outside the hotel. 'Of course. Yes.' He had known of the conference. He remembered it being mentioned at the daily briefing late last week. A planning meeting, the finishing touches to Operation Schwarz. How could he have forgotten that? 'Thank you, Captain. So there was much traffic?' He knew he sounded inane, but he needed to keep Kessler talking.

'Especially in the early part of the evening of Saturday. The conference ended on Saturday afternoon. Most of the attendees were returning to their units at the time.'

'Most?'

'Some stayed on at the hotel, I believe,' replied Kessler. There had been staff cars parked at the hotel this morning. Maybe connected to the conference. Maybe not. 'During an event such as the conference, we receive a copy of the list of authorised attendees. We check their arrival off against the list. On such occasions, unless the incident is egregious, normal traffic duties can be suspended or superseded. Therefore, what is listed will be only unusual incidents. Not improperly inflated tyres, or smudged or illegible registration, or overloading. That is why I can assure you no incident was reported that would seem to impact upon your investigation.'

Reinhardt looked down at the ground, at oil stains and gravel and the marks of tyres, but what he saw was the investigation withering away in a series of dead ends, or foregone conclusions. He ran his fingers around the back of his neck, where the muscles were still tight, and thought of photographs of soldiers. 'Whom do I ask for a list of the attendees at that conference?'

There was a pause. 'You would need to check with the commandant's office, Captain,' replied Kessler. 'If you think that information would be of some use.' The Feldgendarmerie captain kept his voice flat, but Reinhardt heard the question in his words. He had no idea if the information would be useful. It would certainly be risky to ask for it, and certainly risky to do anything with it, but it was all he had at the moment. This case was bundled tight; any loose thread was something he could hang on to, pull on, see what unravelled with it, and hope it did not unravel all over him.

Kessler stared at him, leaning back slightly. 'But surely you do not think there is any connection...' His voice faded away, his feet shifted. Putting distance between himself and Reinhardt. Between himself and whatever it was Reinhardt was after. Again, Reinhardt left the question hanging. Let the man draw his own conclusions, and his own implications of his own role in this. Whatever *this* might be, it was clear no right-minded soldier wanted any part of it, and it was clear that was what Kessler thought of himself.

'I do not think anything, at the moment,' Reinhardt said. 'I am merely investigating.'

'Of course,' said Kessler, turning away to his vehicle. 'Well, as Major Becker said, once you have written authorisation, any assistance we can provide will be yours. Until then, a very good day, Captain.'

'So?' Claussen asked, as Reinhardt slumped into the *kübelwagen* next to him.

'So, nothing much,' replied Reinhardt. 'Did you remember that planning conference out at Ilidža?' He glanced over at Claussen to see him narrow his eyes and shake his head. 'Kessler just reminded me. I'm pretty sure Freilinger alluded to it this morning, but I just didn't catch it.'

'You think there's a connection?' asked Claussen.

Reinhardt pushed his chin out, pursing his lips. 'I've no clue,' he sighed. 'Take me back to the offices. I really hope Freilinger's back. Then we need to think about getting a look at that Ragusa place.'

Reinhardt looked at the Miljačka as Claussen drove back up Kvaternik. With the summer's heat, the river was low; in some places it was a dry jumble of stones. A group of boys played in the flow of water that still ran down the middle of the river's channel, jumping from rocks into the water. 'Freilinger told me you used to be in the police,' he said, suddenly.

Claussen twitched his eyes towards the rearview mirrors, then shot a quick look at Reinhardt. 'Nearly twenty years. In Dusseldorf,' he replied.

'Why'd you come back into the army?' asked Reinhardt.

Claussen took a moment to respond again. 'Didn't much like some of the changes that were… you know, that we had to go through,' he said after the moment. 'And the army, well, it was always sort of my first home.'

'You mentioned Naroch. Back at Vukić's house.'

The sergeant nodded. 'Yes, sir. Eastern Front 1915 to 1917. I was wounded, and sent home. Joined the police when the war ended.'

Reinhardt stared ahead at the road in front and the blank façades of the buildings on the left. Claussen's experience was close to his. Very close, but as much as it seemed they might have much in common, there was almost certainly as much, if not more, that separated them. A silence grew, and instead of welcoming it Reinhardt cursed himself at starting a conversation he did not know how to finish.

Claussen pulled up in front of HQ and Reinhardt, still feeling a prickling awkwardness, sat for a moment before turning to face the sergeant. 'That was good work you did. At the Feldgendarmerie station, pointing me in the direction of Kessler.' Claussen said nothing, only looked back at him. 'That's something I'll need from you, Sergeant. Any time you have something like that, a feeling, something to say about this investigation, speak up.'

'Very good, sir.'

Reinhardt could not put a finger on how, or why, but he was sure Claussen felt he had just been insulted. Or patronised, he thought, remembering a time, long ago, a similar conversation with Brauer. Claussen was not Brauer, and Reinhardt did not have the time or strength to invest in forging a relationship with him that resembled in any way what Reinhardt and Brauer had once had as soldiers, then as policemen, as friends.

'You have the address of this nightclub you mentioned Hendel went to? Let's pay it a visit tonight. Bring Hueber and meet me at the barracks at eight o'clock.' Reinhardt got out of the car, turning as he closed the door. 'Until then, you are free to do as you will.'

Back at the offices, Reinhardt was told Freilinger had returned and was expecting him. On his way up, Reinhardt stopped quickly in his office and retrieved from his desk the notebook he used to record information within Abwehr. He flicked through the pages until he found what he needed, folding the top of the page to mark it. The major's orderly ushered him into Freilinger's spartan office, where the major was standing with his hands clasped behind his back, looking out the window. Reinhardt came to attention.

'Sit down, Captain,' Freilinger rasped, turning back and moving to sit down behind his desk. He shook a mint from his tin and leaned back in his chair. 'Tell me what has happened in this case. Just the facts, for now.'

Reinhardt kept his report simple, especially as there was not much to report on. He told of the interviews with Frau Hofler and with Vukić's mother. He told of the failed attempt to elicit information from the Feldgendarmerie. Freilinger listened in silence, his clear blue eyes rarely blinking. When Reinhardt had finished, he sat silently for a moment, then folded one hand within the other under his chin. 'Now, tell me of your impressions, your feelings about this case.' He twisted and flexed his hands, dry-washing them together.

'Well, sir. I have an infamous Croatian journalist who worked hard and, apparently, partied harder. Influential. Well connected. Politically active. Who seemed to like soldiers, experienced ones. Older ones. To have some kind of fixation on them, judging by the photographs in her house.' He paused, going over what he had just said. It seemed to make sense, to fit with the nascent feelings he had about the investigation, about her. The dull rasp of Freilinger's hands did not change. 'I have an unhappy and recalcitrant police officer for a partner and liaison with the local force.' An officer steeped, he did not say, in ideology and trained in police techniques that Reinhardt despised. That assigned crime and criminal impulses to people based on social and racial background, rather than motive and opportunity. 'The Sarajevo police's methods seem a bit… dated' was all he said. 'Because of the increasing political pressure that they are coming under to find someone to take the blame for Vukić's murder, I am concerned the Sarajevo police are not interested in finding the real culprit, only someone to blame it on. They are experiencing high-level pressure from Zagreb. Putković will want this wrapped up soon, I'm sure.'

'Is it too early for a suspect of your own, Captain?'

Reinhardt looked back at Freilinger, at the shift and slither of his hands. 'Yes, sir. Too early.'

'The most likely, in your opinion?'

'Sir, respectfully, I must decline to be drawn on that.'

'Oh?' Freilinger's hands paused in their movements, fingers interlinking and falling still. 'Your next steps, Captain,' he said, dropping the subject.

'Sir, I have an appointment with Inspector Padelin tomorrow to speak with members of Vukić's production team. I will also speak with Major Gord. He is in the propaganda companies and was mentioned by Vukić's mother as being friends with her daughter. I will be visiting a nightclub tonight that Hendel and Vukić apparently frequented. I also hope I may have greater success with the Feldgendarmerie in reviewing their traffic records.'

'Yes, that you should have,' rasped Freilinger. 'I do not know what happened with my request, but I made it in good time and order. Becker may be playing games with you, and I'm sure not much I could say would change your mind about that. But someone over there is not treating this with the urgency I requested. If you do not have what you need tomorrow morning, I will personally intervene.'

'Sir, in addition to their traffic records, I would like to see a list of attendees at the planning conference for Operation Schwarz.' He did not mention he had completely forgotten about it. He opened his notebook to the page he had marked.

'We were briefed about it last week, on Tuesday,' he said, scanning his notes. 'Final preparations for Operation Schwarz. All divisional commanders. Hotel Austria, in Ilidža.'

'Why do you need that?'

'I have Vukić's murder taking place close, far too close, to a gathering of soldiers who could have stepped out of her photos. I find it hard to believe she would not have known of such a gathering and taken steps to attend it. Personally and professionally, it would have been well worth her while to have done so. Additionally, I must assume the murderer was affected by what he had done. Emotionally, and physically. It would have been next to impossible for a civilian to move around unseen out there at that time. But a soldier might have been able to.'

Freilinger watched him from under hooded eyes. 'That information could be useful, and I could get it for you. But I will not give it to you until you can satisfy me more that there is a link.'

'Sir, I must protest,' replied Reinhardt. He clenched his fingers hard around his notebook. 'How can I make a link if information is denied to me simply because of whom it might importune?'

'Reinhardt,' said Freilinger, as he shook a mint from his tin, holding it between the tips of his fingers. 'I will not have you pestering every officer of general staff rank as to his whereabouts and whether he was familiar, or even intimate, with a woman like Vukić. Not without very good information that such questioning would be merited. Certainly not at this time.'

'Sir, what you call "pestering" I would call –'

'Call it what you want, Reinhardt,' Freilinger interrupted. Reinhardt felt a rush of blood rise to his face and knew that it showed. 'Find out she was there; that would be a start. Establish that she knew any of the officers attending. That would be another. But I'm not having you *pestering* senior officers and their staff with this. Not until you have a lot more to pester them with.' He fixed Reinhardt with his cold blue eyes as he popped the mint into his mouth. 'Dismissed.'

8

Reinhardt drove himself back to the barracks. The duty officer gave him a letter that, from the handwriting, was from Brauer, and he turned the envelope in his hands as he went back up to his room, feeling suddenly drained. He flopped onto his bed, watching the long light of the sun as it shone through his window, resting the envelope on his chest. A drink would be nice. In the little park in front of the barracks, down by the river. Or maybe on the square. He closed his eyes.

The grass is heavy with a night's rain. The smoke from a thousand cook fires drifts through the trees like mist. The rustle and creak of the accoutrements on the men around the terrified young officer sound like thunder. Across the meadow, shapes move in the trees, commands shouted in a strange language. Somewhere, artillery rumbles across the sky. Grey-clad infantry are drawn up in ranks to either side, and the young Reinhardt tries desperately to swallow, finds he cannot. The rustling and shifting of the men suddenly quiets, and Reinhardt feels someone behind him. He turns, and the colonel is looking at him with those grey eyes. From across the meadow comes a guttural roar.

'Ouraaah! Ouraaaaaaaah!'

The colonel rests a gloved hand on the lieutenant's shoulder. 'Are you frightened, sir?' All the lieutenant can do is nod. The colonel nods back, squeezes his shoulder firmly, leather gloves creaking softly. 'Remember,' he says, as another battle cry rolls from the woods opposite, and the dim shapes swell and coalesce into a mass of men, rifles tipped with bayonets swaying into the wind of their passage, 'so are they.'

Reinhardt gasped and sat up, the letter falling to the floor. A thin film of sweat covered his head, and the light had lengthened, but not by much. He could have been asleep only a few minutes, but the dream… He had not dreamed that one in a long time. His first taste of action, at the Battle of Kowel. The first time he had met the colonel. Tomas Meissner. The man who all but became the father he had always wanted, and a centre around which to build a life. Until he met Carolin and found that his centre was only one of two competing poles of attraction, and him in the middle. He had not contacted him in a while now. That was wrong of him, even if he had been told it would have to be that way. Reinhardt owed the man his life, many times over.

He leaned down and picked up the letter, then walked to the window. The park in front was in shade, and there was a band playing this evening. He could see them warming up, but he fancied something else. Picking up a fresh pack of cigarettes, he walked back out past the sentries and headed upriver. He crossed at the Emperor's Bridge, along a little alleyway and onto Baščaršija Square over to a small café on its western side. He sat at a table, ordered Turkish coffee from a thin waiter with distant eyes, and lit a cigarette, watching the world go by, letting his mind drift over the case and the slow shuffle of people along and through and around the square.

Women went by hunched under the burden of food or firewood, followed by an old man who leaned heavily on a cane. A pair of policemen with rifles on their shoulders; three children and their mother who gave them a wide berth. Men washed their hands and feet in the fountain at the top of the square, and the hammers of the metalsmiths in the tiny alleys that wound around the foot of the old Ottoman mosque that stood at the corner of the square never seemed to stop. The roofs of the wooden-walled shops and cafés that lined the square were all of red tile. A couple of shops had swastika flags hanging over the entrances, or the NDH's red-and-white checkerboard *šahovnica*, more an invitation to the soldiers who usually thronged the city than out of any political allegiance, he was sure. A group of tank officers in black uniforms saluted him as they went by and vanished into the alleys to visit the craft shops that sold trays and plates and cups of beaten and worked metal, and beer tankards with *Gruss aus Sarajevo* on them that the men sent home as souvenirs.

What little joy this city's citizens had, it seemed, they took together, in places like this, and it gave Reinhardt some peace of mind to watch them. Friends walked with friends, and couples strolled together. Children played across the square's cobbles. Elsewhere, in the ruins of the Jewish neighbourhoods, in the squalor where the thousands of refugees from the countryside eked out a precarious existence, and in the Serb quarters where people moved cautiously the city was dark, crouched around itself. And always, above and around, the mountains that sometimes seemed to cradle the town in the folds of their slopes, and sometimes seemed poised to clench and crush it.

His coffee came in a little silver pitcher on a round tray, with a small glass of water. He dropped a piece of sugar into the foam at the top of the pitcher, letting it settle in as he had seen others do. The sugar turned brown and slid into the coffee with a ripple. Quicker than it used to. The coffee seemed weaker every time he came, but it was still better than the swill they poured out in the mess. He stared slowly around himself and thought again about how, despite the fear and loathing generated by the war, and which the city's narrow confines seemed to sometimes stir to crazed heights, despite the veiled glances that always came his way, the place sometimes still made him think of a costume party that never stopped.

The costumes he had once thought of as Eastern, as Oriental, were worn here by as wide a variety of men and women as he could never have imagined, many of them far less Oriental than the popular imagination he once was a part of would have had it. A man as blond as a Saxon went past dressed in the loose trousers and shirt that marked him as a Bosnian Muslim. There went a man in a suit and hat with the look of a lawyer who would have fit anyone's image of a Turk back home. A dark young woman in a headscarf sitting on a step averted bright green eyes as he looked at her. The crowd was dotted with men in black suits and red fez, or white turbans, or wide-brimmed hats of Western fashion. Peasant women in veils and baggy pantaloons and slippers that curved up at the toe and stooped under heavy loads walked by, talking and laughing quietly among themselves, followed by a pair of ladies in long dresses and jackets.

From Vratnik, he heard the call to prayer begin, and he glanced up at the mosque on the corner of the square to see the muezzin climb out of the top of the minaret and cup his hands to his mouth. Behind Reinhardt, around the corner at the big Husref Bey mosque, he heard the call taken up, then heard it to the left and right on the slopes of the city. He stirred his coffee, waiting a moment for it to settle, then poured it, and worked his mind around how the murderer, or murderers, was moving around. Ilidža was a long way out, and the murders had taken place late on Saturday night. It was not that there was no traffic along that road at that time, but not much that was not military, and just about every civilian car would have been checked either by the police or by the Feldgendarmerie checkpoints at Marijin Dvor and out at Ilidža itself.

He sipped from the little white cup. The coffee was thin, slippery in his mouth, but it still felt right to be drinking it, out here on the square. The murderer drove out to Ilidža, he thought, testing the way the idea sat in his mind. Hendel drove out there. The murderer had to have left. As he saw it, that was a lot of driving, and a multiplication of risk. Kessler had told him the Feldgendarmerie had nothing in their records, but he had to see for himself. And get Padelin to do the same for the traffic police. Someone who had done what the murderer had done, it would be sure to affect you. He might have been pulled over for speeding, or driving erratically. If he had been, the Feldgendarmerie ought to have noted his plate number. The Sarajevo traffic police might have stopped him, although they would not have been able to do anything with a German and were unlikely to have made a record of any such incidents.

He sat staring at nothing for a moment, then took Brauer's letter from his pocket. He held it by the bottom corners, then opened it slowly, pulling out two sheets of paper with Brauer's crabbed handwriting across it. He sipped from his coffee and began reading.

Brauer was Reinhardt's oldest and closest friend. It was not a friendship either of them had ever thought possible. Brauer was Reinhardt's company sergeant when the young Gregor arrived on the Eastern Front in 1916. Brauer was twenty-two and already a hard-bitten veteran soldier in Meissner's regiment. The two of them had lived and fought together for nearly four years. The Eastern Front, then the transfer into the stormtroops and assignment to the Western Front at the end of 1917 through to the end. Defeat. Retreat. Wounds. The turmoil of 1919, the drift into dissolution in 1920, then the offer of hope in the police.

If there was one bone of contention between them, unspoken for nearly all their friendship, it was the gulf in education. In the Wehrmacht, particularly in the army, education was key to an officer's promotion. Reinhardt had his military college training, and his higher degrees in criminology. Brauer had a secondary school education. When Reinhardt had got over the injury he sustained in September 1918, he had been accepted into the Weimar police as an inspector, but Brauer had walked a beat for several years until at last Meissner managed to use his influence to get Brauer accepted for the test for inspector, and Reinhardt had sat and coached him for the exams.

When the time came to go back into the army, Reinhardt's education and background had got him a captaincy. Brauer's had secured him an NCO's billet. In many ways, Hitler's army had not changed from the Kaiser's. It was still riven by divisions along class lines. Brauer had been mobilised into the infantry as an instructor. He lived in Berlin with his wife, but, he now wrote, they had moved out to the country to stay with his in-laws. The implication – unwritten, to get past the censors – was because of the bombing. Details followed, this and that, small things. Then the news that made Reinhardt go cold.

They have released more names of those fallen at Stalingrad, Brauer wrote. *I am afraid Friedrich's name is not among them.*

Reinhardt slumped in his chair. His son had been with the Sixth Army. A young lieutenant in a panzergrenadier regiment. Reinhardt had not wanted his son to have a military career. But in an echo of what Marija's mother had said that afternoon, what Reinhardt wanted had stopped being important to his son a long time ago. Much as it pained him to admit it, Reinhardt had lost his son to the Nazis. Not, he would sometimes comfort himself, that there was very much he could have done about it. Friedrich had been thirteen when the Nazis came to power in 1933. The Hitler Youth, the warping of history lessons in school, the endless parades, the oaths, the songs, the summer camps, the after-school activities, the discipline and uniforms and militarisation of school life, all produced a child increasingly alien to his parents.

It was a strange thing, Reinhardt remembered, to look at your child and look at a stranger. It was a stranger thing to feel scared of your child, to the point sometimes of not wanting to go home. There were stories in those days of children reporting on their parents. As a policeman then, he knew it sometimes happened. Father and son diverged on nearly everything, and only Carolin seemed able to maintain any sort of space where they could still, from time to time, be a family. Friedrich had watched Reinhardt's struggle with his conscience over the politicisation of the police with contempt, and had joined up himself on his eighteenth birthday. Reinhardt had not seen or spoken to him until last year, but only followed the news from Russia with increasing worry and trepidation.

Reinhardt was pulled out of North Africa in early September, wounded when a British aircraft strafed his convoy. Recuperating in Italy, with time on his hands and his mind skirting the implications of the censored news from the east, he finally wrote to his son. The first letter in years, written with a hand that trembled. When a reply finally came several weeks later, delivered by an officer on leave and thus free of the censor's black, Reinhardt could hardly bear to open it for fear the son still rejected the father.

Friedrich had been wounded and was recuperating at an army sanatorium on the coast of the Sea of Azov, not far from Mariupol. The letter was long, written over the space of several days, and not all of it made sense. Friedrich talked of many things. Of his war, his comrades. There were hints of things seen, and done, but not mentioned. Things perhaps too awful to contemplate. And nothing about the past. Nothing of them as a family. Reading the letter, Reinhardt could see, though, the spite and the spleen of his teenage years had been burned out of him. The Friedrich that came through the long, scrawled lines was purer, somehow. It was something Reinhardt recalled happening to him, in the first war. Everything not necessary for survival got burned away.

Mostly, Friedrich wrote about Stalingrad.

The worst thing, Father, the worst thing about it is nowhere is safe. Nowhere. They come at you from everywhere. Out of the sewers. Down from the roofs. From under the rubble. Out of factory chimneys. From ground you've fought over and liberated ten times. You live your life with your head down and your shoulders hunched. Every day is like a week, and you live every day as if it's your last.

But, Father, fear cannot be all I feel. Yes, I am scared. We all are. But there is purpose to this. I must believe that. I passed a hospital train, yesterday. It was full to the brim with casualties, mostly from Stalingrad. Looking at it, your heart twists around its own contradictions. You rejoice it is not you among them. You envy them their ticket home. You hope for yourself the end comes clean if ever it does. You wonder what the future holds for such as they.

If I could hide them from the world, I would, though. Some things bear a heavy price, and not all prices are worth revealing. I now understand better what you went through as a young man. No one can know what it's like who hasn't gone through it. No one, Father, no one must know what it's like. What we suffer for them. Promise me you'll tell no one.

There was a photograph with the letter, and Reinhardt had to look carefully to recognise his son. Friedrich was burned away, whittled down, looking ten years older than he actually was. Reinhardt read and reread the letter, trying to find perhaps some hidden meaning. Some indication that what Friedrich had experienced might have opened his eyes, if only just a little, to what the Nazis had done to him. To them, as a family. But the faith was still there. Even after all he had seen and done and suffered.

Even if Reinhardt had wanted to write back, he could not have. Friedrich's letter arrived at the beginning of December, just over a week after the Red Army coiled itself around the city. He spoke only to Brauer of Friedrich's letter. Christmas leave in Berlin, hunched over glasses of beer, heads close together, Brauer had listened to Reinhardt in silence.

'Do you think we're different this time?' Brauer had asked. 'You and me?'

'How?'

'That we haven't burned away enough to get through this.'

Reinhardt had nodded slowly. 'It's different. We're different. This isn't our war.'

'Not our war,' he whispered, pushing his pack of cigarettes around the table, knowing it was only with Brauer he could say things like that, and even then… Stalingrad had fallen. The Sixth was wiped out, they said. Only a few survivors. He tossed a handful of *kuna* on the table for the coffee. He had to get moving or face another evening that would end with him at the bottom of a bottle, or staring down the barrel of his pistol.

9

The Ragusa was in the heart of the Austrian city, sandwiched between Kvaternik and King Aleksander Streets. The roads all ran at right angles to each other, and the buildings were much alike, heavy carved stone façades rising three or four floors, doorways flanked by columns or statues, all so different from the serpentine jumble of the Ottoman city. At the club's entrance, Reinhardt stared up at a brightly lit sign: *Ragusa* written in gold on blue, thick red stripes above and below the lettering. He looked at the cars parked in front of the club. A couple of army staff cars, but most of the vehicles were private, including one impressive-looking Maybach. 'Claussen, you stay out here with the car, please. Hueber, you're with me.' He pushed open the doors and strode into a short hallway with what looked like fishing nets hung on the walls, with shells and other nautical paraphernalia wound into the strands, along with a big painting of a coastal city, thick stone walls wrapped around a crowded port. The hall ended in a tall set of opaque glass doors. The strains of what sounded like a Gypsy orchestra became suddenly louder as he opened those and stepped into the club proper.

A lectern stood just inside the entrance, a book open on its surface. Reinhardt paused a couple of steps in and looked around. The place smelled strongly of alcohol, cigarettes, and roasted meat. It was dimly lit, what lighting there was glowing through clouds of smoke or reflecting back off pictures arranged haphazardly around the walls, a mix of photographs of revellers and imitation prints of coastal scenes and cities. More fishing nets were draped across the walls. The overall colour was a heavy red, on the tablecloths and wallpaper. Round tables were spread across a surface split into two levels, the farther level lower than where Reinhardt stood. Down there was the stage, with a group of four musicians in traditional costume playing on what looked like fiddles, a clarinet, and a small handheld drum. Most of the tables were taken by men in uniforms, but some men wore civilian clothes. A few women were scattered around the tables, flecks of colour in a sea of black and field grey. Waiters moved to and fro, wearing brightly coloured waistcoats with white shirts and black trousers.

A man in a tuxedo slid smoothly behind the lectern. His hair was black and shiny, brushed straight back and held with some sort of pomade. Reinhardt could smell it. 'Yes, sir? May I help you?' The maître d' spoke perfect German, offering Reinhardt a reserved smile as he took in his uniform.

Reinhardt glanced at him, then around the bar again. 'I'd like some information, please.'

The maître d' put his head slightly to one side, the smile tightening somewhat. He managed to flick his gaze up and down Reinhardt without losing eye contact, taking in the captain's field uniform and the wear and tear on his boots. 'Information, sir?' He took his time looking over Hueber in his corporal's tunic, who flushed under the maître d's gaze, which was unfortunate as it turned his acne an even darker shade of red. 'What kind of information could that be?' From the accent he was Bavarian, thought Reinhardt.

'Information,' repeated Reinhardt. He fixed the maître d' with his eyes as he took Hendel's photo from his pocket. He put it on the lectern. 'Have you seen this man before? An army lieutenant.'

The maître d' leaned over the photograph for a moment, then back up. He looked at Reinhardt, and Reinhardt could see him pondering whether he had the weight to ask what this was all about. A maître d' in a place like this? Popular, frequented by all kinds of officers… He might just feel confident enough to do it. Overimportant maître d's had been an occupational hazard back in Berlin. Especially once the Nazis had begun to colonise all the best restaurants and hotels, turning everywhere black and brown with their uniforms, and leaving men like this maître d' out at the front, pretending the barbarians had not taken over and everything was normal.

'Yes,' said the maître d', finally. 'He is a frequent guest here. But not tonight. I'm sorry,' he said, handing the photograph back.

Reinhardt left him with his hand out, the photograph in it. He looked around the club again. 'He won't be coming back. He's dead,' he said, turning back to look at the maître d' as he spoke. The man blinked, the hand with the photograph drawing back, and down. He looked at it again, then up at Reinhardt.

'I am… sorry to hear that,' he said. He proffered the photograph again, wishing to be rid of it.

'Murdered, in fact,' said Reinhardt. 'What is your name?'

The maître d' looked back at him. 'Name… ?'

'Your name,' said Reinhardt, moving closer to him, still ignoring the photograph. 'I am conducting the inquiries into his murder.' He said nothing about his unit, his function, letting the maître d' draw his own conclusions.

'Dietmar Stern.'

'You have worked here long?'

Stern nodded, tentatively. 'Nearly one year, now.'

'You say Lieutenant Hendel was a frequent visitor?'

Stern nodded, again, the photograph hanging forgotten in his hand. 'Every few nights.'

'Alone? With friends?'

'He would often come with friends, yes. Excuse me, one moment,' said Stern, as a man in a grey suit and burgundy tie came in. The maître d' put the photograph down, took the man's hat, and escorted him to a table. Reinhardt stepped up to the lectern, picking up the photo and looking down over the list of bookings and reservations. Stern came back over, saying nothing as Reinhardt scanned the book, then stepped back.

'When was the last time he was here?'

Stern ran a finger down one of the pages, turning back one. He tapped an entry. 'Thursday night.'

'This last Thursday?' Stern nodded. 'Was he with anyone?' There was a burst of applause from the patrons as the band ended one song and started another.

'The entry does not say, sir,' said Stern.

'Do you know Marija Vukić?' asked Reinhardt.

'Of course I did. She was a regular guest here. It is terrible, what happened to her.'

'Did Hendel know her?'

Stern nodded, frowning. 'He did. I believe they met here quite frequently.'

'When would have been the last time?' asked Reinhardt, motioning at the ledger. 'Check, please.'

Stern looked back to his book, then back up at Reinhardt. 'Also Thursday. But she was with someone else.'

'Who?'

'A General Paul Verhein.'

The name meant nothing to Reinhardt. Sarajevo was full of generals these days. 'Is there anything that comes to mind about Hendel?' he asked. 'Anything at all. How he behaved. How often he came. Who he talked to.'

Stern shook his head. 'I'm afraid I would not really know, sir. You might ask Dragan, the barman.'

Reinhardt held Stern's eyes a moment longer. 'Down there?' He turned to Hueber, motioning him to follow.

'Sir,' Stern said, softly. 'Your cap, if I may.' He did not offer to take Hueber's forage cap, but the corporal took it off and folded it into one of his tunic pockets.

Reinhardt threaded a path through the tables, past German and Italian officers, Ustaše, men in suits and women in dresses that were probably fashionable a few years ago, before the war. Reinhardt flicked his eyes from German officer to German officer, hoping not to make eye contact with any of them. Some looked up at him as he passed. Most turned away; those that looked longer had eyes more for Hueber than for Reinhardt. A corporal in a club like this was not usual and would eventually cause comment.

He walked past the last table and into a space in front of the bar, with the band playing to his left in front of a long mirror that gave a poor illusion of space and light. He felt terribly exposed, imagining all those who might be watching him from the smoke-shrouded gloom behind him. A couple of men, an Ustaša in his black uniform and a man in a suit, stood at the bar, shoulder to shoulder in conversation. A barman in white shirt and black waistcoat stood to one side, polishing a glass with a cloth. Reinhardt walked to the far end of the bar, motioning to him to join him.

'What may I offer you for drink?' asked the barman, eyebrows raised and head tilting back slightly as he spoke. His German was thick and accented.

Continuing the place's nautical theme, the bar was decked out with fishing paraphernalia. Reinhardt scanned past nets and seashells and a ship's lantern and sepia-toned prints of coastal towns along the limited display of bottles behind the barman, and noticed a bottle of red standing open, with what looked like a Mostar label. 'Give me a glass of that.'

The barman poured with an exaggerated care, filling the wineglass almost to the brim, then placing it in front of Reinhardt. He made to move away, but Reinhardt raised his hand, slightly. 'One moment,' he said, as he raised the glass to his lips. The wine was cold, the way they drank it here. Despite that, it was still heady and thick, lying heavy on the tongue.

'Is all right?' the barman asked.

Reinhardt turned his lips in between his teeth and squeezed the tip of his tongue. 'Fine,' he nodded. It was diabolical. Reinhardt took another sip. 'Mr Stern said we should talk to you, Dragan.' The barman looked back at him expressionlessly, flicked his eyes at Hueber, then picked up his cloth and began drying a glass.

'About?'

'About a lieutenant. Called Hendel. Do you know him?'

Dragan nodded. 'I know him. He come often here.' He ran his cloth around the glass with a practiced move and put it away in a rack over his head, taking another from just below the counter.

'When was he last here?'

The barman wiped and dried the glass, his eyes turned inward and somewhere else in a ploy that, to the policeman in Reinhardt, was transparently one to gain time. Dragan could not know what this was about, but he was surely not wanting to get in the middle of whatever was making a German Army captain ask questions about a lieutenant's whereabouts. 'Maybe I think last week?'

'A day?' replied Reinhardt.

Dragan stayed expressionless as he cleaned his glass, his eyes elsewhere, then focused back on Reinhardt. 'Thursday?' he said, at last.

'You remember anything special about him?'

'Special? Sorry, my German. Not so good.'

'Hueber, please,' said Reinhardt, half turning away from the bar and motioning the corporal forward. 'Ask him what he remembers in particular, if anything, about Lieutenant Hendel.'

Dragan frowned at him as he spoke to Hueber, and then his frown deepened as Hueber began talking in Serbo-Croat. The barman's eyes flicked back and forth between the two of them, then settled on Reinhardt as he began to talk back. Hueber held up a hand after a moment.

'Sir, he said Lieutenant Hendel was in here twice, sometimes three times a week. He usually drank at the bar. He liked the ladies. He did not cause any trouble.'

'Does he know who Marija Vukić is?'

'I know. Of course, I know,' said Dragan, stepping forward as if to push Hueber out of the conversation. 'She is here many, many times.'

'Did you ever see the two of them together?'

Dragan nodded. 'Yes. Two, maybe three times.'

'What do you remember?'

Dragan opened his mouth to speak, then paused. He looked between the two of them again, and then, as if deciding that Hueber was the lesser of two evils, began to talk to the corporal. The Ustaša at the bar peered over his companion's shoulder at them, making the other man turn and look as well. Reinhardt looked back at them expressionlessly until the civilian turned away, and the Ustaša shrugged, and they went back to their drinks and conversation.

'Sir,' said Hueber, again. 'He says that Vukić was a frequent guest here. She was usually here with guests, and their parties were always quite wild. A lot of drinking, and singing. He remembers her with Hendel because the times they were together were unlike any of her other visits. She came alone, and they talked alone. The barman says he thinks that Hendel was interested in her but she was not interested in him. He was...' He broke off for a second, asked something in Serbo-Croat to which Dragan replied. Hueber nodded, and resumed. 'He was not her type.'

'What was her type?' asked Reinhardt, guessing the answer.

'Officers. Older ones. With gold on the shoulders,' said Dragan, not needing Hueber to translate that one.

'Anything else?'

'Yes, sir,' replied Hueber. 'The barman remembers that while they were talking, others would come up to greet her. She was courteous, but she did not allow others to join them. Some of the men were annoyed with that. He knows because they came to the bar to complain. Afterwards, when she was finished talking with Hendel, she came to the bar, and she would laugh and joke with those men, and then everything was fine.

'There was just one time when there was trouble. There was an officer who always tried to talk to Vukić. She did not like him. When she did not like someone, it was very clear, but this officer was persistent. The last time Dragan saw Vukić and Lieutenant Hendel together, this officer tried to join them. She told him to go away, and he was insulting to her, and apparently he tried to pull rank on the lieutenant. It did not work, and he came to the bar angry, talking with friends and asking what he did not have that a mere lieutenant did. He tried to cause trouble for Lieutenant Hendel, but his friends persuaded him out of it, and Vukić threatened to make his life a misery if he persisted in his attentions. This was on Thursday, last week.'

'Yes,' said Dragan. 'Then Vukić, she go in back room with Hendel. To be private.'

'Back room?'

'Is private room. She go there sometimes.'

'Does he know who the officer was?'

Hueber looked desperately uncomfortable. 'Only that he is SS.' At the mention of that, Dragan looked hard at Reinhardt, as if imparting to him how much this information could cost him.

'No name?'

Hueber turned to look at Dragan, but the barman shook his head. 'I don't know name. But he is one of us.'

'Not a German?' Dragan shook his head again. 'A Yugoslav? A Croat?' Dragan paused, then shrugged, a movement that meant more yes than no but still managed to convey his discomfort. 'What unit?' asked Reinhardt, pointing to his collar and shoulder boards.

Dragan shrugged again, switching back to Serbo-Croat. It did not really matter, thought Reinhardt. There were not that many SS units around Sarajevo at the moment. That could be checked fairly easily.

'Sorry, sir,' said Hueber. 'He does not know.'

'He is not good guy, this SS.' Dragan polished a glass hard, glancing up. '*Pomalo*. He crazy,' he finished, tapping a finger on his head. 'He take knife, stick it hard into the bar. Just there,' he said, pointing at a scar of whiter wood in the bar's surface.

'A knife?'

'Big knife,' said Dragan, measuring out a distance with his hands. Reinhardt thought for a moment, digesting what he had learned. Hendel was a frequent guest, as was Vukić. According to everything he knew of the journalist, Hendel was not her type, however much he might have wanted to be. They met here several times, the last time two days before her murder. Someone, an SS officer, was sufficiently annoyed at her spending time with a lieutenant to get threatening about it. Not that there was no truth in any of it, but it all seemed a little obvious. 'Was there anyone else here who knew Hendel? Who spent some time with him?'

Dragan had gone back to his glasses, another one vanishing into the folds of his cloth. 'Are singers. With band,' he said, motioning with his head over to the ensemble. 'Florica and Anna.'

'Tonight?' asked Reinhardt, hearing himself slow down in his speech to match the barman. 'Are they here, tonight?'

'No,' replied Dragan. He frowned as he put yet another glass away and leaned forward with both hands on the counter. 'But why you asking these questions again?'

'Again?' He frowned and turned to Hueber. 'What is he talking about? Has someone already been asking questions?'

As they talked, Reinhardt looked over his shoulder back into the club. From out of the gloom was a gleam of eyes from beneath shadowed brows, the crescents of faces over the angles of hunched shoulders. And here, there, faces looking back at him, like moons.

'Sir,' said Hueber. Reinhardt turned back, feeling more and more exposed down here at the bar. 'Someone has already been asking questions about Lieutenant Hendel. From the description, it sounds like the Feldgendarmerie. He says we should talk to the two ladies he mentioned. Apparently the Feldgendarmerie roughed them up a bit.' Reinhardt looked at Dragan as Hueber spoke. The barman's eyes were fixed on the young corporal and swivelled to Reinhardt when Hueber had finished, then back to Hueber.

'*I policije*. Don't forget to say about police.'

Hueber gave a distracted nod. 'Yes. *Da*. The Sarajevo police were also here. It was Padelin.'

'Padelin was here?' Reinhardt said it more as a statement. He looked at Dragan. 'When?'

'Was today. After lunch. They took Zoran. One of the waiters.'

'Did they say why?' Dragan shrugged, his eyes dull and flat. Reinhardt sighed, slowly. 'Where are the girls now?'

'At home,' shrugged Dragan, again.

'I want to see them. Do you have an address?'

'You ask manager.' He motioned over to the other side of the bar, where a small door stood almost unnoticed. Reinhardt walked back along the bar, past the Ustaša, who looked at him over his friend's shoulder, and over to the door. Dragan pointed at a small brass handle, which Reinhardt pushed down on. A crack of dim light arrowed up the side of the door, widening as he pushed it open and stepped into a short corridor.

Like the bar itself, the corridor was red. Red wallpaper on the walls, red shades on the lights. Photographs hung on the walls, pictures of guests seated around tables, the photographer's flash caught in wide liquid eyes and on the stems of glasses and the necks of bottles. Reinhardt paused in front of one of them. Vukić was seated in the centre, slightly side on to the camera. Her dress rode high and tight up her thighs, and she had one arm around the shoulders of a rather self-conscious-looking general. Again, Reinhardt found himself taken with the sheer animal attraction of her. He remembered that one dance with her, at Christmas, the giddy sensation she had left him with. He could only imagine the effect she must have had when she focused the searchlight blaze of herself on someone she was truly after.

There were three doors at the end, one in front of him and one to each side. The one in front was slightly ajar, and the sound of a wireless playing music came through softly. Reinhardt walked up to the door, knocked, and pushed it open, stepping into a small office. It was neatly kept, with a small wooden desk behind which sat a dark-haired man in a suit tapping a pencil against the top of the table, his head propped on his other hand. The man looked up from the papers he was going through as they came in, a slight frown of annoyance at the interruption swiftly replaced by a more neutral expression at the sight of a pair of German soldiers. The pencil went still in his hand.

'Yes?'

'You are the manager of this club?'

'I am Robert Mavrić. Can I help you?' he asked in heavily accented German.

'I am conducting an investigation into the death of a German officer. This officer was a frequent guest here.' The manager's face narrowed, took on a pinched and haunted look, and he slumped back in his chair. 'Two people who work for you were friends with this officer. I need to question them, and so need their addresses.'

Mavrić's eyes moved between the pair of them. 'You know, I gave you this information yesterday morning.'

Reinhardt stared back at him, letting the silence grow. He hated to do it, but there were times when the uniform, and the weight of oppression implicit in it, were useful, like now. That, and the fact he was digesting what Mavrić had just said. Yesterday morning was Sunday. Vukić was not discovered until today, Monday morning. Mavrić tapped his pencil a few more times and then tore a piece of paper from a pad. He scribbled down an address and handed it to Reinhardt.

'Where is it?' Reinhardt asked.

Mavrić pursed his lips. 'It's in Terežija. Just over the Čobanija Bridge. Five minutes from here.'

Reinhardt turned to Hueber. 'Go and give this to Claussen. Tell him we're going straight there and that he knows how to find it.' Hueber took the paper and turned smartly on his heel and left.

Mavrić tapped his pencil on the desk again. 'Is there anything more I can do for you, sir?'

'Did you know Lieutenant Hendel? The officer whose death I am investigating?'

Mavrić sighed, flipping the pencil onto the desk. 'Like I told the others, I knew of him. He was a guest here. He behaved himself. He tipped well. He was well liked. He wasn't any trouble.'

'Whom did you tell?'

Mavrić frowned at him, a retort clearly on the tip of his tongue, but he bit it back. 'I don't know who they were.'

'Describe them.'

The owner's frown deepened. 'I don't know,' he repeated. He cast his eyes around his little office. 'One of them was a cop. One of ours. Tall, dark hair.' He rummaged on his desk a moment, held up a card. 'Padelin,' he said, looking up at Reinhardt. 'He was here earlier today. The other was one of your Feldgendarmerie. Reddish hair. Shorter than you. Glasses.' He shook his head. 'He came on Sunday. Really, nothing else.'

Reinhardt stared back at Mavrić a moment longer. The description sounded like Becker, but the important thing was the Feldgendarmerie were at least a day ahead of him, and Padelin had been and gone as well. He nodded. 'The police. They took someone?'

'Zoran Zigić. One of the waiters.'

'They tell you why?' Mavrić snorted and shook his head. Reinhardt could guess, but he would find out tomorrow. 'Very well. Thank you for your time.'

Mavrić nodded, coming around the desk over to the door and opening it wider for Reinhardt. His evening suit was loose on him, the sleeves bunching over his wrists and ankles, as if it were made for someone taller. 'My pleasure. I am sorry about Hendel, but you understand, I don't want any trouble here. This is a good club.'

Reinhardt stepped out into the corridor and paused, looking at the two closed doors. He turned back to Mavrić. 'Those are the private rooms?' Mavrić nodded. 'Show me the one Vukić used.'

Mavrić's mouth tightened, but he pulled a small bunch of

keys from his pocket and squeezed past Reinhardt to open the door to the right. There was a table, low, polished, surrounded by a curved sofa and other comfortable chairs, and there was a thick carpet on the floor. It was light, though, not because it was not red, but because of the long mirror that hung on the back wall to the right of the door, and the one that covered a large part of the ceiling. To the left, there was a window, and Reinhardt realised he was looking into the club from behind what he had thought was a mirror. It was a one-way glass. People could be in here, private, intimate, and yet look out there and observe the goings-on in the club. Reinhardt walked up to the window, looking at the backs of the band as they played. The sound of their music came through faintly. The room was well soundproofed.

Reinhardt turned around, seeing himself reflected in the mirror along the back wall, seeing the bar behind his reflection. 'Vukić liked this room in particular?' he asked, remembering the bedroom in Ilidža and the mirrors on the wall and ceiling there.

Mavrić looked startled. 'Yes,' he said, after a moment. 'She was often a guest in here. She enjoyed her privacy. Whenever she was out there, she was always on show, she would say. In here, she could relax. Be herself.'

Reinhardt glanced around the room again, not having to try very hard to imagine what might have gone on in here. 'Zoran,' he said, the moment the thought occurred to him. 'Zoran, the one the police took? He worked in here, didn't he?' Mavrić took a slow step into the room, looking blankly at him, and nodded. Reinhardt gave one last look around the room. 'Thank you for your time,' he said again, as he made for the door. It sounded so inane.

'Yes, of course,' replied Mavrić as he stepped backwards into the corridor to give Reinhardt space. His hand strayed out, hesitating. 'Please, err… Captain,' he said, glancing at Reinhardt's collar tabs. 'Please, I do not want any trouble. There will not be trouble for me? Because of this?'

Reinhardt looked at him a moment. Mavrić's eyes blinked hard around a fixed stare. 'I do not know,' he said, turning away. He paused at the door back into the club and looked back. Mavrić looked haunted, a man in clothes too big for him. 'I would worry more about Zoran,' he said, pushing open the door.

The noise was louder. The band had left its little stage and was playing around one of the tables. It was filled with drunken Ustaše, who were getting stuck into a folk song. Glasses in their hands, they sang with gusto, their throats and faces straining at the words. Reinhardt ran his eyes around the club quickly, watching as heads turned his way, some staring, some turning away. From the bar, Dragan motioned him over with a twitch of his head. 'That SS, the one I say of. He is here. He is asking about you.'

Reinhardt nodded his thanks. He turned and began making his way back through the tables, keeping his eyes fixed firmly on the maître d' where he stood by his lectern in front of the frosted glass of the entrance. He was passing the last of the tables when a waiter glided in front of him, round silver tray held against his chest as if to shield him. The man inclined his head slightly and gestured with his free hand. Reinhardt frowned at him, faked a small smile, and shook his head as he made to move around the side of the waiter. The man took the smallest of steps to block him. 'Sir. Please,' he said. This time, he made his gesture into an invitation, his arm extended to point across the back of the club, into the far corner. 'One of the guests would like to talk to you.'

Four men were sitting there. The light was dim, but Reinhardt could see that at least two of them were SS. There was nothing for it but to follow the waiter, who made to pull out a chair for him, but one of the officers hooked a boot around the chair leg and stopped him. The waiter froze, unsure of what to do, then backed away. Reinhardt did the only thing he could do and came to attention before them. In the quick glance he gave them, they were senior to him.

The officer who had hooked the chair was SS. His collar tabs bore the oak leaves of a Standartenführer – a colonel in the army – and his left cuff, where his arm rested on his table with his hand around a glass of beer, had a *Prinz Eugen* band. Seventh SS. Recruited mostly from the Volksdeutsche, Reinhardt remembered, the ethnic Germans. Sudetens. Hungarians. Yugoslavs. They were German, according to the Reich's definition, but they were touchy about it. The man was long limbed, obviously very tall, with limp blond hair and eyes of a pale blue – so pale, they were hardly visible in the dim light. His cheeks, though, bore a high red flush, maybe from the heat, or alcohol.

'Captain. What are you doing?' The voice was languid, a slur discernible in it, and an accent, just as the barman had said.

'Standartenführer,' said Reinhardt. 'I am on official business, conducting an investigation.'

'Into what, exactly? You've got the whole place astir with your questions.' The accent was Croatian, maybe Slovene, Reinhardt was sure of it.

'The murder of a German officer, sir.'

The officers glanced among themselves. The two SS grinned. The fourth man was an Ustaša, a squat lump of a man crammed into his black uniform like rubbish squeezed into a sack. 'Is that all you're doing, Captain?' asked the Standartenführer, as he sipped from his beer glass. His right hand rested heavily on the butt of his pistol, thumb tucked tightly behind his belt, and his fingers tapped a rapid tattoo on the holster.

'I'm not sure I follow,' replied Reinhardt.

'You're asking about Marija Vukić, as well.'

'Yes, sir. She was found dead with the officer. Therefore, she forms part of my inquiries as well.'

'Right,' said the officer, his glass held to his mouth and only his eyes visible over its rim. 'And what have you learned?'

'With all due respect, sir, I am not at liberty to divulge such details.'

The Standartenführer snorted, and the others around the

table made various motions of amusement, like a ripple across a pond and him the source of it, like a rock tossed into water. 'Sounds like a Jew, don't you think?' he asked his companions. '"*Not at liberty to...*"' he repeated, with a little whine in his voice. He said something to the Ustaša and the man laughed, his cheeks quivering like slabs of suet. Reinhardt flushed under their gaze. The officer's fingers tap-tapped on his holster, and he looked for a moment at Reinhardt's Iron Cross, his eyes narrowing. 'Are you Feldgendarmerie, Captain? You don't look like a chain dog.'

'Abwehr.'

The Standartenführer smiled, a wet gleam that slid rather naturally into a sneer. 'Yes. Well, would you like to ask me anything, Captain? I knew Miss Vukić rather well, you know.'

'By all means, sir. Are you able to shed any light on her movements in her last days, or perhaps offer information as to the motive behind her death?'

The Standartenführer's nose twitched. 'Marija Vukić was a slut, Captain. Don't let anyone tell you differently.'

'Come on, Mladen,' said one of the other officers. 'Take it easy.'

The Standartenführer ignored him. 'I saw you come out from the private rooms. I presume you saw the mirrored room? Yes? They told you, that was her hideaway? Her little sex parlour, for the fortunate few. And I say that with a pinch of irony, Captain. She'd fuck just about anything.' There was a snicker of laughter around the table.

'Present company excluded, of course, Standartenführer,' said Reinhardt. The table went still, but the SS officer's fingers continued their tap-tapping. Although Reinhardt felt himself break out in a sudden, icy sweat, he refused to be cowed, turning a deaf ear to the voice within that, aghast at his temerity, was urging him to back away. No good came of provoking men like this.

The Standartenführer stared back at him with dead eyes, then snorted. 'What was it I said?' Half to himself, half to his friends. 'Just like a Jew. Picking up the little details. Sniff-sniffing around.' He leaned forward, a sudden shift. The officer sitting behind him reached out a hand, left it hanging. Reinhardt saw it all from a distance. They were obviously used to a certain kind of behaviour from this man. Violent, probably unpredictable. 'No, Captain. I never had that dubious honour. Thank God. I'll bet you can still smell the stink of her rutting in there.'

Reinhardt allowed himself to breathe a little easier and gave that note of inner caution its head. 'There was something, indeed, sir,' he agreed. He needed to get away from there, and placating this officer was the best way out.

'A word of advice to you, Captain. This is a respectable club. Don't come back here asking questions and spreading rumours. And don't let me hear of you bringing noncoms in again.'

'Thank you, sir. And may I have the honour of knowing to whom I have been speaking?'

The officer took a long drink from his beer before answering. 'Standartenführer Mladen Stolić.'

'My thanks to you, Standartenführer. With your permission?' Stolić nodded a lazy dismissal, watching through heavy-lidded eyes as Reinhardt clicked his heels and inclined his head in salute.

'And you can take your salute and shove it up your arse. We did away with that in the SS a long time ago,' Stolić said, rising to his feet. 'This is the way it's done.' He slammed his heels together, his right arm pistoning up. '*HEIL HITLER!*' he bellowed. It felt as if the bar had come to a standstill. He held the pose a moment, then relaxed, his right hand coming to rest on his belt buckle. He smiled. 'Now. Your turn, Captain.'

Reinhardt stared back at him, then blanked his mind. 'Heil Hitler!' he returned, fixing his eyes on the wall behind Stolić's head. For a panicked moment Reinhardt thought Stolić would make him do it again, but he just smiled, took his seat, and resumed his conversation. Reinhardt took a step back and turned for the door. Stern came around from behind his lectern to open the door, handing him his cap and inclining his head courteously as Reinhardt went past.

'I trust your inquiries were successful, sir,' he murmured. 'A very good night to you. Do come again.'

10

Reinhardt stood out in the street; holding his cap by the visor, he flipped it onto his head, working his mouth around the memory of those words. Hueber waved at him from a little farther down the street, where Claussen had parked the *kübelwagen*. Reinhardt acknowledged him, taking the time to light himself a cigarette and calm down. The night was hot, though far cooler than the club had been. Reinhardt could smell the smoke and sweat stink of it on his clothes. He wondered what someone as glamorous as Marija Vukić found in it. Maybe it was the only place like it in town. Beggars couldn't be choosers, he thought as he climbed into the car.

Claussen wound his way through a series of narrow roads until he came to Kvaternik, where he darted over and across a bridge, turning right at the end of it. He glanced at a map scrawled hastily on a piece of paper he held in one hand, counting off streets to his left before hauling the *kübelwagen* into one of them and bringing it to a stop, the engine clattering into silence.

The neighbourhood was one of those built by the Austrians not long after they began their occupation. Designed along functional rather than ascetic lines, the houses and buildings were blocky, most of them two floors, some with three. There was no street lighting, only a few lights were on or visible, and there was the smell of wood smoke and cooking in the air. Voices drifted through the night. A child cried somewhere, a woman shouted, a man answered back.

'What was the address?' asked Reinhardt. Claussen flicked on a torch, shining it onto Mavrić's piece of paper. 'No number,' said Reinhardt. 'Fourth on the left. Claussen, stay with the car again. Hueber, with me.'

The sergeant took an MP 40 machine pistol from between the seats, cocking it as Reinhardt and Hueber set off down the street. The arrival of the car could not go unnoticed. Faces appeared at windows only to vanish just as fast. Curtains twitched. A door cracked open as Reinhardt walked past, a child peering out. There was a frantic burst of whispering, and the child was pulled backwards and the door pushed shut. There was the sound of a blow, and the child began to cry.

The fourth house was a two-storey affair, with a wooden staircase up one side of it. Not knowing which floor to take, Reinhardt knocked on the front door. From behind the curtains drawn across a small window next to the door, he could see a line of light, so someone was home. He knocked again, heavier. A quavering voice came from behind the door, an old woman by the sounds of it. Hueber stepped up to the door and called through it. The voice answered back, and Hueber motioned up with his eyes.

The wooden staircase creaked alarmingly under their feet as they climbed. It ended in a small landing with a carved wooden railing. There was a door, slightly ajar, a wash of light like a candle's playing across it. The sounds of women's voices came from the apartment within. Two women, singing together softly, then a pause, and laughter. Soft and crystalline, the sound of something metallic shaking, like chains. The sound made him stop, made his heart suddenly clench. How long had it been since he had heard a woman laugh?

Reinhardt swallowed hard and walked up to the door. He knocked softly, then again, harder. The door gave under his hand, and he saw as the light flickered over it that the frame around the lock was broken, shards and splinters of pale wood showing against the black. A woman's voice called something, and he stepped into a cluttered room, piled with costumes and dresses, shoes and boots of all kinds all over the floor. A pile of boxes was stacked haphazardly in one corner, and as he came in farther, he saw in the other corner a small table with pots and bowls of makeup. A woman with long blond hair sat staring at him in a mirror under a pair of lanterns that hung from the ceiling, the light inking the cracks that crazed the rough plaster of the walls. A second woman looked up at him from a low stool next to the other, her dark, heavy features of the sort Reinhardt automatically associated with Gypsies. Full lips, liquid eyes, and thick black hair she was combing into a tress over her left shoulder, letting part of it hang over her forehead, over her eye and cheek, and Reinhardt was fairly sure it was all in order to hide the bruise that blackened her left temple.

There was silence as he looked between them. The Gypsy lowered her hands and straightened her shoulders, sending a necklace of coins sliding and tinkling over what was, Reinhardt realised, a quite substantial bust. Whether it was because she saw his gaze slide down then back up, or because of who he was, or because she would have done the same to any man who walked in on her, a fire bloomed in those big eyes.

'Ko si ti, i što želiš?' The challenge in her voice was unmistakable.

Reinhardt did not bother turning to Hueber for a translation. He took another step into the room. 'Do either of you speak German?' he said, looking between the two of them.

The women exchanged glances, and the Gypsy looked about to speak when the blonde put out her hand. 'I speak German,' she said softly. The Gypsy subsided, but the fire remained bright in her eyes as she crossed her arms under her considerable breasts. 'What do you want? Didn't you cause enough harm before?'

'Your names, to start with,' replied Reinhardt, ignoring the accusation.

The blonde sighed, gently. 'I am Anna. This is Florica.'

'The barman at Ragusa, Dragan, said I should talk to you,'

said Reinhardt. The Gypsy frowned and muttered something darkly under her breath. 'You knew Lieutenant Hendel?' Anna nodded. 'You are aware that he has been killed?' The blonde nodded again, face blank. 'How did you know him?'

'He would come to the club, often. He liked our music.'

'That was it?'

Anna shrugged. 'He said he liked me.' She pursed her lips, looking straight at him. 'He was kind. Generous. We spent some time together. How much detail do you want?'

'You do not seem too surprised at his death.'

'Your chain dogs told me. Last night, when they came looking for Peter.'

Reinhardt noted the colloquial reference to the Feldgendarmerie, but what surprised him more was the fact that Becker had told him nothing this morning. 'Hendel's first name was not Peter.'

Anna frowned slightly. 'I know. It was Stefan. They were not looking for him. It was Peter Krause they were looking for.'

Reinhardt ran his bottom lip across his teeth. 'Who is Peter Krause?' Something jogged his memory. Why did he know that name?

'A soldier,' replied Anna, simply. 'One of Stefan's friends.'

'And the Feldgendarmerie were looking for him?' Anna nodded. 'Did they say why?'

'They said he was a deserter. But I don't think that's what it was. They kept asking whether Stefan had ever given him anything, or had he left anything with us. They turned this place upside down,' she said, motioning around the room.

'And gave your friend that black eye, correct?'

Anna nodded. Florica, who it was clear spoke at least some German, drew herself up, which had the unfortunate side effect of pulling her dress even tighter across her bosom, and glared at them. Her eyes were liable to strike sparks and it was lucky for her, thought Reinhardt, the Feldgendarmerie had left her just with a bruise.

'What did they think Krause had?'

'They didn't say. They just kept asking, and I kept saying I didn't know. But I think it was some pictures. I heard them talking. Especially the one in charge, the second time they came.'

'They came twice?'

'The first time was on Sunday, in the evening. The last time was this morning. They were in a big hurry to find whatever they were after. The one in charge was very angry. He hit us.'

'A tall man, blond? Big chest?' Reinhardt asked, pushing up his shoulders.

'No,' replied Anna. 'Thin, and quite short. And he had thin hair. Dark, like red,' she said, tilting her head down, and checking for Reinhardt's reaction through her eyelashes. She tilted her head as Florica whispered something at her. 'And glasses. Little metal ones.'

She had described Becker quite accurately, despite Reinhardt's attempt to throw her off. Why had he stymied Reinhardt? 'What did they want?' he asked, again.

Anna sighed. 'Do you maybe have a cigarette?'

Reinhardt shook a couple of Atikahs from his pack and offered them to her and Florica, who refused with an imperious shake of the head. Reinhardt lit a match and Anna leaned forward. She cupped her hand lightly around his as she lit the cigarette, closing her eyes as she exhaled a long cloud of smoke.

'They wanted what, you said?' Her hand was warm and soft where it lay around his.

She shook her head and opened her eyes. 'I didn't say,' she said. She let go of his hand, slowly. 'I don't know. I said I think it was pictures. They kept asking if Peter had a camera, and where it was. Or if Stefan was a photographer.'

'Were either of them?'

'I never saw either of them with a camera.'

'Krause,' said Reinhardt, after a moment. 'Can you describe him?'

Anna and Florica exchanged glances, the Gypsy shrugging expressively. 'Sort of, nothing special, really,' said Anna. 'Brown hair. A little bit fat.'

'His rank?' Anna shook her head, pursing her lips slightly, and drew deeply on her cigarette again. Reinhardt turned, taking in the room, the jumble of possessions. The Feldgendarmerie were looking for something, more than someone, but the someone was unknown to Reinhardt. Someone completely new to the investigation. 'Were they often together, Hendel and Krause?'

Anna nodded, thoughtfully. 'I think so. They were often at the club together. And here, sometimes.'

'How did Hendel seem to you? The last time you saw him.'

Anna exchanged a glance with Florica. The Gypsy stared back at her. 'He seemed excited,' said Anna, finally, still looking at the other woman. 'Something at work, he said,' turning to look at Reinhardt. 'I know it had something to do with Marija Vukić, but he did not say what.'

'Do you know what kind of relationship the two of them had?'

Again, that exchange of glances between the women. Florica snorted and turned away, exasperated. Anna hissed something after her, her eyes darting back to Reinhardt, then back to the other woman. 'I know the kind of relationship he wanted to have,' she said, finally. 'But she was not interested.'

Florica spun back towards Anna, hissing something at the blond girl. Anna snapped back, the two of them whispering urgently, their voices dragging at the back of their throats. Reinhardt turned to Hueber. The young corporal was fascinated by the two of them, his eyes flicking back and forth between them. 'What are they saying?' asked Reinhardt.

'They're saying, sir…' He cut off, and Reinhardt looked back at the women. They were both staring at the boy like cats at a wounded bird. Hueber blushed bright red again. 'They're saying, at least, Miss Florica is saying, that Hendel, that is, Lieutenant Hendel, could not have Miss Vukić, so he used Anna as the next best thing,' he finished desperately, his embarrassment written plain across his face. Anna's face coloured, but when Hueber had finished speaking she held Reinhardt's eyes nevertheless.

'Very well,' he said, finally. He brought his heels together and bowed his head to each of the women. 'My apologies for the interruption, and my apologies especially,' he said, looking at Florica, 'for the way you were treated.' The pair of them looked more than a little taken aback at the courtesy. 'I wish you both good night.'

Clattering back down the steps, Reinhardt looked up at the stars. They shone bright here, even in the city. There was almost no light to rival them, just the mountains to frame and block them. Stepping back onto the street, he looked for a moment towards the looming bulk of Mount Trebević to the south, along the rise and roll of its long summit where it cut the night sky in two, then turned back towards the car. In the darkness, with no one to see, he lifted his hand and smelled Anna's perfume where it lingered faintly on the back of his fingers.

There was a metallic clack as Claussen stepped out of the shadows, putting the safety back on the MP 40. He had turned the *kübelwagen* around so it was pointing back towards the city, and he wasted no time in gunning the car down the narrow street and back towards the bridge.

Back in his room, Reinhardt slumped back against the door as he closed it, feeling drained. It had been one of the longest days he could remember in quite a while. The difficulty of thinking like a policeman again. The stress the city always engendered in him, with its labyrinthine character. The hostility of the people. The mistrust of his own side. But in the middle of that, he felt a sense of lightness. Of completion. A thread to long ago, a memory of a better man, better times.

He sat on his bed, emptying his pockets on the table. He poured a drink and knocked it back, poured another, and unholstered his pistol, watching the light ripple across its matte surface. He turned it up, looking down the shiny roundel of its muzzle. His finger slid across the bruise at his temple, then gently beneath his nose, smelling Anna's scent. He reached for his glass. And then his mind went suddenly blank, and he saw it – the motorcycle and sidecar, parked in front of Vukić's. Two men. Hendel and Krause. God, what a fool he'd been.

He looked down at his hands. He saw himself as if from far away, with the eyes of the man he used to be, and he did not like what he saw. Pistol and glass. His two faithful companions. This macabre ritual. With a stir of self-loathing, he put them both away, kicking off his boots, throwing an arm over his face. It was enough for today. Tomorrow would bring as much, if not more.

11

TUESDAY

As arranged with Padelin, Reinhardt arrived in front of police headquarters at nine o'clock the next morning. For once, he had slept well, and it was only the rumble of heavy convoy traffic down the Appelquai that had finally dragged him from bed. The receptionist at police headquarters called up to Padelin and indicated to Reinhardt that he should wait. Reinhardt pantomimed waiting outside, and the clerk nodded vigorously that he had understood. He bought a couple of newspapers from a kiosk and found a little patch of sunlight and scanned the headlines and some of the text.

Vukić's murder had made the front page of all of them. The *Novi Beher* had a big picture of her meeting Pavelić, the leader of the Croats. He could not make out whether a suspect had been named, although he saw Putković's and Padelin's names. After a while, he folded the papers, lit a cigarette, and waited, thinking back to the morning briefing at HQ. The Feldgendarmerie had reported that the police had been shaking the city down all night, cars showing up here with suspects for interrogation. Reinhardt knew from experience it was hard to find anyone with a dragnet like that, and it was more a case of rounding up the usual suspects and putting on a good show before the senior official that Padelin had mentioned arrived from Zagreb.

The doors to police HQ opened, and a policeman stepped out, holding the door for a woman dressed in black. She came slowly down the steps and fitted a hat to her head, placing it carefully over her ash-blond hair, and he recognised her as Vukić's mother, whom they had interviewed yesterday. Reinhardt straightened as he watched her walk slowly away, something in her bearing, in the way she seemed to be holding herself up and together, demanding that he stand in the best way he could. She did not see him, her eyes somewhere very far ahead. He watched her, her shoulders braced as if she walked into a high wind, one only she could feel, until she turned a corner and was gone, but his eyes stayed fixed on the point where she had been.

When he got home from the hospital the day Carolin died, Friedrich was there. The day had unspooled itself in shreds, the light wavering, people moving like marionettes, as in those old silent films. Somewhere distant he seemed to hear the sound of a piano, like the one they played in the cinema when he was a boy. A scratchy reel of notes just out of rhythm, and that tinny soundtrack to the mess his life had become had eventually led him home.

Reinhardt saw the bags on the floor of the hallway as he opened the door, and the soldier, tall and slim in his grey uniform. His son looked at him, looked him up and down. Reinhardt flushed, twisting his hat in his hands, feeling like a supplicant. In his own home.

'You've been drinking,' was all Friedrich said.

He had not. Not that day, but Friedrich would not believe that, so he said nothing, only shrugged out of his coat. Another soldier walked out of Friedrich's room, a bag in his hand. Hans Kalter. A year older than Friedrich and the model his son followed. A corporal already, Reinhardt saw. Kalter said nothing, watching with the confident air of a man who knows the outcome of a particular fight. Reinhardt hung up his hat and coat and walked past Friedrich into the kitchen, shying away from that coldness he always seemed to feel around him. He felt Friedrich looking at him as he shifted slowly around the room, lighting the gas for water to boil.

'Nothing to say, Father? Nothing about the uniform? Didn't you say never to come back here wearing it?' Playing to the gallery, and sure enough, Kalter straightened, seemed to swell with indignation.

'What are you doing here, Friedrich?' Reinhardt asked, finally.

'I'm picking up the last of my things. What does it look like?'

'That's what it looks like,' Reinhardt agreed, quietly. He spooned tea into a small pot. Blue china. The one Carolin always used. He almost never drank tea. He felt Friedrich watching him. He had seen it too. Their eyes met. Something sparked deep behind their flat sheen, behind the blank façade his son seemed to hold up for his father.

'Where is she?'

'She died last night. Early this morning, in fact,' he finished, as the kettle began to whistle. He poured the water slowly, as she used to, hearing it purr softly over the leaves, watching it rise up the inside of the pot, watching the steam curl up and out. 'Would you like some tea?'

Friedrich was white. 'When were you going to tell me? Were you just going to leave me to guess?'

'When would I have told you, Friedrich?'

'When you walked in.'

'I just did.'

'You waited. You did it on purpose.'

'You're a grown man, now, Friedrich. That's what you keep telling me...'

'That's what you won't believe!'

'... and so a man needs to pick and choose his words like he picks and chooses his fights...'

'Like you? Like you?!'

'... as otherwise he'll be left looking like a fool.'

'Are you calling me a fool, Father?'

'And if you accuse your father of being a drunk...'

'You are. You are. A bloody drunk.'

'... don't be surprised if the conversation takes a turn away from where it might have gone.'

There was silence. How fast they had come up against each other. Fallen into the rhythm of their assigned roles. Parry, riposte, words skirling, useless hard scrabbling against each other.

'A fool?' Friedrich blustered, after a moment. 'My choices foolish? My choices are Germany's, Father. Are Germany's choices foolish?' He opened his stance, inviting Kalter into the conversation.

Kalter stepped forward. 'I would have thought a German man, a veteran, would know better than to treat his son in this manner.'

'When you've got one of these, Corporal,' he said, jerking his thumb at the black dress ribbon of his Iron Cross where it was fixed to his lapel, 'or better yet, when you've lost a leg or an arm, then come back and lecture me about the duties and responsibilities of a German soldier.' Reinhardt put Carolin's blue cup and saucer on the table and sat there looking at her chair, his mind beginning to skirt around the understanding that she had filled not one space, but many. And he was only beginning to learn just how many, and where.

'She died in her sleep, Friedrich. They say she felt no pain.' Reinhardt looked at him but felt nothing anymore. No connection across to the boy he had been, and still was, in so many ways.

Friedrich swallowed hard, his jaw tendon tight. 'You just want to make me feel guilty. You always...'

'Get out, Friedrich. Do as you said. Don't come back.'

He sat there, the blue china pot and the blue cup and saucer in front of him, watching the steam writhe in the air as the door slammed at the end of the hall and an emptiness suddenly gaped underneath him, within him.

He sat there until the tea went cold, and the night came down on that day, which had unspooled itself like a film. And as with a film, it always ended the same way, each of them playing out a role, even if one of the actors was missing now.

Reinhardt sat in his little patch of sun, his mind far away, until Padelin showed up about ten minutes later, coming heavily down the stairs with his jacket under his arm, rolling his shirtsleeves down. Reinhardt could see that he looked exhausted. His eyes were dark, his hair lank, and he had not changed his clothes. They shook hands, and Reinhardt noted the swelling and bruising across the knuckles. 'Busy night?'

Padelin looked down. There were flecks of blood on the cuffs of his shirt. He turned those heavy eyes on Reinhardt and nodded. 'You could say that.'

'Anyone confessed?'

'Not yet.'

'Right.'

'You have had breakfast yet?' asked Padelin. 'No? Then let us have something.'

Padelin took them to a place on Zrinjskoga Street, around the corner from headquarters. It was obviously a policemen's haunt. Heads came up and greetings were offered to Padelin. From the tone of voice and the laughter and shoving that ensued, not a few of the comments were on what he had been doing to get in the state he was in. To a chorus of cheers, a policeman even bigger than Putković raised Padelin's arms over his head like a prizefighter. It made Reinhardt nostalgic and uncomfortable in equal measure. He remembered the party they had thrown for him and Brauer when they finally caught Dresner, the Postman. The big officer grinned, brought his head close to Padelin's, and said something, one hand patting the back of his neck. Padelin turned and indicated Reinhardt. The huge policeman looked him up and down, then nodded and left with a final ruffle of Padelin's hair.

'Who is that?' asked Reinhardt. 'Your fan club?'

Padelin shrugged as they sat at an empty table. 'That's Bunda.' He said it like that was all that needed to be said.

'Looks like a man you wouldn't ever want to have angry at you.'

Padelin allowed a small smile to flicker across his mouth. 'No. You would not. Like I said, Vukić was popular. People want her killer found. I must wash. I will order something,' he said, and left.

The atmosphere of the place was thick with smoke. Despite the warmth of the morning, no windows were opened. That, the low hum of conversation, and the glances at him over hunched shoulders and crossed arms, and Reinhardt began to feel uncomfortable. Bunda appraised him openly, staring at him through eyes sunk deep under heavy brows, a cigarette like a toothpick where it poked out between his thick fingers. It was with a surprising degree of relief that he saw Padelin coming back. He had combed his hair and found a fresh shirt somewhere. Coffee and rolls arrived as he sat down, and Padelin began to eat with that methodical, head-down attitude he had shown yesterday. Reinhardt sipped his coffee and winced, forgetting that Croats often served their coffee already sweetened, and there was too much sugar in it.

Padelin finished his breakfast and ordered a second cup of coffee. 'I talked with our traffic police, but they have nothing for the times we're interested in. Here.'

Reinhardt took a couple of sheets of paper, with handwritten entries between ruled columns. He flipped between the two. There were only a few entries on each page. He noticed the word for *fire* and pointed to it, his eyebrows raised.

Padelin leaned over, and nodded. 'Yes, there was quite a big fire on Sunday night, in Ilijaš. I heard about it.' He scanned the entry. 'Looks like they had to call in one of the fire engines from here to help put it out.'

'Forensics?'

'Still being worked on.'

'Pathologist?'

Padelin reached into his coat and pulled out some papers and handed them over. There were two pages, folded lengthways down the middle, and then in half, in the manner they used in Yugoslavia. It was the little differences in things that always struck Reinhardt. 'There's the report. Nothing we don't already know. Severely beaten. Stabbed to death. Any of three wounds in particular would have killed her. One to the heart, and two to her lungs. There were signs of sex. The pathologist does not think it was rape. Hendel, well, we know what happened to him. But the pathologist said that, given the entry and exit wounds he suffered, it was not a nine-millimetre round that killed him. Something smaller.'

'Probably 7.62 millimetre, then,' said Reinhardt. 'Can't say it narrows it down that much, but it's something. I talked with some of our people yesterday. It seems there was a planning meeting in Ilidža over the weekend. There were a lot of senior officers in the Hotel Austria, not far from Vukić's house.'

Padelin looked at him. 'Your point being?'

Confronted with such apparent lack of interest, Reinhardt was at a loss. 'Maybe something. Maybe nothing. You saw the collection of photographs at Vukić's house? You remember what her mother said, about her being attracted to men of power and authority? It's something to consider. No?'

'I suppose so,' said Padelin, his eyes looking out the window.

Reinhardt felt a flush of annoyance. 'What about your side of things?' Padelin raised an eyebrow. 'Has anyone had a look at the darkroom? Been able to catalogue what might be missing? What about Vukić's movements? When she was last seen. Where she was last seen.'

'The maid was the last person to see her.'

'So she says,' replied Reinhardt, willing Padelin to tell him about the Ragusa and whatever else was going on.

Padelin pursed his lips and shook his head. 'She didn't lie to me.'

'No,' replied Reinhardt. 'She probably didn't. But that doesn't mean she's right. About being the last person to see her. What about before that? We have all of Saturday to account for, at least.'

Padelin nodded ponderously and raised a placating hand next to his coffee cup. 'Saturday, yes. Friday, she was working. I have confirmation of that from this man we're going to see now. She worked late with her film crew, then told them she was going home.'

'So, apart from the maid, the last time anyone saw her we know of would have been Friday evening. That's a lot of time to account for.'

'She was at home. The maid confirmed it.'

'When did the maid arrive?'

'Saturday morning.' A frown touched Padelin's face.

'And she can testify Vukić was there all day, until she left?'

'Yes.'

'She had no visitors?'

'No.'

'She made or received no telephone calls?'

'I don't know.'

'So we still have two gaps. Friday evening to Saturday morning. And from when the maid left until she came back and found the body.'

'Reinhardt.' There was an edge to Padelin's voice, people looking up from other tables. Reinhardt felt a sudden wash of fear as the big detective's eyes sparked. 'What point are you trying to make here?'

Reinhardt looked back at him. The fear was gone as fast as it came, replaced by something much colder and more calculating. This was the first reaction he had really elicited from Padelin. He leaned in close. He had to get close. He could not afford to show fear in front of Padelin. Especially not here, in this bar. 'That it's a bit too soon to be *interrogating* suspects,' he said, with an edge to his own voice, 'and celebrating closing a case, when we can't even begin to account for something so simple as her movements.' He stared hard at Padelin, then sat back, shaking his head slightly. 'When were you going to tell me about the Ragusa?'

'What?'

'Ragusa. You arrested one of the waiters. Zoran Zigić. Last night.'

Padelin stared back at him for a long moment. '*Jebi ga*,' he muttered, finally, and then belched softly for a man of his size, to which a couple of the policemen at the nearer tables offered what must have been pithy comments as it set off a new round of laughter in the bar. The ghost of a smile touched Padelin's lips during all this, and Reinhardt could not help but smile back, but Padelin's next words wiped it away. 'I think I said before, I don't need to be told how to do my job. I am satisfied in my knowledge of Vukić's movements, and her death is my affair. That part of the investigation I take care of myself.' He stopped and swirled his coffee before knocking the rest of it back. 'Zigić is part Serb. We also think he's closely related to a senior member of the Communist Party, here in Sarajevo. Someone we've been after for a while. And we think the Communists are involved. So, arresting him, we – how do you say? We take two birds with one stone,' he said, sitting back in his chair. 'Are you afraid we will solve this before you?'

Reinhardt shook his head, the skin around his eyes crinkling in frustration. 'Padelin, it's not a race.' Then he thought of the Feldgendarmerie. Becker's stalling. A day ahead of him, and Padelin filled in what was suddenly racing through his mind.

'Of course it's a race, Reinhardt,' he said, shaking his head. 'Maybe you just don't know it yet, but you should.' Reinhardt stared back at him, struck speechless. 'You are fortunate, in a way, that this case has not attracted so much attention on your side. Still, you are hoping your investigation does not lead you into trouble with your commanders, right? That you can solve this in the proper way. The way you would like.'

'*My* investigation?' repeated Reinhardt. It was all he could manage. Any thought of telling him about Krause was gone, at least for now.

'My mistake,' said Padelin, placidly, and not at all sincerely. 'I misspoke.'

'All right. So now, we're going to see Vukić's film crew, correct?'

'Just one. Her sound recorder.'

'Sound engineer?' Padelin nodded, covered a yawn with his hand, and pinched the bridge of his nose. 'Ready when you are, champ.'

Padelin endured a series of loud farewells as they left. Picking up Reinhardt's car, the detective directed Reinhardt towards Bjelava, to a relatively new area of housing and businesses at the western entrance of the town, constructed between the two wars, laid out in blocks. They stopped in front of a five-storey building. Following Padelin into the foyer through a door that squealed on rusty hinges, he scanned the address boxes for what he wanted. 'Second floor,' he said. The door was opened to their knock by a thin young man with floppy blond hair and glasses. He was what Reinhardt took to be fashionably dressed, with a burgundy knitted waistcoat on top of a blue shirt, its top button undone over a loosened, dark blue tie.

'Jeste li policija?' he said. His eyes were red, and puffy, as if he had been crying. Padelin showed him his identification and gestured at Reinhardt as they talked. 'Jeste, I can speak German,' the man said, as he let them in into a broad, open room. Filmmaking equipment was scattered all around: screens hanging from the walls, projectors, film reels, tripods and lights and other gear standing in corners. At one end of the room was a huge mirror, a tatty old couch under it covered in newspapers, magazines, and photos, like the kind of glossy prints film stars had made of themselves. On a big table in the middle of the room lay a disassembled camera, one of the big ones used for making films, surrounded by parts and tools. An overflowing ashtray and a pack of cigarettes sat next to a pile of newspapers. Beneath the smell of tobacco was a sharp chemical tang, as in Vukić's darkroom.

The young man motioned them towards some high stools at

the end of the big table. He lit himself a cigarette without offering one. He held his right forearm vertically, his elbow cupped in his left hand, and held the cigarette lightly between his fingers, wrist tilted back. It was a strangely effeminate gesture. Reinhardt wondered if Vukić had smoked, and if she had, had she held her cigarettes like that. 'I am Duško Jelić. What can I do for you?'

'You were told we are investigating the murder of Marija Vukić?' asked Padelin.

Jelić nodded, his eyes welling up again. 'I am sorry,' he sniffled. 'I cannot seem to stop crying. You know? Since I heard.'

'Yes,' said Padelin. 'We are sorry for your loss. Did you work with her a long time?'

'About two years,' said Jelić, around a deep drag of his cigarette. 'I was the sound engineer. It was Branko took care of the cameras and films. He's not here. He had to go back to Zagreb on Friday.'

'And when was the last time you saw her?'

'Friday as well. She was here.' He motioned towards one of the doors that led off from the central space. 'She has… had an editing studio. Just a small one. We were cutting the film we took in Višegrad. She sat just there.' He pointed at the couch. 'We talked, and laughed, and had coffee.' His eyes watered over.

'How did she seem to you?' Reinhardt looked at the mirror and the couch, remembering the room in the club, and for a moment he imagined Vukić sitting there. Her legs crossed at the ankles as she read a magazine. No, too demure. Too like her mother. Crossed with one leg on her knee, like a man, and she was slumped back in the couch, one hand around a cup of coffee as she laughed and joked.

Jelić shrugged and looked at them with wide eyes. 'What can I say? She was normal. Happy. Funny. She was looking forward to the weekend. There was a man coming, I think. But she was also very engaged in this film. She wanted it to be right,' he continued, 'because they were going to show it in Zagreb, to

Pavelić. She kept Branko here so late, I was sure he would miss his train, but she drove him down to the station herself.'

'This man you just mentioned,' said Padelin. 'Did you know who it was?'

Jelić shook his head as he stubbed out his cigarette with short, sharp movements. 'No.'

'Nothing at all?'

'I wasn't her keeper.'

'No,' agreed Padelin. 'No one is saying you were. But you were close to her. You knew her. And we believe this man may have been the one who killed her.' Reinhardt blinked at that. They had no reason to think that yet, least of all Padelin. The Sarajevo police already had their suspect, so what was this line of questioning? Just stringing things along? Keeping the nosy German happy?

The technician squashed the butt flat and looked up at them with rebellious eyes. Almost adolescent eyes. Reinhardt had seen that look in the eyes of his son, many times. Padelin seemed to see something too, because he sat up straighter. The sniffling man was gone, replaced by something that looked more like a jilted lover. 'Look, I didn't keep track of her men. You know what they say about sailors, right? A girl in every port? That was Marija for you.'

Reinhardt leaned forward. 'We understand she had a thing for older men.'

Jelić laughed. 'Yeah. And in uniform if she could get them. The truth was, though, she would fuck anything she took a fancy to that could move its hips fast enough and that wasn't dead.'

Without saying anything, Padelin rose and calmly struck him a thunderous blow across the ear with the flat of his hand. The slap reverberated around the room, followed by the crash and clatter of Jelić and his stool hitting the floor together. Jelić groaned in pain, his hand to the side of his ear. '*Picku materinu!*' he croaked. He sat up on the floor, his head down between his knees, gasping and swearing in Serbo-Croat. Padelin sat down as if nothing had happened and folded his big hands on the table. Jelić looked up and seemed to remember Reinhardt, and that he had an audience. '*Fuck!* What the *fuck* did you do *that* for?' he moaned, switching back to German. 'Did you see that?' he said to Reinhardt. 'Did you see what he just did to me?' Reinhardt nodded. 'And you're just going to let him do it?'

Reinhardt raised his eyebrows, more shocked than he wanted to let on. Padelin's sudden ferocity had awakened a slew of bad memories, of the last months and weeks of his service in Berlin, when that sort of casual violence had become commonplace, accepted. 'He's your problem, not mine.'

Jelić sneered. 'Fucking cops. You're all the *fucking* same.'

'Keep a civil tongue,' said Padelin, heavily. 'Or I'll give you another one to go with it. Sit down.' The technician picked up his stool and righted it, sitting down a respectful distance from Padelin's hands. 'And tell us about Marija Vukić, and what you know about the men she frequented.'

Jelić worked his jaw and winced. He straightened his glasses on his nose, and his hand crawled across the table to his cigarettes. He lit one, all the while keeping Padelin in sight out of the corner of his eyes. His hand shook as he held it. 'Look, all I know is Marija liked them… mature. And she liked to hurt, and to be hurt. That was her thing.'

'Masochism, is that what you're saying?' said Reinhardt.

'Right, that's it,' Jelić replied, still working his jaw. 'She was into pain. Watching it. And giving it. She got some sort of kick out of it. Some of the stuff we saw in Russia. And here. Jesus.' He trailed off, his eyes far away. 'Look, there was this story, right? I don't know if it's true. It was before I joined her crew. But I heard it like this. There was this Serb, rich, good-looking, someone important in Banja Luka. Banja Luka's a nice enough town. Nice river. Mostly Serbs. Rather, it was a nice town in which a lot of Serbs used to live. Until we came along, right?' He suddenly giggled. 'So, this Serb, he was famous before the war for something or other, I don't know. Music, maybe.' He took a furious drag on his cigarette, his other hand cupping his cheek.

'So, he's got nothing, he's due for deportation, and she sees him. In a line, or a queue, whatever, and he's with his family, and she takes a fancy to him, and she tells the Ustaše to give him to her. For something like a week, she takes him. Takes care of him, dresses him, feeds him, and she's fucki –' He flinched, looking at Padelin. 'And at the end of the week, they're in bed, and she cuts his throat, and leaves the body there and walks away.'

There was silence. Reinhardt and Padelin looked at each other, and each knew the other was thinking of that bedroom in Ilidža, and the knife wounds that had killed her. Could it be, wondered Reinhardt? Could it be that Padelin was right, and this was vengeance, pure and simple? 'Like I said,' Jelić said with his mouth all stretched out, eyes looking inward, trying to work out where it hurt the most, 'it's a story I heard. Might not be true. I never worked up the guts to ask her, even though we'd been through all kinds of hell together. But it's got enough of the Marija I knew for me to believe it. Angel and demon. Light and dark. Someone who cares for you, and someone who takes away all you have. Shows you the highs, and leaves you in the lows.' Reinhardt looked at the couch, and imagined Vukić on it, and something began to gnaw at him.

'Where were you before you came back to film in Bosnia?' asked Reinhardt.

Jelić got up and went over to a small stove. 'You want coffee?' he asked. They both shook their heads, and Jelić continued. 'Russia, until November last year,' he said, pouring a cup, then taking a small sip. 'Then back to North Africa, but that didn't last long because the Afrika Korps was getting kicked out by the British. That made her cross, as she had designs on Rommel.' Despite what was gnawing at him, Reinhardt could not suppress the grin he felt at her audacity. Jelić grinned sheepishly as he came back to the table, wrinkling his glasses on his nose. Only Padelin stayed expressionless. 'She wanted to go back to Russia. Thank Christ that one was turned down. She was angry about that, so we went to Stokerau, in Austria. We interviewed some of the surviving Croat soldiers from Stalingrad, watched the training for the new 369th Division. They're here now, you know. We filmed some of them up in Višegrad. Some of them remembered Marija from Stokerau. God, they were happy to see her…'

He trailed off, staring at his cigarette, then sniffed and took a deep draw on it. 'Italy, for a bit, earlier this year,' Jelić continued, 'filming the training of this new Croat division that the Italians are putting together. The Legion, they call it. We got back here about three months ago.'

'Did anything like this story you told happen in Russia? Or anywhere else?' asked Reinhardt.

'Not that I know,' replied Jelić. He seemed subdued now, turned in on himself. He lifted his cup to his mouth, then paused. 'There were three guys I know of who she was seeing in Russia. One of those affairs was just crazy. But that was pretty much straight-up sex, if what I heard was right.'

'And here?' demanded Padelin. Jelić shook his head. 'And you? Did you… ?' Padelin trailed off. Reinhardt looked at the table, trying to work out what was bothering him. Why was he thinking of mirrors?

Jelić shook his head. 'Not that I didn't want to.'

'What were the names of the men she was seeing in Russia?' asked Padelin.

'One was an SS general, but he was killed. The other two…' He sighed. 'I can't remember. There was one of them, though. Christ, half the division could hear them having sex. That one ended badly, apparently. That's all she'd say about it, but I wouldn't be surprised to hear they'd picked up where they left off.'

Reinhardt and Padelin sat up, Jelić cowering back from the big detective. 'What do you mean?' demanded Reinhardt. Mirrors. Why was he thinking of *mirrors*? Vukić in front of mirrors. At the club. Here. Her bedroom.

'Yeah, yeah. One of those guys she was seeing in Russia. I heard he was here. Heard his name, something like that, don't know, about a month ago, and asked her wasn't that one of her... one of her men.' His eyes glazed over a bit, as he focused inward, then back out at them. 'You know, she had the strangest look when I mentioned it. She said she knew he was coming. She knew he was coming, and she had it all planned out.

'Something happened between them, in Russia. I don't know what it was, she never talked about it. I'm pretty sure it was some kind of argument. Maybe a lovers' quarrel. Maybe he'd had enough of her, told her to get lost. That was something no man did to Marija. She'd never let them get away with it.' He looked between them. 'Hey, I mean, emotionally. Never let them get away with it *emotionally*. She'd find some way to get back at them.'

'Mr Jelić, do you think you'd be able to identify this general if I found a picture of him?' said Reinhardt.

The man pursed his lips. 'Look,' he hesitated, 'I don't *know* he was a general...'

'There's a good chance, correct? From what you've told us about her, and about what she liked?' said Reinhardt. Jelić shrugged, and nodded. 'We'll arrange it, then.' He pulled out a notebook. 'Give me the dates you were in Russia, please, when Vukić was seeing this man.'

Jelić swallowed and squirmed on his stool. 'Look. Sir. I really don't want anything to do with this. I mean, come on. Look at me. I don't want to get mixed up in stories like this. I wouldn't last a second.'

Reinhardt said nothing, just held his gaze as Padelin glowered next to him. Jelić's eyes narrowed and twitched, and he sighed out. 'Errr... it was last year. Hang on. I think I've got the dates somewhere.' He went over to a desk and, opening a drawer, pulled out what looked like a journal. Reaching out for it, Reinhardt was disappointed to see it was some kind of ledger, not one of the missing diaries.

Padelin peered over his shoulder, and turned a few pages with a thick finger. 'It's... how do you say?' He looked at Jelić.

'Accounts,' said Jelić. 'It's an accounts book. A ledger.'

Reinhardt flipped it around and handed it back to Jelić. 'The dates, please.'

Jelić lit another cigarette as he leaned over the book. 'Russia, Russia…' he muttered as he turned pages. 'Here. We arrived 4th August, 1942. Left…' He turned a page, then another. 'Left on 6th November.'

Reinhardt jotted it down. 'You have locations in there?'

Jelić puffed his cheeks and breathed out heavily, and coughed. 'Some. Hotels usually. Let's see. We flew in to Kharkov from Stokerau, stayed there a few days. Hotel Chichikov. Christ, what a dump that place was. Then out to the front, to join up with the 369th Division around… Selivanova. Back to Kharkov… then Glazkov with the division. The boys were refitting. Ah, yeah,' he said, looking up. 'Pavelić made a trip out to visit the troops.' He grinned. 'Yeah, that was a good evening. Medal parade in the afternoon, then dinner with the officers. That German general, what's his name? The one in Stalingrad… Paulus?' Reinhardt nodded, transfixed. 'Paulus. He joined us. First good food we'd had in a while, but Christ, you should have seen the way they were all over Marija. She had 'em wrapped around her finger. Pavelić, he was…' He looked up, as a man might look up expecting clear skies and instead the horizon was draped in thunderclouds. Jelić took a look at Padelin's face and went back to the book.

'That was the 24th September, and the end of the good times. The 369th went into Stalingrad a few days later. We hung around. Marija wanted to get into the city to do some filming, but the closest we got was the airfield at Pitomnik, and that was close enough.' He looked up at Reinhardt. 'We could hear the guns during the day, and during the night it burned. You could see it from miles away. You've got to feel sorry for the poor bastards who were in there. You know they say all the Croat boys are dead.'

Padelin snarled something at Jelić in Serbo-Croat, and Jelić snapped back, the detective's earlier violence towards him forgotten. Whatever it was he said, Padelin folded his hands on the table and just stared at him with those heavy eyes. 'I know what I saw,' Jelić said, quietly, staring back, and switching back to German. 'And I know what I've heard. None of them are coming back,' he finished, looking back down at the book. Reinhardt looked at him and swallowed in a dry throat, thinking of Jelić's description of the city where his son had vanished.

'Listen,' said Jelić, turning pages and then looking up. 'Do you need anything else from me?'

Reinhardt nodded. 'Do you know when Vukić met up with this officer in Russia?'

'Yeah, sometime in late August, early September. We left the 369th in Glazkov, and joined up with some Germans as they advanced towards Stalingrad. We were in Voroshilovgrad on 28th August. The Hotel Donbass. I'm pretty sure that she had met up with him by then, but I can't be sure. Rostov in early September. Then back to Glazkov, like I said.'

'When did they break up, Vukić and this officer, you remember that?'

Jelić shook his head. 'I really don't.' He stared at the pages. 'It was after we spent the first couple of weeks with the 369th. After Rostov, but before Pitomnik. So, sometime in September. Mid-September. She actually took off with him and his men for a few days while Branko and I stayed in the hotel. But the actual dates… I'm sorry, I really can't remember. Branko will probably remember better than me. He's usually good at dates. I'm hopeless.'

'Very well,' said Reinhardt, tapping his notebook with his pencil. 'Padelin? You have anything else?'

'Yes,' he nodded. 'Jelić, you can come down to headquarters. We have some suspects in custody you can look at. Let us know if you ever saw them together with Miss Vukić.' Jelić nodded again, although it looked like the last thing he wanted to do. 'And I want an address for Branko… ?'

'Branko Tomić,' finished Jelić. He scribbled a name and a Zagreb address on a piece of paper. 'I've no idea if he knows what's happened. Poor guy. He's been with her for years.'

'You've been most helpful, Mr Jelić,' said Padelin, with ponderous finality. 'I will be in touch to arrange a time to come to headquarters. No, don't get up.' He raised a hand. 'We'll see ourselves out. And put some ice on that jaw, or it will swell up.'

They left him in his studio, hunched over, watching them with feverish little eyes through a cloud of cigarette smoke. Downstairs, Padelin turned to Reinhardt. 'Did you get anything useful out of that?' His tone made it clear he had not.

Reinhardt drummed his fingers on the *kübelwagen*'s windshield and nodded. 'I did,' he said, distantly. 'Look, something he said is gnawing at me. Going around and around in my head,' he explained, seeing Padelin's look of incomprehension. 'Something about mirrors.'

'Mirrors?' grunted Padelin. He looked at Reinhardt, then away.

'I want to go back to the house in Ilidža for another look. Do you want to come?'

'You don't know what you're looking for?' demanded Padelin.

'Maybe nothing. Maybe something. But I need to see.'

'Very well,' he replied. 'I will come. It will be better if I do, in any case. We're supposed to be working together, yes?'

The road out to Ilidža was relatively empty of military traffic, and Reinhardt was able to drive fast all the way. Padelin sat quietly next to him, flexing his wrists and fists over and over again. They pulled up outside Vukić's and surprised the police guard who was dozing along the shady side of the house, next to the motorcycle and sidecar. The man blanched at the look on Padelin's face and fumbled the keys to the door, eventually getting it open and almost dropping his rifle as he stood aside and saluted them in. Reinhardt took the stairs quickly up to the second floor, through the living room and into the bedroom.

The curtains had been drawn open, the two lights at the foot of the bed were turned off, and the bed had been stripped. Otherwise nothing had changed. The head of the bed was still covered in blood, and it had soaked into the mattress. Reinhardt walked to the bedside table and looked back. He could see himself standing in the other mirror. A glance up, and he saw that the roof of the four-poster was also a mirror. Padelin watched him from the doorway.

Mirrors. She liked to watch, he thought. She liked to watch others. She liked to watch herself. He looked back and forth between the two mirrors, the one by the door and the one at the headboard. The blood on the light switch at the entrance caught his eye again. The mirrors. It was all a setup, he thought. Set up so that she could see. So that whoever was with her could see.

But it wasn't enough just to watch. This was elaborate. Why waste it? He turned in the room, looking for he knew not what, and came back to the two mirrors, and the blood on the light switch, and the two lights. This was like a set. A film set. She was a filmmaker. He walked slowly back towards the door and stopped, looking at the light switch. He pushed the top button, and the lights at the foot of the bed came on. He pushed the second, and lights in the roof came on. He frowned, not knowing what he had expected, but not that. Nothing that simple. He stood in front of the mirror, looking past his reflection, trying to look inside it. He took the mirror's frame in his two hands and pulled it. Nothing. He pushed, each side, shook it. Nothing.

He tried harder. The mirror did not move, seemingly bolted to the wall. He stepped back, and knocked the wall, stopped. Stared. He hit the wall again, harder, as he looked at Padelin. The wall boomed hollowly under his hand.

'There's a room behind here,' Reinhardt said. His eyes ran over the wall, stepped back. There was no entrance he could see, nowhere he could work out where one might be. Back and forth went his eyes, and then he looked down, imagining the space beneath him, and took off back downstairs.

The kitchen was gloomy, cool, like it seemed to be holding its breath. Reinhardt paused again and focused on that cupboard he remembered from his first time. The one with the big double doors, padlocked shut. He took the lock in his hands. It was a big, old-fashioned lock, a round hole in it for a key. He rattled the ring, and the shackle came loose from the lock. He froze, stared at it, then turned the lock in his hands and slipped the shackle through the ring. The padlock sat heavy in his hand, and he realised as he pushed the shackle down into the lock, then pulled it out again, that it would not work without a key. Someone had tried to put it back on the door but without the key it would not lock shut and so they had left it, made it seem nothing had happened. He pulled the doors open, looking into a deep space that was all but empty save for a ladder standing against one wall, an old broom, and a few boxes. Nothing else.

Reinhardt's mouth twisted as he stepped back. He had been so sure... He frowned, looked closer. The ladder was not standing against the wall. It was too upright. It was fixed to the wall. He looked up, seeing where it vanished into the ceiling. He reached up with his fingers and pulled at what looked like a latch, and the ceiling swung down, suddenly, releasing a wash of light that etched out the inside of the cupboard. He ducked, took the weight on his hands, then manoeuvred it past his head, looking up. The ladder continued up into the light. He exchanged a quick glance with Padelin, then began pulling himself up.

The ladder passed through a flimsy ceiling, into a space braced by a crisscross of beams, then up into a small room, bare of any furnishing, only one thing in it. The floorboards creaked softly under his weight as he crossed over to a tall rectangle of light and looked out into Marija Vukić's bedroom. There was creaking from the ladder as Padelin began to haul himself up. His head poked up, and then his shoulders heaved up and around, and the two of them stood squeezed into the small space, Padelin swearing quietly under his breath.

Reinhardt felt a lurch in his stomach, like one feels at the edge of a great height. A camera stood on a tripod, mounted in front of the mirror, its lens like a wet, black eye. He swallowed in a dry throat and reached out to open the film case, but it was empty.

12

Reinhardt thought about the ransacked darkroom as he stared at the camera. He thought about Anna, who thought the Feldgendarmerie were looking for pictures. Not pictures. Film. A film, he thought, glancing over at the bed, that probably showed Vukić's murderer. Whoever killed Vukić must have found out about this, or what she liked to do, and taken everything she had, just in case. He thought about the disassembled camera in the studio at Jelić's apartment, the chemical smell of the place.

'I need to get back to headquarters,' said Padelin. 'Can you drive me back?'

'*Christ*, Padelin!' exclaimed Reinhardt. Padelin's eyes went flat. 'This is *important*! Whatever happened here on Saturday night, it was probably filmed. And someone's got it. We need to search this place again. Question the maid. The gardener. The handyman, if there was one.'

The muscles in the sides of Padelin's jaw clenched, once. 'I need to get back,' he grated, 'and report this.'

Reinhardt clenched his jaw as well, then sighed and nodded. 'Very well.' Taking a last look around, he followed Padelin down the ladder and back out of the house to the *kübelwagen*. Padelin balled and rolled his fist again, flexing it back and forth. Reinhardt gestured at Padelin's hand. 'You all right there?'

'Fine,' replied the detective as he got into the car. 'I couldn't punch him. Jelić. My fists hurt too much already.'

Reinhardt said nothing during the drive back into town. The day was sweltering hot, and the heat was only slightly alleviated by the wind of the *kübelwagen*'s speed. He pulled up outside police headquarters, where Padelin got out. Two policemen on duty outside the entrance stopped talking to look curiously over at them.

'Padelin,' said Reinhardt. The detective turned to face him. Reinhardt felt a weight in his chest. A weight of words, and feelings, about how people like them, people with authority, should behave. But he knew he would get nowhere with them, and so he tamped down hard on them, pushing and squeezing those words and feelings down. 'I am going to try to speak with Major Gord. You recall, the soldier that Mrs Vukić mentioned she thought knew her daughter.' Padelin nodded. 'Are you interested in accompanying me to that interview?'

'Reinhardt,' he said, a sense of finality obvious in his voice. 'I am available. But I think my investigation will be ending soon. I am confident we have a suspect for Vukić's murder.'

'Fine,' sighed Reinhardt. He looked away a moment, then back. 'One thing you might consider, however, is finding out how many places in Sarajevo could possibly develop a film like the one that might have been shot at Vukić's place.' Padelin stared back at him, expressionlessly. 'Not many, I would think. Might be worth your while checking up on them.'

'What about where we just met Jelić?'

'Exactly,' said Reinhardt, taken aback that Padelin had given it any thought at all.

Padelin stepped back, shrugging into his jacket and pulling the knot up on his tie, and nodded goodbye. Reinhardt watched him walk up the steps into the building and saw the way the two policemen on duty straightened as he approached, saluting him, one going so far as to shake his hand. They smiled at each other as they resumed their hipshot stance and slouch against the wall, knowing looks, a thumb jerked in the direction Padelin had taken.

Reinhardt stared at them and then at the white-knuckled

grip he had on the wheel. He forced his hands to relax, to unclench, and then continued back to HQ, where he parked and walked up to his office, trying not to think about the bottle of slivovitz – the local plum brandy – he knew was in the bottom drawer. Looking at his in tray, he sifted through the usual correspondence, his mind elsewhere. He sat in his chair, the leather squeaking as he settled himself, his hand going to his knee. Glancing up, he stared at the map of Bosnia that hung on his wall, his eyes wandering from Sarajevo, east to Goražde, then south, down to Foča, Kalinovik, Tjentište, imagining the forces gathering there for the upcoming operation.

'Your case,' he muttered. '*Your* case.' In his mind, he saw those two policemen again, the respect they had shown Padelin. Their new hero. They must have someone, he thought. Someone who had confessed. Vukić's killer, who they would parade. Hendel's killer, well... Maybe they would pin that one on the poor bastard as well. Otherwise, they would just leave Hendel to the Germans. He felt a cold sweat break out over him at the thought of what that must mean, at what must have been going on in the cells under police headquarters, while he wandered back and forth across Sarajevo. Padelin had to know, *must*, that whoever they had did not do it.

Reinhardt jerked away from the desk, away from the drawer with that bottle. He knew he was prevaricating, shying away from the discomfort he had felt about the way Padelin had behaved. God only knew, he thought to himself as he stared at the map's contour lines and rubbed the ridges of his scarred knee, he had seen and heard and read of enough horror in his four years back under the colours to last him a lifetime. It was not that, he knew. Padelin was a policeman. Policemen, he still believed, should not act that way. Policemen, he still wanted to believe, despite all he had seen over the past few years, could be better than the system and the laws they served.

He had clung to that belief as long as he could, until the time, that one and only time, he had raised his fist to a suspect. That moment when the temptation, the pressure to conform, to be *just like all the others again* became too strong to resist. That one time, down in the cells under Alexanderplatz, knowing he could wipe away the sneer of that criminal with his fists, the goading from the other policemen to do it, *do it*, and he had. Then how he had run through Berlin's darkened streets, hammering on Meissner's door. Cowering in the corner of the colonel's drawing room with a bottle clutched to his chest as Meissner watched him from beside the fire, and the decision was made. The flight back to the army. Back to his first home.

'Gregor,' the colonel asked. 'Are you sure you want this?' The question went right through Reinhardt. That memory came to him again, of Kowel, and how Meissner's calm words reminded Reinhardt he was not the only man who was scared, turning a terrified and lonely young man into just a terrified one. Reinhardt had bound his life to Meissner's that day, the boy-man finding in the colonel a father like he might have wished for, and in the soldiers of his regiment the brothers. In memory of that day, Reinhardt had never lied to him. And he would not now.

'I am afraid. Of letting you down. But more than that. I am afraid I have lost whatever faith I might once have had that the work I was doing served for anything.'

'Will you go back in?' Meissner asked, finally.

'I'll do it for you, sir. For nothing else.'

Meissner sighed softly, then nodded, the fire playing across his white hair. 'Thank you.'

Reinhardt uncurled from his corner, putting the bottle down. 'Will that be all for now, sir?'

Meissner nodded. 'For now. We will talk later.'

As Reinhardt opened the front door, Meissner's hand came up gently on the wood and stopped him. Reinhardt looked down at his old colonel, now a senior member of the Foreign Ministry. There was a faint expression in Meissner's eyes, a glint hidden in their grey depths. 'You know, Gregor,' he said, softly, 'it is not such a bad thing. Joining the Party. They do not ask for much.'

Always this came back to haunt him. The Party. The bloody Party. 'Why did you do it, sir? Join it?'

The expression in Meissner's eyes never changed. 'I thought it was the best way for them to leave me alone to do my job. Why did you not do the same?'

Reinhardt's throat was dry as a bone, and he pressed his fingers tight against themselves, the pressure painful on his ring finger. God, he needed a cigarette. 'I suppose... I thought I could do mine without them.' He stopped, frightened he might have gone too far. 'I was right, for a while, no?' Meissner said nothing. 'But really, it was because of Carolin. She never had any time for them. You knew her. Social Democrat till... till the day she died. And... and because of her cousin.' He smiled wryly, made what was even to him a pathetic attempt to lighten an atmosphere gone suddenly heavy. 'I am just glad you never asked me to. I don't know what I would have done, torn between the two of you.'

The faintest nod. 'And if I asked now?'

Reinhardt knew he could never refuse this man anything. 'Please. Do not.'

'She is gone, now.'

'But I like to think the best of her will stay with me. I could never forgive myself for doing it. Even if... even if I knew she probably could.'

Meissner's hand fluttered down, away from the door. He stepped away. 'Go now, Gregor.'

There was a knock at the door. Reinhardt snapped around from the map, his mind flailing for a moment, caught between the here in his austere office and the there, Meissner's study and the crackle of a fire burning low as he closed the door on one life and opened a door on another. Claussen stood in the doorway. He cleared his throat and offered him a handwritten sheet of paper. 'Units taking part in Schwarz,' he said.

'Very good,' said Reinhardt. He scanned the list of units. 'Where did you get this?'

'From Vogts, downstairs in dispatch. If you want names to go with the units, I suppose you'll have to see someone in Abteilung III H.'

'Hmm,' murmured Reinhardt. He put the handwritten list on his desk and placed his hands to either side, leaning over it. 369th (Croat) Infantry Division. 1st Mountain Division. 7th SS Prinz Eugen, recalling his run-in with Stolić last night. 118th and 121st Jäger Divisions. 'Speaking of paper, here,' said Reinhardt, taking Padelin's pathology report on Vukić from his pocket. 'Can you get that to Hueber, or someone else who speaks Serbo-Croat? I want a verbal translation as soon as possible.'

'Yes, sir,' replied Claussen, slipping the report into a pocket.

'What about that appointment with Gord?'

Claussen shook his head. 'Gord's not here. I left you a message.' He flipped through some of the papers on the table. 'Here. Gord and the whole Propaganda Company are in Foča, covering Schwarz from there. Have been since 3rd May.'

Reinhardt remembered that with Brauer, sometimes they would start talking about a case. Just talking, ideas moving back and forth, and sometimes the investigation would take off or move in another direction. 'The Croats have someone. Someone's confessed, or is about to.' He felt, all of a sudden, that he had crossed a line, letting Claussen take the place Brauer once occupied. Still did, even though he was a continent away.

'A put-up job?' asked Claussen, quietly.

'I'm sure of it. There's tank-sized gaps in the Croat investigation, but they're not interested in investigating. And they're certainly not interested in investigating Hendel's death, or his involvement in all this.' He paused, chewing softly on his lower lip.

'So?' prompted Claussen, after a moment.

'So, I'm wondering whether our command will be happy

with the suspect the Croats present, or whether I should keep investigating.'

'You think this suspect can carry the weight of two murders?'

'I'm sure he could if we requested it,' Reinhardt replied, quietly.

The two of them looked at each other a moment. It was Claussen who shook his head. 'Kruger works in III H. You should go and see him with that list. He'll sort you out for commanding officers and whatever else you'll need.'

And just like that, it was over. Any hesitation Reinhardt had was gone, swept away by Claussen's simple directness. It was like a weight lifted, a weight Reinhardt had not known was there. 'No time like the present, I suppose,' he said, nodding to himself.

Reinhardt walked slowly downstairs, down a corridor of squeaking floorboards and a wall with peeling green paint, until he found the offices of Abteilung III, responsible for the security of the Abwehr and the armed forces. III H was the subsection charged with army security, and Lieutenant Kruger, who ran it, was a genial chap, expansive of girth and appetite. Reinhardt found him peering over his glasses at a file, a single, dim bulb the only illumination in his gloomy office. All four walls were covered in shelves with files with coded numbers up their spines.

'Captain,' said the lieutenant, standing and pulling off his pince-nez. 'What can I do for you, sir?'

'I need your expertise, Kruger,' replied Reinhardt. 'I need some names to go with some units. These,' he said, placing Claussen's list on the desk.

Kruger flipped the list around to read it, raising his eyebrows and lowering his mouth at the corners as he placed the pince-nez back on his nose. 'Pretty easy,' he said, walking to a row of files. 'What do you need this for?' he asked, over his shoulder.

'Oh, just updating my files,' replied Reinhardt. 'In advance of Schwarz.'

'Right,' said Kruger. He pulled a file out and flipped it open to a cover sheet that bore a list of typed names, all of which save for the last were crossed out. 'Here you go. 369th Infantry Division. Lieutenant General Fritz Neidholt commanding.'

'The same for the others, please?'

Kruger went through the list one by one, adding a commanding officer next to a unit that Reinhardt jotted down into his book. 1st Mountain, Lieutenant General Walter Stettner Ritter von Grabenhofen. 7th SS Prinz Eugen, Obergruppenführer Arthur Phleps, handing over command to Brigadeführer Karl Reichsritter von Oberkamp on 15th May. 118th Jäger Division, Lieutenant General Josef Kübler. 121st Jäger Division, Lieutenant General Paul Verhein commanding.

Reinhardt knew that no self-respecting general would be without his staff officers, and he would have liked to be able to note them down as well. They probably would also have been accompanied to the conference by their intelligence officers, and likely by some of their senior regimental and battalion commanders, but that was asking for too much. This was a good start, but before he went any further he would have to know whether this really was an avenue worth pursuing. Reinhardt stared at his list as Kruger looked over his shoulder. What he really needed was to cross-reference this with service history, to find out who among them had served in Russia.

Kruger snorted. 'Good luck with that. I don't have that information.'

Reinhardt froze. He had not realised he had spoken out loud. 'Who might?' asked Reinhardt, trying to keep his voice normal.

'Paymaster might.'

Reinhardt sighed long and softly. 'A lot of bureaucracy involved in getting anything out of them.'

'Unless you owe them money,' quipped Kruger, as he began putting his files away. He came back to his desk and paused with his hands on another. 'I'm sorry, Captain. I'm not sure how else I can help you.'

'That's fine, you've been very helpful.'

Kruger removed his pince-nez, rubbing the bridge of his

nose. 'What's an officer's Russian service history to do with your updating your files, anyway?'

Reinhardt froze, feeling a cold sweat suddenly break out down his back, knowing his mouth had run away with him. He looked at his list a moment longer, then raised his eyes to Kruger, forcing the cold he felt inside out of his gaze. 'Need-to-know basis, Kruger. Need-to-know.'

'Right,' said Kruger with a lopsided grin as he put his file away. 'Sorry.'

'No harm done. And thanks again,' said Reinhardt, through a parched mouth. Reinhardt walked back upstairs to his office, the cold sweat that had risen after Kruger's question drying away.

13

Back in his office, Reinhardt tossed his notebook on his desk and paced around his room. The bell at the cathedral began to toll, and he counted off the bells to midday. As the tolling faded away, a muezzin's call sounded from somewhere to the east, then another, and another. He decided to give Claussen another five or ten minutes to find Hueber, and then he would go for lunch. He thought a moment, then pulled a pencil and paper towards him and began to sketch out what he had so far on the case. He wrote *Vukić* in the centre of a blank page, and *Hendel* next to it. Then he jotted down what they knew, which was next to nothing – the car, and the cigarettes, what they knew of Vukić's life, what he knew of Hendel's duties. He wrote *murderer*, and stared at it. Then added a pair of parentheses to the end of *murderer* and added an *s*. More than likely there was more than one of them.

More names appeared on the paper – Freilinger's, Padelin's, Becker's – and the various organisations they served – the army, the Ustaše, the police, the Feldgendarmerie. Jelić, almost the last person they knew of who had seen Vukić alive. The map took shape, lines connecting names, sundry information jotted down next to names. Motives, such as he assumed them. Facts, such as he knew them. Avenues of investigation... Padelin's choice of a politically expedient suspect. Reinhardt's own investigation.

His stomach growled. Glancing at his watch, he saw that

nearly three quarters of an hour had gone by while he worked and wrote. He folded the map into his breast pocket and drove out through the heavy midday heat to the barracks. The officers' mess was a long, narrow room, overlooking the Miljačka and the strip of garden in which the band had played last night, and mercifully cool. Tables with white cloths were spread across most of the space, with a bar at one end of the room and a corner where a motley collection of armchairs and settees had been drawn up into a smoking and reading area. A swastika hung on the wall above the entrance, with a portrait of the Führer to the right. The walls were covered in unit plaques and other memorabilia. The place stank of cigarettes and pork and beer.

Most of the officers were done eating, but a sizable crowd was holding up the bar, and a group of senior officers Reinhardt did not recognise, mostly colonels it seemed, had colonised the reading area under a fog of smoke. Reinhardt chose an unoccupied table by the window and sat with his back to the bar, hanging his cap off his chair. A waiter appeared with a menu under one arm and a decanter of water in his other hand.

'Good afternoon, Captain,' the waiter murmured as he poured Reinhardt a glass of water.

'Afternoon, Kurt,' replied Reinhardt. 'What is it today, then?'

'What is it ever in this city, Captain?' the waiter replied, brushing away an almost imperceptible crease in the white tablecloth. 'Pork chops. But we do have some runner beans. Quite fresh.'

'Fine, Kurt. Thank you.'

'Thank you, Captain,' replied the waiter, inclining his head. Reinhardt watched him go, remembering out of the blue the time that Kurt had confided in him he had once waited tables at Medved's, the Russian restaurant in Berlin. *Certain standards,* he had said, *once learned, can never be unlearned. No matter where one finds oneself.* He laughed to himself at the trite irony of a waiter's reminiscence and attempt to maintain his own standards, and the parallel with his own situation. His own standards. There was a blast of laughter behind him, and he instinctively hunched his shoulders up and his head down and away from the noise. He felt wound so tight.

His meal arrived, and Reinhardt ate it quietly and methodically, sitting back when he was done. Kurt removed his empty plate and replaced it with coffee and a small dish of rice pudding. Reinhardt drank the coffee, which was awful watery stuff compared to what could still be had in the city, and left the pudding. He took the map from his pocket and spread it on the tablecloth, staring at the blank area where his investigation should be.

He put his elbows on the table and held the map in two hands, running the paper between thumbs and forefingers. Reinhardt glanced quickly at this watch, then stood. It was half past one. Time for one drink, and then he had to find Claussen and see what had been done about translating the pathology report.

There was still a clutch of officers at the bar, and a group of colonels in the armchairs. Reinhardt walked to the end of the bar, ordered slivovitz, and spread his map out again. A couple of the officers looked over at him. He nodded to them cordially, not wanting any contact or conversation. One of them, a solid-looking man with ash-blond hair, looked at him a little longer than the others.

Looking at his map, he saw two options. The first was to investigate Hendel's death by following up in the city, with the people who knew him or might have seen him, or who knew Vukić, but he had neither time nor resources for that, and in any case his remit was to assist the Sarajevo police while concentrating on Hendel's death. The second was to pursue his investigation within the army, following up on the information that Vukić frequented officers of senior rank, and try to find where Hendel fitted into that.

'I beg your pardon, but we've met, have we not?'

Reinhardt started, swallowing his slivovitz a little too quickly and coughing. He put his glass down and his hand over his map, and turned to face the man standing next to him. It was the officer who had looked longest at him, a lieutenant colonel in the black uniform of the panzer troops. He had cropped blond hair and cheeks made florid from drinking. Reinhardt came to attention with his heels together. The officer was rather young for his rank and, as Reinhardt looked at him, he did seem rather familiar, standing there smiling and with a half-drunk glass of beer in his hand.

'Excuse me, sir,' he managed around the burn in his throat, and the burn he could feel on his cheeks. 'You were saying?'

The lieutenant colonel raised his glass and pointed it at him. 'We've met,' he repeated.

'Forgive me, sir, but I am not sure I can recollect when I might have had that honour.'

The officer clicked his fingers repeatedly, staring at Reinhardt with his smile seemingly stuck on his face. 'I've almost got it,' he exclaimed. 'R... Ran... Rein... Rein something or other. Damn it, it's on the tip of my tongue!'

'Reinhardt. Gregor Reinhardt.'

'That's it!' he exclaimed, a finger in the air. 'And you don't remember me! You need a clue, *Monsieurrr*?' he asked, dragging out the French word and almost gargling it at the back of his throat.

That was what did it, though. Reinhardt smiled, offering his right hand. 'Johannes Lehmann. 1st Panzer. Although you were a captain last time I saw you, sir.'

'What can I say? Promotion comes pretty fast in a panzer unit! But fancy meeting you here. Long way from France, no?!'

'A long way, indeed. When was it, then? May, June 1940? Dunkirk, right?'

'That's it,' Lehmann replied, jovially. 'We had just finished chasing the Tommies into the sea, and you were what, doing interrogations or some such?'

'Debriefings of captured enemy officers,' said Reinhardt.

'That's what they call it, do they?' snorted Lehmann, taking a swig from his glass. 'Well, you must've had your work cut out for you, because we certainly gave you plenty of officers to debrief.'

'No complaints from me on that score,' said Reinhardt. He breathed deep and slow to cover his surprise. 'Last time we saw each other was, when? Paris, wasn't it? Christmas?'

'Christmas in Paris! Those were good days. France. The weather. The wine, the parties. The girls,' he finished, with wide eyes beneath raised brows.

Reinhardt would have added *victories* to that list of good things. There were not that many of them anymore, especially for the tankers, since the glory days of 1940. 'You were divisional intelligence, weren't you?'

'Still am. Still am. And you? Still with Abwehr?'

'For my sins,' said Reinhardt. He glanced at Lehmann's decorations. He wore the gold-and-silver panzer assault badge pinned to the breast of his coat, the white tank destruction ribbon on his right arm, and the red, white, and black stripes of the Winter Campaign medal made a diagonal slash of colour across the big lapels of his black uniform. He raised his glass at them. 'You've been busy, I see. Where has the war taken you?'

'Poland and Russia mostly. We were with Army Group North. Got to within sight of Leningrad before we got pulled back. We were beaten up pretty badly,' he said, swigging from his beer. 'Then Rzhev, for about a year. We were pulled out again and sent back to France for refitting in January this year. God, what a relief that was! You?'

'Since Dunkirk? Here, until the end of forty-one. Then North Africa until September last year. Italy for a bit. Then back here.'

'Riding with Rommel, eh?' Lehmann's eyes flicked over Reinhardt's map, then back up. 'You still in counterintelligence?' Reinhardt nodded, as he slowly folded his map away. 'Look, I'm here as advance liaison for the division. We're deploying out of here in June, to Serbia and Greece mainly. I'm getting the official line from all the right people, but I'd appreciate any information you have that could be useful to us, especially on the Četniks, seeing as we're going to be in Serbia. Something a bit more local. Anything to put things in perspective.'

'I understand,' replied Reinhardt. 'And I'm at your service, sir, of course.'

'C'mon, don't make it sound so formal. Just talk, over drinks or something. Like whatever you've got about the politics here. They seem pretty messed up. Like nothing we've experienced anywhere else.'

'They are labyrinthine, indeed. But you said you'd be in Serbia, and my area of operations is Bosnia, so I'm not so sure what use I'd be to you.'

'Well, there's Serbs here, and Serbs in Serbia. Right… ?'

'Granted, but it doesn't mean they've the same motivations.'

'Does my head in,' said Lehmann, putting his empty beer glass on the bar top. He pointed at Reinhardt's glass. 'Another?' Reinhardt hesitated a moment, then nodded, glancing quickly at his watch as Lehmann called the barman over for their drinks. 'So, in Bosnia you've got Serbs, Muslims, and Croats. No Croats in Serbia, right? For which I've been made to understand I should be eternally grateful. Then you've got all these damn organisations. Četniks, Ustaše. I'm still trying to get that straight. I went through it all again at that conference the other day. It made sense then, but now it's fading. Here, cheers,' he said, handing Reinhardt his slivovitz.

Reinhardt clinked glasses with him. 'Firm ground under your tank,' he said, running what Lehmann had just said back over in his mind to make sure he had understood.

Lehmann snorted. '"Firm ground". I like that,' he said, taking a swig from his beer. 'What it all means,' he continued, 'is that a simple tanker like myself can't make head nor tail of it all. It was easier in Russia. There, it was just us and them.'

'History is layered here, like anywhere else, really,' said Reinhardt. 'Each people's version of the past, and the present, like the carpets you see for sale in the market. But the layers don't just lie one atop the other. They clash and rub up against each other as each side's fortunes wax, then wane, and the versions compete for the truth to the exclusion of any other.

Compromise is not easy in such situations, and each side invariably expects – and receives – the worst from the other.'

'Well, what do you expect?' mused Lehmann into his beer. 'Always been the way.'

That did not seem right. It seemed… easy. Stereotypical. And coming from a German soldier… 'Well,' Reinhardt said, finally, looking inward at himself and feeling disappointed he could not come up with more. He sounded weak. 'It's not, actually. Relations have often been strained, but actually they aren't any more prone to fighting themselves than anyone else, and often when they've fought its because they've been dragged into something bigger.'

'What?' snorted Lehmann. 'Like this war, y'mean? So it's our fault these people keep falling out with each other?'

Reinhardt smiled, feeling it strained and shallow. 'Some might say that. But, for instance, here, in Sarajevo, the communities help each other more than not. Serbs in the countryside massacre Muslims, but the Muslim authorities here have often defended the city's Serbs against Ustaše depredations. And the Ustaše are Croat, but many of the city's Croats resent their behaviour.'

'So it's complicated.'

'It's complicated,' agreed Reinhardt. 'Like I said, this war in Bosnia is many wars all piled up. You need to understand the many to understand the whole.'

'But the Muslims are with us, right?'

Reinhardt sighed, sympathising with Lehmann's need for simplicity in the face of complexity even if he did not agree with it. 'The Muslims don't have a big brother to look after them, and they have nowhere else to go. So, the way they see it, to survive this they keep their heads down, or they ally up either with the Croats or, more and more, with the Partisans, or with us.' Lehmann's eyes seemed to glaze over. 'You said you were here on a conference?' asked Reinhardt, sipping his slivovitz.

'Yep,' Lehmann replied, licking foam off his lip. 'Senior officers planning for Schwarz. I was there as advance liaison for the division, as part of the area that the op will cover is in Serbia.'

'That's right,' said Reinhardt. He felt nervous, hesitant, like someone on a high diving board for the first time, screwing up the courage to jump. This might take him somewhere. It might take him nowhere. 'I'm hopeful for some good material coming out of this operation. Counterintelligence has been a bit slow lately.' He winced as he said it, it sounded so weak.

'Ah, well, some of them are here. The chaps from the conference. You could try to talk to them now, couldn't you?'

'I'm sure they have better things to do than chat with a captain of the Abwehr.'

'Nonsense, come on. I'll introduce you.'

Caution got the better of him, clenching a firm hand around his innards. That, and the memory of Freilinger's ice-cold eyes. 'No, really, sir, you've been very kind to offer. I wouldn't want to bother any of them.'

'Well, fine then. But come, let me introduce you to a couple of my men, at least. I'd like you to meet them. Tomas, Pieter,' he called. Two other panzer officers in the huddle of uniforms at the far end of the bar turned. Lehmann ushered Reinhardt down to them, a pair of lieutenants. 'An old acquaintance from our first time in France. Gregor Reinhardt, of the Abwehr.'

Reinhardt shook hands with them, exchanging pleasantries. The two officers laughed when Lehmann recounted Reinhardt's joke about firm ground under their tanks. More jokes followed. Reinhardt listened with half an ear, his eyes scanning the officers sitting around the reading corner, and found himself holding a glass of beer as well as his slivovitz.

'What's all this, Johannes?' The four of them turned to see a colonel standing behind them. Reinhardt and the two lieutenants came to attention. 'Share the joke, why don't you?'

'Faber, hello. Meet Gregor Reinhardt, an old friend from France. 1940! Fancy meeting him here, eh? We used to do prisoner interrogations together.'

Reinhardt looked at the colonel's unit insignia. He was from the 118th Division.

'Prisoner interrogations?' repeated Faber, sipping from a glass of wine. 'We don't get too many of them around here, eh?'

'Yes, sir,' replied Reinhardt.

'Oh?' said Lehmann, looking between them. 'Why's that, then?'

'Partisans tend not to surrender,' said Faber. 'And when they do, they tend not to get taken prisoner. And what is Abwehr's take on this operation?'

'Bound to be successful, sir.'

'What are you working on now?'

Reinhardt took a deep breath inside and took the step he had avoided taking earlier. 'I'm actually working on a murder case at the moment.' Lehmann and his two lieutenants went quiet, and Faber's eyebrows went up.

'Somewhat outside the normal writ of the Abwehr, no?'

'Normally, yes, sir. However, given the priority the coming operation is taking in terms of manpower, I was given this assignment.'

'Come now,' said Faber. 'I find it hard to believe the Abwehr has nothing better to do.'

'Quite the contrary, sir. Partly for the reason I just mentioned, and partly because one of the victims was a German officer. In fact, an Abwehr officer. There are standing arrangements for investigating such things.'

'One?' interjected Lehmann. 'You mean there's more than one?'

'The second was a journalist. A Bosnian Croat. A woman. Apparently well connected.'

The calm had attracted other officers, who began to gather around. One or two of them he knew by name, a couple more by sight, members of the garrison. Others he did not know at all. Reinhardt began to sweat, and he put his glass back down on the bar, partly in order to stop himself from drinking, and partly to show he was ready to go, but if any of the officers caught his intentions they ignored it.

'Well, apart from whether it makes operational sense, what would you know about investigating such a crime?' asked Faber.

'Reinhardt used to be a copper.' One of the officers that Reinhardt knew slightly stepped forward, with a broad smile plastered across a freckled face. 'Big star in Kripo. You might have seen his name in the Berlin papers, before the war. What was the big case, Reinhardt? The post box?'

'The Postman, sir,' said Reinhardt. 'Dresner.'

Faber's eyes widened. 'Right, *right*. The Postman. I remember as well. There was another one. Some gangster, wasn't there?'

Reinhardt nodded. 'Podolski.'

'Podolski! *Riiight!* What was it they called him?'

'Leadfoot Podolski.' He looked around at the flushed faces and raised eyebrows. 'He had a habit of weighting his victims down with lead and dumping them in water.'

'And *Paris*! There was something in Paris, no? At the universal exposition, back in thirty-seven. Something to do with the Russians? Yes?'

'Yes,' he said, feeling desperately uncomfortable at talking of his past. If someone here knew enough to link him to the policeman he had been, they might know more about what had made him leave that life.

'Come and tell us of these investigations,' said Faber. 'It would make a change from what we usually end up talking about.'

'Sir, really, I should not take up too much of your time.'

'Nonsense,' said Faber. 'Just one story. A good detective story.'

'Paris! Tell us about Paris!'

'Tell us about the Postman.'

With Faber and Lehmann on each side, Reinhardt was ushered around the end of the bar to the sitting area, where about a half dozen colonels, and as many majors, were standing, sitting, or leaning against the bar. There was a round of introductions, and bouts of hand waving and head nodding as the officers looked towards him, some with the curiosity that they might show to an exotic zoo exhibit, others with dead, uninterested glances. Only a few names stuck in Reinhardt's head, the first ones called out. There was Colonel Eichel, a tall, blond man with limpid blue eyes. Colonel Ascher, who looked like a monk all round and doughty with the top of his head bald, and the hair on the back and sides shaved short. Colonel Kappel, rotund and jolly looking. Reinhardt thought he remembered seeing him at the Ragusa the previous night. Colonel Forster, gaunt and cadaverous, with fingers like cords wrapped around his glass.

There were a few others, men whose names Reinhardt did not try to catch, and at least one or two of whom he was sure were at the club. His eyes, though, his eyes took in the uniforms, the insignia. 369th. A pair of SS officers from Prinz Eugen. 1st Mountain. 118th and 121st Jäger Divisions. All of them were on his list, which felt like it was burning a hole in his pocket.

'Dresner?' asked Eichel. 'Who is this Dresner?' His voice had a slur from his drinking.

'Dresner was a killer! A murderer,' replied Faber. 'Go on, tell us how you caught him.'

'Well,' said Reinhardt. He looked down at his feet a moment. 'I was working with Berlin homicide at the time. It was 1935. A number of people, all men, mostly in their middle ages, had been murdered in their homes. All of them had been stabbed to death, with the killing wound under the left armpit. A very precise wound, either penetrating the heart or cutting the main arteries that led from it. All the victims had had their hands broken with a hammer, and had had their sexual organs crushed.' Some of the listening officers winced, and one pantomimed clutching his groin and falling backwards into a chair. 'There were no signs of forced entry,' Reinhardt continued, 'and no signs of anything having been stolen.'

'A real mystery, indeed,' said Eichel as he tipped his head back for his glass. A couple of other officers shushed him.

'Go on, Reinhardt,' said Faber.

'I was called onto the case following the fourth murder. I was struck by the way the victims were killed. No forced entry, so the killer was likely known to the victims, or was someone who would normally be above suspicion. As we investigated, we realised in two of the murders witnesses had seen someone in a uniform in the vicinity. This, and the victims' wounds, suggested it was the same person doing the killings, but nothing on why or who he might be. So, instead, we began to look more deeply into the victims' backgrounds. We were sure there had to be something linking them together. While we were on those inquiries, another two people were killed in the same way. We eventually discovered that all of them had, at one time, worked in a boys' boarding school that had been closed in the late 1920s due to rumours of abuse by the staff of some of the boys.

'We began to follow up with boys – now men – who were at the school. They confirmed many of the rumours, and although there were variations in the names of the suspected abusers, all of the victims were on all of the lists. Those interviews gave us three more names of teachers and staff members who had been suspected of abuse. Inquiries as to the boys who might have suffered most at their hands gave us a list of a dozen or so names. Further investigation eliminated most, leaving us with four possible suspects who had, so we thought, motive, and opportunity as they all lived in Berlin. One of them interested us a great deal, as he was a postman.'

There was a collective shuffling and straightening of postures among the assembled listeners, some of them looking puzzled, some of them starting to smile as they saw the picture coming together. Kappel peered into his beer glass and belched.

'So, now we had someone in uniform. Someone who could reasonably expect to be welcomed into a stranger's house. Someone normally above suspicion. That information and those suppositions led us to fasten on one Ferdinand Dresner, a postman, who worked at the central sorting office for Berlin and had easy access to addresses. And, in Dresner's case, someone who was also a former medical student.' More of the officers began to grin and nod. Reinhardt gave a small smile back, nodding with them, the memories coming thick and fast, almost enough to push back the desperate discomfort he felt whenever he had to relate anything to do with his career. 'Which led me back to my suspicions about the killings, and the wounds, that they were too well placed to be coincidental. And it got us thinking, what was a former medical student doing working for the post office.' To one side, Eichel ordered another drink and turned away to talk with one of the other colonels. Ascher, Reinhardt remembered. Ascher inclined his head to listen to Eichel but kept his eyes on Reinhardt and the story.

'We put Dresner under surveillance and then, after interviewing them, also put the three remaining members of staff under watch as well, believing that sooner rather than later he would seek to kill them. When we talked again with some of the ex-pupils, they confirmed that Dresner had experienced quite sadistic treatment from some members of the staff, and had undergone psychiatric care as a consequence, and had dropped out of his studies. And, sure enough, he attempted to kill again, and we were able to apprehend him as he tried to commit another murder. And that was it.'

There was a round of applause and a chorus of bravos. 'Brilliant. *Brilliant* work,' enthused Lehmann. Eichel glanced at him, Ascher's eyes glinting over his shoulders.

Reinhardt ducked his head. 'It was merely patient detective work, following up on all leads, examining all possibilities until they could be eliminated, and keeping an open mind.' Nothing about the political interference they had run into, the pressure to pin the murder on someone, anyone, just to end the publicity about the killings. The competition from the other squads on the case, the procession of suspects rounded up, taken down to the basements under Alexanderplatz. The resistance they had met from the Nazis who clung to the belief that the murderer was a Gypsy, or some other undesirable. Nothing about their ideological refusal to countenance the possibility of an Aryan serial killer, which led to the bungle when Dresner had actually been interviewed by one of the other squads but released because he was above racial suspicion.

'What about the wounds? The stabbing, and the mutilations?' called an officer.

Reinhardt nodded. 'Yes. As we suspected, Dresner's medical training indicated where to stab into the heart. He then said that, although he killed in cold blood, he was afterwards taken by rage. Rage at what these men had done to him with their fists, and... in other ways. So he took his revenge on them as best he could.'

'So, tell us more about this investigation you are on now,' asked Faber. 'Another drink?'

'What's that, then?' asked several officers.

'Well, it's not advisable for me to talk too much about the case. No, thank you, nothing more for me to drink,' Reinhardt demurred.

'Ah, come now. You can talk with us, surely?' said Faber, clearly enjoying himself. Over by the bar, Ascher raised his hand to someone behind Reinhardt, gesturing him over.

'Well, I am working with a detective from the Sarajevo police. He is investigating the journalist, while I am concentrating on our officer.'

'Journalist? What's going on?' asked an officer.

'Any leads, then?' interjected Lehmann.

'What's this about a journalist?' demanded a couple of officers. Lehmann turned to them, keeping an eye on Reinhardt as he briefly outlined the murders in Ilidža.

'No leads, not really.'

'Where were they found?' someone called.

'At her house.'

'Where's the house, then?'

Over at the bar, Reinhardt saw Standartenführer Stolić join Ascher and Eichel. His throat clenched, and he swallowed. He had to get out of there, but that giddy sense of invulnerability pulled him on. The feeling he got when on the trail of good evidence that things were right, just right. 'In Ilidža. Behind the Hotel Austria.'

'When were they killed?'

'Late on Saturday night.'

There was a babble of excited talk.

'Wasn't there a party there that night?'

'You were there, weren't you?'

'Yep. The high point of that bloody planning conference.'

'Hey, just think, boys, a murder like that happening next door!'

'Saturday night?' repeated one of the officers, with mock relief, clapping his hand over his heart. 'Thank heavens, that counts me out. I was in Rogatica. Just ask the ladies at Petko's bar!' Several other officers joined in the laughter.

'But that doesn't rule you out, Ascher,' blurted a colonel with ruddy cheeks, quite obviously some way into his cups. 'You were there, weren't you? You and Kappel, and... and...' He trailed off, looking around the assembled officers with watery eyes.

'Where what?' asked Ascher, turning from his conversation with Stolić and Eichel. Stolić looked over his shoulder. His eyes, as Reinhardt had guessed from the dim light of the bar last night, were indeed very pale. They fastened on Reinhardt, and he saw recognition jolt through them, followed by what could only be fury.

'Careful now,' joked one of the officers. 'Do we need alibis?'

Reinhardt smiled back. 'I don't know. Do some of you think you *might*?'

Conversation just died away from the men around him. At the bar, Stolić and Ascher exchanged glances. Reinhardt breathed shallowly over the awful lump that sat sodden and heavy in his chest, aghast at what he had just said.

Faber's eyes narrowed. 'Captain,' said Ascher, from where he stood against the bar. 'I am sure you cannot be insinuating anything.'

'Nothing at all, sir,' he replied, forcing a tone of levity into his voice.

'Good. Then I am quite sure you are stating nothing, either.'

'Correct, sir.' God, what had he been *thinking* to say what he did? Was it the drink? Recounting the past? From a time when he was someone, when what he did counted for something? Things were just right. They were always *just right*, until the moment they were not.

'Just a minute,' said Stolić, coming forward. As they had last night, his cheeks bore a high flush. Ascher half raised a hand to stop him, but the Standartenführer ignored it. 'Just a bloody minute. You say you are investigating a murder that occurred in and around the same place and time that some here were present? And you told us *nothing* of this? What, you tried to insinuate yourself into our confidence? To sound us out?' Stolić's face became further suffused, his eyes becoming even paler as a result, and his voice rising as he spoke. He took a step, then another, until he loomed over Reinhardt. All conversation stopped, all heads turned. To Reinhardt, they were nothing but a row of pale ovals in his periphery. 'Just who the hell do you think you are, *Captain*?' In the face of Stolić's aggression, Reinhardt froze. Coming to attention was all he could do, directing his gaze to a point just behind Stolić's head, ignoring the blaze of humiliation that roared through him.

'A captain of the Abwehr, apparently,' said Ascher. 'An ex-policeman. Of course he was sounding you out. He was sounding all of us out.'

'Is this true, Reinhardt?' grated Faber.

Reinhardt had not been the focus of so many men who could do him harm in a long time. 'No, sir,' he said, with as much confidence as he could muster, keeping his eyes front and focused on nothing. He had wanted to sound them out, but God knew the way things were progressing it would have been a terrible idea. It was bad enough now, when he had not even meant for any of it to come out. 'If you will recall, sir, I came upon your invitation.'

'That's true,' said Faber, half to himself, half to Stolić.

'Don't be so bloody gullible, Faber,' Stolić snarled. His teeth, Reinhardt suddenly noticed, were in bad shape, and the man's breath was pinched, acidic. 'The man's a policeman. Deception's in his blood. I'll bet he planned it all.' He stepped back, raking him up and down with his eyes, then swinging them around to look over the others. 'I caught him sniffing around the Ragusa last night. Who the *hell* thought it was a good idea to spring him on us?' The officers shifted and muttered, looking left and right, most of them looking to Faber and Lehmann. Faber looked hard at the tank officer, who went red with embarrassment.

'Who is your superior, Reinhardt?' demanded Ascher.

'Major Freilinger, sir.'

'Good. He will be hearing from me about this.'

'Now,' said Stolić, stabbing Reinhardt's chest with a finger, right on his Iron Cross, and then pointing over his shoulder. 'Fuck off.'

14

Reinhardt forced himself to walk back through the halls to the courtyard. He looked straight ahead, praying he would meet no one he knew, but as he approached the door to the parking lot, he paused; checking that there was no one behind him, he collapsed backwards against the wall, feeling his knees trembling as if they were about to give way on him. He breathed deeply, a slow, ragged, shuddering breath. 'Gregor,' he whispered. 'Gregor, why couldn't you have left it alone?'

Voices had him standing straight, tugging at the hem of his tunic as he walked briskly back out into the courtyard, into the blaze of heat and light to his car. He drove back to his office, where he found Claussen and Hueber waiting.

'Hueber has that translation you were asking for,' said Claussen as they followed Reinhardt into his office.

Reinhardt sat in his chair and folded his hands in his lap. 'Proceed, Corporal,' he said, tightly.

Hueber shuffled some sheets in his hand, glancing down at a page of handwritten notes, and began reading. It was a fairly standard pathology report. Dates, times, places, findings of the autopsy, which, it seemed, barely qualified as one as the pathologist had stopped at the knife wounds and gone no further. The corporal finished, saw Reinhardt staring hard at him, and blushed.

'You said something about the wounds and the knife. Go over it again.'

'Sir. Err... the wounds. Average depth three inches. Deepest penetration six and a half inches. Errr... Wounds characteristic of a very sharp, heavy knife with a bottom edge curving up to a point, and a top edge equally sharp along at least two inches, but showing a pronounced... err... hook? A hook shape? A curve...' The corporal trailed off. 'I'm sorry, sir. I'm not at all... sure of the words. That seems to be what they are describing.'

'A hook shape?' repeated Reinhardt.

'Yes, sir.'

'What kind of a knife is hook-shaped...?'

Hueber went red, reading over the report, and then his notes. 'Sorry, sir. It doesn't say.'

'Don't worry, son. It's not your fault.' He sighed. 'Nothing much, eh?' Claussen nodded in agreement. 'Very well. Thank you, Hueber. You are dismissed. Type those notes up for me.'

The corporal left, and Reinhardt sighed, suddenly deflated. He slumped on his elbows. Looking down past his knee, he could see the drawer where he kept that bottle of slivovitz. The temptation was strong, but he stood instead, walking over to look at the big wall map. His eyes ran back and forth between Ilidža and Sarajevo, and then over and up around the thread of the city's streets. The whole place was so small, but wound in and built up upon itself. He put his hand on the map. With his thumb on Ilidža, he could almost stretch his little finger out to Sarajevo, and when he put his palm on the map it almost obliterated the city. And yet to get anywhere, it seemed you had to turn and turn and turn again...

'Captain Reinhardt?' Reinhardt looked up and away from the map at the tone in Claussen's voice. 'Is something wrong, sir?'

Reinhardt paused, then related the incident in the bar. Woodenly. No expression. At the end of it, Claussen just stared at him and shook his head slightly.

'What does that mean?' hissed Reinhardt through tight lips, life surging back into his voice. 'I didn't ask to get dragged into entertaining a bunch of colonels like that.'

'No, sir,' Claussen replied, imperturbable in the face of

Reinhardt's anger. What was it about sergeants and their ability to do that to him? Brauer had had the same effect on him. Like a father staring down a guilty son, although Reinhardt was sure he had never managed that same stare with Friedrich. Perhaps, if he had been able to, things between them might have been different. 'But you didn't walk away from it, either.' The two of them stared at each other, but it was Claussen who stepped back. 'Will you be needing anything else for the time being, sir?'

'Yes,' said Reinhardt. 'Find out who Peter Krause was. Is. I've no rank, but I'm guessing he was a lieutenant like Hendel. You are dismissed for now.'

With Claussen gone, Reinhardt had nothing to occupy his mind while he waited for the inevitable summons from Freilinger. He unfolded his map, stared at it, put it away, unfolded it again, and added *Stolić* to the names on it, linking it to Vukić's, thinking of the way Dragan described Stolić and his knife. He checked in on Maier and Weninger. He found Weninger this time, a small and taciturn man, who pointed at Hendel's sorted files with a pencil and had his head back down in his own material as Reinhardt walked out with them back up to his office. There was a lot going on in the building. Frantic last-minute arrangements for Schwarz, mostly. Reinhardt passed through it, feeling detached, alone.

Hendel's material was not much, Reinhardt thought, as he looked at the stack of paper and cardboard standing in the middle of his desk, but he should have looked at it earlier himself. He checked that it was ordered chronologically and then began to go through the files one after the other, starting with Hendel's activity log. Hendel's work was internal army security. He had made log entries fairly regularly upon arrival in Sarajevo at the end of December, but they had begun to tail off around the beginning of March. Flipping through the log, he saw no references to Vukić. He went back through the log more carefully, looking for euphemisms, initials, some kind of internal code, and found nothing.

He sat back, drumming his fingers quietly on the desktop,

not sure what to make of that absence. He lifted the case files one by one, glancing at the titles as he went. A couple were for operations he knew of, mostly targeting the Croatian Army for Partisan infiltrators or leaks. Unlike the Ustaše, the Croatian Army – the Domobranstvo – was not what anyone would call ideologically inclined or committed and suffered high rates of desertion and low levels of morale, particularly among its Bosnian Muslim conscripts. Most of the Croats in its ranks were from Croatia proper, far from home and desperately homesick. At the command level there was a sustained level of mutual loathing and distrust between the Domobrantsvo's officers and the Ustaše. In that, they were not too different from the way many German officers felt about the SS. Some of the files had the names and ranks of soldiers on them, mostly Germans, none of whom he knew, and none above the rank of major, with the exception of one file belonging to a colonel of the Domobranstvo, one Tihomir Grbić.

Out of interest more than anything else, Reinhardt opened the file, which, from the date stamped on the cover, was one of the last files that Hendel opened before his death. The case against Grbić seemed to be one of cowardice in the face of the enemy. He scanned down the front page, and the name of Standartenführer Mladen Stolić leaped out at him. Reinhardt flipped to the after-action report, which stated that Grbić's men had failed to press home an attack against the Partisans made in conjunction with units from the 7th SS. It was not the first time Grbić's men had failed in action, but from reading over a summary of Grbić's service record, it was clear the man himself was anything but a coward. He had served with the Croatian Army in the USSR until he was seriously wounded in the fighting around Stalingrad. The man was a veteran, thought Reinhardt. It was his troops, all new and mostly conscripts, who were probably unwilling. That seemed to be the emerging gist of Hendel's investigation, such as it was recorded in the file.

Reinhardt sat back, not knowing what, if anything, to make of this. There was a clear connection from Hendel to Stolić, and from them both to Vukić. It was clear Stolić knew of, and disliked, Hendel. What was wrong here? Too obvious, perhaps? Too clear a link? For a moment, he seemed to hear his old probationary officer's voice. *It's the little things, Gregor. Always the little things.* Where was the little thing in this, he wondered, seeing Claussen appear at the door.

'What do you have, Sergeant?' Reinhardt asked, shaking an Atikah loose from a packet.

'Lieutenant Peter Krause, sir,' said Claussen, stepping into the room and reading from the page. He passed through the beam of light, the light snapping and dividing around him, sending the motes of dust into a new frenzy of movement. 'Works in transportation. Movement supply officer. Been posted here since June last year.' He passed the paper across Reinhardt's desk.

Reinhardt scanned down the handwritten notes. 'They've reported him missing?' he asked as he lit his cigarette.

'Reported missing to the Feldgendarmerie yesterday morning.'

'And yet we know Becker's been looking for him since Sunday.' Reinhardt snapped back in his chair, staring hard at Claussen. He clicked his fingers and pulled his cigarette from his mouth, pointing his fingers at the sergeant. '*That's* where I know Krause's name from. The list of deserters and wanted men. He was on that list I saw in the Feldgendarmerie's HQ while I was waiting to see Becker yesterday afternoon.' He twisted his mouth in an ironic smile. 'Bloody hell,' he muttered. He took a long drag on the cigarette, pulling the smoke deep into his lungs.

'One interesting thing, sir,' said Claussen. He leaned over the desk and pointed to the bottom of the page. 'Krause is Volksdeutsche. His mother was Slovenian. He speaks the language.'

Reinhardt nodded. 'So if he's gone to ground, he'll get by a lot easier than we would.' He trailed off, twisting around to look at the map again, imagining where someone like Krause might run to from Ilidža. Not only where, but to whom. He glanced back at the files on his desk. What would Hendel, an Abwehr officer on post here less than five months, be doing with a lieutenant of transportation troops? What was the link between them? There had to be one, beyond the fact that the pair of them seemed to like to drink and chase skirts together.

'Captain Reinhardt?' A corporal stood in the door at attention. 'Major Freilinger's compliments, sir, and you are requested to report to him immediately.'

'Inform the major I will be there directly.' Reinhardt stood, tugging his uniform into place, and breathed out heavily through pursed lips as he stubbed his cigarette out. He exchanged a glance with Claussen, who looked back at him expressionlessly. 'Wish me luck,' Reinhardt muttered, walking out.

15

Freilinger's offices were one floor up, in the corner looking west along King Aleksander Street. The sun was low, barely over Mount Igman, and the light was short and bright. Freilinger was standing at his window again. He looked around, moved his mouth around as if there were something in it, then motioned Reinhardt to take the seat in front of the desk and turned to look back out.

'There's something about this city. In the evenings,' Freilinger said, the rasp in his voice low and leathery. 'Sometimes it seems like a labyrinth. No way out. And then, there's times like this when it seems there's openness and light.' Reinhardt looked at Freilinger, hearing the echo of thoughts he had had himself, so often, since he first came here. Freilinger was looking out the window, into the light. His eyes, always so pale, were almost invisible, and with a lurch Reinhardt saw Freilinger's face as he saw it in his nightmares, awash in the blaze from the fire, and he stiffened in his seat as he imagined the acrid stench of smoke. He looked down, breathing slow and deep to cover his fear, and when he looked up Freilinger was staring hard at him.

'Reinhardt, was I not clear enough last night?'

'Sir?'

Freilinger walked back to his desk, never shifting his gaze. 'Do not "sir" me like some damned sergeant,' he snapped. 'Was I not clear enough last night?'

'You were, sir,' said Reinhardt.

'Remind me, what was it I was clear about?'

'That I was not to go pestering officers about this investigation.'

'Correct,' said Freilinger. 'And so *why*,' he shouted, with a hoarse roar, slamming his hand on the desktop, 'do I find myself dealing with a half dozen complaints about your inappropriate behaviour this afternoon in the officers' mess? Accusations. Insinuations.' He picked up a piece of paper by its corner. '*Alibis?* For *Christ's* sake.'

'Sir, if I may explain?'

'It was a rhetorical question, Reinhardt,' replied Freilinger. 'I'm not interested in explanations. I'm only interested in dealing with the consequences, which so far,' he said, fingering through some of the pages on his desk, 'have involved me talking to four colonels, an SS Standartenführer, and a general. Put up to the task by his chief of staff, Colonel Forster. A civilised sort of dressing-down. Nevertheless, dressing-down and complaint it was. From a general.'

He stopped, screwing up his mouth and swallowing hard against the tightness in his throat. Reinhardt sat as still as he could, feeling the cold sweat in the small of his back and the flush he knew was colouring his cheeks.

'Reinhardt, I gave you this investigation for several reasons. The first is that Hendel was one of ours. The second was that I am not blind to what you are going through here.' Reinhardt locked eyes with the major. 'You are not happy.' He paused. 'None of us is. We have all seen, and done, things that might make lesser men weep. I thought, perhaps wrongly, that work similar to what you did in the past, and did well, might be of some help. The third… well, Reinhardt, have you forgotten so quickly the consequences to the local population for the death of a German soldier? Have you?'

'No, sir,' he managed, finally.

'Perhaps you will remind me of them,' said Freilinger, quietly, sitting down. His eyes bored into Reinhardt. They both knew what the other was thinking. 'Remind me of General Kuntze's directive.'

'Sir. When a German soldier is wounded, the lives of fifty prisoners or civilians are forfeit as a reprisal. When a German soldier is killed, the lives of one hundred prisoners or civilians are forfeit.'

'Correct, Captain,' said Freilinger, picking up a piece of paper. 'Let me perhaps *refresh* your memory further. Directive of 19 March 1942, from the commander of 12th Army, Belgrade. I quote: "*No false sentimentalities! It is preferable that fifty suspects are liquidated than one German soldier lose his life. If it is not possible to produce the people who have participated in any way in the insurrection or to seize them, reprisal measures of a general kind may be deemed advisable, for instance, the shooting to death of all male inhabitants from the nearest villages, according to a definite ratio.*"' He put the paper down. 'One wounded German, fifty dead Serbs. One dead German, one hundred dead Serbs.'

Freilinger sighed and looked down for a moment. 'I wanted you on this case because I thought we could avoid something like this,' he said, pointing at Kuntze's directive, 'coming to pass if you found me a suspect, or the one who pulled the trigger. Not that I thought such reprisals were that likely. Not here. There aren't enough Serbs in any case, and it's not as if Hendel was killed in an uprising. Still' – he swallowed – 'stranger things have happened. And now, thanks to this incident in the mess, I am being asked why the directive is not being applied. I know that at least one, if not two, of the colonels you offended this afternoon are making these points to the army staff in Banja Luka.'

He sighed again, his throat moving painfully as he fumbled open his tin and popped a mint into his mouth. 'Why are we wasting manpower and resources on an investigation of this kind, at this time? Why are we not letting the Sarajevo police take care of it? These are the sorts of questions I am fielding. And so, with all that, what can you tell me of your investigation, Captain?' He clasped his hands under his chin and waited.

Reinhardt licked his lips, thinking carefully. 'Sir, I can

almost certainly confirm one thing. The police only began investigating on Monday morning, when the maid reported it. But Hendel's death was known to the Feldgendarmerie on Sunday already.'

Freilinger's brow creased as his hands continued their slow movement. 'Go on,' he said.

'One of the last places Hendel visited was a nightclub, called the Ragusa, also frequented by Vukić. The Feldgendarmerie interrogated staff there on Sunday, and they interrogated two singers who were, apparently, intimate with Hendel. On Sunday, and again on Monday. But they weren't looking for Hendel, or searching for evidence as to who killed him. They were looking for a Lieutenant Peter Krause, and for something that they thought he might have. Photographs, or film. Someone tipped off the Feldgendarmerie before even the Sarajevo police. I can only believe Major Becker's stalling tactics from yesterday afternoon were not only bureaucratic, but also deliberate.'

Freilinger sighed, running a palm up and then down each side of his face. 'You see, that is what I was afraid you might say.' He raised a hand to forestall Reinhardt's protest. 'I'm not saying you're wrong, Captain. I'm just saying you've no proof to make such an accusation. I know you and he have a long and tortured history and I know he is not always quite what we would expect in our Feldgendarmerie, but why would he do that? What would be his motivation? Who might ask him to do that? Becker will tell you he was looking for a deserter, this Peter Krause. Perhaps it is simply coincidence Krause was a friend of Hendel's. For now you cannot place Krause at the murder scene. Although...' He trailed off. 'Although I will admit it is strange. Very strange...' His hands resumed their dry-washing. 'What else?'

'Sir, I have come across one common element between Hendel's death, his work, and my investigation.' Freilinger raised his eyebrows. 'An SS officer. Standartenführer Mladen Stolić. 7th Prinz Eugen.'

Freilinger nodded, his eyes slipping sideways. 'Go on.'

'He has been hostile and vocal in opposing my inquiries. It would seem he objected to, or was jealous of, whatever relationship Hendel had with Vukić. In addition, he seemed to take an instant dislike to me.'

Freilinger smiled, a faint twitch of his lips. 'Yes, he would. I know of him. Stolić is an angry man. And a rather violent one. He's Volksdeutsche, on his mother's side. He joined the Ustaše in the thirties, hung around Italy with Pavelić and the other exiles, then came back with them in 1941 and joined the Croatian Army. When the Seventh was formed, though, he transferred out, and there's the problem. He's angry not to have seen enough action. If he'd stayed with the Croatian Army, he'd have gone to the USSR, and probably gone out in a blaze of glory at Stalingrad like the rest of them are supposed to have done. He tried to leave the Seventh but was refused. No action, or not enough. No decorations.' Freilinger's eyes strayed to Reinhardt's Iron Cross. 'He won't have liked you on sight just because of that. And he wouldn't have liked Vukić because she was a woman who refused him. To make matters worse, she was a woman who followed the Croats in the USSR almost to the end, and he was jealous of that, too. She went where he could not.'

'Sir, how do you know this?'

'I have my sources,' responded Freilinger, simply. 'I speak to my counterparts in the Domobranstvo, even in the Ustaše. Stolić is well known to them. Mostly for the wrong reasons. And don't forget, Hendel was Abwehr. He reported to me.'

'I see.'

'The case Hendel was working on, involving that Croatian Army colonel… ?'

'Grbić, sir,' supplied Reinhardt.

'Grbić was anathema to Stolić because of his service record and because he was a decorated veteran. Stolić detested him. There was always trouble between them.'

'I see,' said Reinhardt, again. It seemed to be all he could manage.

'So you keep saying,' said Freilinger, drily. Reinhardt flushed. 'You might find this interesting. The only real action Stolić has ever seen was in Spain, back in thirty-seven. He volunteered for the nationalists and came back with a reputation for being rather brutal with captured prisoners. A reputation he has wasted no time expanding upon here in Bosnia. He favours knives and hatchets, apparently, and is known to frequent a particularly nasty Ustaše officer, called Ljubčić. One of those Black Legion men –' Freilinger paused, and Reinhardt wondered whether that could have been the Ustaša at Stolić's table at the Ragusa the other night. 'What else?'

'We interviewed Duško Jelić, a member of Vukić's film crew, with Inspector Padelin. He provided a lot of background information on Vukić's movements over the past few months, as well as some personal details on her... predilections. Apparently she had rather distinctive tastes in men, preferring older men, especially decorated soldiers.' Freilinger raised his eyebrows, and there was the ghost of a smile at the edge of his mouth that Reinhardt affected not to notice. 'She also had particular sexual tastes and a rather voracious sexual appetite. According to what Jelić said, and from what I have been able to determine, neither Hendel nor Stolić would have been attractive to her, and I know Stolić took that badly.

'The reason I mention her sexual activity,' he continued, 'is after the interview with Jelić I found a hidden room in her house containing a film camera but no film. Her darkroom had been ransacked – that, I noticed on my initial visit to the scene – and I believe the Feldgendarmerie, and whoever has asked them to assist, know or suspect Krause has the film and the film shows her with her murderer.'

Freilinger's hands went still again, his eyes narrowing. 'Now that *is* interesting,' he said quietly.

Pausing a moment to swallow, Reinhardt reviewed the last things he had to say. He knew he needed to be convincing to Freilinger, as he could feel any control he had over this investigation slipping away. 'Jelić told us Vukić had an affair while she was in the USSR with a senior army officer sometime in September last year. It was apparently rather tempestuous, and ended quite badly, and Vukić bore some kind of grudge. Jelić told me the officer in question recently transferred here, and he and Vukić had met, or were planning to. According to Jelić, Vukić did not play the role of jilted lover very well and it would not have surprised him if she planned some sort of revenge.'

'A revenge that went wrong, and someone may have the proof of it...' Freilinger grunted, looking away from Reinhardt for a moment.

'At the moment, it's all I have to go on.'

'In any case,' Freilinger sighed, looking back at him, 'it is all somewhat irrelevant now. I received a call from Major Becker. The Sarajevo police have their suspect. He has admitted to killing Vukić. Becker tells me we can almost certainly pin Hendel's murder on him, too.'

Reinhardt leaned forward in his chair, shaking his head. 'Sir, whoever the Sarajevo police are putting forward is a scapegoat. The police are running a purely political investigation and are pretending there is no link between Vukić and Hendel.'

'Well, you may be right, but after today's little show in the mess and with Schwarz about to kick off, I don't think anyone's going to care. Do you?' Reinhardt stayed mute, if only because he did not dare speak around the swell of frustration in his chest and the feeling of helplessness that threatened to overwhelm him. 'We are invited tomorrow morning to police headquarters. There's to be some sort of official gathering at which they'll present their findings and suspect. You will go. And then I expect we will be told to bring our investigation to an end.'

Reinhardt looked back at Freilinger, wanting to protest, to keep him away from that mockery, but the steely look in the major's eyes kept him quiet. As if assuring himself of Reinhardt's quiescence, Freilinger leaned across to the side of his desk and pushed two blue folders towards him. 'Feldgendarmerie traffic records. As we requested.' Reinhardt put the folders in his lap, resisting the temptation to consider them as useless now.

Freilinger stood and walked over to his window, clasping his hands behind his back. The sun was much lower now. From where Reinhardt was sitting Freilinger seemed outlined in light, his close cap of grey hair shining almost silver, but the rest of him just a dim suggestion of back and arms and legs. 'It's not over, Reinhardt,' he said, finally. Reinhardt had to strain to hear him. 'I have not received orders yet to end this. So keep at it, but whatever you're doing, get it done soon, one way or the other. When Schwarz starts, no one will care about a dead lieutenant. But they will care about a captain getting in the way and asking questions.'

He turned back to face him. 'I will look into recent transfers of senior army officers. You think of general's rank? This year?' Freilinger scribbled a note, then fastened his gaze on Reinhardt. 'You know this is the beginning of the deep water? If you're not already in it, you soon will be if you keep this up.' Reinhardt nodded as Freilinger straightened up. 'I can protect you so far and no further. Very well, then. Dismissed.'

16

Reinhardt managed to control himself on the walk back downstairs to his office, but once there he shut the door and then let his frustration boil out. He flung the Feldgendarmerie files at the wall and slammed his fists up against his map, keeping his teeth clenched hard against the scream raging in the pit of his belly. Putting his head on the wall, he rolled his forehead from side to side, pressing it hard, breathing deep and ragged.

When his head began to hurt more than he could bear, he turned and slumped against the wall, sitting with his legs splayed out in front of him. He looked at his desk, wanting that bottle in the drawer, but put his head back, staring at the wiring and the light fitting in the ceiling. He scrubbed his hand through his hair, then jerked it down as his fingers stole treacherously to his temple and the memory of the bruise left by his pistol. He flinched from the sudden acrid tang of smoke, knowing he was only imagining it, but it was enough to pull him back.

He thought of Freilinger's last words, about protecting him so far and no further. Was there another meaning there that he had not caught? Something Freilinger had wanted to say but could not? He let his hands drop to the floor, and they brushed up against the Feldgendarmerie files. He looked down where the paper had spilled out, and he sniffed and hauled himself up and onto his haunches and began picking everything up. He tossed the files onto his desk and looked at them. If what Reinhardt suspected about Becker was true, if there was anything that would have been of use to him in those records, then he would probably have had it removed.

But still. Standing in front of his desk, he leafed through the pages. There were only a couple of sheets per file, one file for Saturday and the second for Sunday, and it was, as far as he could tell, fairly anodyne. Going through them, he found no trace of Hendel. No report of a motorcycle going either way. He took the Sarajevo police traffic records for the same period, intending to compare them, but he realised his heart was not in it and put it to one side. Trying to do this now, in the state he was in, he would miss something. Overlook something. What he wanted to do, and where he needed to be, was over in police headquarters.

Once he realised that, he straightened and went down outside. He walked past his car, past the sentry, and into the narrow street that led to Kvaternik. He needed to walk. Needed the time to think, or he would arrive and do something stupid, or ridiculous. He walked fast, feeling his knee twinge, down the street as it curved gently, following the channel of the Miljačka to his left. It was early evening. A curfew had been announced that morning, and it would be coming into effect in an hour or so. People were strolling quite briskly along the street: couples, families, mostly walking away from Baščaršija behind him, back to their homes. He felt their eyes, their whispers, feeling it run off him, for once, leaving him uncaring. Perhaps because of the uniform, perhaps because of the expression that might have been on his face, perhaps both, they parted in front of him. Or rather, he thought, as he strode through the orange light, with the sun low in the sky in front of him, it was he who stayed still and life that parted around him, like a branch poking up above the water in a river. A branch, twisted and ragged, the ends split and splayed like fingers, he thought, with that sense of macabre self-consciousness that had saved him in the past, usually from himself.

He arrived with his head no clearer than when he had set

out, and the frustration that simmered in his gut had spread all through him. At police headquarters, he ignored the guards who made a half step towards him and he stopped inside, looking left and right. There was a big set of double doors in front of him, two doors to his left, and a flight of stairs leading upward on his right. There was a receptionist's booth under the angle of the staircase, with a policeman behind the counter, looking back at him.

'I want to see Inspector Padelin.' The policeman gestured with his arms, a shrug as if to say he did not understand. 'Padelin,' repeated Reinhardt, slowly. '*Padelin.* Your new hero.'

The policeman's face lit up with a smile. '*Da, da, Inspektor Padelin.*' His smile became something of a grimace. '*Žao mi je, neće biti moguće da ga vidi.*' He shook his head. '*Nije dostupno.*'

'I don't understand a bloody word you're saying,' grated Reinhardt. 'I want to speak to Inspector Padelin. *Now!*' He raised his voice on the last word, and the policeman took a step back, those arms coming up again to placate, or to ward off. He said something again, slowly, painfully, as one does to a foreigner. Reinhardt's face twisted. He felt it go out of his control for a moment. Horrified at himself, he lurched back from the counter, into the middle of the foyer. He smelled smoke, again, that damned memory of smoke.

'Padelin!' he shouted. '*Padelin!* Get down here and talk to me!' The policeman was calling something, coming out from behind the counter. '*Padelin,*' he shouted again.

He went over to one of the doors on the left and pulled the handle. It was locked. He felt a hand on his shoulder. Unthinking, he reached up, squeezing the fingers and pushing them up and back. He heard a yelp, saw one of the policemen from outside. He shoved him back, seeing the man's face go red with anger. Reinhardt ignored him, pulling on the handle of the second door, but it was locked as well. He heard voices behind him, the clatter of feet on the steps.

'*PADELIN!*' he bellowed.

'Captain Reinhardt.'

He turned at the quiet voice, his last shout echoing up into silence. Dr Begović stood there, looking very small and rumpled, a brimmed hat in one hand and a bag in the other. His eyes were large behind his thick glasses. Two policemen stood behind him. He took one step towards Reinhardt. 'Captain. Please. This is not helping anyone.'

Reinhardt found he was breathing heavily. 'No?' he managed. 'What the hell would *you* know?'

Begović took another small step. 'I might know a great deal, Captain, of what goes on in this building, and who it goes on to.' He shifted his arm, ever so slightly, the one carrying the doctor's bag. Reinhardt's eyes were drawn to the movement, then back up to Begović's face. It was carefully blank, calm, and Reinhardt felt abruptly and completely a fool, but no less angry. The anger just felt more focused.

'You should come away, Captain. You can do no good here.'

'I want to see Padelin,' said Reinhardt. He felt foolish saying it in front of the doctor but could not see any way around it.

'He isn't here,' said Begović, simply. 'No one here can help you.'

'Padelin,' Reinhardt repeated. 'I need to see him. He has the wrong man, you see.'

Begović stared back at him. 'The wrong man?'

'The wrong man for the Vukić killing. Whoever he has, he couldn't have done it.'

Begović's mouth moved, as if he wanted to say something. The two of them stared at each other for what seemed like a long moment, and then Reinhardt felt the rage begin to drain away. The anger stayed, and he held it tight, hoping it would keep him focused, but he nodded to Begović and stepped away from the door. The doctor turned, ushering him towards the exit. The two policemen followed him out into the dusk, looking at him warily. Reinhardt walked down the steps slowly, feeling drained, empty.

'I did warn you, did I not?' Reinhardt jumped, startled. He had been so lost in his thoughts he had forgotten the doctor, standing quietly just a few feet away. 'About these people?'

'Who is he? The man they've got?' asked Reinhardt.

'There are two of them. One is a waiter. The other is his uncle. Both Serbs, although the waiter is half Croat.' Reinhardt shook a cigarette into his hand, offering one to Begović. He lit his, finding his hand shaking. He let the match go out, clenching his fist hard for a moment, before lighting another one for the doctor. Its flame pitched Begović's pasty pale face into sharp relief and woke answering glints in his thick spectacles. The match flickered out, and they were plunged back into that peculiar deep gloom dusk sometimes brought on.

'What have they really done?' asked Reinhardt around a deep lungful of smoke. He felt more than saw Begović look at him, the pause as the doctor obviously wondered how much to tell him.

'The uncle is a member of the Communist Party. His name is Milan Topalović. They say he's one of the Partisans' contacts in the city. The police have had their eye on him for a while. What is it you policemen often say? "Motive and opportunity"? Unfortunately for him, Topalović lives in Ilijaš, not far from Ilidža. They've witnesses – including that old Austrian woman, Frau Hofler – who said they saw him, several times, near Vukić's house. So he had the opportunity, apparently. And he's a Serb, allegedly a Partisan, and Vukić hated both, so that's motive. Apparently. The waiter's just a boy really. They used him to get to Topalović. He's his only relative. They said if Topalović confesses to the Vukić killing, they'll let the boy go.'

Reinhardt finished his cigarette and tossed the butt into the road. 'Thank you, Doctor. I wish you a pleasant evening.' There was a foul taste in the back of this throat, and he wanted to be away from there.

'Wait,' said Begović, coming after him. 'You're walking? You didn't bring a car?' Reinhardt shook his head. What little light there was ran up and down the frames of Begović's glasses as he turned his head from side to side. 'It's not safe for you to walk alone. Not even here. I will come with you. I'm going your way in any case.'

Reinhardt smiled, somewhat bemused that this little man thought to protect him. Then he tensed as a shape suddenly loomed out of the shadows. The man exchanged a few words with Begović in Serbo-Croat. Reinhardt could not see him well, only the gleam of his eyes above the shape of his beard as he listened to the doctor. He nodded, reluctantly, it seemed, and stepped away. Begović smiled as he answered Reinhardt's unspoken question. 'That's Goran. You saw him yesterday. My driver cum assistant cum handyman. He doesn't like me walking about after dark.'

'Your friend is right, Doctor. It will be curfew any minute now. You should not be out.'

Begović patted his jacket pocket. 'I have a doctor's permit.'

Reinhardt inclined his head courteously, putting his heels together. 'In that case, it would be my pleasure, Doctor.'

The two of them walked in silence down to the end of the street, then left on Kvaternik. There was some street lighting here, shining creamy from lamps atop wrought-iron posts that stood along the quai, on the side nearest the river. Without speaking, the two of them crossed over and proceeded down towards Baščaršija, following the little pools of light winding down the road and around the corner. The shrunken river trickled quietly past them. There was something calming about walking. It was something Reinhardt seldom was able to do anymore, and the doctor was a strangely comforting presence. He was obviously fairly well known as he tipped his hat several times to people he passed as they hurried to get off the street before curfew, stopping once to talk to a woman with a little boy. He tickled the boy under the chin as he said goodbye, but the child only had eyes for Reinhardt. Big, wide eyes over a solemn mouth, the sort of face that expected the worst from people like him. Reinhardt looked away, suppressing a shiver of memory.

As the boy and his mother left, Begović caught Reinhardt

looking at him. He gave a little smile, then let his eyes slip, looking over Reinhardt's shoulder at the opposite bank. He took a couple of steps over to the parapet that ran along the pavement. 'You know, I was born just across there. In Ćumurija.' He looked down at the water. 'We used to play down there. I can remember the Austrians building this, it was called Appelquai in those days. Very exciting. All that machinery. We used to play on the building site all the time; it drove the workers crazy. They would thrash us if they caught us, but it never stopped us.' He gestured with his head across the river. 'It used to flood all along and over there, quite regularly. I remember once, we were washed out of the house. It was the most exciting day of my life.' He smiled at the reminiscence.

'That's a nice memory,' said Reinhardt, more out of politeness than anything else. He hesitated a moment, wondering if he should be polite and offer a memory of his own, but he had nothing like that to offer. His childhood had been happy enough, but austere in its way; school, the church, duty, holidays once a year at Wismar on the Baltic.

'Then the Austrians strengthened the other bank too, and it never flooded again. This place' – he gestured down at the river – 'became too dangerous to play in. Because of the new banks, the waters would rise too fast and too quickly.' Begović looked up, then around and behind him. 'This city and water have always gone together, you know. There's the valley, and the Miljačka. There's the Željeznica, and the Bosna. The water flows through in the way it wants. Sometimes gently. Sometimes not. Like life. The Ottomans understood that, I think. All the Austrians could do was dam it, and channel it. Make it work for them and call it progress. Which,' he sighed, 'I suppose it was, in a way.'

They carried on walking up to the Emperor's Bridge, which led back over the Miljačka to the barracks, where they stopped. Reinhardt waved away a pair of policemen on foot patrol. He looked up at the night sky. 'You know,' he said, 'there are times I hate this place. The mountains. The streets. They seem to hem you in. You move and move and never get anywhere. Whichever way you turn, there's always a wall.'

Begović looked up as well. 'Walls have doors, Captain. And windows. Have you been to Travnik? No?' He smiled, running his eyes up and along the roll of Trebević against the night. 'Now there is a town squeezed in between its mountains. I can see how you might think that of Sarajevo, Captain, but I don't see walls, or confinement. My city is a flower. A rose, in the shelter of her mountains.' He looked up at Reinhardt. 'This is my city, Captain. Mine. And she is beautiful.'

Reinhardt offered his hand, and Begović took it after a moment. For some reason, Reinhardt was absurdly grateful that the doctor had not looked around to see if anyone might be looking before shaking the hand of a German soldier. 'Thank you, Doctor,' he said. 'For your help, back there. I do apologise for my behaviour.'

'Think nothing of it,' replied Begović. He paused. 'If it can help, I can tell you Topalović will not suffer much more. It will soon be over for him. For them both.'

Reinhardt's mouth twisted. 'Yes. A show trial and an execution. Very quick, if it's done properly.'

Begović blinked at him past his thick glasses. For a moment, it seemed to Reinhardt he wanted to say something else. Share something. 'I wish you a good night, Captain. Until the next time we meet.' He tipped his hat and was gone, a small, thin shape disappearing into the night.

17

Reinhardt ate alone in the officers' mess, making a point of not staying away as much as he wanted to. He sat at a table facing the bar and the corner with the easy chairs. Kurt served him in silence with his usual impeccable style. Pork again, in some sort of cream sauce. The bar was not as full as it might have been, with so many troops gone to the front. It was mostly officers from the Sarajevo garrison, most of whom ignored him, a couple looking his way just long enough for him to be sure that word of what had happened that afternoon had spread. A couple of times he heard whispering, barely restrained snorts of laughter, but he ignored it, even if it did make the flush rise that bit higher in his cheeks and neck.

When he had finished his meal, he made himself go to the bar, but the only other person he exchanged a few words with was Paul Oster, a captain he knew in medical corps, who sat slumped against the bar, exhausted by the preparations for Schwarz.

'Now all we can do is wait for the casualties to come in,' he muttered into his beer. 'Got everything ready. From here to Mostar. Clean sheets. Soft pillows. Sharp saws. A train ticket home for the lucky ones,' he giggled, staring into the bottom of his empty beer glass. 'But those badly wounded will be lucky to get up those bloody roads out of the valleys and through all these damn mountains. And as if that weren't enough, the idiots have to keep getting themselves hurt,' he said, as he nodded thanks to the beer Reinhardt bought him.

'What's that?'

'Oh, you know. Carelessness. Idiocy. Self-inflicted wounds. Treated a pair of infantrymen for burns the other day. Quite bad ones, actually. Stupid buggers. They said it was an accident but I'll bet they were burned siphoning fuel for the black market or some other brainless bloody stunt.' Oster slurped from his beer, his eyes glazed with fatigue and booze. He left soon after, waving a bleary goodbye as he weaved off.

Reinhardt stayed a while longer with his drink, absently tracing his fingernail through the wood grain on the bar top. There was a pile of magazines and newspapers at one end of the bar, and he flicked through back copies of *Signal* and *Das Schwarze Korps*, half hoping to find something by Vukić. He thought back to what Padelin had said about her work. He remembered the sparkle she brought to that Christmas party when she had danced with him and could imagine the light and warmth she must have brought to the lives of soldiers far from home. He could easily see her posing for a photo sitting on a tank with her arms around a couple of lucky men or leading them all in a song.

'Are you Reinhardt?' He jerked slightly. A captain of infantry stood behind him, a cloth-covered helmet under his arm with a pair of goggles strapped to them. An unloaded MP 40 hung across his chest and a long pair of leather gloves were shoved behind his belt. His uniform, with the red stripe of the Winter Campaign medal, was covered in dust and his face was dirty, his cheeks showing the crescents of his goggles. 'Reinhardt?' he asked, unscrewing the top button of his uniform. Reinhardt nodded, cautiously. 'Hans Thallberg. Good to meet you,' he said, offering his hand. 'Barman,' he called. 'Give me a wet cloth. Been driving most of the day,' he said to Reinhardt as he dropped his helmet on the bar. 'Come on, man, quickly now,' he snapped as he was handed a towel. He wiped his face and hands on it vigorously, wadded it up, and tossed it back over the bar. 'Anyone drinking that?' he asked Reinhardt, pointing to Oster's half-empty glass. Reinhardt shook his head and Thallberg knocked it back. 'Barman, don't go away. A beer. Tall and cold. And… another slivovitz?' His nose wrinkled. 'You've a taste for that stuff, do you? A slivo for the captain.'

Reinhardt watched him, somewhat bemused by all the breeze and bluster. Their drinks arrived and Thallberg's beer went down his throat in three gusty swallows. 'If you've a moment, I'd appreciate a word,' he gasped, wiping his mouth with the back of his hand. 'Table over there? Barman,' he barked. 'Another beer.'

The two of them took their seats at a table in the corner of the mess, a couple of battered armchairs arranged around it. Thallberg put his helmet on the table, unstrapped his MP 40, and laid it with a metallic clack on the floor next to him. His equipment belt followed, and he sank into his chair and stretched his legs out. His second beer arrived, and half of it went straight down. He sighed in pleasure, scrubbing fingers through his cropped blond hair. 'By Christ, I needed that. This is not bad stuff,' he said, twirling his glass in his hands. 'They make it here, you know. Sarajevo Brewery. Just up the hill, in fact. Built it right on top of a freshwater spring. Haven't got a cigarette, have you?' Reinhardt lit one for each of them and sat back.

'What do you want, Captain?'

'Hans, please.' He sat up in his chair, sipped from his beer, and spoke quietly, the happy-go-lucky demeanour suddenly gone and replaced by something more serious. 'I understand you're investigating the murder of Stefan Hendel?'

'That's not common knowledge, Captain,' said Reinhardt, looking straight at him.

'Not common knowledge?' Thallberg snorted. 'After your little rumpus in the mess this afternoon with the colonels? How quick do you think word like that gets around? Relax, Gregor,' he said, quietly. 'I'm not here about whose toes you might have trodden on.' He shoved his cigarette into the corner of his mouth and, reaching inside his jacket pulled out a small, green booklet. Reinhardt knew what it was but opened it anyway, seeing the two photos of Thallberg inside, one of him in uniform, a second of him in civilian clothes. 'I'm Geheime Feldpolizei. Hendel was one of mine.'

Reinhardt flipped the ID shut and handed it back. 'Let me see your warrant disc as well.' Thallberg handed it over. Reinhardt twisted it in his fingers, flipping it over to see Thallberg's number stamped under *Geheime Feldpolizei*, and *Oberkommando Des Heeres* above that. Save for that, it looked just like the one he used to carry as a Berlin detective and, he thought morosely, was probably stamped in the same factory that had once made his. 'Secret field police? You are secret field police? As was Hendel?' he asked as he gave it back. Christ, that explained a lot, he thought as pieces of the investigation slid and clicked into place.

'I was down near Foča when word reached me this morning he'd been killed. I came back as soon as I could. He was working on something pretty secret. I didn't know exactly what. His tasking came direct from Berlin, but he was after someone senior, I think. The last I heard from him, he was following up a lead given him by this Vukić.'

'Where would Marija Vukić get information like that?'

'The girl got around, if half the stories about her are to be believed,' replied Thallberg. 'Maybe she got it from someone she was banging. If that's in fact what she had. Hendel wasn't all that clear about it.'

'Did she know Hendel was GFP?'

'The idiot probably told her. No doubt he was trying to impress her. Can't think why he'd want to do that,' he muttered into his beer glass, raising his eyebrows suggestively at Reinhardt.

Reinhardt was finding Thallberg's lurches between levity and seriousness somewhat disconcerting, as it was probably meant to be. Nothing was ever spontaneous, not with the GFP. 'And she was planning on giving him this information when?'

'Apparently, she wanted him to have it at the same time she

confronted the person with it. It sounded like a bit of an elaborate setup, if you ask me. Bit too much like the way it happens in the movies. Which, seeing as she was a film director or what have you, shouldn't surprise us, I suppose. Those sorts of things have a habit of going a bit pear-shaped in real life, though, but I was too far away, and too tied up with work for this attack, so I left it with him.'

'So, what you're saying,' Reinhardt said, eventually, 'is Vukić may have had information about someone senior in German military circles and she wanted Hendel to have this information, but wanted to give it to him in the presence of another person. Who may or may not have been the person Hendel was investigating. Or she might have had information about something or someone completely unconnected to all that, but who was guilty of something or other.'

Thallberg grinned brightly. 'Sounds about right,' he said as he finished his beer. 'What has Krause said about all this? I haven't talked to him yet.'

'Krause?' repeated Reinhardt.

Thallberg looked straight at him. 'Krause. Lieutenant Peter Krause. He usually partnered Hendel in any operations. I told Hendel to take someone with him.'

Reinhardt stared back at Thallberg. 'Krause was GFP as well?'

Thallberg frowned. ' "Was"?' he repeated.

Reinhardt shook his head, annoyed at himself. 'I misspoke. You're telling me Krause, Lieutenant Peter Krause, transport company, is a GFP agent?' Thallberg nodded, frowning at him. 'No, I haven't talked to Krause,' Reinhardt said, finally. So that was the link. Obvious, really. Once you had all the pieces. 'He's missing. Hendel drove out to Ilidža with a motorcycle and sidecar. I presume Krause went with him. If he was killed there, his body hasn't shown up, and he's now reported as a deserter by the Feldgendarmerie. They've been looking for him since Sunday.'

Thallberg ran his tongue around the inside of his mouth and

raised his eyebrows. 'Well, well, well. More work for you?' Reinhardt stared at the tabletop as Thallberg began picking up his equipment and made to get to his feet. 'Me, I need a shower and some food. I'm here tomorrow then I've got to get back to Foča. I presume you've had someone look at Hendel's files, but this stuff wouldn't have been in them. I'll see what we've got and get back to you.'

'Unless you know of a secret place where Hendel stashed his good stuff, good luck finding it. And watch your back,' said Reinhardt.

'Meaning?'

'Meaning the Feldgendarmerie are after whatever Hendel had. They think Krause might have it and have been kicking in doors since Sunday.'

Thallberg grunted, curling his lower lip under his teeth. It was the first apparently unconscious gesture Reinhardt had noticed him make. 'Well, when Krause turns up he'll be able to explain it all.'

'Thallberg, I may be wrong on this, but I wouldn't give a *pfennig* for Krause's chances if the Feldgendarmerie, or whoever is behind this, gets to him before we do.'

'Oh?' said Thallberg. He put his helmet back on the table and rested the MP 40 against his leg. 'You have someone in mind?'

Reinhardt looked at him a moment, then breathed in deeply and shook his head. 'No,' he said. 'I've given you enough. You bring me something tomorrow, and we'll talk more, but I'm not saying anything else.'

Thallberg looked back at him expressionlessly, then flashed his grin. 'Fair enough,' he exclaimed, slapping his thighs. He took a little notebook from his pocket, jotted down his office and extension, tore the page out, and left it on the table. 'You can find me at State House.'

Reinhardt ran his eyes over Thallberg's uniform. His unit insignia marked him down as 118th Jäger Division, and he wore the close combat clasp in gold, and on his right arm the patch that signalled he had destroyed at least one enemy tank with

handheld explosives. 'Captain, are those awards real?' said
Reinhardt suddenly. He pointed at Thallberg's Winter
Campaign medal, fishing in his pocket for his handkerchief.
'Were you in Russia?'

'That's what the frozen meat medal says,' he replied, brightly,
referring to the award by its army slang. 'Although I'll grant you,
as GFP can wear any uniform we like, it's a pertinent question.'

Reinhardt rose and proffered the filter from the papirosa.
'Do you know what this is?'

Thallberg leaned over and sniffed, then put his helmet down
again and took the handkerchief in his hand, looking closely at
it. 'There's a blue smudge down the side... I'd say that's a
Belomorkanal papirosa. The authentic poor man's cigarette.' He
handed it back.

'It was found at the scene of the murder. A witness reported
a man, possibly a chauffeur, smoking them outside the victim's
house shortly before the estimated time of death.'

'None of my chaps smokes anything like that. I suppose if
you find the smoker, you're halfway there.' He hefted his
equipment, flipping his belt over his shoulder, and paused.
'Dreadful stuff, that papirosa tobacco. You've got to really love
that to smoke it out here. Can you believe, of all the things a
man could bring back from Russia, he's got to bring that?
Something on your mind, Reinhardt?'

Reinhardt stared at him, at his Winter Campaign medal. He
hesitated, running his tongue along the bottom of his teeth.
'Look, there is strong reason to believe Vukić was killed by
someone she met in Russia. And that that person has recently
transferred here.'

'Oh? You know that how?'

'Never mind that. You gave me something, about the
papirosa. I'm giving you something back, that you can do
something about. Get a list of recent senior transfers. Officers
who have served in the USSR. Something along those lines.
And get a list of all officers who attended the recent planning
conference in Ilidža. The one they just held for Schwarz.'

Thallberg grinned. 'Sounds like good old-fashioned detective work to me.'

Reinhardt almost smiled back. 'It is. It's slow. Methodical. Sometimes it pays off.'

'I can do that. You used to be a big shot in Kripo, didn't you?' Reinhardt blinked at him, taken aback by the question. Thallberg grinned at his discomfort. 'I've read your file. Gregor Sebastian Reinhardt. One of the best criminal inspectors in the Alexanderplatz. A half dozen big crooks to your name. We liked the look of you for the GFP at one point. That's how I know. Brauer was your partner, wasn't he? You two went through the first war together. Eastern Front. Western Front. Iron Cross First Class. At Amiens, right? 1918? You got the first- and second-class Crosses the same day, didn't you?' he said, answering his own question. Thallberg looked at him, his eyes bright and inquisitive in the white patch of clean skin his goggles had left. 'Quite something. How does Brauer take being a sergeant again? You were both inspectors, weren't you? Now here's you, a captain, and him, a sergeant.'

Reinhardt sat back down and reached for his glass. He looked up at Thallberg as he took a careful sip from it and put it back down. 'You're right about Kripo.' He felt a flush of anger, remembering his conversation with Claussen about being an NCO. Christ, was it only yesterday? He acknowledged nothing else. Nothing about the east in 1916, the transfer to the stormtroopers and the Western Front in 1917, the attacks of 1918 when they seemed to have victory in their grasp, the wound that saw him hospitalised for the last months of the war and almost cost him his leg, the riotous years following it. To do so, it seemed, was an admission that it was fine to distill a man's life down to a few choice nouns, but it grated on him that he was allowing this Captain Thallberg to draw his own conclusions about him. 'As to how Master Sergeant Brauer feels, you'd have to ask him.' His voice seemed to come from far away.

Thallberg grinned that boyish grin. 'I'll be in touch tomorrow,' he said, and with that he was gone.

Reinhardt stayed in his chair a while longer after Thallberg had gone. The man was something of a whirlwind, for sure. He was certainly different from most of the officers around here, and Reinhardt could not but feel strangely attracted to the thought of working with someone like him. As GFP, he would be of invaluable assistance, as long as Reinhardt could manage him and for as long as the GFP saw value in a partnership. The GFP could do pretty much anything. Go anywhere. Be anyone. Wear any uniform, or none at all. Use whatever they needed, when they needed it. What was that English expression… ? Holding a tiger by the tail… ?

All of a sudden, he realised he was shaking, and a spasm ran through his stomach. He glanced quickly around the bar, but no one was paying him any attention, and he folded his arms tightly, pressing his hands to his sides. He hunched around the blaze of stress and confusion and frustration that burned in the pit of his belly and drew a long, ragged breath through his clenched teeth. It was coming up to midnight, and he realised how tired he was and how much he had absorbed that day.

'Enough,' he said to himself. 'Enough.' When he felt steady, he left and crossed the courtyard over to his wing and took the stairs up to his second-floor room. With a trembling hand he pushed the door open to the bathroom and pulled on the light. The bulb flickered on, steadying slowly. Showers to the left, behind a wall of cracked white tiles. Toilet stalls to the right, the toilets mere squats, holes with footrests to either side. A line of sinks down the middle of the room with mirrors in front of them.

His stomach cramped, and he winced. He hunched over a sink, but nothing came up. He ran water and splashed his face, wetting the back of his neck, and drank his fill. Settling his fists, he stared at himself in the dull mirror. He looked dreadful. His face was drawn and lined, a drab fuzz of stubble furring his cheeks, his eyes sunk far back and the whites yellow in the vapid glow of the bulb.

He felt the bile rising again and hung his head over the

sink, breathing hoarsely through his nose, waiting. Nothing came up, but he felt something. His skin began to crawl. He lifted his head, sniffing the air like an animal, and found it. That acrid tang. The same one he had smelled outside Vukić's house. He drew his pistol as he lurched around, his eyes stabbing along the line of stalls. One by one, he pushed the doors open onto nothing, only the stained round hole in the floor, until he came to the end, to the one he often used. There was a window there, there was light during the day, and the smell of men's waste and the carbolic slop the cleaners used was not quite so strong. He pushed the door open. The smell was there. There was a sprinkling of ash down the angle of floor and wall, and there, floating in the water at the bottom of the hole, a finger's length of what looked like cardboard. He fished it out with two fingers. A cardboard filter. A Belomorkanal papirosa.

He backed hurriedly out, hastening back to his room. Feeling in his pocket for his key he saw something. Felt it, more than saw it, he realised, as he leaned over to look at his door. There was just light enough to show him the several small, bright strikes of metal to either side of the keyhole. Glints, where something had been put into the keyhole, and moved around. Someone had tried to force his door. Perhaps had succeeded.

He told himself whoever it was, they were gone now. He unlocked the door and pushed it open with his foot, sweeping the room with his pistol. The room was empty and, as far as he could see in the light coming in the window, had not been disturbed. Taking a quick glance up and down the corridor again, he went inside and locked the door, shoving his ladderback chair up under the door handle.

Whatever strength had held him together until then, it began to slough away like sand in the tide. He lurched across the room and fumbled open the drawer on the little table by his bed, lifting out Carolin's picture in its silver frame. He clutched it to his chest and slid down into the corner opposite the door, drawing his knees up, and, dragging the air into his lungs, he willed the panic, and the stress, and all the pent-up emotions of the day to pass. But as much as he wished for it, he dreaded the sleep that would follow, and the dream that now haunted him, nearly every night.

It is a cool day for October, but his head feels cooked inside his helmet, and his shirt inside the battledress tunic is stuck to his back with sweat. He stands by the side of the road where the Feldgendarmerie have ordered them to stop. Smoke broods over the town; there is the rattle and clatter of gunfire. Here, there, women huddle in desperate groups bounded by the anguished lines of their backs and shoulders, fists clenched at their mouths.

He walks away from where Freilinger argues with the Feldgendarmerie. He turns a corner, another. Doors stand open. A length of fabric hangs torn out of a smashed shutter. The smell of burning is strong. Faces twitch at him from the darkness within houses, from behind the sheen of a window, from behind the folds of a curtain. Another corner, then another, and there is a field, the hassocks stiff with frost, the ground hard and tufted. There are soldiers, and lines of men and boys, just schoolboys with, here and there, the taller figures of their teachers. They are ordered into the field, class by class, the younger ones hand in hand, some crying, some walking bravely. Most just stare at the back of the person in front of them with the fixed resignation of those already dead.

And there, a moment that comes perhaps once in a lifetime. A pivot, around which a life can turn. A line of children, a row of soldiers, people moving, a swirl in the crowd, and two boys at the end of the line are left alone. Brothers, twins perhaps, they stand small and lost and wide-eyed in each other's arms as the crowd eddies around them. He sees them, and they him, and he has but to reach out to them and he can take them away from here. He knows it, they know it, he sees himself doing it – he feels himself doing it – but the boys are gone, taken away. The moment is past, a fading outline of possibilities.

They are all gone, pressed and herded into the field, lined up in front of the ditches with the earth turned fresh and black behind them, and Reinhardt is moving forward, pushing men from his way, but they are heavy, immobile. He comes up behind the rank of soldiers as they raise their rifles, their shoulders swivelling. The crash of gunfire, the screams. Officers step down into the ditch. There is the crack-crack of their pistols. Somewhere nearby, the field is burning; smoke eddies slow and heavy, lying indolently atop the stench of blood and bowel.

A moment of stillness, and calm. It was a pivot, that moment, around which a life can turn. Or a nail, from which it could hang itself.

Part Two

18

WEDNESDAY

He woke with a ragged, tearing intake of breath. The smell of the smoke faded away, but he knew that as long as he lived he would never forget that day in October, in Kragujevac, behind the barracks at Stanovija Polje, when more than two thousand men and boys were executed in reprisal for a Partisan ambush that had killed and wounded some thirty Germans.

It was early morning, and he already felt drained, empty. He winced from the pain of his bladder as he straightened his legs, uncurling himself from the corner. His left knee was stiff and painful, his eyes full of sand from lack of sleep. He cleaned himself up as well as he could, avoiding his eyes in the mirror as he shaved as well as his shaking hand would allow. Downstairs, his breakfast tasted like ashes. More and more, what was within him seemed to leach out into the waking world. That, or the madness the world seemed to have sunk into was leaking in. He did not know anymore, but it was the dream that seemed to symbolise, for him, the predicament he found himself in. A man who loved his country, but who hated what it had become. A man who had found friendships stronger than anything he could have imagined in the army, but who could no longer stand the sight of the uniform he wore. Not for the first time, he longed for someone to confide in, but of the three people with whom he might have done so – Carolin, Meissner, and Brauer – one was dead and the other two far away.

Reinhardt liked to think he was at least somewhat self-aware. He was a man whose formative years were spent in strict discipline and war. His father, a university professor, was a stern taskmaster who instilled in his son two perhaps contradictory ideas: a sense of duty to the state and people, and a respect for learning and independence of thought that constantly brought him into trouble with the university's rectors and eventually forced him from his post. From him, Reinhardt inherited also his taciturn nature. Although he had a keen mind, he was not free with his opinions. Carolin would often chastise him, not for not having a mind of his own, but for keeping it, and his temper, too firmly under control.

She sometimes resented the influence Meissner had over Reinhardt but knew she could not fight it. The debt Reinhardt felt to Meissner was not one he ever thought about repaying. Meissner was a father figure to him who had saved his life several times during the war and from penury after it. She appreciated, although could not fully understand, the deep ties of loyalty and respect that bound them together, and she learned to find a place in that relationship. With Brauer, though, it was different, their two families coming from similar left-wing working-class backgrounds.

As he sipped his coffee, Reinhardt again thought back to the end of 1938, to his return to the colours and the start of the journey that had led him, via Norway, France, Yugoslavia, and North Africa, to where he was now. Reinhardt knew he had been a good policeman. It had been a surprise and a revelation to him how much he had enjoyed it, the security and respect it afforded, after those bitter and tumultuous years immediately after the war. The chance to channel all that anger and frustration from the war into something else, something constructive. But his fall from grace with the Nazis had been rapid, especially once he had refused transfer to the Gestapo for the second time, after he had clashed repeatedly with the new men they were pushing into the police, but more often with the men he had known for years who suddenly, overnight, expressed sympathy or outright support for Hitler and his ideals. He was pushed off the homicide desk and began a descent through the various departments, then out of Alexanderplatz into the suburbs, until he was running missing-person investigations. Which, seeing as just about all missing persons were Jews and just about all of them had been made missing by the people who employed him, was about as low as a detective could go in those days.

But even then he was still of interest to the Gestapo, and by June 1936 he knew there would not be a third offer. They would just move him. There was a lull during the Olympics when, for a few weeks, the city almost seemed to return to normal. Reinhardt was even reinstated back to homicide, but when the Games were over, it all came lurching back. That summer, the Nazis amalgamated the Kripo and the Gestapo with the intelligence agency of the SS and the Nazi Party – the Sicherheitsdienst – and there was no longer any distinction between the forces of the state and those of the Party. He became desperate in the autumn of that year to find a way out.

There was one more reprieve, at the end of the year, when he was posted to Interpol in Vienna. The Nazis were desperate to maintain a semblance of professionalism, and Reinhardt had a good reputation and contacts in England and France. He was their 'face' in Interpol. It was a sop, and he knew it, but it got him away from them, and they left him alone for a while. Carolin's health even seemed to improve, but Vienna's charms wore off fast as the city began the same downward spiral as in Berlin. After nine months there, the farce of Interpol was over as the Nazis moved it to Berlin, and Reinhardt went back into Kripo.

He muddled through that winter, keeping his head down, working nights, taking sick leave, all the while continuing to try to do his best, and clever enough to realise his best was only serving the Nazis. It was then, he knew, his horizons began to narrow, when he began measuring his days against the least he could do to get through them. The shambles of those months made him realise he was a man with few convictions in life, and he found himself with little or no desire or willingness to fight for the few he had. That realisation was horrifying to him. He held to the need to keep working to pay for Carolin's treatment as a justification to stay on the job, but as her condition worsened, and as the work became increasingly surreal in the juxtaposition of formal procedure, extreme violence, and breathtaking political chicanery, he took steadily to drink.

Almost as soon as they returned to Berlin, and against Reinhardt's express wishes, Friedrich joined up and Carolin, increasingly sick and worn out by the constant struggle between father and son, faded away and died. And then, at what seemed the lowest point, Meissner stepped in and arranged, through his contacts, a transfer to the Abwehr. Reinhardt accepted even though the army held no more attraction for him, and the oath to the Führer stuck in his throat, but it got him out of the police and away from the Nazis. The mental weight he had borne for several years eased.

Reinhardt was left only with the friendships of Meissner and Brauer, who had himself quit the force in 1935 after a violent altercation with his new commander. As a rambunctious working-class man with strong left-wing leanings, Brauer was instinctively hostile to the Nazis but smart enough to keep his head down. A self-confessed 'simple' man, Brauer had no illusions about his abilities to resolve a crisis of conscience, so he decided not to have one. From his position in the Foreign Office, Meissner's motivations remained a mystery to Reinhardt, something that, when he thought about it, still gave him cause for concern.

What it all meant to Reinhardt, he realised more and more, was that he had no reason to do any of the things he did anymore. In the first war, he was a young man. Told to fight for the Kaiser, and for Germany, he did so to the best of his abilities, which in the end were considerable, and, truth be told, he had never been as alive as during those days of iron and mud. He would never be younger, never be fitter, one of the elite. But in reality he fought for Brauer, and Meissner, and all the others who shared the hardships of that war, and the riotous peace that followed. All those men from different walks of life, professions, persuasions, and convictions. Lives like threads that came together in one place and time to form one particular pattern of experiences, a unique combination shared by no one else. This time around, he had nothing and no one to fight for, and no one to fight alongside. No one to guard his back, as he once guarded theirs, and so he skulked through this war, keeping his head down, staying in the shadows.

It had been a long time since he had thought of anything like this, and he wondered whether it had done him any good. He knew he was lonely. Sometimes he even revelled in it. He knew he had not been true, really true, to himself for many years. He even knew when it first began, when he had first avoided his own eyes in the mirror. It was the time in 1935 they received the news about Carolin's cousin. Greta was disabled and had been transferred to one of the new sanitoria. A few months later they received word she had died. He knew, though... As a policeman, you heard things.

The last excuse for carrying on and muddling through had been Carolin, and she was gone, and so the question he could not avoid answering much longer was, what made him keep going the way he was? Serving a cause he detested, in a uniform he hated, in an army he could not respect, with men he did not think he could fight for, feeling his convictions falling away one by one. He knew that collaboration and resistance came in many forms. He knew collaboration was not necessarily immediate, coerced, or unconditional, just as he knew resistance was not always instant, fervent, or inflexible. Knowing this gave him no comfort, and he knew that however much he had tried to hew to some kind of middle path, he had done both over the last few years.

Screwing his eyes tight shut against their gritty feel, he knocked back the last of his coffee and then walked up to his room. From a trunk under his bed he took a policeman's extendable baton, spring-loaded, a lead ball at the tip. He checked the action, flicking his wrist and watching the baton snicking out smoothly. He looked at it, wondering why he had come back up for it. Maybe it was the memories, he thought, of times gone by when he was a respectable man doing well in a respectable profession. He collapsed the baton and slid it down into the pocket of his trousers.

19

A fair number of cars were parked outside police headquarters, including an official-looking one with a government pennant on the front bumper. Inside, the foyer was crowded with policemen, most of them in uniform, and a couple of men who could only be journalists, one of them wearing a little red fez. Heads turned to him as he came in, then away, and straight off Reinhardt could feel something was wrong.

He wormed his way through the crowd over to the receptionist and asked for Padelin. Thankfully, the officer on duty spoke a little German, and he dialled a number, waited, talked a moment, and then nodded as he put the receiver down.

'Please. Are waiting here,' he said, indicating the stairs. 'Is coming, Padelin.'

Reinhardt waited on the bottom step, scanning his eyes over the crowd. There was a lot of muttered conversation beneath a grey fogbank of cigarette smoke. Some of the cops looked back at him. Reinhardt recognised Bunda, the giant policeman from the bar where he and Padelin had had breakfast yesterday. The journalist in the fez looked hard at him, but then all eyes were drawn upward and conversation died away. Reinhardt craned his neck around and saw Padelin coming down the stairs. As the detective saw Reinhardt looking up at him, he paused and gestured for him to come up.

The stairs had a tatty strip of green carpet fixed by brass

runners down the middle. It deadened his footfalls as he climbed up. Padelin shook his hand, looking grave as he gazed out on the crowd below. Neither of them said anything as they climbed to the top and through a heavy wooden door into a dim corridor. They walked down to another set of big doors, which Padelin opened quietly, ushering Reinhardt into a large conference room, with a big baize-covered table. Large chairs stood around it, about half of them occupied. Putković sat at the top of the table, next to a short, fat man in a suit, himself listening to what seemed to be a report being given by a uniformed police officer. Somewhat incongruous in this gathering of uniforms and suits, two priests – one an Orthodox with a silver beard – and an imam with a white cap sat listening attentively. And there was Becker, sitting partway down the opposite side. He looked away as Reinhardt came in. Reinhardt did not recognise anyone else as he took the seat Padelin pointed to.

The report came to an end, and the uniformed officer sat back. A line of sweat ran down the back of his uniform, and crescents had darkened under his arms. The short, fat man fixed him with a hard gaze for a moment, then looked around the table. The uniformed officer took the opportunity to wipe a sheen of sweat from his forehead with a handkerchief. As he put it away, his eyes raced around the room, holding Reinhardt's a moment before passing on.

The short, fat man began talking. It was a harangue, if ever Reinhardt had heard one. It did not last long but made up in apparent viciousness what it lacked in length. Reinhardt watched the tips of Putković's ears go white, even as most of the rest of him went red. At one point the Orthodox priest tried to say something, but the envoy cut him off, then cut off both the imam and Catholic as they tried as well. The man spoke fast, and although Reinhardt caught quite a few words, the sense of it passed him by. Then it was over. The man was on his feet, straightening his suit, and the others were standing up. A last few words, and Putković was escorting the man out. They passed close by Reinhardt. The man looked at him uninterestedly. Putković's eyes were flat, and Reinhardt had no idea what the man was thinking. Others began filing out after them.

'What's going on?' asked Reinhardt, quietly.

Padelin looked at the faces of the men going past, nodding to a couple. 'Our suspect is dead,' he replied, without looking at Reinhardt.

Reinhardt frowned up at him. 'Dead?'

'He was found this morning. Dead in his cell.'

'What's with those three?' Reinhardt asked, watching the priests and imam walk out, their faces blank.

'Them?' A strange look came over Padelin's normally blank features. 'These Sarajevans. They stick together. The Orthodox have been trying to get Topalović out. That is ironic, no?'

'Ironic?'

'An Orthodox priest trying to get a Serb Communist out of an Ustaše prison, helped by a Muslim and a Catholic? But that's this city for you. There is the world, and there is Sarajevo. A world of itself. Rules you never understand. A community you will never be part of.'

Reinhardt thought of the way the city's people would often come together, the way he would skirt the edge of that community, and the pressure of eyes that watched him and pushed him away. 'Dare I ask what killed Topalović?'

If Padelin caught the sarcasm he made no sign of it. 'The doctor thinks it was an overdose of morphine.'

Reinhardt's frown deepened. 'Not accidental?'

'No.'

'What is Dr Begović saying happened?'

Padelin looked blankly at Reinhardt. 'I did not say it was Begović who made that determination. Do you know where he went last night?'

Reinhardt's mouth opened, then closed. 'Dr Begović?' he repeated.

'You left together last night.'

'That's correct,' said Reinhardt.

'Did he say anything to you? Perhaps something out of the ordinary?'

'No,' said Reinhardt, perhaps a little too quickly.

'Captain,' said Padelin. Had he heard it, thought Reinhardt? He felt a moment of panic. The detective took a step closer. Just a small step, but all of a sudden he was there, that bit closer, that bit bigger. Reinhardt's skin crawled. He resisted the urge to take a step back and hated that he had to lift his eyes, not so much, but enough, to look Padelin in his. 'You came on foot. You left on foot. That is unusual for a German to do in this town. Your behaviour last night was, apparently, also unusual.'

Reinhardt swallowed in a throat gone dry. He had to try to regain some control over this. 'Padelin,' he said, quietly. 'Are you accusing me of something?'

Padelin blinked, that slow, feline blink, then shook his head. 'No. I am not.' Reinhardt did not miss the emphasis on *I*. Others, apparently, were.

'I did come here last night, looking for you. I was upset, shall we say, over the revelation that you had your culprit for Vukić's murder. I left with the doctor, who said he was going in my direction, and that a German should not walk unescorted at night.'

'He said nothing?'

Reinhardt shook his head, all the while running the doctor's words over and over in his mind. *He would not suffer long*, he had said. 'Nothing,' he replied. 'He said nothing to me last night that would indicate to me now he had a part in this.' But Begović not only knew, he had done it, Reinhardt realised. 'Why can't you ask him?'

'Because he has vanished,' said Padelin. 'Why were you upset with me last night?' he asked.

'Why?' repeated Reinhardt. He blinked once or twice. 'Because…' He paused. What was the point of trying to explain? He had tried before and not made any impression he could tell. 'Because I was unhappy with the way events were playing out,' was all he said.

'Well, perhaps you will be happy with something I have to show you. Please wait here. I must speak with someone, but I will be back.' With that, he was gone, leaving Reinhardt alone in the conference room.

Almost alone. He heard a faint scuff and turned. Again, perhaps a little too quickly. Last night's scare, too little sleep, and too much self-reflection had left him very jumpy.

'So?' said Becker. 'That's it, then?' Becker was standing behind him, slightly turned away, with his head tilted up. He held his glasses in his hands in front of him.

Reinhardt leaned back and sat on the edge of the table and shook a cigarette out. 'I don't know. Why don't you ask them whether they'll go out and try to find some other poor bastard to pin this on?'

Becker snorted. 'Come now, Gregor,' he teased, knowing how much Reinhardt hated it when Becker called him by his given name. 'Don't be so uncharitable.' He smiled and cocked his head, the light catching the rims of his little steel glasses where he held them in his fingers.

Reinhardt lit his cigarette, drew on it, and exhaled, giving himself time. He hated arguing with Becker. It made him feel weak. It reminded him too much of the past, of railing pointlessly against things that could not be fought against. He looked at the Feldgendarme past the stream of smoke, considering. 'You know, I ought to congratulate you. That little scene at your headquarters, yesterday. "I'm a policeman." "Nothing good ever came of bending the rules." You almost had me believing it.'

Becker grinned. 'But it was true, Reinhardt. Nothing *good* ever *did*. That was always the point. You never got it, though.' He shifted, his head tilting down as he altered his stance, turning the other way. It was a habit of his, to never stand facing whomever he was talking to. He faced away to his right with his head down. Away to his left, with his head up. Always fiddling with his glasses. Reinhardt hated it for the ridiculous affectation it was, although he was half sure that Becker did not even realise he did it anymore.

'More to the point, where does this leave you?'

'Hmm?' asked Becker, running his finger along a fold in the baize.

'You found Krause yet?'

Becker was good, Reinhardt had to give him that. His finger stopped moving for a moment, no longer. He looked up at Reinhardt, shifting stance again. 'Krause?'

Reinhardt ran his tongue over his teeth and spat a piece of tobacco off his lip. 'Don't try to bullshit me, Becker. You know who Krause is. You've been after him since Sunday. What game are you playing?'

Becker's face hardened. 'Just what are you accusing me of, Reinhardt?' he said, tightly. 'And call me "sir", damn you.'

'Take your pick. Sir.' Reinhardt blew smoke at the ceiling. Becker's face twitched at the insolence, as it always did. He looked back down at the Feldgendarme. 'Obstructing my investigation. Assault on a woman. Complicity in a blatant cover up. The usual mix of what you're good at.'

Becker's face was white now. He stepped closer to Reinhardt. He had none of the physical presence of Padelin, but Reinhardt still tightened in around himself, his hands wanting to tremble. 'Careful, Gregor. You're clutching at straws, here.'

'Spare me your bleating, Becker. I know you.' He blew smoke in Becker's face, feeling a sudden edge of recklessness begin to stir inside, just like yesterday in the bar, except he knew he could control this confrontation. 'Sir.'

'The *hell* you do!' snapped Becker. 'I'm looking for a deserter. Reported as such. You can't prove I knew anything about Hendel's murder before the rest of us did.'

'That's interesting. Sir. I never said anything about you knowing Hendel was dead before the police found him and Vukić.' Becker's face went blank, but Reinhardt could see the tension in the corner of his eyes, in his neck. He shifted stance again. 'Who is it that's called in this favour, Becker? Who has you looking for Krause? Hmm?' He raised his eyebrows. 'What's in it for you? There's always something, isn't there? I mean, why should Sarajevo be any different from the way things used to be in Berlin?'

Becker's mouth tightened, then relaxed. He turned to the left, raising his head, grinning. Reinhardt could see the confidence flowing back, all the cocky catch-me-if-you-can arrogance Reinhardt had hated so much back in their Kripo days. 'Gregor, Gregor.' He shook his head. 'Always so uptight. You need to get laid more. You always did, even back in the old days,' he smirked.

Reinhardt ignored the jibe at Carolin. It was an old dig. It still hurt, but not nearly as much as it used to. 'Is it women? Money? A transfer?' Becker's grin slipped, just a little. 'It's a transfer, isn't it?' Becker swallowed, his grin slipping further away. 'Figures. You always were a cowardly little weasel.'

For a moment Reinhardt wondered whether he had pushed Becker too far, then decided he no longer cared. Becker's grin came back, that shit-eating grin he wore so well. 'Gregor the crow,' he said, but his throat was tight and his voice was hoarse. 'Still cawing and flapping about stuff no one cares about.'

'What are you scared of, Becker?' asked Reinhardt. 'I know you're scared. You're shifting left and right again. Playing with your glasses. Not looking at me straight.' Becker coloured. His hands tightened on his spectacles, his arms half coming up as if he meant to put them on, then stopped, and he smiled, suddenly.

'Captain Thallberg's quite something, isn't he? A real live, poster-grade Aryan superman.' Reinhardt forced himself to reveal nothing, say nothing. Becker must know Thallberg was GFP, but if Reinhardt was reading Becker's actions right, he did not know Hendel and Krause were. Becker could only guess what Thallberg could bring to the table. What he might know. 'What's all that about? Finally giving up the solitary life?'

'It's what you've always told me to do, isn't it?'

Becker chuckled. 'You've got to be careful with those supermen, Gregor. You remember Berlin, back in the old days. People like him stomping around in brown shirts, smashing glass and breaking bones. Beating their breasts over how German they were. They're nuts.'

'This is you telling me this?'

'I'm garden-variety nuts, Gregor. People like Thallberg are something else. They move and think and see the world in different ways.'

Much as it pained him, there was something in what he said, and Reinhardt had felt it himself, but he just held Becker's eyes as Padelin opened the door, looking between the two of them, frowning at the tension that must have been evident between the two Germans.

Reinhardt stubbed his cigarette out. 'You're looking well, Becker,' he said, no pretence anymore that he was a captain and Becker a major, but then, it always ended this way between them. 'I wish you a very pleasant day, and happy hunting.' He walked out after Padelin, not looking back.

Becker still managed to have the last word, though. 'My best to Major Freilinger,' he called. 'And to Captain Thallberg.'

Padelin glanced in at Becker as he closed the door after Reinhardt. 'Old history,' said Reinhardt, shortly, willing himself to unwind. 'Forget about it.'

Padelin shrugged. 'This way,' he said. He led him through the building to an office. It was a dark, dingy affair, overlooking what must have been the building's internal courtyard. There was a desk, obviously shared by two people, covered in files and bits of paper, a ragged bit of carpet. Shelves held more files, books, folders, and assorted bits of junk. Several chunks of blackened metal sat on the desk, and Padelin picked one of them up and handed it to Reinhardt. It was warped, blackened, and twisted by what must have been considerable heat, but it still retained a roundish shape, as did the other pieces.

'You remember that fire, in Ilijaš, on Sunday?' Padelin asked. 'You saw the entry of the fire engines in the traffic records I showed you yesterday morning. These are from that fire. They are film cases.'

Reinhardt's eyes widened. 'You're sure?'

Padelin shrugged. 'Sure as we can be. The fire brigade found them at the fire. It was a big fire. Very hard to control. I am told film burns very intensely.'

'I think I remember hearing about that,' Reinhardt said, quietly. He put the piece of metal back on the desk, thinking. 'Where was the fire?'

'In the forest, near an abandoned farm.'

Reinhardt pursed his lips. 'Last night,' he said, after a moment, 'I talked with one of our doctors. He said he treated a couple of soldiers for burns...' He trailed off, glancing at Padelin. 'What do you think?'

'I think these are the films from Vukić's house. Whoever took them destroyed them.'

Reinhardt nodded again. 'Becker. The Feldgendarme I was just talking to? He is looking for a reported deserter, called Peter Krause. A lieutenant. I think he thinks Krause has a film. The one' – he gestured at the metal pieces – 'these people are looking for, and perhaps thought they had. Almost certainly the one from that camera we found.'

'Why would he think this Krause has this film?'

Reinhardt hesitated. There was only so much he could tell Padelin about the GFP. 'It's complicated,' he said, finally. 'Hendel was Abwehr. Apparently, he worked with Krause from time to time.' It sounded weak to Reinhardt, but Padelin seemed to accept it. 'So, where does this leave you?'

'Leave me?' repeated Padelin, frowning at Reinhardt.

'Your culprit is dead. Where does that leave your investigation?'

'Oh,' said Padelin. He began stacking the pieces of metal. 'Well, he confessed before dying. We'll see if that's enough for Zagreb. I think it will be.'

'Padelin,' insisted Reinhardt. 'You know, you must, that that man did not have anything to do with Vukić's death.'

Padelin paused in what he was doing and straightened up. Again, Reinhardt felt that sensation of something heavy bearing down on him, and again felt that irrational twitch that he had to look *up* into Padelin's eyes. 'I don't know why this is so hard for you to understand, Reinhardt,' said Padelin. 'You were a policeman once, under the Nazis. You should know, better than me.' He went back to what he was doing. 'The man was a Serb. A Communist. People like him will commit crimes, just like Gypsies and Jews. Frau Hofler identified him from photos we showed her. If he did not kill her, he did something else. Besides,' he continued, 'we know he was a senior Partisan. So, at a… how do you say… at a minimum? We have given the Partisans a loss. Who knows? Maybe he was Senka. The Shadow.'

It took a moment for Reinhardt to realise Padelin had actually tried to be funny. He stared back at the detective, remembering that conversation with Begović outside Vukić's house. The doctor calmly smoking his cigarette, sitting contentedly on his rock. 'And the nephew?'

Padelin narrowed his eyes at Reinhardt's tone, then shrugged. 'Nothing, I think. He will be set free.'

'So what becomes of *our* investigation?' he asked. He pointed at the film casings. 'This proves there was more to the murder, no? Someone was trying to cover something up, here.'

Padelin frowned. It seemed to Reinhardt it was the frown of a man trying to be patient with a child, trying to explain something obvious and evident. 'My part is over, I think,' he replied. His frown deepened. 'Yours too. Was that not what you were talking about with Major Becker?'

'No. Are you telling me Becker has received instructions on this case?'

Padelin shrugged. 'I don't know. Putković may have talked with him. I know the police are talking with your army at higher levels.'

Higher levels, thought Reinhardt. That could mean anything, and anyone. He gave a long, slow sigh, then nodded. 'Very well,' he said. He offered his hand, which Padelin shook after a moment, his frown deepening even further. Reinhardt turned and left, feeling the air thicken with confusion behind him. He walked back down the corridors, down into the foyer, past the press of men still waiting for answers, and outside. The air was hot already, heavy with a weight of stone and concrete, but it was fresh and clean after the stale atmosphere inside.

20

He slumped into the car, staring down at the pedals, his mind empty. After the momentary high of finding out the police had lost their suspect, he could feel himself sliding back into the depression that had seized him since last night. Padelin's complacency, Becker's assurance of knowledge that Reinhardt did not have… He raised his head, tracked his eyes along the spartan lines of the Austrian façades without really seeing them. He had no idea what to do now, so he started the engine and began driving.

On purpose, he swung the car left and right more or less at random, taking streets he rarely, if ever, took. The few shops he passed were mostly shut, and the inhabitants of this city had long perfected ways of looking at people like him without seeming to, or avoiding him altogether. People stared ahead, bent their heads closer together in conversation, found the most interesting things in half-empty shop windows, hugged walls, pulled children closer. Like last night on Kvaternik, he thought of water. As if he moved through water, a bow wave of apprehension moving ahead of him, altering behaviour and trajectories, all of it swirling and washing back and forth in his wake, emotions and intentions coming back together.

There were noticeably fewer troops in the city. The endless convoys were gone, off down to the east and south, and a large part of the city's garrison had followed them. Of the soldiers who were left, most were from the Croatian Army, many of them Bosnian Muslim conscripts, incongruous in their German Army pattern uniforms with black fez on their heads. The hats were supposedly a cultural exception. Reinhardt thought they looked like extras in some children's matinee production.

His feet felt like blocks of lead as he climbed the stairs to his office. The day was barely begun and he wanted it over in a way he had not felt for a long time, but there was a note on his desk requesting him to report to Freilinger soonest. He flipped his cap onto a chair and sat on the edge of the desk. As always, in these moments when his mind seemed to drift, he looked without really seeing at the big map of Sarajevo on his wall. East to west, all the way from Hrasnica, on the long, winding road down through Jablanica to Mostar and on to the sea, to Lapisnica and its old Ottoman footbridge where the mountains pinched off the city. North and south of the city were hills and mountains, where he had rarely been. Green rolling country to the north, hills folded and rucked like a bed that had been slept in, but to the south they bulked high, swelling into the great stone bulwarks of the south and east.

It was down there, hidden in fastnesses of stone and wood, moving freely as they wished, that the Partisans had their bases. And it was down there, clustering along the few roads and around the few towns and villages, that the Germans and their allies had mustered their forces. Almost, Reinhardt wished he were with them. This war had, for him, been one of paper and shadows. The war he had known, the first war, had been one of sludge and clay, a blasted horizon slashed and barbed by wire, and the sky at times so full of iron and steel it seemed there could be room for nothing else. But he had sometimes found an honesty in warfare he had found nowhere else. A comfort in the company of men exposed to the same dangers, running the same risks. It was better, sometimes, to face open danger than skulk through the shadows like this.

He sighed and stirred himself. Feeling sorry for his lot would get him precisely nowhere. And nowhere was where he was. No suspect. No investigation. No support. He took the stairs up to

Freilinger's office slowly and found the major much as he had found him the night before, standing by his window, looking west. Freilinger turned as he came in, and Reinhardt was struck by how tired he looked, the lines on his face long and deep. The two of them stared at each other a moment, and then the major gestured to the chair in front of his desk. 'So,' he said, pointing to his telephone. 'I've just spoken to Putković. I understand things have come to a pass?'

'They think their suspect was murdered by one of their own doctors, whom they're now searching for as a Partisan agent.'

'So I hear.'

'Even if he didn't kill Vukić, Topalović must've been important to them,' said Reinhardt, staring out the window. He turned back to Freilinger. 'I mean, Topalović must have been pretty important if an agent as apparently well placed as Begović was blown just to shut him up.'

'Hmm,' said Freilinger, rolling one of his ubiquitous mints in his fingers. He fixed Reinhardt with those blue eyes. 'Putković seems to have it in his head you had something to do with it.'

Reinhardt was too tired to muster up a protest. 'I met the doctor last night when I went to police HQ. I –'

'What were you doing there?' interrupted Freilinger.

'I was angry, sir,' replied Reinhardt. 'What you told me seemed so wrong. I went to try and talk to Padelin, to...' He paused, ran a hand over his face, swallowed. 'It's not important why I went, I suppose. I couldn't find Padelin. The doctor escorted me out of the building and walked me as far as the Latin Bridge. That was it.'

'So it was some sort of mercy killing?' Reinhardt nodded. 'Well, so might this be, I suppose.' Reinhardt straightened in the chair. 'It's over. The investigation. I've been told to bring it to an end.'

'By whom, sir?'

'Staff, up at Banja Luka. It would seem the telephone lines have been buzzing. Some colonel on the commander's staff seems to have a dim view of us wasting resources, getting in the way of senior officers, distracting attention, sowing confusion within our own forces, upsetting our allies...' He rolled the mint around the front of his mouth. 'Seems you've stirred up quite the hornet's nest, Reinhardt.'

Reinhardt nodded once, slowly, closing his eyes as he did so. 'So it would seem, sir,' he said quietly.

Freilinger frowned at him, his lips pursing and moving as he swallowed his mint. He drummed his fingers quietly on the table, one after the other, a rolling little beat that came to an abrupt stop. He leaned forward on his elbows, looking hard at him. 'My God. This has really got to you, hasn't it?'

Reinhardt opened his mouth to reply and found nothing. Freilinger seemed willing to wait, so he tried again. 'It has got to me, sir. You're right. I think... I think it's because you held the door open to a past that meant something to me. And, for whatever reason, I could not seem to join that past up with this present.' He looked away, down at the floor, then back. 'Naïve of me, I know.' He found he had nothing more to say and gave a twitch of a smile in place of the words that would not come.

'Reinhardt,' Freilinger said, after a moment. 'I've no written orders for you yet, but I know you are supposed to stand ready to transfer down to Foča. That's where they're setting up the holding area for prisoners, and they'll want you for interrogations.' He leaned back. 'I'm being reassigned. My replacement's on his way from Belgrade, and I'm off to Italy.'

Reinhardt knew there were consequences here. Implications. For both of them, but he could not think them through, could only feel them, waiting like steps in a road he would have to take. He wondered whether this was what Becker's parting shot had been about. 'It was the Feldgendarmerie making the calls,' Freilinger continued. 'The colonel at army HQ referred specifically to the commandant of the Feldgendarmerie.'

'The commandant? He only knows what Becker tells him.' Reinhardt shifted. 'Is your transfer because of... this?'

'It's been on the cards a while. This has probably sped things up, is all.' He looked down at something on his desk. 'Last night, I promised you some information.' He held up a sheet of paper. 'Recent transfers of general staff officers to Bosnia in the last six months.' Freilinger considered it a moment, then held it out to Reinhardt. 'Not much use to you now, I suppose, but I marked the three officers who served in the USSR.' Glancing at the paper, Reinhardt saw that it listed about a half dozen names and folded it into his pocket. Freilinger watched him, twisted his lips, and sat back in his chair.

'Sir, you talk as if it's over for me. I know that's what Banja Luka told you, but you seemed to be hinting that I ought to continue until orders come telling me otherwise. Was I wrong about that?'

'When I referred to written orders, Reinhardt, I indeed only referred to myself. I have none for you. You may very well consider that licence to pursue your inquiries. Or you may not. Perhaps it would be safer not to.'

'Yes, sir. I ask because I met with someone last night. A Captain Thallberg. Ostensibly an infantry captain, he is GFP. He told me Hendel was as well, as was Krause. They were working for him.'

Freilinger looked back at him. 'What?' he said.

If Reinhardt had been in that kind of mood, he might have taken pleasure in the look on Freilinger's face. One of complete surprise, written blankly across his drawn features. 'They were GFP. Hendel was on some kind of surveillance mission. He was tasked to it by someone senior, not in country. This Thallberg doesn't know who, but he's trying to find out.'

Freilinger seemed to deflate in his chair. His mouth moved. 'GF...' He paused, swallowed, passed a hand across his face, then began to rub his hands together under his chin. That slow movement, back and forth and around and around.

'The GFP are often involved in court martials, aren't they?' Freilinger nodded, slowly. 'Maybe that's the case here. Maybe Hendel was building up a case against someone.'

'Do you know who he was after?'

Reinhardt shook his head. 'I would've hoped to find out eventually. But sir, it has to have been the man Vukić was seeing, who was at her house that night. My belief remains the same. She knew something about a senior member of our armed forces. She had revealed all, or part, to Hendel, who was after the same person. How they met, I do not know. Probably at the nightclub. They arranged a confrontation. It went wrong. Probably, she tried to control too much of it and lost the control she sought. He ended up killing both of them, and Krause is on the run. He knows who did this, and he's terrified.' He tapped the list in his pocket. 'With any luck, he's one of those names you found.'

Freilinger's eyes followed Reinhardt's hand, then drifted away. The silence lengthened. 'Do you think the GFP's involvement really changes things?' Reinhardt asked. He knew it did. It was a nonsensical question. It was just that the silence made him suddenly uncomfortable.

The major's eyes hardened, as if they focused on something, and swung back to Reinhardt. 'Of course it does. Reinhardt, if the GFP are involved, this isn't a murder investigation anymore. It's something else. Who knows what… ? But I do know the stakes will be much higher.' Freilinger paused, swallowing slowly. 'And if you felt strongly before about trying to do this right, then you'll have to fight doubly hard with the GFP. They can do anything.'

'Well. What do I have to lose?'

'We always have a lot to lose, Reinhardt. I would have thought someone like you would know better than to make a flippant remark like that.'

Reinhardt flushed. 'Yes, sir. Will there be anything else?'

Freilinger shook his head, looking away. 'No. Dismissed.'

At the door, Reinhardt paused as Freilinger called out to him. 'Captain. If you will continue with this, with the GFP…' He paused, the words trailing off.

'I will be careful, sir,' replied Reinhardt, stepping into the breach. Freilinger's expression gave no hint as to whether that was what he had wanted to say. If he felt any frustration, if he felt Reinhardt was being obtuse, he showed no sign of it, and only nodded and looked away.

21

There was a message slip on his desk. Thallberg had called and was waiting to see him at the State House. He put the piece of paper from Freilinger on his desk and scanned the names. He took his own list of officers commanding the units in Schwarz and compared the two. Freilinger had underlined three names as having served in the USSR – Generals Grabenhofen, Eglseer, and von Le Suire. Only Grabenhofen was involved in Schwarz, and the other two were not on Reinhardt's list. Of the other transfers on Freilinger's list, one was in command of a unit in Schwarz – General Verhein – but had not served in Russia.

He straightened, stepped back from his desk. This was all getting tangled in his mind, and he needed to straighten it out. He glanced at the message slip again and saw that Thallberg had called about twenty minutes ago. He should take some time, try to make some sense of what he had now. He telephoned downstairs, ordering them to find Claussen and send him up, then shut the door and sat at his desk, flattening his map of the case onto it. He began adding information – *GFP* next to Hendel's and Krause's names. Pausing a moment, he linked Becker's name to the empty circle of the suspect. He glanced at the list Freilinger had given him, and then the list of commanders, and back at his map. For now, he refrained from listing those names. If anyone else came across the map, it would look very bad, especially as he had nothing to substantiate it all with. Underneath the suspect's circle he wrote *senior*, and then *USSR*, linking USSR to Vukić.

There was a knock at the door. 'One moment,' he called. Reinhardt folded up the map, grabbed the keys to the *kübelwagen*, and opened the door. Claussen stood in the hallway. Reinhardt tossed him the keys and they went back downstairs and out to the car.

'Where to, sir?'

'State House,' Reinhardt answered. He settled into his normal position, back wedged between the seat and the door as Claussen took the car out onto Kvaternik, then pulled it around the Rathaus and back down King Aleksander Street. Reinhardt watched the streets go by on the right, the old Ottoman buildings giving way to the drab fronts the Austrians had put up until the car pulled in front of the pillared portico of the State House. A soldier on duty lifted a striped barrier and let Claussen park in the street down the side of the building. Next to the staff cars already there, black and shiny with pennants on their hoods, the *kübelwagen* with its dull grey panels looked like a fish out of water.

The foyer inside was gloomy and heavy. A woman in an army uniform directed Reinhardt to follow the stairs up to the second floor. He passed the offices of the small German civilian security administration that had accompanied the army into Yugoslavia. It was mostly officers from the Gestapo, with a few from the Sicherheitsdienst, the Nazis' own security service. They were mostly here to work with the Ustaše, oversee the treatment meted out to undesirables – Jews, Serbs, and Gypsies, chiefly – and to keep an eye on the ideological behaviour of the Germans. Unlike in Poland and the USSR, though, the Germans had not brought the full panoply of their bureaucracy and administration with them, and the civilians, even the powerful ones with senior Party ranks, were kept pretty much in check by the army. Bosnia was supposed to be part of Croatia, after all, an allied state. So no Reich governorate for Yugoslavia and so much less squabbling between civilians, soldiers, and SS;

much less administrative chaos; and corruption at a manageable scale. And there were no death squads on the scale of the Einsatzgrüppen in Russia, the special action units, the rumours of which were enough to chill the blood. Mass killings were their forte: Jews, the politically undesirable, unwanted populations, resistance fighters... No, for that here they had the Ustaše, who managed very well.

Reinhardt stared at the GEHEIME FELDPOLIZEI sign on the frosted glass of a door, at the blocky Gothic lettering, remembering other signs like it on other doors in Berlin. He had hated those names, bastard amalgams of police and political, but now he just felt detached from it. Was this what it meant to get old and jaded? he wondered. Men walked briskly past and around him as he stood there. Just as at the Abwehr offices, Reinhardt felt untouched by it all. Finally, he knocked and went in without waiting for an answer.

A corporal, tall and wiry in all ill-fitting uniform and with a fuzz of iron grey hair, was just opening the door for him and came to attention. Thallberg was on the telephone, standing in his shirtsleeves by a window that looked out over the road outside and across to a small park with a couple of Ottoman-era tombstones standing crookedly among the trees. His jacket hung over the back of a chair, and his equipment was strewn around an otherwise largely empty office. A camp bed with crumpled sheets stood against one wall. He gestured Reinhardt to take a seat as he listened to the person on the other line. He snapped a terse 'Yes', then put the phone down on his desk and stood looking down at Reinhardt with his hands on his hips.

'So, how are you this morning?'

Reinhardt nodded as he took a cigarette from his packet. 'Fine,' he said, offering the pack to Thallberg, who shook his head. Maybe it was the setting, seeing him in an office in a building like this. Despite his general sense of undress, Thallberg seemed sharper, more competent.

'I'm hearing things,' said Thallberg, as he pulled back a chair and sat down. He put his booted feet up on the desk and crossed his ankles, scrubbing his hands through his unkempt blond hair. 'Things have gone a bit pear-shaped over at police HQ?'

Reinhardt nodded again around a mouthful of smoke. 'Their suspect's dead,' he replied. 'But seeing as whoever he was didn't do it, it still leaves us pretty much nowhere.'

Thallberg grunted. 'And no sign of Krause.'

'Are you asking me or telling me?'

'Telling.' He picked up a mug and peered into it. 'You want some coffee? It's pretty good here.' He spooned coffee into two cups and handed them to the corporal. 'That'll be all for now, Beike, thank you,' he said to him. 'I talked to the Feldgendarmerie this morning and warned them off him.'

'Who did you talk to?' Reinhardt looked at the door through which the corporal had gone. 'And who was that?'

'That was Corporal Beike. My right-hand man, if I'm honest. Memory like an encyclopedia. I trust him. And I talked to the Feldgendarmerie commandant.'

'Colonel Lewinski?' Thallberg nodded. Reinhardt pursed his lips, holding Thallberg's eyes. 'Lewinski's old-school Prussian. A gentleman. Also wholly ineffectual. Major Becker's the one who runs things around here, and he's the one you've got to worry about.'

'You and he have a history together, correct?' Thallberg asked, echoing Claussen's words yesterday.

Reinhardt reminded himself not to underestimate this man who seemed to have so many facts about his own past. 'Becker and I were in Kripo together. He was a bad cop. A dirty one. He hasn't changed. He runs the Feldgendarmerie here pretty much as he likes.'

'*Becker?* Well... he's a bit squirrelly, but he's harmless enough.'

Reinhardt shook his head. 'He's dirty. Whoever killed Hendel has got Becker looking for Krause. Like I told you last night, if he finds him before you do...'

'Fine,' said Thallberg, shortly. 'I'll deal with Becker if I have to.' He seemed to dismiss it from his mind, leaning forward with his elbows on the desk. Reinhardt wanted to stress the point: Becker was not someone you could just turn your back on like that, but he let it go. 'So, what do we have, then?'

'You're supposed to have a list for me?'

'Right.' Thallberg pulled a folder towards himself and took a piece of paper from it. 'Two, in fact. Transfers. And officers attending that planning conference. I had Beike working on that transfer list last night.' He passed it across the table. He yawned and ran a hand over his face, stubble rasping beneath his palm.

Reinhardt looked at the transfer list, squinting past the smoke that spiralled up from his cigarette. Like Freilinger's, it was only a half dozen names long. He ran his eyes down it, considering. He did not want to take out Freilinger's to compare it. Something held him back.

There was a knock at the door, and a soldier came in with two mugs of coffee. 'There's only condensed milk. Sugar's there,' pointed Thallberg as he sat back in his chair with his mug held in two hands. 'I had a look through Hendel's files. These here,' he said, pointing to a pile of paperwork. 'There's gaps. Nothing on what he was doing here.'

'Is that usual? I mean, I don't know how you GFP chaps work.'

'You mean secret handshakes and Teutonic rituals? Silver daggers and oaths by moonlight?' Thallberg smirked. 'No, we leave that kind of crap to the SS. And no, it's not usual. He was supposed to keep files and records. Just like any policeman.'

'You've got nothing as to what he was on?'

Thallberg chewed his lip, that same small gesture he had used last night. 'Nothing.' Reinhardt could not tell whether he was lying.

'So? What do you think?'

Reinhardt looked at Thallberg's second list, which was longer. He folded them and put them on the table. He spooned sugar into his coffee. 'I think it's not much good to me anymore.' Thallberg raised his eyebrows in query. 'Freilinger told me this morning the investigation's being halted. I'm supposed to stand ready to report for new duties.' He sipped the coffee. 'He's being transferred to Italy.'

'Investigation's halted?' repeated Thallberg. 'Who ordered it?'

'Banja Luka. After pressure from the Feldgendarmerie here.'

Thallberg took some coffee, worked his mouth around it. '*Fuck,*' he said, pushing himself back in his chair. He rose and went over to the window. 'Look, *sod* that. I don't care what some *poxy* staff officer said. This isn't over. One of my boys is dead, and I want to know why, and who did it.' He drank more coffee, and seemed to hesitate over something. 'You don't want to give it up, do you?'

Reinhardt felt a lurch, a sudden tilt deep inside. He did not want to give this up, no. But what did that mean? Where would it take him? He looked back at Thallberg before slowly shaking his head. 'No. No, I don't.'

Thallberg grinned, the man Reinhardt had met last night coming out. 'Want to work for me, then?'

Reinhardt forced himself to think slowly. 'Work for you? What would that mean?'

'Just that, Reinhardt. You don't need to pussyfoot around with this.' He came back over to the desk. 'You keep going with your investigation. Find whoever killed Hendel. Give me a name. Anything. I'll take it on, I promise.'

Reinhardt swallowed hard, letting his eyes drift away, then back. 'And then?'

'Then? Well, then we'll have our man. Or at least we'll have Hendel's man. And someone in Berlin will be very happy with us.'

'And that's enough?' asked Reinhardt, quietly.

Thallberg heard it as a statement. 'That's enough,' he said, firmly. 'More than enough.'

'Enough to do what? For what?'

'Christ, Reinhardt, who *cares*?' exclaimed Thallberg. 'Enough to write your ticket out of this shithole, perhaps? Enough to catch the baddie? Isn't that what you old-time coppers were all about?'

'Nice of you to make the distinction,' said Reinhardt, covering his confusion by drinking from his mug. Thallberg grinned, and Reinhardt felt a growing excitement. The chance to pursue the investigation, perhaps even finish it. With someone like Thallberg backing him up, it could be done. But the risks, to dance with the devil on something like this. Behind Thallberg's boyish exuberance there had to be someone ruthless, merciless. He could never afford to forget that. 'All right, then,' he said, riding roughshod over his own misgivings, reaching out to grab the tiger's tail.

'Good,' said Thallberg. 'Well done.' He took a piece of paper from a drawer and wrote quickly on it, then walked to the door and called for Beike. He smiled, self-consciously, it seemed. 'It's strange, Reinhardt. You know, you and all those other Berlin coppers were heroes to me when I was a boy. And now, here I am, working with one of you! It's a bit like living a dream.'

Thallberg handed his paper to his corporal and Reinhardt kept his face blank, even as he struggled to understand who Thallberg was, and what he had just done agreeing to work with him. The GFP officer seemed to lurch between almost childish enthusiasm and a semblance of ruthlessness. Reinhardt had not yet seen that harder side come out, but he knew it was there.

'So, where will you start?' Thallberg asked, closing the door.

'At the beginning, I think.' Reinhardt put his coffee down on the table. 'I'll start by retracing the moves the killer probably made. I'm going to go back out to Ilidža and start from Vukić's house. But first,' he said, smoothing out Thallberg's transfer list, 'let's have a look at this. Where did you get these names from, did you say?'

The captain came around to Reinhardt's side, looking over his shoulder. There were seven names. 'From here. General staff records.'

'So it's about as reliable as it comes, then,' said Reinhardt as he read the names off. He pulled out his list of units involved in Schwarz, comparing the COs to the list of transfers. Only two names matched up: those of Generals Verhein and Ritter von

Grabenhofen. Two other names were listed as having served until fairly recently in the USSR – Generals Eglseer and von Le Suire – but their units were not involved in the operation. He circled all four names with a pencil. 'What do you know about these ones?'

Thallberg raised his eyebrows. 'Grabenhofen, not much. Pretty tough fighter. Got involved in some rough stuff in the USSR at the beginning of Barbarossa. Verhein, I know a bit more about. Up and coming. Very brave. Loved by his men, apparently. Le Suire... typical Prussian aristocrat. Also pretty brave. Good with the ladies, they say,' he added. 'And Eglseer. Well, he's a rough old bastard. Been in the army all his life.'

'Yes, I think I know him, as well,' said Reinhardt. 'From the first war. Very well,' he sighed out. 'We've got four names. We can place them all in Sarajevo at the conference. Now, we have to match them to Vukić.'

'Steady on, Reinhardt,' said Thallberg. 'Back up a little. What's the reasoning behind that?'

'Right. I owe you something of an explanation. Vukić travelled a lot. She was a member of the propaganda companies, in fact. She often visited the troops, and when she travelled she had a technical team with her. One of them is in Sarajevo now. He told me about her movements in Russia. She was there towards the end of last year and, according to him, she had a pretty tumultuous affair with a senior German officer that ended badly.' Reinhardt paused, drank some coffee, and gestured at the list. 'According to him, whoever that officer is, he transferred here not long ago, and Vukić was aware of it. Again, according to him, Vukić was not the sort of woman to come second best in love. She was certainly planning something this officer wouldn't like.'

Thallberg seemed fascinated, hanging on Reinhardt's words. It made him feel alternately uncomfortable and somewhat gratified. Something in the way Thallberg looked at him suddenly reminded him of when he was the mentor to a young detective called Sander, and the way he had absorbed

Reinhardt's advice, of the way he had seemed to look up to Reinhardt, the famous criminal inspector. Right up until Sander had joined the SS in 1934, claiming that police work was too much like hard work. Whichever it was, Reinhardt wanted to feel none of it.

Thallberg flicked his eyes over the lists. 'So we need to compare movements.'

'Correct. I have hers. Now we need to match them up to these four.'

The door opened and Beike slipped inside, putting a sheet of typed paper on Thallberg's desk. 'I don't know, Reinhardt. It's pretty thin stuff, isn't it?'

'I've built up good cases with less,' replied Reinhardt, with a bravado that he did not quite feel. He had indeed done that, but in other places, at other times, and with a little less riding on the outcome.

'All right, then,' said Thallberg. 'Leave them with me and I'll start looking up more details. Shall we check back together later on today?'

Reinhardt nodded. 'I'm going out to Ilidža. See if anything new occurs to me.'

'Let's hope so. I need to be getting back down to the front tomorrow.' Thallberg went back around to his chair, suddenly all business and efficiency. 'This is exciting, but I don't want to miss the battle.' He glanced at the paper, scrawled his signature over the stamp, and handed it to Reinhardt. 'Until later, then?'

Walking back outside, Reinhardt paused on the steps, lighting a cigarette and looking across the junction at the little park, then down at the letter of authorisation he held in his hand, naming him as a GFP auxiliary. He drew deeply on the cigarette, drawing the smoke around the roil of emotions he was feeling. Satisfaction, even a sense of exhilaration, that he was still on the case. Trepidation, uncertainty at his new ally. Folding the letter away, he spotted Claussen waiting at the corner of the building and gestured that he should join him across the road.

He walked across to the park, over to the tombs. The stone was white, pitted, and the way they jutted out of the grass was like bones from a grave. Flowing Arabic script was carved into their sides, and the head of each tombstone was shaped like a turban. His hand feeling furtive, he took Freilinger's list from his pocket and unfolded it. He stared at it, then stared at Thallberg's, his eyes moving back and forth between the two. He was not wrong. The two did not compare. One name was different.

22

He was quiet on the long drive out to Ilidža. The jarring rattle of the *kübelwagen*, the slap of its tyres on the crumbling road, he blanked it all out, his attention focused on that name and on why Freilinger might have failed to mark it, to draw it to Reinhardt's attention. An oversight? Unlikely, but possible. An attempt to draw him away? Why? It was Freilinger who had put him on the investigation. Why would he then obstruct him? He was still worrying it over as Claussen parked the *kübelwagen* in front of Vukić's house, and he realised he had not paid any of the attention he had intended to on the trip out.

Cursing under his breath, noting the policeman rising to his feet from where he had been lying in the shade under a tree in the garden, he stood in the lane and looked around. Quite some distance away, through the trees on the other side of the road, he could make out the white walls of the Hotel Austria. To his right, the lane arrowed straight on up to the source of the Bosna. He pushed open the gate, walking up to the front door, cursing himself again for not bringing Hueber as the policeman stood in his way.

The man was young, nervous looking. Reinhardt gestured at the house. 'Speak German? *Njemacki govorish?*' The policeman shrugged, a pained smile on his face. 'Padelin. You know Padelin?' The policeman nodded vigorously, repeating the detective's name. Reinhardt's hands fluttered back and forth as he tried to pantomime his relationship with him, struggling with his pidgin Serbo-Croat. 'Me. Padelin. Good, yes? Friends. *Drugi. Kolegi.*'

'*Da, da, razumem,*' said the policeman, apparently coming to some kind of understanding. '*Nema problema.*' He hitched his rifle onto his shoulder and took a key from his pocket. He pushed open the front door, standing to one side, and gesturing with his hand that Reinhardt could go in.

Reinhardt walked slowly in, the policeman standing uncertainly just to one side of the door. His boots waking the wood, which creaked softly underneath, Reinhardt walked the length of the hallway, opening the doors to either side and peering in. There was nothing in the rooms except furniture covered in sheets and the smell of dust and disuse. He went upstairs, up past the pitted stain on the wall where Hendel had been killed, up to the third floor. Pausing on the landing, he looked down and around. Just dust, as Claussen had said.

Back down to the living room, into Vukić's bedroom, eyes passing across the blood-soaked mattress, the big mirror, imagining the room behind it. Someone had to operate that camera, but from where? He went back into the living room and sat down gingerly in one of the armchairs, feeling the leather creak comfortingly around him. He looked at the doorway to Vukić's bedroom, at the stain of Hendel's blood, at the righted drinks cabinet. A showdown, a setting for a denunciation. What were they thinking, those two? What had they hoped to accomplish? What made them think it was a risk worth taking? Moreover, why had Hendel gone along with it? Reinhardt was fairly sure his orders would not have countenanced something like this. So what was it? Had Vukić convinced him? Bewitched him, somehow?

He rubbed his hands briskly together, then put them to his mouth, sighing out and shaking his head in frustration. The policeman was still standing by the front door, his eyes uncertain on Reinhardt as he paused at the foot of the stairs and went into the kitchen. There were three doors, and none of them led down to a basement. He checked the ground-floor rooms without finding anything either. Wondering if there might be an entrance outside he walked briskly out, past the policeman, and made a tour of the house.

He found a garden shed in a far corner, almost hidden behind a big rosebush. The door was not locked, but dug into the ground as he pulled it open in fits and jerks. The interior was dim, the walls lined with tools and plank shelves on which rested the usual bric-a-brac of a garden shed. He ducked his head and walked in and, past a wheelbarrow and a lawn mower with earth and grass still stuck to the blades, saw another door. It was locked, but the lock had been shattered off. He put his shoulder to the door and pushed it open, the bottom dragging at the earthen floor of the shed, and stepped into the little room he had found. There was a table and chair, and along one wall under a dirty little window was a neatly made-up camp bed. The chair was incongruous, the wood dark and lustrous, with a plump red cushion and, on the table, resting on old newspaper, was what looked like the parts of a disassembled camera, together with an array of tools. A bottle and a glass turned upside down stood to one side, as did a pipe in a bowl, a little tin of tobacco next to it, and the slumped remains of a candle in a jar.

There was nothing else in the little room, and the surge of excitement he felt at finding it faded fast as he pawed through the junk on the shelves and peered into the shed's corners. Someone had obviously beaten him to it, but he seemed to have found the place where Vukić's cameraman waited. He could see no sign of any film, no photos, nothing hidden away. The floor of the shed was bare earth with no sign it had been disturbed. It was all detail. Useful detail, but nothing he could see brought him any closer to what he was looking for.

Back outside, he walked slowly down the side of the house, his feet crunching the gravel of the path. An army car drove slowly up the alley, towards Vrelo Bosne. The soldier driving peered at him as he drove past. Reinhardt followed the car with his eyes, and then his gaze fell on a stretch of path where the gravel had been scuffed and pushed, exposing the dark earth beneath. He paused, frowned. He turned to the policeman, standing by the now-closed front door. He pointed at the spot of disturbed earth.

'There was a motorbike, here,' he managed. 'A motorbike. *Brroom, brrroom,*' he said, miming revving the handles of a motorbike.

The policeman nodded. '*Motocicl, da, da. Mi ga je dao natrag. Errrr...*' He trailed off, then pointed away, through the trees, over towards the hotels, his hand fluttering. '*Tamo, je...*' He looked flustered, then pointed at his throat, his finger moving back and forth, tracing a shape.

Reinhardt frowned, then understood. A crescent. 'You gave it to the Feldgendarmerie?'

The policeman smiled. 'Feldgendarmerie,' he repeated, his finger making the sign of a gorget again.

Reinhardt took some Atikahs from his pack and offered them to the policeman. He lit one for him, thanked him, then walked quickly to the gate. 'Claussen, I need you to take me to the Feldgendarmerie checkpoint by the bridge.'

'Sir,' answered Claussen as he started the *kübelwagen*. Reinhardt did not know what he might find, but he remembered one of his first lessons from his old police mentor. *It's the simple things in life, kid*, he had said. *The simple things are usually the right things in any case. Nothing complicated.* Why were Hendel's files missing? Probably because he had brought them with him, to confront whomever it was he was after. It was Vukić who had staged it all, but Hendel would be the one to bring it to an end, and for that he would need evidence, and if Reinhardt's hunch was right, the evidence was waiting in plain sight, where it had waited nearly a week.

Claussen pulled the *kübelwagen* over in front of a low grey building that stood across from the bridge over the Željeznica. Remembering another of that old copper's lessons – *bullshit baffles brains, kid* – Reinhardt walked inside and up to a

Feldgendarme on duty behind a battered wooden desk. He flashed his papers as the guard rose to his feet and saluted.

'Corporal, my name is Captain Reinhardt, with the Abwehr. I am on a mission of internal army security.'

'Sir,' exclaimed the soldier. 'I am afraid my lieutenant is not here at this time.'

'Of no importance,' replied Reinhardt with a flick of his wrist. 'Tell me, do you have a parking lot, here? Yes? Then take me to it, immediately.'

The corporal took Reinhardt into the back of the building, down a short corridor, and through a kitchen area where a squad of Feldgendarmes were eating at a table. There was a scrape and clatter of chairs as they rose to their feet and stood at attention. Reinhardt waved them back to their meal as he followed the corporal outside to where a handful of cars were parked. Reinhardt strode past them, stopping as he came to the end of the row.

'This vehicle,' he snapped, pointing at a motorcycle and sidecar. 'Where did it come from?'

'Sir, I do not know.'

'When was it left here?'

'A day ago, I believe,' stammered the Feldgendarme.

'You *believe*?' sneered Reinhardt, putting as much into it as he could. 'For Christ's sake, Corporal, get back in there and find me someone who can answer my *simple* questions.'

Reinhardt waited a moment after the corporal had scurried back inside, then bent over the sidecar. The seat would not move. He ran his fingers down the side, finding nothing. He checked underneath the tyre fixed to the front of the sidecar. Nothing. He leaned forward, peering into the sidecar's well. Nothing there either. On the off chance, he reached his hand in, running it all around the interior, and felt his fingers brush up against something bolted to the underside of the top of the sidecar. A shelf, or pocket of some kind. His fingers scrabbled around as he heard voices and footsteps, and his hand closed around the soft edge of a file.

His heart hammering, he pulled it out, put it behind his back, and rose to his feet just as the corporal came out with a sergeant, who cracked off a salute. 'Sir, may I be of assistance to you?'

'I most certainly hope so, Sergeant. What can you tell me of this vehicle?'

'Sir, the police left it here two days ago.'

'Police?'

'The city police, sir.'

'Ahh,' said Reinhardt, with wide eyes and raised brows. 'And did they show authorisation? Did they show identification? Did they give a reason?' The sergeant's mouth moved, searching for a response to Reinhardt's questions. 'No? Nothing? *Fools!*' he shouted. '*Incompetent fools!* You allowed unknown individuals to park a vehicle of unknown origin within the premises of an army installation? What kind of idiots are you? What if there had been a bomb inside it? Well, what of it?' He gave them a moment, just long enough for the sergeant to open his mouth. '*NO!*' he raged, stamping forward. 'No excuses. It is simply *unacceptable* behaviour. The kind that leads straight to a penal battalion on the Eastern Front. What do you have to say for yourselves? Well, then?'

The corporal looked as if he were about to be sick. Again, he waited just long enough for the sergeant to start to say something, then cut him off. He had to be careful not to overdo it. 'My task is to evaluate the state of alertness across the city. Our enemies, and they are many, may strike at any time, in any way. Remember that. Dismissed.' He gave them both a withering look and stalked past and back through the kitchen, the other Feldgendarmes leaping rigidly to attention as he came through. He regally ignored them, muttering under his breath with his hands clasped behind his back and striding out to the *kübelwagen*, where a somewhat bemused Claussen was waiting for him. A car had just arrived, and a pair of soldiers, little and large in ill-fitting uniforms, jumped aside as Reinhardt stomped out.

Reinhardt stared straight ahead as Claussen drove away and across the bridge, and then, little by little, allowed himself to relax. After a couple of kilometres, he recognised the spot where Padelin had directed them off the road the other day. He found he was terribly thirsty and hungry, and he needed to see what was in the file. He directed Claussen off the road, the *kübelwagen* bumping over the track until he parked it in front of the little restaurant. The same three-legged dog came hobbling up, and a few elderly men sitting around cups of coffee and a game of chess stopped talking to look at him a moment. Claussen said he was not hungry, so Reinhardt took a seat alone and ordered water and *burek* from the waiter, then sat back and looked at the file.

It was just a plain, yellow, soft cardboard file. He took a long, slow breath, and opened it. There was no cover sheet, no index of contents. He flicked through the pages quickly, about a dozen reports containing typed and handwritten information, and some photographs, which slipped down and onto the table. Reinhardt pushed them back inside the file, feeling guilty, furtive, like a child spying on his parents, looking up as slowly as he dared to check if anyone was looking. Only Claussen, sitting in the *kübelwagen*, looking back at him.

23

The first item in the file was an after-action report, typed up by one Obersturmführer Gehrig, a member of Einsatzgrüp D, which had been active in Ukraine during the invasion of the USSR. It was dated 3 August 1941 and concerned an action taken to liquidate Jews and other undesirables in a town near Zhytomyr. The report was typed up in dry, bureaucratic language and detailed with painful exactitude the number of people shot (278, all men), rounds of ammunition expended (443), time taken (five hours and six minutes from start to finish, including transportation to and from the execution site), and so forth. Most of the report was devoted to recommendations concerning the logistics of future operations (an improvement here, an improvement there, all humbly suggested), and a rather detailed observation into the moral state of the men who had done the executions (mostly Ukrainian collaborators, with German assistance). One of the main improvements suggested concerned tighter cooperation with the army, with Gehrig noting the lack of assistance rendered from the divisional HQ staff of the 189th Infantry garrisoned in and around Zhytomyr.

The second report, similar to the first, was written by an Untersturmführer Havel. Another action, this one much bigger, a week or so later. The third report came after the fall of Kiev at the end of September. Another SS officer, a Hauptsturmführer Kalb. Another major Einsatzgrüp operation. Thousands of Jews killed, now including women and children. Yet more details on how and when and how long it took, and more exhaustive examinations of the mental and physical state of the troops. An analysis of the recently introduced execution method known as 'sardine packing', which apparently had been hard on the morale of some of the men. There was a note on several soldiers who had broken down, and one who had refused to fire, and a recommendation to transfer them to other, less strenuous, duties.

Reinhardt's attention was distracted for a moment as an army car passed slowly in front of the restaurant. The waiter brought the food then, and Reinhardt paused, feeling cold, trying to imagine the horror these terse lines obscured. He knew horror, had seen it and experienced it in the first war, but not so far in this one. Not this butchery rendered as terse lines in poor ink on shabby paper. He imagined the officer writing it, hunched over his lists and reports by the light of a flickering lamp, probably cold, tired, hungry, wanting to be done with this so he could go to sleep, or join his friends for a drink and a game of cards, but wanting to get it done *just right*... He stared at the *burek* and could no longer stomach the idea of eating, but only sipped from the water and went back to reading.

Apart from the similarities in the actions, something else linked the three reports together. He leafed back through them to be sure. It was the army. Lack of assistance. Obstruction. Criticism. The first two reports cited the divisional staff of the 189th; the third mentioned the chief of staff of the 128th Motorised Infantry. A colonel who refused to countenance his men being involved in such an operation and who, the report cited in particular, did not provide assistance to hunt down fugitives. The same officer, in fact, who had been part of the headquarters staff of the 189th. A Colonel Paul Verhein.

Unlike the other reports, the one written by Kalb had been brought to the attention of the SD. Verhein's actions were the subject of a follow-up report, also included in the file. Verhein defended his actions as refusing to become involved in activities unworthy of an officer, in addition to which his men were needed for combat duties, not police actions. Verhein's commanding officer defended his rather impetuous subordinate by reference to his impeccable service record, which was attached. If only half of it was true, the man was as brave as a lion. A first war veteran, in this war Verhein had citations for battlefield valour and leadership from Poland, France, Yugoslavia, Greece, Crete, and the USSR. Holder, among other decorations, of the Knight's Cross with oak leaves of the Iron Cross, given to him by the Führer himself after the invasion of France. Holder, as well, of the Pour le Mérite, the Blue Max, the highest battlefield decoration of the old Imperial German Army.

The inquiry exonerated Verhein but concluded by querying his ideological convictions – noting that the Führer had decreed that all activities that contributed to the destruction of world Jewry and Bolshevism were activities worthy of a German officer, and Verhein would do well to remember that – and recommending more ideological rigour.

The fifth report was an internal one from the SD regional office in Kiev, reporting on a range of comments purported to have been made by Verhein, including disparaging remarks about fellow officers and units, derogatory assessments of his superior officers, and criticism of racial policy in the occupied territories. This note had been forwarded to the SD in Berlin, to a certain Sturmbannführer Varnhorst. The sixth, seventh, and eighth reports were replies received to queries sent by Varnhorst to the SD in France, Serbia, Greece, and Poland, inquiring after the conduct of Verhein during his postings there in 1940 and early 1941. Only the response from the SD in Paris offered anything out of the ordinary: details into an incident in July 1940 in a village called Chenecourt when he intervened in the treatment by an SS unit of captured French officers of Jewish origin, humiliating and injuring an Untersturmführer in the process.

The ninth report was another after-action report, very

detailed, but not written by anyone in the military. It dated from September 1942, concerning an incident in southern Russia, not far from the Volga, near the town of Yagodnyy. A Sonderkommando, a detachment from the main Einsatzgrüp, had rounded up the region's Jews and taken them out to an abandoned collective farm for execution. The action was getting under way when an army unit came through, moving up to provide reinforcements against a Soviet counterattack. The two units became clogged up in the farm. The weather was foul, the roads mired in mud, the fields choked with unharvested wheat. Tempers frayed, cracked. Through it all the prisoners wept and wailed. Some were killed, most huddled like sheep. Some ran for their lives. A few fought back against their tormentors.

The army commander and the chief of the Sonderkommando came to blows. The Sonderkommando chief was killed. Other members of his command were shot down as they tried to respond. Jews grabbed weapons from the dead and added their own weight to the fight. It did not last long, but when it was over, all the Sonderkommando were dead. The action was in ruins, Jews were fleeing all across the steppe, and then the Red Army joined in. The day ended with the Soviets in retreat, the farm in flames. All of it was witnessed by Marija Vukić, who was travelling with the Sonderkommando and had typed it up while the memories were still fresh. The photos were hers, Reinhardt saw. Black-and-white images of dilapidated buildings on fire, bodies strewn across streets, and a grainy photo of a soldier – tall, big, a head of white hair – standing with a drawn pistol over another German. He turned the photo over. A date, and a name. Verhein.

There was an investigation, the possibility of a court martial, but Verhein was exonerated; there were no witnesses among his men, and in any case no one really cared as Stalingrad was pulling in all available troops. Verhein's command was all but destroyed in the fighting in the city, but he survived. Wounded. Another medal. A transfer away from the front and an assignment to create a new unit – the 121st Jäger.

It might have stopped there, but for chance. For one of those things that could make or break an investigation. The tenth and eleventh elements in the file were explosive. The tenth report was a sworn affidavit from one Lasse Künzer, made shortly before his execution for forgery in April 1942. Under interrogation, Künzer admitted to forging a variety of records over decades. He gave places, dates, what he did, and for whom. Several of the names caught the attention of the case officer, who forwarded them on to another department, who forwarded them on again until they came to the attention of Sturmbann-führer Varnhorst, who began to put two and two together. Two of those names were of Paul and Nora Verhein. Künzer swore Verhein had paid him to alter his, and his sister's, birth records in November 1933.

Reinhardt sighed as he read this. If the rumours one heard back then were true, it had been a common enough practice in the days after the Nazis came to power, though never easy. He remembered that more than one of his colleagues in Kripo had had it done in the frenzy and uncertainty that followed the Nazis' coming-to-power in 1933, paying good money to have their birth records altered, removing Jewish or, in one case, Gypsy blood from the family tree. He even knew of at least one case in some convoluted power struggle within the SS where the reverse had been done, and an officer's records altered to show a Jewish grandparent where there was none. The officer had ended up in Dachau. Becker had told him the story, laughing uproariously as he did.

The eleventh report was a request, and response, from Varnhorst to Section VII of the Reich Main Security Office ordering a racial search made of Verhein's parentage. The response was positive. Four German grandparents. Purer blood than that would be harder to find in Nazi Germany. If Künzer was telling the truth, his work lived on long after he was guillotined at Plötzensee prison.

The last page was Hendel's orders from Varnhorst. Hendel was actually an SD operative working under GFP cover. His orders dated from June 1942 and directed him to conduct surveillance on Verhein with an objective of gathering evidence of treasonable conduct. There was nothing in the file to show what, if anything, Hendel had found in the year he had been investigating Verhein, during which he had followed him from Russia to Poland, back to Germany where the 121st was being trained up, and then to Yugoslavia. But, Reinhardt mused, flicking back over the file, for sure probably the only things stopping this investigation becoming more overt were Verhein's impeccable combat record, his abilities as a leader of men, and, he speculated further, his friends. A man like Verhein made friends as well as enemies. Almost certainly, someone was looking out for him. He could not fail to be aware he was being watched.

Reinhardt took out his map of the investigation. He looked at the circle he had drawn for the suspect, then took his pen and wrote *Verhein* in it. The link was there, but what Vukić had on him to make him kill her, Reinhardt had no idea. Yes, she was a witness to the incident at the farm, but an inquiry had exonerated him. So what, then? He sipped some water and picked a corner off the *burek*. Vukić was a journalist. She found something out, he thought, as he chewed slowly. She dug. She connected with Hendel, and through him to Varnhorst.

Paging through the reports, he added dates under Verhein's name. July 1940, the first incident in France, in the Ardennes. August 1941, the first two incidents in Ukraine, near Zhytomyr. September 1941, near Kiev, the third. Nearly a year before the fourth, in September 1942 at Yagodnyy, but by which time Varnhorst already had Künzer's statement, dated April 1942. He matched the dates to the notes he took when they had interviewed Jelić. They more or less matched. Verhein's unit was undoubtedly the one they had travelled with, and Verhein was almost certainly the man with whom Vukić had been having an affair.

His was also the name on Freilinger's list that did not match with Thallberg's. Reinhardt took the file, piling the reports neatly back inside it. He stared at it where it sat on the table, then looked at his map. Happenstance. Chance. Künzer's evidence. It was a funny thing. What were the odds he was telling the truth, and that it would come to the attention of an SD officer? And, he thought, as he toyed with his pen, running it around and around one of the names on the map, what were the odds Künzer's evidence would end up on the desk of that particular SD officer, Sturmbannführer Varnhorst who, one day in July 1940, was humiliated by Verhein, in France, over how he chose to treat a handful of French Jewish officers… ?

It did not mean much. It meant everything, perhaps. But what it really meant, Reinhardt realised now, slumping to one side, was that General Paul Verhein, currently commanding the 121st Jäger Division, decorated officer, was almost certainly a Jew.

24

Claussen swung the *kübelwagen* into the broad, white gravel driveway of the Hotel Austria and parked the car in front of a low flight of steps. Getting out of the car, straightening his tunic, Reinhardt realised he should have come here already, here where all those generals and colonels had met for that planning conference. In Berlin, in any normal investigation, he would have, but here the simple things, the straightforward things, such as establishing a timeline, establishing the presence of a suspect, were anything but.

The hotel was not particularly large, and it was not particularly grand, but with its twin, the Hungary, facing it across a broad round swath of perfectly manicured lawn, it stood out, as it was meant to. This was the heart of the Austrian spa, itself built upon and around a much older town that dated back to Roman times. If Reinhardt remembered correctly, the Archduke Ferdinand and his wife had stayed here on their fateful visit to the city in June 1914. Reinhardt had been sixteen that month. They say the end of innocence comes for everyone, sooner or later. It came for him that summer. Military academy that year, the Eastern Front two years later.

The hotel was fronted by a wide, arched portico supporting a terrace running the length of the building. Reinhardt walked into its shade and into the main entrance of the hotel. Across an expanse of creamy carpet an elderly gentleman in a suit stood behind a reception desk of heavy, deeply carved wood. A pair of staircases rose up to either side of the desk. To the left was a bar with wicker chairs and tables and a grand piano with its top down. To the right was a dining area, a checkerboard of tables with white cloths, plush armchairs drawn rigidly against them. Waiters chinked and chimed among the tables, setting out cutlery and glassware.

As Stern had done at the Ragusa, the receptionist behind the desk was able to size up Reinhardt as he walked across the lobby and to make his displeasure evident behind a façade of professional attentiveness. 'Can I help you, sir?' His German was fluent, the accent Austrian. He had white hair combed back from a high forehead, and a pair of spectacles hung around his neck on a golden chain.

'Yes, you may. I am with the Abwehr,' said Reinhardt. 'I need to see the registry.'

The man put on a slightly quizzical expression. 'I'm not sure I understand you, sir.'

'Your registry. I need to see it.'

'May I ask why, sir?'

'You may indeed,' replied Reinhardt, leaning one elbow on the desk.

The receptionist flushed but maintained his composure. 'I'm very sorry, sir, but I'm afraid that will not do. We cannot give out that sort of information to just anyone who asks.'

'I told you. I'm with the Abwehr. I'm not just anyone.'

'That may well be, sir.' Was it Reinhardt's imagination, or did he have the faintest of smiles?

'Something about this strike you as funny?'

'Indeed not, sir. But you will have to forgive me… Captain,' he said, with the slightest of pauses and a glance, a perfectly superfluous glance, Reinhardt was sure, at his insignia. Reinhardt had to give the old bastard credit. He was good. Much better than Stern at the Ragusa. Kept his nerve. He probably saw and dealt with a lot worse than Reinhardt on any given day. 'We get many requests here, for all kinds of things, from all kinds of people. Most of them, shall we say… senior to you. This is a private establishment. We have the comfort and privacy of our guests to think about.'

'Where are you from?'

'Well, that would be neither here nor there, sir. And in both cases, unless this were official, which I feel it is not, it is none of your business.'

'What are you afraid of?' asked Reinhardt, leaning both elbows on the desk and swivelling to face the man directly. He leaned back slightly, as if to keep Reinhardt at arm's length.

'Afraid?'

'Yes. Afraid. Something to hide, perhaps?' The receptionist frowned, drawing himself up, and Reinhardt wondered if he had gone too far too quickly. 'Very well,' he said, quickly. He nodded at a door to one side, marked PRIVATE – MANAGER. 'Let me speak with him. Now.'

'What, may I ask, is so urgent?'

'Well, I said you could ask,' said Reinhardt, glancing around the lobby. Apart from the waiters in the dining room, there was no one.

'In that case, I'm afraid I am not able to help you, sir. Good day to you.' The man sniffed, then picked up a pen and began to write in a small book. He looked up after a moment, seemingly surprised to find Reinhardt still there. 'Was there something else, sir?'

'Your manager. Go and get him.'

The receptionist's face flushed, the wrinkles around his eyes whitening. 'I told you –' He broke off as Reinhardt slapped Thallberg's letter naming him a GFP auxiliary down on the desk. He looked at Reinhardt before polishing his glasses on the edge of his waistcoat. He pulled his nose tight as he put them on, then picked up the paper. With a last look at Reinhardt over the top of his glasses, he sighed, as if giving him a last chance to leave, and then began to read. Within moments the man's eyes flicked up at Reinhardt, then back to the letter. He finished it and put it down on the counter. He took off his glasses, his fingers nervous on the frames, and looked up.

Reinhardt grinned, the most insolent grin he could come up with. 'Changes things?' The receptionist cleared his throat. Reinhardt made the grin go away, looking hard at the man. He did not like acting like this, and the man was polite and just doing his job. It felt wrong, but it was part of the role he had to play.

'I am not sure it does, sir,' said the man, but he sounded noticeably less sure of himself.

'Oh, I assure you it does. You either help me now, or I come back with a squad of Feldgendarmerie and turn this place upside down. Now. For the last time. Your manager.'

The receptionist knew when he had lost. 'Yes, sir. Whom shall I say is calling?'

'Captain Reinhardt. Abwehr.' He flicked a dismissive hand at the paper. 'Just as it says on the letter. Show it to him.'

'Very good, sir,' said the man. He straightened his suit jacket with two hands, and stalked off with his head high over to the manager's office. He knocked once, cleared his throat, then opened the door and stepped inside.

The moment he did, Reinhardt reached over the counter and hauled up a big ledger, bound in black leather, the pages thick and white. He looked quickly at the date, flicked back a page, finding the weekend. He ran his fingers down the list of names, his eyes leaping over the looping signatures of generals, colonels, majors... Some of the names he recognised. Most of the names of the officers from the bar were there. Faber. Forster. Lehmann was there. *Verhein!* There he was. Colonel Ascher's name was next. His chief of staff, Reinhardt remembered. He had been at the bar as well. Two other colonels from the 121st were there: Gärtner and Oelker. He made to put the ledger back, then paused. Why bother? He had been thinking furtively, like someone doing something wrong. He *was* doing something wrong, but the person he was supposed to be would not think that way. He swallowed, hot and embarrassed, feeling how close he was to skirting that line he had always tried to stay away from. He feigned a nonchalance he did not feel, forced himself to lean on his elbow on the counter as he lifted another page.

The receptionist came back out, Reinhardt's letter in his hand. Seeing him with the ledger, he stopped dead for a moment. 'What do you think you are *doing*?'

'Where's the manager?'

'Absent.'

'Very well. You'll do just as well. By the way, your name is?'

'Ewald. Alfred Ewald.'

'Well, Mr Ewald, may I have my letter back?'

He put his hand on the ledger as Ewald reached for it. 'I declare, of all the *insolent*…'

'Mr Ewald, I am on official business. *Official* business,' he repeated. 'You can either help me or hinder me. In both cases, I get what I want. In one case, you come out worse. Decide which it will be.'

'The manager will complain about your behaviour. Believe me he will. To the *highest* levels.' Reinhardt stared back at him, expression even and blank. Ewald clenched his jaw and then seemed to calm. 'Very well. What do you want?'

'For now, just to look at this. If you will permit me… ?' Reinhardt looked at the date entries for Verhein. Checked in on Thursday. Checked out on Sunday. As did all of his officers. But Reinhardt had seen Ascher just on Tuesday, in the officers' mess when he had made such a fool of himself. He jotted the dates down in his notebook.

'Are you aware of the murder of Miss Marija Vukić? On Saturday?' Ewald nodded. 'Well, I have reason to believe the killer may have been one of your guests.'

'One of our…' he said. Reinhardt watched him as the light in his eyes seemed to fold back and away, and he stood straighter, as if braced.

'Yes. One of your guests. Now, think back to Saturday night. Did anything happen you thought then was strange? Or think now was strange? Anything at all. Take your time.'

'Nothing, sir,' said Ewald. 'Nothing comes to mind.'

'Nothing?' Reinhardt pursed his lips. 'A woman was murdered not five minutes' walk from here, by someone who had almost certainly stayed in this hotel, and you can tell me nothing.' He sighed. He felt deflated suddenly, but he saw that his sigh had a different effect on Ewald. He saw an officer, a security officer, an apparently frustrated security officer. 'Who was on the front desk that day?'

'That was me, sir.'

'Hmmm. There was a conference here that weekend, no?' He motioned at the ledger. 'All those officers. There was a dinner? A reception?'

'On Saturday night, yes,' said Ewald. 'But dinner was quiet. There was quite a bit of drinking afterwards, though. Not too much. I mean, I've seen much worse,' he finished, a sickly sort of smile creasing across his face. It looked wrong on him.

'Were there any guests? People invited to the dinner?'

'Oh. Yes. Only a few. All officials of the state.'

'No women?'

Ewald looked scandalised. 'This is a *respectable* establishment.'

Reinhardt shook his head in exasperation. 'Not those sort of women. Guests. Of the officers.'

'Ah. No.'

'When did the dinner finish?'

'Around nine o'clock, sir,' said Ewald.

'And then?'

'Then? Well, I believe most of the guests went to their rooms. Some went to the bar. Not many. Perhaps a few may have gone out, probably into town, or perhaps across to the Hungary.'

'Did you find any of that normal?' Ewald raised his eyebrows and cocked his head. 'Officers unwinding after an event like that usually make more of an occasion of it, no?'

'I have seen things get a little out of hand in similar circumstances, sir, yes.'

'But not this time?' Reinhardt nodded, looking at Ewald. 'I would like to have a look around the hotel.'

The receptionist gave a grudging nod. 'I remind you, Captain,

I will be complaining about your behaviour,' he said. Then he paused, turned back, and picked up a set of keys.

Reinhardt followed the receptionist upstairs. Ewald looked back, once or twice. Reinhardt just gestured to him to keep walking. The receptionist led him up to the second floor, then down a wide corridor before Ewald stopped at the end, in front of a wide window. Reinhardt looked at him. 'I want to see the room General Verhein occupied.'

'Ah. It's on the first floor.' Ewald showed him back downstairs to a spacious room, dark red carpet, the bed linen and drapes of creamy linen. There was a small bathroom in white marble. The cupboards and drawers were empty, and the room smelled faintly of whatever cleaning product had been used on it. 'Has it been occupied since the general left?' Ewald shook his head. The room gave onto the long terrace that ran the hotel's length, with a view of the round lawn that separated the Austria from the Hungary. Vukić's house was away around the back of the hotel, not visible from here.

Reinhardt walked back into the room, staring at Ewald where he stood calmly with the keys in his hands. He looked at him without speaking, hoping that perhaps his silence would shake something out of him. He walked back out into the corridor, then paused at the landing. Ewald stopped behind him.

'You know, it's interesting the way people can sometimes anticipate what others want. I imagine you do that a lot, working in a hotel.' Ewald said nothing. 'I asked to see around the hotel, and you took keys without being asked. You led me up to the second floor, without being asked. To the end of a corridor. It's a funny place to bring someone. You seemed surprised that I wanted to see the general's room.' Ewald stayed still. 'Was there really nothing unusual on Saturday night? Speak freely.'

'Freely?' Ewald repeated. There was a sudden bitter cast to his face. 'There is no such thing anymore, Captain.' He paused, then swallowed, looking much older. 'You know, Captain, you may not believe me, but I once was the concierge at the finest hotel in Klagenfurt. I liked my work. I was respected. This,' he said, looking hard at Reinhardt, 'is not where I ever thought I would find myself.'

Reinhardt sensed this was just Ewald's way of working himself up to speak. 'You know, you sound much like another man I know. Kurt Manfred is the chief waiter at our barracks. He used to work at Medved's, in Berlin, and always tries to keep his standards up.'

'I know the feeling, sir,' he replied, softly. 'It is not always easy.'

'What's up there you thought I might want to see, Ewald?'

'How should I say it? There was… a guest who had rather a lot to drink that night. He held court, so to speak, in the bar downstairs. There was some trouble. A fight. More than one. The Feldgendarmerie had to be called to calm things down in the end.'

'And you thought it was his room I wanted to see?' Ewald nodded. 'Who was it making trouble?'

'It was an SS Standartenführer. You understand… people like that can make life impossible for someone like me.' Reinhardt nodded, but said nothing. The old man sighed. 'His name is Stolić. He comes here quite often when he is in town and invariably causes trouble.'

'What kind of trouble?'

'Oh, his kind never need much of an excuse. He drank a lot with dinner, and more afterwards. One of the other officers was playing the piano, and he argued about that. Then he got into a fight with a Croatian Army officer. One of the other colonels managed to calm him down, but then Stolić got upset again, and the colonel told me to call the Feldgendarmerie.'

'Who told you?'

'Colonel Ascher. The Feldgendarmerie arrived quite quickly but were not happy about taking on a Standartenführer, so they themselves called for more help. Meanwhile, Stolić got into another fight. I don't remember what it was about. He was very drunk. Out of control. Then a Feldgendarmerie officer arrived, and he calmed things down. That was the last I heard of it.'

'Do you know what time the Feldgendarmerie officer came?'

'Perhaps… around midnight. No. Closer to one in the morning.'

'The officer. Did you recognise him?'

Ewald nodded. 'Yes. It was Major Becker.'

Reinhardt looked at him. Ewald held his eyes, and then they shifted. 'There's more, isn't there? Why did you want me to see his room?'

Ewald sighed. 'The next morning, the maid who cleaned Stolić's room… He was still in it. Asleep. She said…' Ewald looked up at Reinhardt. 'She said… on the floor. On the floor… there was a knife. It was covered in blood.'

25

I want to go to that church. The one down at Marijin Dvor,' said Reinhardt, as the houses began to thicken on the approach to Sarajevo.

'St. Joseph's,' Claussen replied. 'Finished just before the war,' he continued.

'What makes you so familiar with Sarajevo's churches?' asked Reinhardt.

'I attend mass,' replied Claussen. 'Every Sunday I can.'

Reinhardt said nothing, only thinking how far he had drifted from the religion of his youth. Church every Sunday, singing in the choir, altar service. Light through stained-glass windows. The comfort of simple truths that just seemed to unravel as you got older.

Claussen stopped the car in front of the church. The façade was all square, white stone, a rectangular steeple with a clock at the top pushing up one side. He looked up at it, thinking. He did not have all that much to go on, but the way the killer had arranged Vukić's body would not leave him alone. He picked up the file. 'I'm going in to see if I can speak to someone. You're welcome to stay with the car. Or go in, say a prayer. Light a candle.'

If Claussen appreciated the irony in Reinhardt's tone, he gave no sign of it, but he did follow Reinhardt up the steps to the tall wooden door. Inside, the church was like all churches in Reinhardt's experience. Gloom pierced by the light from high windows, the smell of incense and beeswax, the sense of voices far away but just around the corner. Claussen stepped quietly away as they came in, moving over to a bank of votive candles.

Apart from a couple of old women kneeling over to one side, and another running a mop over the tiles under one of the Stations of the Cross, the church was empty. The red light of the host drew his eye, and he sat down on one of the front benches. The wood creaked warmly under him, soft and honeyed, awakening a whole different stream of memories. He kept his eyes on the host, letting it keep his gaze until he felt them begin to close, and tried to remember when places like this stopped being places of solace for him.

He opened them to the sound of whispered footsteps. A priest turned along the front row of benches, genuflecting to the altar as he crossed the aisle. He looked down at Reinhardt, looking like every priest one imagines. Portly, balding, grey hair cut close around the sides of his head.

'Can I help you, my son?' the priest asked in German, glancing at the file on Reinhardt's lap.

Reinhardt stood up. 'Perhaps, Father. I am investigating the murder of a young Catholic girl.'

The priest tilted his head backwards in a sign of understanding. 'Ah,' he said. He gestured at the bench for them both to sit. 'You are investigating poor Marija's death, no?' His German was good, an accent riding along behind his native Bosnian one.

'That's right, Father. How did you know?'

The priest smiled, sadly, it seemed. 'This is a small enough town, my son.' He looked at Reinhardt's insignia. 'Captain?' he asked. Reinhardt nodded. 'Word gets around easily enough. Marija was very well known to all. She was a parishioner.'

'Did she usually attend mass here?'

The priest shook his head, and his mouth firmed a little. 'Not regularly. Without wanting to speak ill of the dead, and without wanting to take anything from her achievements, I must say that Marija's behaviour left something to be desired, Captain.'

'You know your ranks, Father.'

'Oh, only sometimes. I've been known to mix my sergeants with my colonels on occasion,' the priest replied.

'Father… ?'

'Father Petar,' he said.

'What time is the first mass on Sunday?'

'At seven o'clock.'

'Is there another service?'

'Yes. At ten.'

'Did you serve either of the masses?'

'I was there, yes. At both of them.'

'Father, did you notice if there were any Germans in the congregation?'

'We get a lot of German soldiers in here. Many, these past few days. From the barracks just up the road. Praying, for success mostly.'

'Success in what?'

'The coming offensive, of course. Against the Partisans. The archbishop gave a most rousing sermon on it just this Sunday.'

Reinhardt had met Archbishop Šarić once and, as an intelligence officer, read translations of his newspaper articles. The man was a rabid Ustaša, a committed fascist. He had also read some of the tawdry poetry the man produced, paeans of praise to Pavelić and his ilk, venomous tracts against Jews and Serbs. The way it had been explained to him, Šarić was one of the instigators behind the mass conversions to Catholicism that were often forced on the Serbs by the Ustaše. Just before they were hacked to death and dumped in mass graves.

Petar brushed down the front of his cassock, then stood up. 'If you will excuse me, Captain? I have things to see to.'

Reinhardt wanted to get out of there before he became maudlin, or said something and regretted it. Not that he would be sorry for what he said. He would be sorry to have lost control of himself and said it. That, as Carolin would say, he would dare to express an opinion outside a police case. But he had not yet got what he came for.

The two of them walked down the aisle to the entrance. 'Your German is very good, Father.'

'Thank you, Captain. I spent some years studying for the priesthood in Bavaria. A most pleasant time.' There was a moment of silence, the church drinking up their words. 'And will you be taking part in the coming attack, Captain?'

Reinhardt shook his head. 'No. Nothing quite so rewarding for me.'

'Perhaps not anymore,' Petar said. He motioned at Reinhardt's Iron Cross. 'But once it was.'

'Thank you, Father. You have been most helpful.' Reinhardt paused, looking back into the church. There really was nothing here anymore for him. Such a long road he had walked from the days of the boy he was, the boy he was brought up to be. Of the comfort he had once taken in the rote and ritual of the church, war, the years he had spent policing the filth and squalor of Berlin, and of watching his wife pulled away from him, had driven a wedge between then and now. 'You must excuse me, Father,' he said, with a smile meant as self-deprecating. 'God and I have drifted quite far apart, but I like to think we were once close enough.' He opened the big door and stepped outside into bright sunlight.

Petar followed him out. 'God is never far from you, my son. You only have to reach out to him wherever you are. But it is funny how often I hear such similar things from your fellow soldiers.'

'Who said what to you, Father?' Claussen was standing just outside, his hands clasped loosely behind his back.

'That many of you feel that you have drifted too far from our Lord.' Petar paused, looking down at the flagstones that lined the church's entrance. 'I talked not long ago, Sunday in fact, and again yesterday, with an officer who felt like that. A very erudite man who had a very Catholic upbringing. A most remarkable knowledge of the Bible. We talked of much. He seemed... troubled. Borne down by a great weight.'

'Well, if he was heading for the front, I suppose that's only to be expected before battle.'

'Yes, indeed. Doing God's work is never easy on mortal men.' Reinhardt had heard this kind of speech in the trenches. Us against them. *God with us.* Except here, it had taken on a measure of virulence he had never known. 'No, it was not fear of battle. It was something else. Some inner demon he needed to exorcise. A fear that there was no way back for him. For those like him. We spoke much of forgiveness, and absolution. I offered him confession, but he refused.'

'Perhaps he knew its limits.' Petar frowned at him. 'The limits of forgiveness,' Reinhardt repeated. 'What some of us have seen, and heard, and done, here in this country, will remain with us as long as we live.'

The priest smiled, but something seemed to shift behind his face, and for a moment Reinhardt caught a glimpse of someone else – *something* else – behind his eyes. 'I am sure it must be difficult, my son. But what you do is for a great cause. The Serbs. The Jews. Communism. These are most terrible afflictions. They must be swept away by men of courage and iron conviction. What you do in that cause, you will be forgiven.'

'Father. There is perhaps one way you can help me.'

'Tell me.'

'Father, please think about this. Did you notice if any of the Germans who came to mass on Sunday, or since, acted strange?'

'Strange, Captain?'

'Nervous. Withdrawn. Panicked. Perhaps someone acting untowards. Someone who seemed distressed. Or perhaps a new face... ?'

Petar frowned, shook his head. 'I am not sure what you are getting at, Captain.'

'May I tell you something in confidence? Yes? I have a reason to believe Marija was killed by a German soldier. And I have reason to believe that soldier may well have come here. Perhaps to confess. Perhaps to seek solace in prayer. Of course, the confessional is sacrosanct. But, perhaps, did you notice anything in church that Sunday?'

The priest's eyes had gone flat at Reinhardt's words. 'What are you alleging, Captain?'

'Nothing, Father. I am following up a line of inquiry. A feeling. Marija's murder was horrible but her killer arranged her body as if she were at rest, afterwards. It seemed to me an act of remorse. And that such a man might seek... solace... in a place like this.'

'I had read the Partisans were to blame for Marija's death.'

'Perhaps,' said Reinhardt, noncommittally. 'But for instance, I would be more interested in hearing about that soldier you talked with.'

'No, Captain. You will not get that from me. I know what you Nazis have done to men of the faith. You will not hound that man for it, nor for his doubts.' Reinhardt made to speak, but Petar cut him off. 'Enough, Captain. I feel you have misled me. That you manoeuvred me into speaking of such things.'

It sounded so much like what Stolić had said in the officers' mess that Reinhardt blinked. 'I am sorry you think that, Father.'

Petar nodded, his eyes considering. 'Well, even if I cannot applaud your line of reasoning, there are enemies all around, Captain. Where we least expect them. And even if you have, as you say, drifted far from your faith, go with my blessing.'

He touched Reinhardt on the shoulder. It felt like something caustic, and something seemed to come apart then, deep inside. Reinhardt was not sure what it was, only that something small, but something important, broke. Snapped. 'You know, this medal,' he said, jerking his thumb at his Iron Cross. 'I got it taking a British redoubt at Amiens, in France. 1918. I attacked it, and then I defended it. I lost nearly all my men. At the end, there were just a few of us standing. Three, in fact. We all got the Iron Cross. One of them was a Jew. His name was Isidor Rosen.'

He lit an Atikah and blew smoke at the sky, feeling Claussen's eyes heavy on him. Isidor Rosen. Big and bluff. A shock of red hair. A real prankster who fought like the devil, who used to joke he liked fighting the English because at least with them he knew where the enemy was, and whom Reinhardt had tried to save after the war, using Becker's illegal network. 'After the war, Isidor became a fireman. He died, trapped in a burning house, while his fellow firemen just stood around outside. A house someone set fire to deliberately, in order to kill him. I know that, you see, because I conducted the investigation into his death.

'Do you wonder what I mean by all this? I wonder myself, actually. A few things I know. The last war was easier than this one. Just us against them. And the Jews? Funny thing about Jews is,' he said, inhaling deeply, 'there's really nothing mysterious about them, once you've seen one blown in two, his guts mixed up with any other German's. Or a Tommy's. I hear a lot of people say they're all around. Behind all this, manipulating us.' He shrugged with his mouth. 'Could be the conspiracies are right. Or could be people will believe anything they want. But I know that in 1918 I knew where to find a lot of them, and that was in the trenches with me.' He looked hard into the priest's eyes, searching for the utter conviction that drove the man. Searching, so he could do what? Crush it?

As fast as it came, whatever drove him was gone. Perhaps what was broken inside had mended. Perhaps he had needed to say what he had just said. But whatever it was Reinhardt fancied looked out from the priest's eyes was still there. Nothing he said or did would ever drive what motivated the priest away.

So he turned and left, motioning to Claussen, a sudden lift in his step. The lift lasted as long as it took his knee to twinge painfully as he took the steps down to the square too fast. As he got into the *kübelwagen* he looked back. The priest was still standing by the door looking down at him. 'Back to the barracks, Sergeant.' Reinhardt resisted the urge to wave a cheery goodbye as Claussen drove away from the church.

'You heard all that?' he asked Claussen, hooking his arm over the door and staring up at the hills. He looked over at the sergeant. 'Well?'

'I heard, sir,' replied Claussen, flicking his eyes up at the mirror.

'And?'

'And what, sir?'

'What do you think, Sergeant? Was I unkind to a priest? Did I say anything that shocked you?'

'I'm sure I don't know, sir.'

'I'm sure you do, Claussen,' snapped Reinhardt. 'You were in the last lot. You were a copper. In Dusseldorf, weren't you? We're not so different.' Down in the river, boys were playing on the rocks again. One of them watched him go by. Reinhardt waved, but the boy did not wave back.

Claussen was silent a moment, his lower lip moving as he chewed it. 'I can't say I was shocked, sir,' he said, finally. 'I heard what you said, about Jews and the trenches. I can't say I ever had much use for a Jew, sir, but they were there right with us then.' Claussen swung the car up to the main entrance to the barracks. A soldier swung the striped barrier pole up, and Claussen drove through, the tyres thumping on the cobbles of the courtyard, and parked. He turned the engine off and sat looking down, then turned to Reinhardt. 'After the war, in Dusseldorf, there were a couple on the force. I got friendly with one of them. Walked a beat with him. Got drunk with him. In and out of scraps. Played football together. Went to his house. A couple of Passovers, things like that. Funny thing, though,' he said, a small, tight smile on his face. 'He would never come to mine. For Christmas, or Easter. Still,' he continued, after a moment. 'He was a good copper. He was kicked off the force in thirty-four, I think. He took on whatever work he could find, managed to get his family out, but he didn't make it. He got beaten half to death by a group of SS one night. He was brought into the police station where I was watch sergeant. Died in the cells from his injuries.' Claussen paused, looking emptily out across the parking area. 'I suppose that was it for me, really.'

'What was?' asked Reinhardt.

Claussen pursed his lips as he shrugged. 'The end of being a copper. I mean, what was the point?' He glanced around. 'The lunatics had taken over the asylum, hadn't they? It must have been the same in Berlin.'

Reinhardt nodded. 'Yes, I suppose it was.'

'What about you, sir?'

'The last straw?' Claussen nodded. 'I tried to arrest an SA man who had thrown a homosexual out of a fifth-floor window. He was known for it. Everyone knew who did it. They knew nothing would come of it. It was not as if it was the first time, but something snapped that night. It was... not long after my wife died. I got blind drunk and tried to arrest him in the bar he always went to...' He trailed off.

'And... ?' prompted Claussen.

'They laughed at me until I pulled a gun on him, and then they beat the shit out of me. Dumped me on the street. Spent the night in jail. Official reprimand for breaching the peace. Drunk on duty. Conduct unbecoming, et cetera, et cetera... The writing was on the wall for me, so I jumped before I was pushed.'

'And now, here we both are,' said Claussen, after a moment. He stared at his hands as he ran them up and over the steering wheel. The engine tinkled as it cooled. Reinhardt thought back over what he had said and how easy it had been to tell it to this bluff man. He listened to the tone he thought he could hear in Claussen's voice. The one that matched his own feelings. That here was a chance to do the right thing, and that doing the right thing was not something he could do on his own. He needed someone with him, and it might as well be Claussen because there was no one else.

'Hendel was GFP,' Reinhardt said, after a moment. 'So was... is... Krause. Hendel was investigating someone senior. This someone was a friend of Vukić's, almost certainly her lover. Whoever this someone is, Vukić had something on him. Some kind of blackmail. She was working with Hendel to expose him, but it went wrong, and they both ended up dead and Krause is on the run. Krause has a film, or photographs, and the Feldgendarmerie are chasing him because someone's told them to get that evidence back.'

Claussen puffed his cheeks and blew his breath out. 'God,' he muttered.

'Quite,' added Reinhardt. 'And to finish it off, it seems I've pissed off enough people that they've told Freilinger to bring the investigation to a close. He's being transferred to Italy, effective immediately.'

'And you?'

'Orders'll come, for sure.' Reinhardt got out of the car and paused with his hands on the door. 'In the meantime, I'm working with this GFP captain. Or maybe for him. Who the hell knows with that lot?'

'What about Krause, sir? Where is he, do you think?'

'Sergeant, if you were Krause. If you were on the run. Where would you go?'

Claussen looked back at him, unblinking. 'The Reds,' he said, firmly, with barely a pause for thought.

'The Partisans,' nodded Reinhardt. 'I think you're right.' He tapped his hands on the door frame. 'I want you to go over to the main hospital. Ask for Dr Oster, on my behalf. Remind him he told me about a couple of soldiers he treated for burns the other day. See if he's got records of them. Names. Units. Bring them back to me here if you get anything.'

'Yes, sir. Captain. Just one thing, sir. I'd like to understand. About the church.'

'It's a guess, Sergeant. It's the first church on the way in from Ilidža. I thought if my hunch about the killer's remorse was true, he might have wanted to pray. That would have been the first place he came to.'

'What time do you think?'

'Seven o'clock would have been too early and too noticeable.' He looked at Claussen, saw the tightness in the corner of the sergeant's eyes, the bunch of his chin. 'Ten o'clock would have been more likely. Is there something you want to add, Sergeant?'

'Sir. There was someone there at ten. He was there before I arrived. He was still there when I left. On his knees. Hands in front of his head, head right down. Kept himself at the back. Didn't come for communion. I'd not seen him before and I only now just thought of him, as you were talking to that priest.'

'Rank?'

'Couldn't really see. An officer, I'm pretty sure. Smallish. Thin hair. Bald at the back.'

Reinhardt shrugged. 'It could have been our man. Could equally have been someone else.'

'Yes, sir. He moved his hands a lot.' Claussen demonstrated, his hands clasping and unclasping, running back and over each other. 'Like they were dirty.'

The two of them stared at each other a moment, the one seeing the scene as it was, the other as he imagined it. There was an echo of truth, suddenly, all around. As if a little piece of the puzzle had shifted, revealed itself. Then, without any further words being exchanged, Claussen drove away and Reinhardt went inside and over to the administration office. He felt tired. Drained. But in a good way. Like he used to feel sometimes after working a case with Brauer. He ordered a call placed through to Thallberg. He held the receiver in the crook of his shoulder as he shook a cigarette out and lit it. His knee ached, and he reached down to rub it absentmindedly. He thought about the officer the priest described as the line clicked, hummed, and then Thallberg's voice came on.

'Reinhardt?'

'It's me,' he replied. 'We should talk.'

'When?'

'Meet me at the fountain, on Baščaršija.'

'Half an hour,' came the reply, and the phone went dead.

Reinhardt unbuttoned his tunic and slipped the file under it, nestling it against his ribs. Giving his knee a last rub, he crossed over the bridge to Baščaršija and sat at the little café where he always went and ordered Turkish coffee. It was that time of day again, the people of the city coming together, pushing away the cares of the war. There was something in the air; Reinhardt could feel it. He always found himself reaching for it, straining, but never managing to experience it, to capture whatever it was the people all around him seemed to feel.

A man came out of the barber's next door to the café, brushing his shoulders. He wore a dark suit and a white shirt with no tie, and carried a newspaper, which he folded and put under his arm. He leaned into the café, called his order, then sat down at the table next to Reinhardt, unfolding his paper. Their eyes met for a moment, and the man nodded a cautious greeting, one patron to another. Reinhardt nodded back as his coffee came. The waiter got his finger caught under the tray, and it clattered as he pulled it out from underneath. Reinhardt glanced at him, and the waiter gave a tight smile of apology as he backed away. Reinhardt dropped some sugar into the pitcher, watched it turn brown and sink. He stirred the coffee, let it sit, absorbed in the ritual, the comfort of the same gestures repeated time after time by him, by those around him, on the square, in houses across the city, in cities across the country.

'Captain Reinhardt.'

He kept very still, then looked up. The man reading the paper was not looking at him, but Reinhardt could tell all his attention was focused on him. Moving slowly, Reinhardt unfastened the catch on his holster.

'Please do not be alarmed,' said the man, as he turned a page, tilting his head to read the headlines. 'I mean you no harm.'

Forcing himself to move calmly, Reinhardt poured his coffee, waited a moment, then sipped. The man turned another page, tutting at something he read. Another waiter brought the man his coffee. Reinhardt glanced at him, and the man looked back. He was big, broad, no subservience in his eyes as he went to stand by the café's entrance, seemingly relaxed, his hands behind his back, but his eyes roamed over the square.

'How do you know who I am?' he asked, finally.

'That is not important. If you agree to accompany me, someone would like to talk to you,' he said, rattling his paper into shape.

'Who?'

'I cannot tell you.'

'Where to?'

'Not far.' The man folded his paper in half, held it in one hand as he put sugar in his coffee and stirred it. His German was strongly accented, but good.

'You do not offer much in the way of assurances.'

The man poured his coffee, letting it sit while he turned another page. 'Captain. If we wanted to harm you, we could have done so. For assurances, I do not have any to offer. But,' he said, folding another page, 'perhaps this might suffice. Two men have been following you. They followed you out to Ilidža and back. We cut them off at Marijin Dvor. So they don't know you are here.'

Reinhardt sipped from his coffee and watched the muezzin at the mosque on the corner of the square unlock the door to the minaret. 'Men?'

'Germans,' he replied, sipping his coffee. 'Soldiers. I am going to get up and leave in a moment. If you wish to come with me, please wait approximately thirty seconds before following me, and keep your distance.'

Folding his paper back under his arm, he rose and strolled across the square, towards one of the little lanes that branched off Baščaršija and into the warren of houses and workshops that clustered tightly around the old mosque and around the back of the Rathaus. The muezzin stepped out at the top of the minaret, his fingers gripping the balustrade. As Reinhardt watched him, he took a deep breath. Reinhardt took one too. He finished his coffee and began to walk across the square, the hoarse cry of the muezzin floating over and behind him.

26

The alley was very narrow, cobbled, lined with shops with white walls and wooden fronts that hinged down to make benches or shelves upon which the merchants sat or displayed their wares. Several of them had unfolded little mats in their shops and were on their knees, praying. Others called out to him, gesturing him to come in, brandishing little cushions with embroidered swastikas, or cannon shells worked into minarets, but he walked past them, his eyes on the man in front of him, and on the men he went past. It was clear that some of the merchants knew him as their eyes fixed on him a moment, then slid away.

The man turned down another, narrower alley, darker than the first, with no shops on it. Reinhardt hesitated, looking behind him. He could see no one following him. The man was only a silhouette ahead of him. He followed him, his steps echoing on the cobbles. The place smelled of stagnant water and waste. It was quiet all of a sudden. The alley turned, turned again, and then there was brightness at the end of it, and an abrupt wash of colour and noise as a tram went past on the main street. Reinhardt saw the man come to the end of the alley and turn left. Hurrying, he came to where the alley opened onto the street and saw no one.

Reinhardt was standing on King Aleksander Street, not far from where the street turned sharply around the Rathaus, which lifted its ochre walls with their amber bands just a few hundred metres to his right. Across the street was another lane, leading up into Bentbaša, and the man could only have gone in there. Stepping across the tram tracks, trying not to hurry, he walked into the alley. It was very crooked and dark, the cobbles uncertain under his feet. The houses were in the Ottoman style, wooden partitions like boxes with windows protruding from the first floor, hanging over the alley. The doors were low, built into thick walls of stone, or plaster, with heavy knockers or bells hanging from them. He looked back, but King Aleksander Street was lost in the twists and turns of the alley. He felt suddenly more alone than he had felt in a long while. He put his hand on the butt of his pistol and walked carefully on.

A cat jumped into the alley and froze as it saw him. It flattened itself against the wall, then streaked away, back the way he had come. He watched it go, then saw an open door just ahead. He looked up and down the alley, but again saw no one. Taking a deep breath, he walked slowly in, taking his time, letting his eyes adjust to the dim light. It was a bare room, only a wooden bench running around it. Another door directly in front opened onto a corridor that led farther into the house.

There was strong daylight at the end. Someone stepped into the doorway ahead. With the light behind him, it was hard to see who it was, and in any case his attention was drawn to the man he had followed this far. He stood to the left, in the shadow of the open door, and he held a pistol in his hand. Another man stood in the other corner, dark skinned and with hair as black as coal, an MP 40 pointed at Reinhardt.

'Captain,' said the man from the café. 'Your pistol, please.'

'You said I would not be harmed.'

'You will not be. If you do not give me your pistol, you walk back out of here. Your choice.' His face was as flat as his voice.

Whoever it was ahead of him turned slightly. An inviting gesture. 'Please. Come in, Captain.'

Reinhardt felt some of the tension go out of his shoulders at the voice. He pushed the door to the street shut. Raising his right hand, he drew his pistol slowly with his left, holding it between thumb and forefinger, and handed it over to the man. Then he walked through into a sitting room, furnished in the Ottoman style, with low divans and tables, dark carpets on the floor, and dark wood on the walls and around the windows. The beamed ceiling was quite low, but the room was full of light that shone in from the house's courtyard, breaking around the man who stood there.

'Dr Begović,' Reinhardt said. The two of them shook hands. 'A pleasure to see you.'

'Likewise, Captain,' replied the doctor. His eyes were wide and bright behind his thick glasses. 'Will you take a seat? Perhaps some coffee?' A brass pot and some little cups stood on a carved wooden table. Three cups, Reinhardt saw, as he sat on one of the divans with his back to the window, facing the door. Begović sat next to him. There was a silence, but not an unpleasant one.

'I would like to say I'm surprised, Doctor,' said Reinhardt, at last. 'But somehow, I'm not.'

'No?' asked Begović as he poured. 'A shame. I do so like surprises.' There was a hint of a smile in his voice as he handed him a cup. He took one for himself and leaned back in the divan. He watched Reinhardt as he took a sip, then another. 'I find myself in something of a bind, Captain. I have something that I think may be of use and interest to you, but I am not, as you may be starting to understand, commonly in the business of making the lives of you and your colleagues easy.' Reinhardt watched him, letting him talk. 'Those with whom I work are also of the same opinion. They don't like my talking with you.' He looked at the man who had led Reinhardt here as he walked slowly across the room and through a door that he shut behind him. The other man stood quietly by the door, his machine pistol slanted across his chest.

'So why are you?' asked Reinhardt, fastening onto the opening the doctor left.

'Why indeed?' murmured Begović as he sipped from his cup. He wrinkled his nose, pushed his glasses a bit farther up, and looked out at the garden. 'Why do we always do things that don't seem to make perfect sense, Captain? There's never any rhyme or reason to it. Maybe it feels right at the time? We hear a small voice – our conscience, perhaps – telling us it's the right thing to do? Let's just say you were kind and considerate, Captain, not least of all to me. You were kind when that is the last thing someone like you needs to be. You were considerate when you didn't have to be. You tried to do your best in this investigation. It was no fault of yours things turned out the way they did. And word reaches us. Of Captain Reinhardt, of the Abwehr. A tricky interrogator. A tough man, but a fair one. I think – and I am not a poor judge of character, Captain – that you are a good man. A good man, in the wrong place. Am I right, do you think?'

Begović looked away, letting his eyes rest elsewhere. Perhaps he had seen the sudden rush of blood to Reinhardt's face, the wet sting in his eyes. Reinhardt felt ridiculous, reacting the way he did, but it had been a long time since anyone, least of all a Partisan, had called him a good man. 'Why am I here, Doctor?'

'I think you need help, Captain,' Begović replied. 'And I am ready to give it to you.'

'Doctor, not that I'm ungrateful, but someone like you doesn't help someone like me without hoping to gain from it.'

Begović gave a small smile. 'Of course, you are not wrong, Captain. You will hear what my motivations are. In the meantime, though…' He rose to his feet. 'Simo!' he called. A door opened, and the man whom Reinhardt had followed from Baščaršija stepped into the room. He looked at Begović, then at Reinhardt before stepping aside to allow another man in. The man was heavy, balding. He took a hesitant step, then another, walking slowly up to Reinhardt, moving with a pronounced limp. He looked uncertainly between him and Begović, fixed Reinhardt with his eyes, and spoke in hesitant, accented German.

'I am Branko Tomić.'

Reinhardt felt his breath go tight inside him. Begović invited them all to sit. 'Branko's German is not very good, so I will translate for you,' he said. He said a few words to Tomić, who only nodded, looking back at Reinhardt. He had smooth, shiny skin, which showed a sheen of sweat. He carried a bag, which he placed at his feet as he sat.

Reinhardt looked at this man, whom he knew only from what Jelić had said. One of Vukić's oldest collaborators, supposedly in Zagreb. The two of them were looking at him, and he did not quite know what to say. He picked up his coffee and sipped. 'Were you at the house of Marija Vukić on Saturday night?' He watched Tomić carefully as Begović repeated his words. The man knew some German, as he gave a small nod before Reinhardt had finished speaking.

'*Da*,' said Tomić. '*Ja sam bio tamo.*' His voice was light for a man of his size.

'Yes,' translated Begović. 'I was there.'

'Can you tell me what happened?'

Tomić nodded, looking down, twisting his hands one against the other. He had big hands, meaty, heavy. He looked up finally, his eyes flicking between the two of them. 'She asked me to come,' he said, finally. 'To set up a camera for her. I –' He stopped as Reinhardt held up his hand.

'I know about the camera. I found it.' Tomić looked surprised, taken aback, as if a script he had been planning had been rewritten without his knowing. He looked at Begović, who looked back expressionlessly. 'Just tell me what happened that night, please.'

Tomić nodded. 'If you found the camera, then you know that Marija… she liked to watch herself with her men.' He looked distant as he talked, as though he spoke of something of which he disapproved, or that embarrassed him. He glanced at Begović, who had his head down as he translated, his eyes on the floor. 'That Saturday, I set things up for her. She was very excited. I had seen her that way many times. It worried me. She told me she would make someone pay for the way they had treated her.'

'You knew who this was?' asked Reinhardt.

'Yes. A German officer. General Verhein.'

Reinhardt felt a wave of relief pass through him. 'How did she know him?'

'They were lovers in Russia, but he ended it.'

'Do you know why she would do what she planned that night?'

Tomić gave a small shrug and paused before answering. 'I am not sure. Marija… she was complicated. I knew her ever since she was a girl. Even then, she could be difficult. We… you know of her work as a journalist?' Reinhardt nodded, and Tomić continued. 'We travelled with Verhein's men for a while. The two of them began an affair. One day, though, Marija went away with some men from your Einsatzgrüppen. She went to cover one of their actions. Me, and Jelić, we didn't want to go, and we stayed behind. When she came back we knew there had been a problem. Something was very wrong between her and Verhein. They didn't talk, and we went away the next morning. She wouldn't say what happened.'

He paused and said something to Begović, who poured him a cup of coffee. Tomić took it with fingers that trembled and lifted it to his lips. 'She said nothing more about it until about two months ago. She found out Verhein was here, and she told me she was planning something, and she wanted me to help to preserve it…' He looked down again, his face twisting as if around a memory he found particularly difficult. 'I did not like it. I often argued with her, but I could refuse her nothing. Ever since she was a girl. But this time, I knew it was different.

'There was that officer, the lieutenant. He was involved, and I did not know what or why. So, that Saturday, I set up the camera for her, and then I waited. I had a room in the shed in the garden.' He took a quick sip of coffee before continuing. 'But then I heard shouting. I went into the garden. The noise went away. I went back to my room. I waited. But then…'

'How long did you wait?'

'Some time. More than an hour.' Reinhardt nodded for him

to continue. 'And so then I heard a shot. I heard her scream. I…
was so scared, I did not dare to go up. I hid. Someone ran past
me and jumped over the fence and into the fields. Another
person chased him, then came back. I heard a car drive away. I
waited, and then I went up. I found her dead. I took the film,
and I ran.' He spoke all this in a rush, Begović frowning as he
tried to keep up with the flow of words.

Tomić paused, and Reinhardt held up his hand. 'Slow down,
Mr Tomić, please.'

He nodded, then resumed, more slowly. 'I hid in Ilidža the
rest of that night, then I made my way into Sarajevo, to the
studio. I waited for nightfall, then used the studio to develop
the film. Then…' He seemed to deflate, suddenly, as if he had
reached the end of something.

'Then he came looking for us,' finished Begović.

'When you took the film, did you leave the padlocked door
open?' Reinhardt asked.

Tomić frowned as he tried to remember. 'I don't know. I
think so. I was rushing to get out.'

So that explained how the killer knew of the film, and why
he had turned the darkroom upside down looking for it. It also,
Reinhardt realised, meant the killer would have had to have
gone back to the scene as otherwise he – they, he now realised
– could not possibly have known about it.

'Tell me about Verhein. Did he come alone?'

'I didn't see. But he usually had a driver. An Asian,' said
Tomić, his two fingers pointing to his eyes. 'Like a Mongol.
Nasty. Devoted, like a dog, to Verhein.'

'Anything else? Anything about what was planned for that
night?'

'You are judging her, aren't you?' Tomić looked between
Reinhardt and Begović. 'You are.' He looked down, looked far
away. 'Maybe… maybe I should tell you something about
Marija, before you judge her.'

'Mr Tomić,' Reinhardt interjected. 'It is all right. You don't
need to say anything.'

'I do. Because you are judging. I can see it. And if you judge her, then you judge me. I knew her since she was a baby. I was a friend of Vjeko. Her father. We were in the first war together. The Austro-Hungarian Army. I was... badly wounded. After the war, Vjeko took care of me. I started working for him. Then Marija was born. Such a lovely girl. But difficult!' For a moment, a smile crept across Tomić's face, a memory. Then it was gone.

'When Marija's parents divorced, Marija spent more time with her father than mother. Me and Vjeko raised her. He was a loving father, but he was tough. When she was sad, it was to me she came. Then Vjeko began getting more and more involved in politics. With the Ustaše. The Ustaše were not for me. Vjeko was my friend, but I could not follow him in that. But she loved her father. Very much. Marija was... pulled into that circle. She became a believer. The Ustaše used her, as well. She was young. Beautiful. She had talent. But... she changed. She still seemed to be the same sweet girl, but I knew better. Inside, she was changing. She was becoming twisted. They were... not good men, some of them. I tried to stop it, but I couldn't.'

He paused, his eyes still far away. 'She began to take lovers. Older men. Men of experience, she called them. Once, she even tried to seduce me.' He swallowed, looked down. 'I could not. Not the daughter of my friend. And, in any case, I was not able. My... my wound,' he said, his hands waved at his groin as he looked up at Reinhardt. Begović caught his gaze as well, his face straight but his eyes sympathetic behind his glasses, and they seemed to be asking him how much more did he need to hear? 'And anyway, despite everything, she was still a little girl. Despite the... the men. The drugs. The drinking. The politics. The... other things. When things got too much... when she was hurt, she would come to me. I tried to help her. Calm her. Sometimes... sometimes I could. Sometimes, I could not...' He trailed off, stopped. 'When I could not, then it was better not to be around her. But when the passions were spent, she would always need someone to turn to. To comfort her. And that person was me. And she was a little girl again.'

'Mr Tomić. Do you have something you would like to give me?'

He nodded, reached into the bag at his feet, and pulled out a film case. He looked at it a moment, then handed it to Reinhardt. 'You will see…' he began, then stopped. He looked at Begović, who waited for him to go on. 'Never mind,' he said. 'Use it. Make sure… just make sure he pays for what he did to her.'

Reinhardt turned the film case over in his hands. 'You have not watched it?' Tomić shook his head. 'Thank you,' he said. He did not know what else to say.

Begović spoke to Tomić, and then they stood up and Tomić left the way he had come, walking slowly, limping heavily. 'What will happen to him?' asked Reinhardt.

'We will keep him safe,' replied Begović. 'He is useful and sympathetic to us. Unlike Marija Vukić.'

'She was no friend of yours?'

'She was no friend of ours,' Begović repeated. 'She was a monster, and I must confess I have a hard time seeing the little girl Tomić so clearly doted upon. What she wrote about us was one thing. What she did to some of us, what she incited her people to do through her films and her writings… you know, Topalović was onto her. A couple of times he went to her house, trying to see how she might be got at. Funny, isn't it, they got him for her murder and he was nowhere near her that time.'

The two of them were silent a moment. 'You said you would tell me something of why you are helping me,' said Reinhardt. Simo came back into the room and stood quietly by the door.

'The Ottomans had a saying. *Kuru ağaca kan bulanmaz.* Don't sprinkle blood on a dying tree. It means, don't do things which will serve you nothing. Like helping your enemies. But I will not lie to you, Captain. I think I will help you. And I think my helping you will assist me as much as you. If I am not wrong – and I do not think I am – you are a good man, and a good man deserves help. I wish to help you to find this murderer. It is the right thing you are doing, and helping a good man do the right thing cannot be bad. But also, I am a Communist. I am a

Partisan, and a patriot. As such, I will confound and confuse the enemies of my country to the extent I can. This man you are after is a senior officer in your army. A general, no less. In helping you to investigate, possibly even arrest, this man, I cause disruption in your ranks. Perhaps just enough to throw off your attack against my comrades. Perhaps just enough to allow a few to escape who might otherwise have not.' Begović poured himself some coffee and looked Reinhardt in the eye. 'So, Captain. You still wish to walk away with what Tomić left? You will do this deal with the devil?'

Reinhardt could not help but smile at this little man with an apparently big heart. Small, bespectacled, he seemed so strong, so sure of himself. Was there ever a time when he had been like that? 'Yes, I will take it.' He paused. 'Doctor, there is perhaps one more thing you might consider doing for me.' Begović raised his eyebrows but said nothing. 'There was a second man with Hendel. A man called Krause. I know this because he was Hendel's partner in...' He hesitated, not wanting to reveal Hendel as having been GFP, but then wondered what the point of hiding it was anymore. 'Hendel was secret field police. Krause was his partner. He was the one Tomić said ran past him and into the fields. I need to find him.'

'Why do you think we might be able to help?'

'Because the soldier – Lieutenant Krause – is half Slovenian. He speaks the language. He's been missing now since Saturday night. Deserters usually turn up fast, or they turn up dead. I'm willing to bet he's gone to ground somewhere in the city. If you should hear of something, or if you could put the word out...'

Begović tilted his head and narrowed his eyes. 'You do know most people around here, finding a German soldier on the run, will either bar their door to him or do their best to do away with him.'

'I know. But now you know he is GFP, and I'm pretty sure you would love to put your hands on him. I've just given you a reason to look for him, and one for keeping him alive.'

Begović shrugged with his mouth – his lips pursed, his chin

bunching up as his eyebrows lifted. 'It's possible.' He looked at Simo, but if he was looking for help, or inspiration, he found none. The big man just stared back at him. Begović sighed, pushed his glasses up on his forehead, and pinched his nose. 'Very well,' he said, letting them drop back down, and there was the faintest of smiles on his mouth as he looked at Reinhardt. 'If we find him we will find some way of letting you know.'

'The coffee shop on Baščaršija. You can leave a message for me there.'

'The old man who runs that shop has been there since my father's day, and his father served coffee to my grandfather. Most of the city has drunk his coffee at one time or another, I would imagine. I would not lightly put that man at any risk and we would be doing that, you and I, if we tried to pass messages through there.' He paused. 'I will think of something and let you know.'

There was a silence. 'What now?' asked Reinhardt.

'Now, Simo will show you out. You may return to Baščaršija. Do what you like with the film.'

'I meant you, Doctor,' said Reinhardt. 'What becomes of you? They are looking for you.'

'Me? I can take care of myself. Didn't I tell you this is my city? It does not belong to you. Or the Ustaše. It never will.' Begović smiled. 'I may have to move quietly for a bit, but I won't need to stay in the shadows much longer, I think.'

'You're that confident, are you? Of defeating us.' Begović only nodded. 'And then what? How will you resolve all the differences between all of you? Between Serb and Croat and Muslim?' He regretted the words as soon as he spoke them, felt them ring flat like argument for argument's sake. He remembered his conversation with Lehmann, when he had taken the opposite tack, tried to convince him of the natural complexity that existed here, the history of coexistence that the wars seemed always to overshadow.

'Ah, Captain. Almost, you disappoint me.' Reinhardt flushed, embarrassed. 'The differences? Yes, they exist. Show me a people without differences, and I will show you a land that existed before time. Before man, even. But did we ask for this war? Was it inevitable? Or were there those among us who took advantage of turmoil elsewhere to enact their vision of what this Yugoslavia should, or should not, be? War was brought to us. As it has been so often throughout our so-called bloody history.'

'Even without war, isn't there more that divides you as a people than unites you?' Again, as he spoke them, Reinhardt felt the hollowness of the words. Argument for argument's sake, just like with his son. As he said them, he wished them back.

'Take Simo. He is a Serb. Or take Karlo, there,' he gestured at the other man. 'He's a Croat. You might say there is much that would divide us all from each other. The religions of our parents. The cities of our birth. Our education. Our class. Perhaps, once, we would have faced each other across a field of battle. Them under their crosses, me under the crescent. Now, we are united in the search for something greater than all of us. That something is a new Yugoslavia. This time, Communism will unite it, sure as a return to our prewar parochialisms will destroy us again.'

'That kind of idealism… it rarely survives the crucible of war.'

'Or the realities of peace, you might add. You think I don't know that?'

'I don't know what you know, Doctor.'

'Then I will tell you something of what I know. I was born in Sarajevo into an old family of landowners. I was educated here, and in Zagreb, and in Berlin. I am a doctor. I am a Muslim. I am descended from men who converted to Islam following the Ottoman conquest for reasons we can guess at, but never truly know. The Ustaše call us Muslims the flower of their nation, and claim us for themselves so they may argue that Croats outnumber all other peoples. The Četniks call us interlopers, Turks, and would extinguish us from this land, and forget their forefathers settled here from Serbia to escape the Ottomans or to fight for the Austrians. I am a Partisan. What, if any, of those things defines me more than another? I say none of them, and all of them, and if anyone has to choose, it is me. I am what I chose to be, not what others want me to be. I am a Yugoslav. This is my land. I have nowhere else to go. That is a little of what I know.'

'You talk to me of choices?' said Reinhardt. 'I only know that the choices life makes you take strip away the person we wanted to be. Builds us up into something we never wanted. Until you look back on life, and you see that the track of your life is a scar that hides what might have been.'

Begović looked at him, his eyes focused, intent. 'If we had more time we could talk, you and I. Of what happened to you, to make you this way...'

'What made me this way? Life, I suppose. Choices.' Reinhardt paused, looked down. 'Maybe I would say everything good in my life happened to me despite me. And nothing bad happened that I should not have been strong enough to prevent.'

'You are an interesting man, if I may say that.' Begović gave the smallest shake of his head. 'I don't say what we hope for will be easy. We can but try.'

'Well, good luck to you, even so.'

'Thank you, Captain. And good luck to you as well. I think you will need it more than me. But I think,' Begović said, smiling, 'that the tree still shows life.'

They rose to their feet. There was a sudden moment of awkwardness, and then Reinhardt extended his hand. 'Thank you for your help, Doctor,' he said, as they shook.

'Captain Reinhardt will be leaving now, Simo. Please see him on his way.' Begović stepped back and looked at Reinhardt again. 'Until we meet again,' he said as Reinhardt walked past Karlo's flat gaze.

At the door onto the street, Simo handed Reinhardt back his pistol, then the magazine. He shut the door behind them, then pointed down the street, the way Reinhardt had come. 'Here,' he said, handing Reinhardt a small brass shell casing, carved into the shape of a minaret. 'You came to buy something. You bought that at the shop opposite the entrance to this alley. You understand?'

Reinhardt nodded. 'I understand. For if anyone asks.'

'And if they ask, the man in the shop will tell anyone he sold it to you for three *kuna*.'

Reinhardt nodded again. 'Three? Cheap at the price,' he said as he put it in his pocket.

The ghost of a smile flickered across Simo's face, and then he turned away and was gone. Reinhardt put the film case under his arm as he walked slowly back down the alley, putting the magazine back in his pistol before he holstered it. As he came up to the exit to the little street, he saw across the road the man who had been the waiter at the coffee shop. The man was looking at him and made the smallest of motions to Reinhardt to stop. He looked left and right, then back at him and nodded, and then he was gone too, and Reinhardt stepped out of the alley into the sunshine.

He walked quickly back to the coffee shop, feeling a lift in his step. Thallberg was not there. He glanced at his watch. He had been gone about forty-five minutes. He should be here. He put his head into the shop and asked the old man as best he could if he had seen him. The old man came squinting out from behind his row of blackened kettles, wiping his hands on a rag. The pair of them talked past each other for a moment, and then Reinhardt gave up. He smiled, patted the man on the arm, and went back outside. He looked around the square, looked at the film case, and then knew where he needed to go.

27

Padelin hammered on the door, short staccato bursts of three, until it finally opened. 'Can you play this?' Padelin said, showing the case of film to Jelić. He took the case, turned it over in his hands, and nodded. 'Do it now,' said Padelin, pushing past him into the studio.

'Come in, make yourself at home,' Jelić muttered under his breath. From the look on his face, it was clear Jelić had not expected them back. He pointed to the big table they had sat at earlier while he inserted the film in a projector and began making adjustments. Padelin sat at the table with his big hands folded one within the other, the knuckles stark and pale. Reinhardt shook a cigarette loose and stared at him. What was he thinking, he wondered. Was he frightened of what he would see, of seeing Marija Vukić in a way that he might have imagined but would never have thought possible?

He felt Reinhardt looking at him and turned those flat, catlike eyes on him. 'This had better be worth it,' he said, again.

'I think it will be,' said Reinhardt, around a mouthful of smoke.

'And you cannot tell me where you got it from?'

'Not yet, no. I'm sorry.' Padelin worked his mouth as if around something noxious.

'Over there, on that screen,' Jelić finally said as he switched off the lights and drew the curtains. A white light shone on the screen, then flickered grey and black, and an image juddered

into life. It steadied into black and white and showed the
bedroom in Vukić's house, with the bed made up. There was no
sound. In the mirror on the wall over the bed, they could see
movement, reflected movement. Someone, two people, moving
around in the living room.

They came closer, into view, and it was Vukić and someone
else. They stumbled from side to side, clutched in each other's
embrace. Vukić, and a man. Taller than her, a head of grey hair,
almost white, close-cut. Big shoulders, big arms came into view
as she pulled a white shirt from his back. He had a belly on him,
this man, but it seemed he was made more of muscle and bone
than fat. They came closer into view, turning and stumbling,
and Reinhardt leaned towards the screen, trying to see.
Trousers. If he was a general, he would have a stripe down his
trousers. But nothing. He had taken them off elsewhere and
stood with his backside bare towards the camera. Vukić turned
him and pushed him down onto the bed. He bounced on it,
shuffling himself excitedly up onto the pillows with his arms
outstretched to her. With a thick mat of fur on his chest, with
his thick arms and legs, he looked like a bear. He looked like the
man in the photo from Hendel's file.

Vukić sauntered towards the end of the bed, with the faintest
flicker of her eyes towards the hidden camera. She undid the
back of her dress and let it slide to the floor. She stood clad only
in her garters and belt, stood in such a way that they could see
her in the other mirror, at the head of the bed. Reinhardt felt his
breath go thick in his throat at the sight of her, and he could feel
as much as see the man on the bed go still with desire. She lifted
one knee onto the bed, then the other, sliding up and over and
then astride him as if he were a horse, and she its rider.

There followed then what seemed to Reinhardt to be an
interminable blur of limbs and quivering flesh, and a shifting
kaleidoscope of positions. They were not two people making
love. Not even two humans having sex. They were two animals
rutting. When it was finally over, the man was kneeling behind
her, the line of his thighs and back taut with his pleasure, and

his hands clamped around the flesh of her buttocks. He collapsed onto the bed next to her, his chest rising and falling, and she lowered herself to her stomach. After a while, he got up, passing in a blur of white in front of the camera, and returned with two glasses and a bottle of champagne. He poured, and they lay in bed, talking and drinking and smoking. Another period of time passed, and he rose from the bed again. Vukić lay there a moment, then stretched like a cat. She looked right at the camera, smiled, and rose from the bed. In the mirror on the other wall they saw her walk into the living room and out of the camera's view.

Reinhardt swallowed and let out a breath slowly. Padelin had sat still throughout the film, unbending, every line of his body screaming a kind of outraged severity. Now, it seemed as though there were a tremor deep inside him, a quiver that seemed to move from within to without.

'There's more,' whispered Reinhardt. 'There must be more.'

More time went by. Reinhardt concentrated on the mirror, where it showed something of what was happening in the living room. Something lurched into view, a blurred scramble of grey and black and white in the doorway as reflected in the mirror. Movement suddenly erupted onto the screen, two people struggling arm in arm. Vukić and the man, half dressed. He ducked his head beneath the swing and clutch of her fingers, gripped her head in one hand, punched her with the other. He hammered at her with his fists, and she fell to the floor. He kicked her in the side, slammed his foot down on her back. He took her by the hair and dragged her up, twisted her around, and punched her once, twice, a third time. She went limp. He hit her again, and again, and then his fist paused, stayed raised. He let her go, and she collapsed backwards and rolled onto her back. The man struggled to his feet, one hand on his knee, the other raised to his face. His chest heaved, and then he stepped back and was gone.

More time passed. Eventually, she stirred, hauled herself onto the bed, where she lay. Rolling onto one elbow, she pushed herself up and stumbled into the bathroom. She came out, holding a towel wadded to her mouth and leaning against the wall. She stumbled past the camera, into the living room, and was gone. The film ran on. In the mirror, Reinhardt could see movement from time to time. Probably her. Then it was over. The film juddered to a halt, and there was the clatter of the end of the reel going around and around on the projector.

Reinhardt drew in a long, slow breath around the weight he found in his chest.

'*Picku materinu!*' grated Padelin.

There was the strike of a match behind them. Jelić cleared his throat. Reinhardt had forgotten he was even there. 'Now that,' Jelić said, around a cigarette, a tremor in his voice, 'is the Marija I remember.'

Padelin rose from his seat in a calm eruption of energy. Reinhardt stayed staring at the screen as he heard Jelić's yelp of protest, and the sound of Padelin's hand, the open palm, and then the meatier thud of his fist. Blow after blow, Jelić's cries fading into grunts, and then the ragged whimper of something broken, and then nothing. Through it all, Padelin made not a sound, and Reinhardt had eyes only for the screen, blank now. If the film could have run a little more he might have seen the end, her death, seen the man who wielded the knife. There was a part of him that felt this was all a show. A stage, and her the player, and as in a film she would rise from her bed when it was all over, show that it was all just theatre, fake, managed and directed by her.

Eventually, he stood and turned. Jelić cowered in a corner, weeping quietly, his face a mask of blood. Reinhardt ran his eyes over the room, spotting a sink in a corner with a cupboard over the top. Opening it, he found a bottle of slivovitz. He poured a measure into a glass he found standing in the sink, knocking it back and wincing as it burned its way down. He poured another and took it over to Jelić. The man watched him coming like a dog that expects only its master's boot, and only stared at the proffered glass through eyes that were already swelling shut. He finally took it with a quivering hand and turned into the corner with it.

Padelin was nowhere to be seen, but Reinhardt spotted that the door was ajar, not shut. He looked at the projector, not knowing what to do with it. 'Jelić,' he called. The man ignored him, twisted inward with the glass resting on his broken lips. 'Jelić,' he said, sharper. The man looked up, screwing his head up and around to see through his swollen eyes. 'The man on the film. Was that the one from Russia?' He nodded, eventually. 'Jelić. Can you take the film off, please?' The man stared up at him with his head canted sideways. 'The film. Please take it off.'

Jelić swallowed slowly, then rose to his feet. He flinched, a hand going to his chest as if to keep something in, and shuffled over to the projector. He flipped switches and clips and detached the case of film. He handed it to Reinhardt without a word and went back to his corner, folding himself into it and around the glass. Reinhardt watched him for a moment, then turned and left, knowing words were unnecessary, and wholly inadequate to whatever pain Jelić felt.

Downstairs, he found Padelin sitting on a concrete block in a patch of late afternoon sun. A handkerchief was wrapped around his fist, spotted with blood. Reinhardt tossed the film into the *kübelwagen* and walked over to him. Padelin looked up as he approached, his eyes hooded. 'Was that absolutely necessary?' Reinhardt asked. Padelin blinked, that slow blink of some great, ponderous beast at rest, and said nothing. Reinhardt looked at him, then shook his head and went back to the car.

He picked up the film case and turned it over and over in his hands. The *kübelwagen* shifted and creaked as Padelin sat in the seat next to him, his jacket folded over his lap, and rested his elbow over the car's door, for all the world a picture of a man off for a drive in the country.

'I'll take you back to your headquarters,' said Reinhardt, starting the car. 'I need to show this film to my superiors and see if anyone can recognise that man. I'll see if I can't get you a copy.'

As Reinhardt dropped Padelin off at his headquarters under the dull gaze of a pair of policemen on duty outside the main entrance, the big detective paused as he opened the door. 'It may not be needed, the copy,' he said. Reinhardt blinked at him, saying nothing. Padelin glanced at his watch. 'But I do want to know where you got it from.'

'Padelin, I don't understand you,' said Reinhardt, staring straight ahead.

'There is nothing to understand. Marija Vukić was killed by one of your soldiers. Apparently this officer she knew in Russia.'

'Did you see her murder on that film? Did you?' He stared hard at the detective, and this time it was Padelin who would not meet his eyes. 'I didn't. I saw a man who beat her, yes. I also saw a man who seemed to stop himself from going further than he did. I saw a man who seemed upset at what he had done. Which means we still don't have a suspect for her death. We have someone we need to interview. That's it.'

'Who gave it to you?' Padelin grated.

'It doesn't matter.'

'It does.'

'Why? Why should it matter? I mean, not much of material value to this investigation has mattered to you until now. Why should this?'

Padelin clenched his jaw, the muscles bunching as he ground his teeth. 'It matters,' he said, slowly, 'because otherwise I... we... have been made to look like fools.'

'Like... ?' Reinhardt raised both hands to his head, taking his cap off and scrubbing his fingers through his hair. 'Padelin, do you honestly think that matters? And honestly, can you look at me and tell me that, through all this, through these past days, you have not acted like fools? Not acted against the evidence? Went where you wanted things to go, instead of following where the evidence suggested you go?'

'Well, if you won't tell me, maybe Jelić will.'

'Jelić? Oh, for Christ's sake, Padelin. You can't be serious.' Reinhardt looked hard at him. 'Padelin. That boy had nothing to do with it.'

'So you say.'

'So I say. Leave him out of this.'

'Why? What is he to you?'

'Nothing.'

'Well, then.'

Reinhardt ran his hand over his forehead. His skin felt thick, clammy, as if he had a fever. 'Padelin…' he began. 'Padelin. You think I have never felt the need to battle my enemies without constraints? There's nothing unusual in that. We would not be human if we did not struggle against what restrained us. It is *that* which demands our attention. Not the urge to action, or to violence. But what holds us *back* from it. As policemen, we might have such wishes. It does not mean we will act in the way we want when the restrictions are removed.'

'I have no restrictions other than those the law places upon me.'

'Padelin, you may believe that. I tell you it is not true. And even if it were so, what does it mean if the law itself is no restriction? If the very law we uphold is what pushes you to excess, or what tolerates it? The law that you – that I – operate under tolerates no restrictions other than its own belief in itself. There is no boundary to what it will do, no threshold it will not cross. You know that.'

'This law… my law, is the expression of the…'

'… will of the people. My Volk. Your Narod. I know. It holds no secrets for me. I was dealing with it long before you ever put on a uniform. But you know… you *know*, Padelin, that not everyone is equal before that law. Some it recognises over others. And those others have no recourse other than the restraint you, as a policeman, choose to exercise.'

'Reinhardt, what are you talking about?'

'I'm trying to tell you… it's like someone saying, "Hold me back, hold me back or I'll kill that person. I'll kill that murderer.

That rapist. That Jew. That Serb." But maybe what that person really means is, "*Because* you are holding me back, I can say I want to kill that person." Because I know I will not. I will not because it is wrong, because the law will stop me. Because my friends, my colleagues, will stop me.' He could see he was losing him. Padelin frowned, his mouth clamped tight shut, but he pushed on. He had to say this. 'So the question, Padelin, is this: if a policeman is allowed to act without restraint – to the boundaries of what is permitted, and perhaps even beyond – will he do so? If not, what will constrain him? What holds him back? Will the law, will his society, his conscience, show him clearly not every goal sanctifies every means? And perhaps even there are means that cannot – ever – be sanctified.'

'Sanctified? Reinhardt, I do not understand you. I don't understand that word.'

'Sanctified. Means "accepted".' Padelin looked down at his knees, where his hands rested on them. He spread his fingers, then bunched them back up. 'What I am saying to you is, you have reached this boundary. You may even have gone over it before. Once. Twice. Many times. It does not mean you must always do so. There has to be something to come back to.'

Padelin nodded, then got out of the car. He closed the door and looked down at Reinhardt. 'What I know is we had someone for Marija Vukić's murder, and now that person is dead. We have been made to look like fools. *You* are making us look like fools. I don't like that and the people I work with will like it less.' He stepped back from the door, holding Reinhardt's eyes. 'You should maybe trust us more. We are your allies, after all. You will, I am sure, be hearing from us soon.' With that, he was gone.

28

Reinhardt pushed open the door to his office to find Thallberg sitting slumped in one of his chairs. He had his feet up on the edge of the desk and the chair back on two legs. He jumped to his feet as Reinhardt came in.

'Where the *bloody* hell have you been?!' he snapped.

Reinhardt put the film case on the desk and raised a placating hand as he pulled out his cigarettes and lit one. Thallberg looked hard at him as he inhaled and blew smoke at the ceiling. 'I was called away,' he said, finally.

'Reinhardt, you're going to have to do a bit better than that.'

Reinhardt held up a hand again. 'Yes. Yes, just a moment, I need to think some things through.'

'Think what through? You told me on the telephone you had information for me. You said you'd found "him". Well? And what's that?' said Thallberg, pointing at the film.

'That's what I was called away to pick up. It's a film.'

'I'm guessing it's not the latest offering from the Universum studios.'

Reinhardt pulled his chair out and sat down, drawing smoke deep into his lungs before answering. 'It turns out Vukić liked to sometimes film herself with her lovers. On the night she was murdered, she arranged to have herself filmed. That's it.'

'*Christ*,' breathed Thallberg. Then his eyes narrowed, and he stared accusingly at Reinhardt. 'How long have you known about this? About her doing this?'

'Almost from the beginning. She had a sort of studio in her house. It had been ransacked, all the films taken, and then I found a two-way mirror with a camera behind it…' He stopped as Thallberg held up a hand, shaking his head irritably.

'Wait, later. Later. Go back a bit. Your telephone call. Who do you think you've found?'

'I've found the man Hendel was tailing. And I know who he was reporting to in Berlin.'

'And?'

Reinhardt drew deeply on his cigarette, thinking of the bottle in its drawer and how much he needed a drink. 'I found one of Hendel's files,' he said, shifting in his chair as he pulled the file out from under his tunic. 'If you can believe it, he'd put it in the sidecar of a motorbike he and Krause took out to Ilidža. The bike was parked in the Feldgendarmerie station out there. Just sitting in the lot, where the police had dropped it off. You want something to drink?'

Thallberg frowned irritably, staring at the file. 'Sure.'

Reinhardt filled a cup and handed it to Thallberg, then poured himself a shot and knocked it back. He breathed out slowly, took a drag of his cigarette, and saw Thallberg looking at him with a sardonic glint in his eyes.

'Well, I wanted one. You certainly *needed* one.' Reinhardt flushed, a hot sweep that came suddenly up his neck. He stared back, and then, feeling defiant and ridiculous at the same time, he poured himself another, then corked the bottle.

'The file?'

'Here,' said Reinhardt, tossing it across the desk. Thallberg swept it up and began to read. Reinhardt sipped from his mug, trying to slow the racing of his mind, waiting for the other man to finish. Thallberg looked up, his eyes and face full of a kind of confused blankness, which Reinhardt was sure had been in his own gaze when he had finished the file. Thallberg sighed, then took a long sip of his drink, eyes squinting against the taste.

'Looks like you needed that,' observed Reinhardt.

Thallberg puffed out a breath and had at least the good grace to look sheepish. 'Well, I said I was after something big, but this…' He puffed out his breath again. 'This Varnhorst suspects Verhein of being a Jew? Verhein's a hero, you know. Medals for everything. Everyone's favourite soldier.' He frowned, sipping again from his slivovitz. 'God, I hate this stuff,' he said, putting the mug back on Reinhardt's desk, barely touched. 'Give me a beer every time. If I'm not mistaken, Verhein's being lined up for a post at Army High Command. The Führer's apparently mad keen about him.' He shook his head. 'Someone like Verhein? A general? A *Jew*? You know, a lot of people are going to look like fools if this is true.' Reinhardt said nothing, only feeling a surge of bitterness in his mouth as Thallberg echoed Padelin's words to him earlier. 'Who gave you this?'

'Her cameraman. We – the police and myself – thought he was in Zagreb. Turns out he was here and he's been in hiding since that night. With that.'

'You've seen it?' Reinhardt nodded. 'Who does it show?'

Reinhardt breathed deeply. 'It shows her having sex with, and then being beaten by, a certain General Paul Verhein.'

Thallberg put his hands behind his neck, then drew them slowly down and around over his mouth. 'Christ,' he said again. '*Christ!* Wait,' he said, suddenly. 'It doesn't show her being killed? Or show Hendel?'

Reinhardt shook his head, looking at the red tip of his cigarette. 'The film ends before that.'

'*Fuck!*' exploded Thallberg, jumping out of his chair and beginning to pace around the room. 'So we've got an army general caught on film getting his end away with this Croat skirt, then slapping her around. Then nothing. Then two dead bodies, one of them one of my men. Oh, Christ,' he said, putting his hands in the small of his back and stretching, looking at the ceiling. 'What a mess.'

'Has been from the beginning,' muttered Reinhardt. He followed Thallberg with his eyes as the captain paced around the room.

'You recognised Verhein? On the film?'

'I didn't,' replied Reinhardt. 'I've never seen Verhein but the man on the film looked like that man in the photograph in the file while Vukić's cameraman identified him as the man she was seeing in Russia last year.'

Thallberg puffed air out, drawing his fingers back and forth across his lips. He eyed the file where it sat on Reinhardt's desk. 'So what do you think?'

'Honestly, I don't know.' He put his elbows on the desk and stubbed out his cigarette. He ground the butt out methodically, taking time to run his mind back over the rush of the day. 'All right, then. A couple of things. I think you need to see the film, to confirm what I saw, and to possibly identify Verhein. You can identify him, can't you?' Thallberg nodded. 'I'm not convinced Verhein killed Vukić. He may have killed Hendel, though, but the timing is all off.'

'Why?'

'She lay on the floor after she was beaten, and she must have been lying there a good ten, fifteen minutes. I don't think he would've hung around. He'd have gone. He was scared. Of her, and of what he'd done.'

'So what're you saying?'

'I'm saying...' said Reinhardt, slowly, 'I'm saying he's a general. And generals don't usually do things for themselves if they can avoid it.'

'His staff,' said Thallberg after a moment.

'His staff,' agreed Reinhardt. 'A witness reported a car that night, parked in front of Vukić's house. And a man. Almost certainly his driver.'

'You think the *driver* killed the girl? And Hendel?'

Reinhardt shrugged, leaned back in his chair, and put his hands behind his neck. He thought for a moment. 'Vukić's cameraman said Verhein had a bodyguard or servant who was devoted to him. An Asian, apparently. From Russia.'

Thallberg grunted. 'Probably a Tartar. I know a few who joined up. Mad buggers, all of them, capable of anything. Some of the stuff I saw them do in Russia you wouldn't believe.'

'No. Again, the timing's wrong. Or at least, if he did it, he'd have had to come back to do it.' He thought for a moment. 'And it's not exactly in a driver's or servant's job description, is it?'

'What, to clean up an officer's mess? I know a few who have done just that.'

'But this is murder,' protested Reinhardt. 'You can't exactly order a driver to do that.'

'Someone else, then,' said Thallberg.

'Someone else,' agreed Reinhardt. He fished in his pocket and took out the list he had made yesterday. 'A general's usually got his men close by him. Chief of staff for sure. For that planning conference, almost certainly his divisional intelligence officer. Maybe we could start there.'

Thallberg nodded. 'Good a place as any, I suppose. Going to take some time, though.'

'What can you do? Get access to personnel files? See who he's got around him?'

'Something like that. I'll have to do it at the State House, so you may as well come with me. It'll go faster if we're together.' Thallberg looked at his watch and Reinhardt stifled a sudden yawn, glancing behind him out the window. The sun was still up, but it was getting on for late afternoon. He realised he was exhausted. He rolled his head around on his neck, feeling the pull of tension on the muscles in his back. His shirt felt heavy and sticky, clinging tight around his neck and arms. 'I think I was followed today.' Thallberg raised an eyebrow but said nothing. 'They weren't yours, were they?'

Thallberg snorted. 'No, Reinhardt. I don't have anyone following you.' He rose and stretched as well.

'I'm also pretty sure that someone tried to get into –'

There was a knock at his door, and it began to open. Both Reinhardt and Thallberg froze, looking at the file on the desk. Thallberg made to move towards it, but Reinhardt shook his head before turning to see who was coming in. It was Freilinger.

The major looked between the pair of them as they came to their feet, his eyes fastening on Thallberg.

'You are?'

'Captain Thallberg, sir. 118th Jäger.'

Freilinger looked at Reinhardt. 'Is this the one you told me about?' Reinhardt nodded, ignoring the slightly accusatory look Thallberg sent him. Freilinger's eyes fell on the file on the table, but he said nothing about it. 'You are making progress?' he asked Reinhardt. He held an envelope in his hands.

Reinhardt nodded, suddenly unsure how much he could confide in Freilinger. That difference in the lists came suddenly to mind. An oversight, perhaps. But perhaps something else. In any case, Reinhardt realised, where did he himself stand now? That morning's talk with Freilinger had seemed pretty clear. Reinhardt was on his own with this. Who, Reinhardt asked himself, did he actually work for? 'Yes, sir,' he replied. 'Good progress. I think I have the main suspect.'

'Oh?'

Again, that hesitation. Reinhardt resisted looking at Thallberg. 'I can confidently place General Paul Verhein at the scene of the crime that evening, and I know it was him who beat the woman, Marija Vukić.'

Freilinger's expression did not change. 'Verhein?' he repeated. 'Commander of... 121st Jäger? You think he's involved?'

'I don't think, sir. I know.' Freilinger raised his eyebrows, inviting him to go on. 'I have a film that shows him sexually involved with Vukić the night of her murder. I know they were having an affair in Russia and I now know Hendel was following and reporting on him to the SD in Berlin.'

Without taking his eyes from Reinhardt, Freilinger took his tin of mints from his pocket and put one in his mouth. 'Well, well,' he said, his voice a dry rasp. He looked at Thallberg. 'Quite something, wouldn't you say, Captain?'

'Yes, I would say so, sir.'

'I would say so,' Freilinger repeated, quietly. He worked his mouth around his mint and turned those blue eyes on Reinhardt. 'What now?'

'Now,' answered Reinhardt, with only the slightest hesitation, 'we are going to continue our research. At the State House.'

'Will you confront him? Verhein?'

Reinhardt and Thallberg looked at each other. 'I don't know, sir,' answered Thallberg. 'We still need more evidence, and we haven't much time. So if you will excuse us... ?'

Freilinger nodded. 'Carry on,' he said.

'Was there something you needed, sir?' asked Reinhardt.

Freilinger put the envelope on Reinhardt's desk. 'This is for you.' He stepped back, and it was then Reinhardt saw it. A tension in the major's bearing, his arms stiff at his sides, and the knuckles showing white across his closed fists. 'Perhaps you will let me know later what you find.' He paused and swallowed, slowly. 'Well done, Reinhardt. Well done, indeed. Gentlemen,' he said to them both, and left.

Reinhardt felt a flood of tension wash out of him he had not known was there. He picked up the envelope and took out a sheet of typed paper. He read it with a mixture of relief and disappointment before folding it back up and putting it in his pocket. He looked at Thallberg, who was waiting for him, his face expressionless. 'State House?' Reinhardt asked, picking up the file and the film case, not wanting to let them out of his sight. Thallberg nodded. 'Then after you,' he said.

29

Thallberg kicked his office door open, holding the rebound for Reinhardt. 'Coffee?' he asked, as he swept up the sáme two mugs from earlier that day. It seemed like Reinhardt had been drinking it all day long, but he nodded anyway. Thallberg leaned into the corridor and hollered someone's name. As he waited, he pushed open his window and chucked the dregs out, apparently not caring on whom they might fall. Reinhardt found himself peculiarly struck by that act. Seemingly nonchalant, throwing coffee out of a window in a place like the State House, but he had seen him not a half an hour ago, crippled with sudden nervousness at the thought of where this case might actually lead him. What might it mean, he suddenly wondered, if it came to the crunch? Would Thallberg fold or stand tall?

Thallberg handed the mugs over to a noncom who knocked at the door. He shucked off his jacket, letting it drop over the back of a chair, and put his hands on his hips. 'Right, then. Now what?'

Reinhardt took out his list of units in Schwarz and the list of conference participants that Thallberg had given him that morning. 'With Verhein and his staff, like we said. Who does he have around him? Who came with him to Ilidža for the conference? Do we have anything on any of them?'

Thallberg gave a small smirk. '"We"?'

'Turn of phrase,' said Reinhardt, keeping his eyes on his lists, but he felt himself colour. He took out his pen and began marking the names on the list of conference participants of officers from the 121st. Verhein. Colonel Ascher, his chief of staff. Colonel Gärtner, divisional intelligence officer. Colonel Oelker, commanding the first regiment, probably the most senior of the combat officers. Major Jahn, divisional medical officer. And a Major Nadolski, divisional quartermaster. Six names. He jotted them down, then handed what he had written to Thallberg.

The captain looked it over. 'So, where will you start with that?'

'Well,' said Reinhardt, as he sat back and lit a cigarette, 'I would start with connections. Someone put the Feldgendarmerie onto this case. Had Becker looking for Krause. What would make Becker do that?'

'Self-interest?' asked Thallberg, his eyebrows raised.

'Possibly,' replied Reinhardt, his voice noncommittal.

'Blackmail?'

'Maybe. Although that's always tricky, blackmail. You might have something on someone and get them to do something against their will. But in doing it, they in turn have something on you. It can get out of hand quite quickly.'

'Friendship?' asked Thallberg. He looked, for a moment, like a boy who had answered a trick question posed by a teacher, and expected any second to be ridiculed for it.

Reinhardt nodded. 'Friendship. That's a powerful force. They all are, in their way. Self-interest. Blackmail. Friendship. Could be any of the three, or something else, but from what I know about Becker, it'll be self-interest. What we're looking for is a connection between one, or more, of these men and Becker.' He drew on his cigarette, then pointed it at the list of names. 'Very likely, someone in this lot murdered Hendel and Vukić, and then brought in Becker to start clearing it all up.'

'Or Becker heard about it, and got involved in return for something?'

Reinhardt inhaled, holding the smoke in his mouth, then

exhaled slowly. The smoke drifted up into his eyes, making him narrow them and squint. He nodded. 'Could well be.' Thallberg looked absurdly pleased with himself. 'Makes our life a lot harder, though. If that's what happened, then we're never going to find a connection.'

'So what, then?'

'So we assume there is one, and work off that assumption for now.'

Thallberg rubbed his eyes, and yawned. 'What do we need?'

'We need to match up Becker with Verhein's staff. For that, we need service histories. I can pretty much lay out Becker's, but I don't know anything about these others.'

'Right, then, let's see what we can do here,' said Thallberg, sighing the words out, almost talking to himself. 'Army administrative files are over at the Kosevo Polje barracks.' He looked at Reinhardt, but Reinhardt felt Thallberg was looking *through* him. 'Want to take a chance? Let's see what we've got here. Gestapo might have something. The boys in the security police might have, too...' His voice trailed off as he jotted something down on the piece of paper Reinhardt had given him and walked over to the door. 'Beike!' he called. Thallberg handed over his piece of paper with some muttered instructions, then took the coffee from another soldier and pushed the door shut with his foot.

'Now what?' asked Reinhardt. Maybe it was because he had worked alone so long, with people he knew either meant him harm or would not stand in the way of any harm which came his way, but Reinhardt could not get over an unease he felt at the way he saw Thallberg sharing tasks and information around without any apparent qualms.

'Now we wait.' Which was what Thallberg did, feet up on the desk, mug held to his lips, eyebrows lowered. He rocked himself slowly back and forth on the two back legs of his chair, apparently lost in thought. Reinhardt would have liked to relax like that, but his mind kept bumping around, back and forth over the events of the day. The morning's depression, the revelations, the elation... the day seemed to be never-ending. He yawned, abruptly. More to keep his hands busy, he began to jot down what he knew – postings and dates – of Becker's career since he had been kicked out of Kripo.

Becker was off the force and out of Berlin by the end of 1936. Reinhardt heard he had gone south, to Munich, tried to set himself up as a private investigator, and then nothing more about him for several years after that. When the war started, he learned Becker was a police instructor at the Feldgendarmerie training centre. How he managed that with his record, and what favours he had called in to secure that post, Reinhardt had no idea. It did not save him from frontline postings, however. Reinhardt knew Becker had been in the invasion of Poland as a company commander in a police battalion. Then Yugoslavia. He had come in behind the initial invasion, back in April 1941, then on to Greece, then back to Serbia. Postings in Belgrade, then Niš, then Sarajevo.

'You know, if we can't find anything here, we might have to call Berlin,' said Thallberg. He looked at Reinhardt over the rim of his cup. 'Ready for that?'

Reinhardt was saved from having to answer by a knock at the door. Corporal Beike stepped inside with several files and papers in his hands, which he handed to Thallberg. 'This is all?' the captain asked.

'Just what we've got. I'm still talking to the Gestapo about what they might have.'

'Any trouble?'

'The usual, sir. No need for you to get involved just yet.'

' "Trouble"?' asked Reinhardt. He stood and came around to Thallberg's side of the desk. There really was not much. Three flimsy cardboard files with loose papers inside them. Ascher, Nadolski, and Jahn.

'The Gestapo doesn't always like to share. It's a common failing of most bureaucracies, I've found. Especially feudal ones like ours,' he said, winking ironically as he passed Reinhardt two folders, those of Majors Jahn and Nadolski.

There was not much. Major Jahn was suspected of being addicted to morphine, of siphoning off supplies of it for his own use and trafficking it to other units. Major Nadolski had been reprimanded for misusing official transport on several occasions, including once to transport a load of women (the women were down as entertainment for the officers). He looked at Thallberg. 'Nothing,' he said, his mouth twisted with frustration. He got up, putting his hands in the small of his back, and looked out the window. 'You?'

Thallberg shrugged without looking up, leafing over a page. 'Ascher apparently put his hand up an altar boy's cassock in Zagreb.' He frowned at the last page. 'There's reference to a previous inquiry, before the war,' he muttered. 'There's a note here about a police investigation in Munich. Something similar, back in thirty-seven. Nothing else.' He tossed the folder down on the desk.

'Jahn likes morphine, and Nadolski misuses divisional transport.'

Thallberg chuckled. 'So Verhein's staff consists of a suspected bum bandit, a morphine addict, and a transport officer who transports things of dubious military value. Pretty tame stuff for these times, don't you think?'

Reinhardt nodded, despite not liking Thallberg's levity. There really was not very much.

'Excuse me, sir.' Reinhardt looked around. Beike was looking at the list of names, the officers from the 121st. He picked it up, and looked over at Thallberg. 'Sir, excuse my intervention, but I believe there is a name missing.'

'Missing?' asked Thallberg, glancing at Reinhardt.

'I believe there is one more officer who should be on the list. Colonel… that is, Standartenführer… Stolić.'

Reinhardt frowned, walking slowly towards Beike. 'Stolić? He's 7th SS.'

'Yes, sir,' the corporal replied. 'He is also the liaison officer to Verhein. Between the 121st and the Ustaše. He was assigned to that duty last week.'

Chance, thought Reinhardt, the first thing that came into his mind. *Chance again. What are the odds that a clerk, a corporal, would see that list… ? And know that information… ?* And the second thing he thought, he thought about the odds that Freilinger did not know that. Had not known it, all the time Reinhardt had been investigating this.

'Who is this Stolić?' asked Thallberg, looking at Reinhardt.

'He's come up a few times in the investigation. A nasty piece of work. Croat Volksdeutsche, in the SS. He had a thing for Vukić, but she wasn't interested in him.'

'What else do you know, Corporal?' asked Thallberg.

'The captain is correct, sir. Standartenführer Stolić has a reputation as a drinker and womaniser. He is also, as the captain said, a "nasty piece of work". There have been several complaints about his behaviour towards captured prisoners of war and against civilians. The Italians in particular have been most vociferous about him. That's why he's been transferred, I believe. The Seventh is operating in the Italian zone and they'll have nothing to do with him.'

'Go on, Corporal,' said Reinhardt.

'Stolić has a sort of band around him. Men like him. According to what I know, most of them met in Spain where they fought for the nationalist forces. Stolić returned from there with a nom de guerre. *El Cuchillo.* I believe it means "the knife".' Reinhardt and Thallberg exchanged glances. 'Stolić is known for carrying one. A very large knife, called a Bowie. According to the way he tells it, he took it from an American he killed in Spain.'

'Thank you, Corporal. You have been most helpful.' He waited until the door had closed before turning to Reinhardt. 'Well? What do you think?' There was a gleam in Thallberg's eyes.

Reinhardt too felt a rise of excitement, but he paused before answering. 'I think it sounds good.' Thallberg grinned, the gleam in his eyes brightening. 'But this is what my old instructor would call an orgy of evidence. It sounds almost too good to be true.'

'Some things are, though, aren't they?' asked Thallberg, somehow giving the impression of a disappointed little boy.

'Some things. Not many. And not usually in this line of work.'

'So where does this leave us, then?'

Reinhardt thought for a moment. 'We have two names. Verhein and Stolić. We know Verhein had an affair with Vukić, and we can place him at the scene. He was at the conference, staying at the hotel, and we have him on camera with her. We know he beat her unconscious. We can also place Stolić at the hotel. I got confirmation of that from the hotel staff. He was upset and disruptive, and we know he had a thing for Vukić. He carries a knife, and Vukić was killed with one. A large one, with a particular shape to its blade. I can also place Major Becker at or near the scene. He was called out to calm Stolić down. And we know the Feldgendarmerie were on the case sooner than I was, and the only way that could have happened was if the killer told them about it.'

Thallberg thought for a moment. 'But that doesn't mean the Feldgendarmerie know or knew the killer was actually the killer.'

'No, but there's a bloody good chance that's what happened. Think about it. The Feldgendarmerie have produced no suspects. They haven't even admitted they're investigating. Why would they do that? Why wouldn't they at least interview the officer or officers who reported the murder?' Thallberg nodded. 'It's because they're in on it. Becker has something to gain from this, but what I don't know.'

The two of them were silent a moment. 'So, what's your theory, then?' asked Thallberg.

'Vukić and Hendel planned to confront Verhein with the evidence that he is a Jew, and that there has been an internal investigation into him for some time. I think Vukić couldn't, or wouldn't, wait for Hendel to get to her, and confronted him herself. Enraged, he beat her. He fled. He spoke to his friends, or to his staff. They agreed to clean things up for him. Stolić was one of them. He hated Vukić for always turning him down, disrespecting him. They went around to her house, finding her conscious. He stabbed her to death. The police doctor always thought the stabbing was the work of a man deranged. I think Stolić fits that bill, and he carries a knife. Becker was brought in to help clean up.'

He paused.

'But… ?' prompted Thallberg.

'But..: there's the question of the blood. The mess…' Reinhardt trailed off again, thinking back to the hotel, the talk with Ewald, and then with the maid. What she said she had seen. What she had not seen…

'What about the mess?'

'There wasn't enough of it at the hotel,' said Reinhardt, still distracted. 'And I can't figure out why and how Becker would agree to be part of this. What did he know? Or see… ?'

'Well, I suppose the only polite thing to do would be to ask them,' said Thallberg. 'Verhein and Stolić.'

'They're at the front.'

Thallberg nodded. 'Then we'll just have to go to them. Ready for that?'

Reinhardt paused before answering. 'We can't arrest them. Not with what we have.'

'Who knows? We can at least question them, can't we? Put the fear of God into them?!' Reinhardt nodded finally, holding Thallberg's eyes, watching that manic grin flash across his face. 'What about Becker?'

Reinhardt shook his head. 'Not a word to him. He may tip them off. And believe me, he's more dangerous than he looks.'

'So you keep saying.' Thallberg blinked. 'Tomorrow, then. I'll need that long to get things ready here. Tomorrow, early morning? Six o'clock? From the barracks? I can take you in the sidecar if you need. How about movement orders? Need anything?'

Reinhardt shook his head, ignoring the rush of words, and thinking of the paper that Freilinger had given him. 'I have movement orders and I can get us a *kübelwagen*,' he said. They were silent a moment. 'Are we really doing this?' asked Reinhardt, half to himself.

'It would seem so.' Again, that abrupt mood swing. Thallberg sat there, looking subdued and turned in on himself.

Reinhardt got to his feet. 'Until tomorrow, then,' he said. The moment felt suddenly formal. Thallberg must have felt it, too, because he rose to his feet, and they shook hands. The moment broke, and the two of them smiled self-consciously at each other.

'Until tomorrow, then,' echoed Thallberg.

With the film and file tucked under his arm, Reinhardt paused on the steps of the State House. He felt light-headed, adrift, despite having as firm a purpose as he had had these past few years. He lit a cigarette and walked slowly to his car in the gathering dark. Before he went anywhere, he knew, he needed to speak with Freilinger. There was unfinished business there, but he was afraid of what it might mean.

Back at headquarters, Reinhardt passed by his office a moment. There was a note from Claussen on the meeting with Captain Oster. The two soldiers treated for burns of the hands and forearms were 121st Jäger. Reinhardt grinned mirthlessly, but the grin faded fast as he leaned down to unlock his desk. It had been forced. Rather expertly, but forced nevertheless. He took a long, ragged breath, letting it out slowly, thinking that the unfinished business just became much harder, but at the same time simpler. He gripped the film case and the file tighter and went upstairs.

Freilinger's orderly was sitting behind his desk. Reinhardt walked past him, hearing the man's chair go scraping back as he lurched to his feet. 'Captain, the major is busy.'

Reinhardt ignored him, raised his fist to knock, then stopped. He waited a moment, then pushed open the door. He walked in, seeing Freilinger look up. The major's eyes narrowed, then went flat as he saw Reinhardt. 'Is this what you were looking for?' Reinhardt asked, holding the film and file up.

Freilinger looked past him, at the orderly. He made a curt gesture with his head, and the door closed quietly. 'It is customary, not to mention polite, to knock at someone's door,' Freilinger rasped. His eyes, though… his eyes battened on what Reinhardt held.

'Is it what you wanted?' Freilinger turned those pale eyes on him, and he flinched as he smelled smoke.

'Yes, Gregor. That's what he was looking for.'

Reinhardt froze, because someone else had spoken. Someone sitting quietly in a corner of Freilinger's office. Reinhardt knew that voice, would know it anywhere. He took a step back from the desk, turning to the corner, at the man who rose to his feet, straightening his jacket and tie. He stepped forward, the light washing across his white hair.

It was Meissner.

30

'Hello, my boy.' Reinhardt was speechless. 'Something of a surprise, it would seem.' Meissner smiled. 'Don't blame Freilinger. I asked him to keep me out of it, especially as I didn't know whether I'd be able to come, or whether I'd be able to see you if I did.'

'Sir,' Reinhardt managed, finally. 'It is good to see you.' And it was.

'And you, my boy.' Smoothly, without thought, he enfolded Reinhardt in a warm embrace. After a moment, Reinhardt brought his free hand around on the old man's back, his palm open against the smooth material of Meissner's jacket, and closed his eyes. He smelled of cologne and cigars and clean cloth. God only knew what he himself smelled like, Reinhardt thought. As if sensing his thoughts, Meissner stepped back. He had that paternal sparkle in his eyes, the eyes themselves framed by a web of wrinkles that deepened across his cheeks when he smiled. 'You look tired, Gregor.'

'I suppose I am.'

'I'm not surprised.' Meissner held on to Reinhardt's shoulder, his hand firm, and looked deep into his eyes. Almost despite himself, despite the suspicions and the fatigue, he felt better. Calmer than he had felt in a long time. 'Come. Sit with me.'

There was a second chair in the corner. Reinhardt sat, the file and case in his lap, Freilinger going back behind his desk. The major seemed far away, and what Reinhardt had wanted to say seemed farther still. 'What are you doing here, sir?'

'Foreign Office business. I'm doing a sort of grand procession through Croatia, then on to Italy. Evaluating our allies. Renewing contacts. Making new ones. Catching up with old friends. Diplomacy, in short.' He smiled.

'And you, sir? Are you well?' Meissner's hair was white, but it had been for a long time. He had felt thin to Reinhardt. Fragile, as if old age had finally caught up with him.

Meissner shrugged, raising his eyebrows. 'Nothing retirement would not solve.' He smiled, wrinkles suddenly spreading like tributaries across his cheeks, and Reinhardt could not help but smile back.

Meissner leaned forward and put his elbows on his knees. The skin of his face, where it stretched across his cheeks and under his jaw, had the fine sheen of parchment. 'Tell me, really. How are you, my boy?'

'To anyone else, I'd say fine. But...' Reinhardt sighed, twisted his mouth. 'It's like I can't see two steps in front of me anymore. I seem to spend much of my time trying to forget. About Carolin. About what I've seen. Friedrich's lost at Stalingrad.' Meissner only watched, and listened. 'You know, we had begun talking again. After a fashion. I had a letter from him.'

'Brauer told me something of it the last time I saw him.'

Reinhardt brightened. 'Brauer? How is he?'

'Making life a misery for new recruits at infantry training. You know how he can be!' They shared a smile. 'He told me he wrote to you recently, otherwise I'd have brought you a letter from him.'

'And the others? What news of them?' The 'others' Reinhardt referred to were some of the officers and NCOs Meissner had taken under his wing after the war. A band of brothers, of sorts. The few who had survived the war and then the fighting in Germany at its end. Some were in the police, some in the army. A few in government, others in private practice. Nothing in common but the war, and each other, and Meissner.

'*Comme ci comme ça*, as the saying goes.' Meissner lifted his hands off his knees, then put them gently back down. 'But tell me, Gregor, tell me something of what you are doing. Freilinger has been spinning the most fantastical tale of murder and intrigue. Apparently he has you acting as a proper policeman again.'

Reinhardt glanced across the room at the major, sitting calmly behind his desk, hands folded under his chin, watching. 'You could say that, sir,' said Reinhardt. Meissner only looked at him, encouragingly. 'Two murders. One of them an Abwehr officer, who turns out to have been GFP, only he was really SD, investigating an army general called Verhein. This general was romantically involved with the second victim, a Croatian journalist. An Ustaša. They both had evidence Verhein is a Jew who has managed to hide his origins. He killed them both, or had them killed. We're not sure, yet.'

' "We"?'

For almost the first time in his life, Reinhardt ignored a question posed by his old colonel. 'Sir, what are you really doing here?'

Meissner smiled, gently. 'It really is diplomacy, Gregor. But...' He paused for a moment, and although his eyes never left Reinhardt's, Freilinger rose quietly to his feet, as if hearing an unspoken signal. He went and spoke to his orderly in the outer office, then shut the door and sat back down. Reinhardt felt a chill rise up his spine.

'Once,' said Meissner, 'you asked me why I had joined the Party. Do you remember? And do you remember I told you it was the best way I could think of to be able to do my work? You know, it hurt me terribly – inside – to think you and Carolin would think the Nazis' work was my work. It is not.' Reinhardt felt colder and colder, and his breathing came short and high over the bands he felt tightening around him. As if sensing it, Meissner gave that gentle smile of his. 'There are only a few of you, you know, with whom I can be this honest. My work is something else entirely, which my functions at the Foreign Office enable me to do. I am opposed – implacably – to the

Nazis. To what they have done to the Germany I love. I have been opposed to them from the beginning. And there are many who feel the same way I do.'

He paused, as if to let it sink in. Reinhardt swallowed. 'The resistance,' he whispered. 'You are talking about the resistance.' These words, these *thoughts*, were forbidden. His mind spun.

Meissner nodded. 'Yes,' he said, simply. There was a pause. 'This does not surprise you?' Phrased as a question, it was more of a statement.

'No,' said Reinhardt, but if he was honest with himself, what he felt was relief as a part of his mind he had sealed away, a part that knew Meissner as a Nazi, was suddenly gone. 'No, I am not surprised. Why?'

'Why? We Germans – or should I say, we Germans of a certain class – are not easily led to oppose authority, and none of us was imaginative enough to foresee what has happened. War, yes – but not like *this*! Their extremes, their laws, their cults, their hypocrisy, their *ridiculous* strutting… The course of the war… The catastrophes, one after the other… The treatment of the conquered… For myself, I could not see visited upon another generation the suffering we went through.'

'How did it begin for you?'

'In the heart rather than in the mind. As thoughts rather than words. Then as words rather than deeds. Then, finally, action came.' Meissner nodded. 'Before the war, it was contacts with friends and counterparts abroad. Meetings. Opinions shared. *What ifs*… explored. Discussing the Nazis as if discussing a particularly nasty illness someone had. One never mentions it by name. All very civilised. The discourse of erudite, worldly men. What fools we were. How *naïve*,' he said, his words all the more powerful for their measured, gentle tone. 'Then it was words exchanged between old friends. Cautiously. Carefully. One could not be too careful. Even more so now. There are many groups, but none with the potential that ours has. We are numerous. Some in high places. Some in low. Some near, some far. And some,' he said, his eyes glinting sharply, 'who do not know they fight for the resistance at all.'

'Me?' Meissner nodded, slowly. He felt the pull of the colonel's eyes, pushed past them to those memories of those last days in Berlin. Huddled in the corner of Meissner's study, seeing it again. Seeing it differently.

'Will you go back in?' Meissner asked, finally.
'I'll do it for you, sir. For nothing else.'
Meissner sighed softly, nodded, the fire playing across his white hair. 'Thank you.'

'Me,' said Reinhardt, again.

'You,' whispered Meissner. 'We placed you carefully. Moved you as we thought best. It was always a difficult business. Now, it is becoming all but impossible. The Nazis are strong, and they are clever. They have broken many groups. Broken many men, and no few women. You may have heard of those young students, The White Rose. Such bravery in ones so young. But the noose is tightening, and I fear it is only a matter of time before it closes around me. For now, although I am free to move around more or less as I please, I have noticed things – small things – are different, and so the work I am doing, the work I need to try to finish, has become that much more important.'

Meissner looked down and away. 'The problem is, for all our good intentions, we are just a group of faceless Prussians, crotchety old businessmen and nobles and pensioned soldiers meeting in the shadows, bumbling on about uncouth Bavarians. My boy,' he said, turning his eyes back on Reinhardt, 'what I'm going to say to you, now, you will not like. My group' – he sighed – 'has been talking to Verhein. We need him. We need someone with his charisma. We need someone with the loyalty he inspires. With the contacts he has in the army.'

Reinhardt swallowed slowly, forcefully, against the tightness in his throat. 'And… ?' he managed. He knew the answer, but he needed Meissner to say it.

Meissner seemed to know that, or at least understand it.

'And, Gregor, I need to know what you know. I need to know what you are planning now that you know about Verhein. And, if possible, I need to know whether you can give me what you've found and be persuaded to look away.'

'Look *away*?'

'Yes,' replied Meissner. His mouth opened as if to say something else, but he stopped.

'Don't,' whispered Reinhardt, hoarsely. 'Don't say it. Don't say "Just this once", because *you* know, and *I* know, that's not true.' He bent forward, hunching around the weight he felt, feeling the frustration, the rising anger. 'I suspected something,' he said, finally. 'I suspected Freilinger was obstructing me. Deftly, I'll give him that. He tried to keep me away from investigating senior officers. He gave me a list without Verhein's name on it. He steered me towards an SS Standartenführer... I didn't know why, though.'

'Freilinger was put in a difficult position. He is one of us. He has tried to talk to Verhein, but the general won't listen.' He looked over at the major.

Freilinger unfolded his hands. 'When the murders happened, I suspected Verhein's involvement and I decided to do something that I suspected you would find distasteful.' He paused, swallowed around the scrape in his throat. 'I decided to let you proceed, to gather evidence, to then try to orient you in another direction, and to use that evidence to persuade Verhein to at least listen to us. Verhein was offered a staff position at Army High Command.' Reinhardt nodded. 'It would have put him at the heart of operations and close to Hitler himself. We needed him to take that post but as one of us. Or with us. He has been refusing it, but all of sudden I hear he is taking it. We think something has happened to make him change his mind.'

The telephone on Freilinger's desk rang. Reinhardt jumped, looking at it. Freilinger ignored it. There were footsteps in the outer office, a voice, and the ringing stopped. 'You are talking about blackmail.'

'We are,' said Meissner. 'I am. Exactly that. We did not know of Verhein's Jewish origins, although we suspected something like it because of what he has done and said – or rather didn't do and say – throughout his military career. Especially in Russia. We did check his records. If they were falsified, they were very well falsified. Now we know. We can use this to talk to him.'

Reinhardt hunched forward again. He screwed his eyes tight shut and shook his head. 'My God,' he whispered. 'You will use this…' He looked up. 'You are asking me to take no further action against a man who may have committed murder, or ordered it done.' Meissner nodded. 'Why? Because you need him?'

'I am convinced Verhein will help us. He already is, only he can't seem to see it. And if he can't bring himself to help us willingly, then, yes, I will force him. I lose nothing but a pawn in a game. He stands to lose much, much more.'

His life. His career. Reinhardt thought back to Hendel's dossier. 'His sister.'

'Yes,' said Meissner. 'His one weakness.'

'You are talking about sacrifice. Two lives for one.'

'No,' rasped Freilinger. 'We are talking about one life for many. For thousands. For hundreds of thousands.'

'Think about it, Reinhardt,' whispered Meissner. 'Think what Verhein could mean for the resistance.'

'I'm thinking, believe me,' snapped Reinhardt. He screwed his palm into his forehead in frustration, and in embarrassment at having talked in such a way to Meissner. 'Do you know,' he said, his head in his hands, then looking up, 'do you know what you're taking away from me? For the first time in I don't know how long, I had found myself again. Found a reason to be. To live.'

'I can give you a reason, my boy. Now you know what I'm doing, what I stand for, you can join us. I can take you with me to Italy with Freilinger. This place is a slaughterhouse. It's bad enough now, just wait until we're gone, and everyone here is at each other's throats again.'

Reinhardt thought about Dr Begović and wanted to shake his head no, to tell Meissner it did not have to be that way, but he was distracted again by a telephone in the outer office, more voices. 'I am sorry, Colonel. I… it just seems… wrong, to me.'

'It's a bit late to get a *conscience*, Reinhardt,' snapped Meissner. Reinhardt froze, as a child freezes under the whip of his father's voice. Meissner's eyes bored into his, then softened. He passed a hand over his face. Reinhardt saw how the hand shook, like an old man's. For the first time, he seemed to see that Meissner's skin was dotted with spots, stretched tight, clawlike, over the bones. 'I am sorry, my boy,' Meissner whispered. 'I should never have said that.'

'No,' said Reinhardt. 'It is a bit too late. But better late than never. I can do this. I can do this right. I need to.' He looked down at the floor, back up. 'Please.'

There was a knock at the door. Meissner and Freilinger froze. The colonel reached into his jacket, then nodded to Freilinger, who rose and crossed the office. Reinhardt saw that Freilinger's holster was unbuttoned. He opened the door, then stepped out.

Meissner saw Reinhardt looking at his hand under his jacket. He swivelled his eyes to look at the office door where it stood ajar. Voices leaked in from the other room, words on the edge of comprehension. Meissner looked back at him with a flat expression, and Reinhardt was suddenly afraid. He did not recognise this man staring at him.

Freilinger shut the door and stood listening at it for a moment. Meissner looked at him, then cocked his head towards the door, eyebrows raised. 'Nothing to do with us,' Freilinger said, looking at Reinhardt.

'Sir. Colonel. Even if I wanted, even if I could help you, I can't control Thallberg. I can make any promise to you but I don't know what he would do.'

'Does he trust you?' Meissner still had not taken his hand out of his jacket.

Reinhardt thought of that childish interest that Thallberg had taken in his past as a detective. 'Maybe.' He thought of the way Thallberg's mood could change, the way something hard seemed to slide into position behind his face. 'I don't know.' He looked at Freilinger. 'What was it about? Out there?'

The major hesitated. 'The police are going to arrest Jelić for Vukić's murder,' he said, finally.

'When?'

'Now.'

Reinhardt rose to his feet. 'Sir...' he began to say to Meissner, but the colonel cut him off.

'Stay out of it, Reinhardt.'

'I can't let that happen.' He looked at Meissner's hand under his jacket, at Freilinger's unbuttoned holster. 'That boy, Jelić, he has nothing to do with this. And don't tell me he has to be another sacrifice.'

'Reinhardt,' said Meissner, taking his hand out from under his jacket and putting it on his knee.

'No. Don't say anything.' He stood by Freilinger's desk, but the major still stood between him and the door. He hefted the film case in his hand, then put it carefully on the table. The file, he kept. 'You have done a lot for me over the years. I can never repay that. But I've done a lot for you too. I've led men to their deaths for you. I've fought for you until I had nothing left to give.' Freilinger looked at Meissner, who nodded. Freilinger stepped aside. 'There was a time when I don't think I would have had to explain something like this to you.' Meissner's mouth tightened, as if Reinhardt's words had struck home with the force of blows. He weakened, as he knew he would. He could not hurt this man to whom he owed so much. 'I will think about... what you have said, sir. I will be in touch with you.'

Meissner came across the room, slowly, moving like the old man Reinhardt realised he was. Old, worn down. He sighed, then raised his arms and put his hands on Reinhardt's shoulders. He patted his hands on Reinhardt's epaulettes and smoothed down the material. 'I have something for you,' he said, giving Reinhardt a small package of soft leather. He began to unwrap it, but Meissner put his hand over his. 'Look at it later.' He gave a small smile, then pulled Reinhardt to him. 'You were the best of them,' he whispered. He pushed Reinhardt away, gently. 'Do what you have to do.'

31

Driving through the city's darkened streets, past blank windows and shadowed doorways, he lost himself once or twice as he tried to find the way back to Jelić's building. He finally found it, recognising it only because of its new construction, its five floors sticking up and out of the rest of the neighbourhood. He drove past the apartment's entrance, feeling suddenly wary, and parked a little way down the street in front of a rusty truck that sat atop four flattened tyres, the rubber parched and cracked. He switched off the lights and let the engine clatter into silence. He shifted in his seat, looking back down the street and up at Jelić's apartment. Slits of light were visible through poorly drawn curtains, but no cars. If the police had been and gone, they'd left the lights on.

He lit a cigarette and waited, his fingers tapping the file where it lay on the seat next to him. The curfew was in its second night and it was quiet. As his eyes adjusted to the darkness and his ears to the silence, the shape of the street seemed to emerge from the night, cautiously, as if wary of men's notice. It felt empty, but it was not. As form coalesced out of the dark, sounds followed. A clink of china. A snatch of conversation. Someone laughed. He knew he was taking a risk. Despite the curfew, he could not stay here long.

He drew deeply on his cigarette, feeling himself calm a little. He thought back to the revelations of the day. Begović a Partisan. Verhein a Jew. Meissner and Freilinger in the resistance, himself a pawn in a bigger game, and finding something that reminded him of what and who he once was. Something that felt right but on the cusp of being taken away. For the first time in years, he felt some lifting in the fog that had held him tight. Some clarity of purpose, something to aim at, a direction in which to go. He watched the reflected ember of his cigarette flare in the windshield as he drew on it, behind it the planes of his face welling out of the darkness, then back again. His thoughts faded in and out like the light. Was he too lost to himself, and to others? Too wrapped up in this selfish feeling of rediscovering himself, unable to see the big picture anymore? Not able to take this chance to strike a greater blow than he could ever hope to strike alone?

He stiffened as he heard a car. It came up behind him, its lights folding the lines and angles of the street from the dark. It parked in front of Jelić's building and three men climbed out. There was a hum of conversation; someone drummed his fingers on the roof of the car. There was a squeal of hinges, a dull smack as a door swung closed, then silence.

Reinhardt hesitated with the file, then slipped it under the spare tyre. If the street had felt quiet before, it was nothing compared to what it was like now. He could practically feel the silence, touch it, hear the thoughts of the people in the street as they hoped and prayed the car was not coming for them. His heart pounding, Reinhardt followed them inside, pulling open the door slowly, softly, so the hinges did not squeal. He paused, listening, then walked quickly up the stairs to the second floor. There were lights under only one of the other apartments besides Jelić's. He listened at the door, hearing the strong sound of voices, the tone forceful, accusatory. Reinhardt's heart lurched, and not giving himself any time to think about it, he knocked once on the door, opened it, and stepped inside.

Jelić stood against the big desk, his face white and drawn where it was not already swollen and battered. Facing him was Putković, his meaty fist bunched in the other man's shirt. Padelin stood off to one side, hands on hips. Both the policemen looked at him, Putković's face red and florid, Padelin's flat and expressionless. Two of them but three had got out of the car...

The door was yanked from his hand and slammed shut, and two huge hands like metal bands came down on his elbows and pinned his arms to his sides. He looked up over his shoulder at Bunda. The man was enormous. Up close, the ursine stink of him was almost overpowering.

'What you doing here, Captain?' asked Putković.

Reinhardt swallowed, then turned away from Bunda and his beady little eyes that shone out from under his cavernous brow. 'I might ask you the same thing.'

'I'm asking questions.'

'Very well. I heard you were coming, and I wanted to make sure you didn't make any mistakes. Again.'

'You heard?' repeated Putković. He exchanged a look with Padelin, who gave the smallest shrug of his shoulders. Putković looked disgusted and muttered something in Serbo-Croat. Reinhardt frowned as he made out several of the words.

'Becker! You just said Becker,' said Reinhardt, moving forward against Bunda's grip. It was like trying to shift a boulder. Putković scowled. 'What has Becker to do with this?'

'That's not important.'

'No,' agreed Reinhardt, changing tack, watching Putković struggle to reassess. The man was dense. Padelin, on the other hand, just watched. 'No, what's important is one of your men has his hands on a German officer.'

Putković grunted. 'Yes. Well, badder things have happened. Don't worry, we won't hurt you. You are our ally, yes?' he finished, with clumsy sarcasm.

'What do you want with him, then?' Reinhardt asked, looking at Jelić.

Putković looked at the young man with an expressionless face. 'He knows something about a film,' he growled, his fist tightening in Jelić's clothes. Jelic made to say something, but Putković shook him, like a man might shake a kitten. '*Šutjeti*,' he hissed.

'I already told Padelin, Jelić doesn't know anything.'

'Yes, is what you said. But you didn't give proof.'

'*Proof?!*' scoffed Reinhardt. 'You haven't been overly concerned with that until now. Why break such a good habit over someone like him?'

'Break is good word, Captain Reinhardt. But not word you know well, I think.'

'What?'

'I will break this Jelić,' said Putković, ignoring him. 'Maybe you will tell me what I want to know. Maybe he will tell me what I want to know. I win both times. And, I have some fun with this Jelić,' he smiled. In a form of repulsive symbiosis, Reinhardt felt Bunda's grip on his arms tighten in what must have been anticipation.

'Putković, there is no need for any of that.'

'What is he for you, anyway?' grunted Putković. 'You fucking him or something?' A dull glint sparked in his eyes, and he snorted something in Serbo-Croat at the other two policemen. Bunda laughed, Reinhardt feeling the huge man shake through the grip he maintained on his arms. Padelin just kept that basilisk stare, his eyes not leaving Reinhardt. 'Hey, bum-boy,' Putković laughed at Jelić. 'This man bothering you? You have something you want to report?' He carried on, guffawing over his own mirth with Bunda egging him on. From the way Jelić's face coloured, Reinhardt knew that some of the barbs were striking home.

Putković gave a final laugh that trailed into a chuckle, and then he was silent, any trace of humour gone. He looked between Reinhardt and Jelić. 'What you doing here, Captain?' he said, again.

'I came to see if he was in trouble. With you, over what you thought he might know.'

'And what you think he might know?'

'Like I told Padelin earlier today, he doesn't know anything.'

Putković let go of Jelić, the young man staggering back and slumping against the big table. The policeman walked up close to Reinhardt and stared at him with his piggish little eyes. 'I don't believe you,' he said. 'Why should German officer stick out neck for someone like him?'

Other than the fact that this was wrong, Putković was right. There was no reason why Reinhardt was doing this, and every reason to stay away. Every reason in the upside-down world this life had become. 'I got the film from Tomić. He was Vukić's cameraman. All right? He was supposed to be in Zagreb, but he was here all the time.' He dared not say more unless he revealed too much about Begović and the safe house. Who knew how things might end then.

'Where is Tomić now?'

'I don't know.'

Putković narrowed his eyes, staring intently at Reinhardt. 'You don't know? Or you won't tell us? There is more. I know it.' He stepped back. 'We hear about you. You soft with Partisans.'

'What? What are you talking about?'

'In interrogations. You soft. Go easy with the Reds. You like Reds? You don't break them. Just talk to them. Talk, talk, talk.'

Reinhardt felt a chill, a curious sense of dislocation, thinking of how Begović had spoken to him of this very same thing. It was like seeing himself suddenly from a different angle, as someone else would. A German officer soft on Partisans? Putković clenched his jaw and said something to Padelin, nodding his head to the door that led farther into the apartment. It looked like Padelin would protest, but then he just took Reinhardt's pistol from his holster. Bunda let go of him, and Padelin took Reinhardt's arm in his own not-inconsiderable grip and pulled him with him out of the room and down a short corridor. 'In there,' he said. Reinhardt opened a door into a bedroom. A rumpled half-made bed, a lit lamp on a bedside table. Padelin pushed him in with a heavy hand in his back. 'Sit on the bed.' Padelin shut the door, put Reinhardt's pistol in his pocket, and took a chair opposite the bed, sitting back with a creak of wood and staring blankly at the wall behind Reinhardt.

It was hard to hear anything in the room through the walls

and doors, and over the thudding of his heart and the pounding of the blood in his ears. What he could not hear, though, his imagination made up for. Jelić did not stand a chance against Putković and Bunda, and they would not waste too much time questioning him. And then what? The Germans and Croats were allies, but it would not take much for these three to get it in their heads that he knew more and then dispose of him somewhere. They could always blame it on the Partisans. Thinking of them had him thinking of this apparent reputation he had. Reinhardt, the interrogator soft on the Reds…

He put his forehead on his fingertips and sighed out slowly through puffed cheeks, looking up at Padelin through the bars of his fingers. 'You don't look very happy, Padelin,' he said, lifting his head and dropping his hands.

The inspector blinked, his eyes fixing on Reinhardt. His mouth firmed, as if to hold something back. 'No' was the short response. 'This is your fault, Reinhardt. You should have told me about Tomić.'

There was something to what he said, and Jelić was now paying for that decision. Reinhardt could not find it in himself to regret it, though. His arms throbbed where Bunda had held him. He put his hands on his knees, ran them up his thighs. He felt something in his pocket. Shifting his weight, keeping an eye on Padelin, he put his hand in his pocket, finding, remembering, the little package that Meissner had given him. He unwrapped it and caught his breath for a moment. It was his Williamson. The big pocket watch that he had left for safekeeping with Meissner. Who had returned it to him…

'What do you know of friendship, Padelin?'

'What?'

'Friendship. Friends. What do you know of that?'

Padelin sighed. 'Just be quiet, Reinhardt, and it will soon be over.'

'I was a fortunate man, by most standards. I had good friends. The best. The sort that would lay down their lives for you. Ever had a friend like that, Padelin? No?' The detective stared at him with his flat eyes. Reinhardt looked back down at the watch. 'Do you think Vukić had friends?'

'Be quiet, Reinhardt.'

Reinhardt fingered the watch, running his thumb over the inscription on the watch's case, at the name engraved there. He had done that so often that the metal was worn smooth, polished to a bright edge. He checked his Phenix and adjusted the time on the Williamson before wrapping it back in its soft leather bag. He thought back to Meissner's words and saw the sense behind them now. Meissner did not know how much time he had left, he realised, and did not want the watch to end up with anybody else. He was tying up loose ends.

He gave a shallow sigh, looking down at the floor. There was a coil of wire by his foot, leading from a plug to the lamp on the bedside table next to him. He shifted on the bed, putting the watch back in his pocket. As he did so, he slid his foot onto the wire, the heel of his boot resting on top of it.

'Mind if I smoke?' He took his cigarettes and matches from his other pocket, letting the baton slip up and out. He straightened his jacket as he did, making it all but invisible where it lay snugly down his leg. There was a sound from the main room. A thud. Someone cried out in pain. Reinhardt stared at the wall, then at Padelin. The big detective blinked, returning his stare with a monk's impassivity. 'I don't think she had friends,' said Reinhardt, lighting a cigarette and taking a long drag. He put his elbows on his knees, folded one hand within the other. 'I think she had people that used her. For sex, mostly,' he said, blowing smoke across the room.

'What?'

'I'm talking about Vukić. The Ustaše's sex symbol.'

'Quiet,' Padelin grated.

'Maybe I'm wrong, though. She had one friend so far as I can see, and that was Tomić. The one you're after. The one you think Jelić can lead you to.' Padelin shifted his hands where they lay on his lap. Reinhardt forced a smile. The sort of shit-eating grin he had seen countless suspects make. The one guaranteed to make a policeman's blood begin to boil.

'Why didn't you say this about Tomić before?'

'I told you. Why should I trust you? But I digress.' Padelin frowned. 'I'm changing the subject. We were talking about Vukić. Tomić told me a lot about her. You know, he was her father's best friend. He was wounded in the war. He got his balls blown off. Imagine that...' Reinhardt shook his head, taking another long pull on his cigarette. 'I know I can't. And God knows I've seen a lot of injuries in my time...' He looked at the tip of his cigarette and tapped ash on the floor. Padelin's eyes twitched. 'He told me she treated him like her father. I suppose because her real one was too busy being an Ustaša, or whatever. He never quite said it, but I got the sense the father was no angel. Didn't treat her too well. Probably tried to pass her around some of his friends. Tomić said she once tried to have sex with him, but, of course, he couldn't. Once she found out, that was when she began to sort of treat him like a father. But of course one she tried to fuck. At least once.'

Padelin breathed in slowly, his chest rising like a bellows. 'Reinhardt, is there any point to this? If not, then please be quiet.'

'I'm just thinking out loud, really. No harm in that, is there?' He smiled, seeing Padelin's eyes tighten again. 'Funny, isn't it? Here we have this beautiful woman. Marija Vukić. Probably pimped out by her own father. Seeking solace from a eunuch. I think a lot of people wanted to have sex with her. She only wanted to have sex with older men. Men of maturity.'

'Reinhardt.'

'Men like me, for instance. You know, if she walked in here now, and she had to choose one of us, she'd choose me.' Reinhardt grinned, swallowing at the back of it against a dry throat. There was another thud from the front room, a rumble of laughter like an engine heard through a wall. 'Man of experience that I am. A touch of grey up here,' he said, fluffing at his hair. 'Medals. I've even got a war wound,' he said, tapping his knee. He dragged his foot a little more, tautening the wire as it led into the wall. He forced his grin wider. 'I think she'd be all over me.'

'Reinhardt, if you don't *shut up...*'

'Oh, for heaven's sake, Padelin. We're just *talking*,' he said, finishing his cigarette. He stubbed it out on the table. 'But I have to ask, what did you think when you saw her dead? Did you think about what it might have been like? You know? To fuck her?' The skin along the collar of Padelin's shirt went white. Danger sign. Reinhardt's blood thudded and pounded through his chest. Padelin filled the room with his immobile menace. Slowly, carefully, Reinhardt pulled on the wire. The cord tautened against the wall, went stiff against his foot.

He looked the big detective in the eyes. 'Jelić was probably right about Vukić. She was a complete fucking slut.' He saw the glaze come over Padelin's eyes, as if a screen had swung shut somewhere inside him. 'What was it he said about her?' Reinhardt leaned forward, let that smile come over his face again, widened his eyes as if in merriment. 'You remember? You do, come on.' He tested his foot again, breathing over and around the fear that squatted in his chest. He leaned to the right, towards the door, watched the slight shift in Padelin's weight as the detective mirrored his movement. 'She'd fuck anything, right? Anything that could move its hips fast enough. But do you think she fucked the dead?'

Reinhardt knew Padelin moved without expression. No sneering, no roaring, no twisting of features. Just movement. Implacable, like a boulder coming downhill. He saw it begin as Padelin's feet went firm to the floor, lifting his big frame in one smooth movement. Reinhardt allowed himself to show fear, real fear, and then he leaned towards the right and slid his foot hard across the floor, feeling the cord come popping out of the wall.

The room was plunged into absolute blackness. Reinhardt flung himself back against the wall, back where he had come from, scooping up the baton where it had lain against his thigh, flicking it up into the air, feeling it extend and snap into place.

He felt Padelin go past him, felt the heat and weight of the man, like a swimmer might feel a leviathan pass beneath him in dark waters. Reinhardt swung his knee up, heard the detective give an astonished wheeze even as his arms scrabbled apelike across Reinhardt's tunic and under his chin, his thick fingers searching for a grip, twisting up and over his face and grasping at his eyes. Reinhardt jerked his head back and away and hacked down with all his strength. He felt the baton thump across Padelin's back, heard the man's gasp of breath as it bent around and across his ribs, the weighted ball at its tip digging deep. Reinhardt jerked his knee up again, connecting with Padelin's chest, and smashed down with the baton once more, and again, across the shoulders.

He felt the ball bite into something soft, and he kicked and thrashed with his knees and feet. This was trench fighting, the kind that left you no room except what you could hack out with your arms and legs. Hack, stab, thrust, swing, and never stop until your man is down, or you are, and the fear was gone, only emptiness where it had been. He felt a sickening familiarity of movement, a vestigial memory of stumbling and brawling through earthen trenches with Russians in brown tunics and Frenchmen in blue uniforms and British in their round tin hats.

Padelin collapsed to the floor, but even as he did, he punched Reinhardt in the side, just below the ribs. His breath sawing in his throat over the blare of pain from where he had been hit, Reinhardt fell on Padelin's back with both his knees digging down, and beat him over the back of the thighs with the baton. He did not want to kill him, although he knew Padelin had had his death in his eyes. With his free hand he gripped Padelin's hair and struck his head against the floor once, twice. He stopped, breathing raggedly, and felt Padelin through his legs, listened to his breathing. Padelin twitched, his torso moving. Taking the haft of the baton in his fist, he placed it on the back of Padelin's neck and drew it back. Judging as best he could in the dark, he struck Padelin across the back of the neck and felt him go stiff, then limp under him.

He remained kneeling on Padelin's back for a few moments, but the detective was still. Light was bleeding into the room. The shutters were limned in a faint brush of silver from outside, a rectangle of white around the door. Drenched in a cold sweat, Reinhardt leaned over, close to Padelin's face, and heard the thread of his breathing. He ran his hands over Padelin's jacket, finding his pistol, and taking the detective's as well. Standing, his hand searching blindly, he found the wall, and he leaned against it a moment. Remembering where the table was, he picked up his cap and, wiping his sweaty face on his sleeves, screwed it onto his head. Feeling calmer, he cracked the door open, listening, before opening it wider and looking out into the corridor.

There was no one. He collapsed the baton, pocketed it, and slipped out, turning for the door at the end, opening it as quietly as he could. There was a thud, a mutter of a man's voice, and then another man's, swearing. Two men began arguing. Footsteps, and Bunda came into sight. A tap ran, and he walked back with a jug. Water spilled across the floor. Using the noise as cover, Reinhardt peered around the door frame, seeing Bunda and Putković standing over Jelić's body.

He stepped quickly into the room, moving over towards the two policemen, who looked at him in bovine astonishment. He aimed his pistol at Putković's head. 'Enough,' he said, quietly. 'Both of you drop your weapons. Tell Bunda to pick Jelić up and bring him downstairs.'

Putković's eyes drilled past Reinhardt, to the door he had come out of. 'Where is Padelin?'

'Alive,' replied Reinhardt. 'Get Jelić picked up. Now.' Bunda clenched his fists, breathing heavily through his nostrils. Reinhardt shifted his aim to him. The man did not even flinch, staring past the muzzle at Reinhardt. 'Move or I'll shoot your pet gorilla and make you carry Jelić.'

'You won't get away with this,' grated Putković.

'Get away with what?' said Reinhardt. He kept his pistol on

Bunda, looking back at him unflinchingly. Bunda was the danger man. Reinhardt could not let him anywhere near him. 'You detained a German officer. Struck him. Disarmed him. Who is in more trouble here?' Putković glared at him, then grunted an order at Bunda. Their pistols clattered to the floor, and then the bull of a policeman knelt, slid his arms under Jelić, and hauled him up and over his shoulder. He stood, shifting the body slightly, and turned back to look at Reinhardt. 'Downstairs. Him first,' he said, pointing his pistol at Bunda.

Outside, on the pavement, Reinhardt kept his back to the wall. 'Tell him to put Jelić in the car. In the back.' Bunda bent over and unceremoniously dumped Jelić across the rear seat. The man moaned through the ruin of his mouth as he slumped into the *kübelwagen*. 'Back, both of you. On your knees. In front of the car.' The two of them knelt slowly, reluctantly. Reinhardt could feel the anger seething off them like heat as he got into the car, managed to turn the ignition, and then the lights. The two kneeling policemen blinked and squinted into the sudden glare as Reinhardt reversed the *kübelwagen*. He slowed as he passed Putković's car and fired a shot into the back tyre, and then he flipped the pistol onto the seat next to him. Bunda hauled himself to his feet and began running after him. Reinhardt floored the accelerator, the engine howling metallically. As he came to the end of the road, he saw Bunda lumbering into the street after him in the juddering image of the rearview mirror, then fading away into the night, like some wild creature of the forest.

32

Reinhardt drove without thinking until he reached King Aleksander Street. He paused there, the engine idling, and it was there his fear caught up with him and came clamouring up against the calmness in his mind that had carried him this far. He took a long, ragged breath and put his head on the steering wheel until his breathing steadied and his hands were firmer. He glanced into the back. Jelić seemed unconscious. At least, he said nothing when Reinhardt called his name. After the frenzy of the past few minutes, Reinhardt was at a sudden loss for what to do. A slow wheezing groan from Jelić sparked him into action, however, and he began making his way through the streets to Bentbaša. Passing only one or two military vehicles, he parked against a wooden garage door and hauled Jelić out of the back of the car, wrapping one of the boy's arms around his neck and putting his other arm tight around his waist.

'Jelić. Can you walk? You have to try to walk. To help me. Please, walk a little.'

Jelić slumped heavily against him, but it seemed he tried to carry a little of his weight. Reinhardt took the pair of them down a darkened alley, his feet turning unexpectedly on the cobbles as he staggered from step to step, his knee twitching painfully. He reached a house and paused, looking up and down the street. Seeing no one, he hauled Jelić's weight to one side, and with his free hand he pushed on the door handle. The door opened soundlessly, and he swallowed a sob of relief in his throat. He had only hoped it would be unlocked.

Moving as quickly as he could, he slipped inside, pushing the door shut with his foot. He staggered into the living room and laid Jelić down on a low divan in front of a set of windows. He straightened, breathing heavily, rubbing his knee. In the kitchen he found bottles of brandy and slivovitz and wet some towels, which he applied to Jelić's face. It felt hopeless, just a gesture. He poured some brandy and tried to lift Jelić's head, putting a glass to his lips. Jelić winced and turned his head away, a murmur of protest slipping from his swollen mouth.

Reinhardt sighed and sat back. He fingered his glass, then emptied it hard against the back of his throat, gasping harshly as he wiped his hand across his mouth. He poured another glass as he looked at Jelić, his mind spinning. What had he done? What was he going to do? Was it the reference to Stalingrad? That Jelić had been so close to Friedrich? Did this boy remind him of his son? They looked and acted nothing alike. Was he perhaps a substitute for those two boys at Kragujevac? The two he had not saved? He blinked hard through the sting of tears, the sudden bite of smoke harsh in his nostrils, and downed the brandy. He made to pour another and as the bottle rattled on the rim of the glass he stopped and put glass and bottle down.

Maybe it was just the right thing to do.

He scrawled a message to Jelić on a page of his notebook to stay put until a doctor came, tore it out, and left it on the table where he hoped he would see it. He wrote another note, tore it out and folded it into his hand, wrote two names on it, and left the house. At the end of the alley he stopped, looking across the road to the shop where Simo had said he had 'bought' his souvenir. He slipped the note under the door, then drove back to the barracks.

Almost forgetting to take the file out from under the spare tyre, he went upstairs to his room, lodged the chair under his door again, and collapsed onto his bed, letting his pistol clatter onto the bedside table. He threw an arm across his face and began to calm down. Checking his watch, he saw that it was coming up to nearly eleven o'clock. He had an early start with Thallberg tomorrow and he had not done anything to prepare for it, and he could not seem to find the energy to do anything about it now. What had Putković said about Becker? He was sure he had mentioned Becker's name.

He shot up in bed as someone knocked at the door. The room was dark but there was an expectation of light outside the window. His mouth felt thick and gummed, and he knew he had been asleep. The knocking came again. He swayed to his feet and picked up his pistol.

'Who is there?' he called, standing to the side of the door.

'Freilinger.'

Reinhardt pulled the chair away from the door, opened it, and stood back, the pistol held at his waist. Freilinger stepped into the room, his eyes squinting against the gloom. He shut the door, cutting off what little light there was from the hallway. 'The light?'

Reinhardt reached past him and flipped the switch, squinting and standing back as he did. Freilinger's eyes paused on the pistol, but he said nothing. 'What do you want?' His watch read four o'clock in the morning. He cursed under his breath, never having meant to sleep so long. Never having meant to sleep at all.

'Thallberg is dead.'

Reinhardt's breath stopped. 'What? *How?*'

'Car crash. It seems.'

'When?'

'He was found about two hours ago. His car looks to have gone off the road into the Miljačka. There was a corporal in the car with him.'

'Corporal Beike,' said Reinhardt, quietly. 'Who told you?'

'I heard about it over the radio and sent Weninger down to look. He said Becker was there, as well as Putković. He got quite an earful from them. He told me they said you've had an interesting evening.'

'Did he see Thallberg's body?'

Freilinger nodded. 'And he couldn't tell if the car crash killed him or not. A bottle of slivovitz was found in his vehicle. And there was quite a bit of booze down the front of his jacket. And the corporal's. Seemed like they'd been having quite the party.'

'Thallberg drove a motorbike. And he preferred beer to whisky.'

'Quite. Well, the issue is not so much who killed him – we can probably guess that – but what he might have said before he died. What were you planning?'

'We were planning on going down to the front. To question Verhein and Stolić.'

'Then you need to get going. Quickly. If they've killed Thallberg, there is every chance they'll come after you.'

Reinhardt stared back at him. '*Now?* How can I?'

'Just do what you planned to do.'

'Just like that? I mean, I don't even know where they are.'

'The 121st is operating south of Foča.'

'Why are you doing this?'

'This is an investigation that needs to end. And I suppose I am taking a chance you might choose to end it in a way advantageous to us.'

'To the resistance.' The way Reinhardt said it, it felt furtive, and that was wrong. He remembered the pistol and holstered it. 'Who told you last night about the police going to arrest Jelić? Was it Becker?' Freilinger nodded. 'Why?'

Freilinger shrugged with his mouth as he tapped a mint into his palm. 'At a guess? He wanted you out of the way while he dealt with Thallberg. I don't suppose he thought you'd end up assaulting three Sarajevo policemen. Who is Dr Begović?'

If Reinhardt had not already been wary of what he said around Freilinger, perhaps the question might have thrown him. As it was, he simply shook his head. 'He is a doctor who sometimes works with the police. Putković seems to think he's also a Partisan. And that I'm helping him in some way or another.'

'Are you?'

'Not so far as I can ascertain, no,' lied Reinhardt, his mind focused on something else.

'Is he helping you?'

'Yes,' Reinhardt said after a moment. 'He gave me the film. You have not been completely honest with me, sir. You told me of the police going to arrest Jelić. You didn't have to do that. What did *you* stand to gain by having me out of the way last night?'

Freilinger gave a small, tight smile. 'One can be too devious, Reinhardt. I should not have told you, but... I did. Just say,' he swallowed, 'that the discussion you had with Meissner moved me. And at the risk of sounding pretentious, you were perhaps due a little action. You have been doing an awful lot of thinking these past couple of days.'

'So you think I should leave?'

'Now. Otherwise I am not sure what Becker might do. I don't think you can do much against him and the police together.'

Reinhardt sat on his bed. He looked around the room. 'I've not had the time to arrange anything.'

'No need. Claussen is downstairs with your vehicle and supplies.'

'*Claussen?*'

'I asked him if he would go with you. He said yes.' Reinhardt gave a little laugh, feeling like flotsam, that the current of events was leaving him no choice, even if... even if this was what had been planned. 'Reinhardt, you need to decide now. You were told to stop this investigation, and you didn't. You are accused by the Sarajevo police of aiding and abetting the Partisans. Becker will come for you if you stay, and you have, if I may put it bluntly, no friends strong enough to cover for you. You are going to be in real trouble here, and I can't deny you're likely to get yourself in trouble if you leave. But if you get going, I can cover your tracks for a while, and you may be able to outrun any word he sends and' – he paused – 'who knows how things might end up turning out.'

It was more the *way* Freilinger spoke – that hoarse rasp – as he outlined the odds stacked against Reinhardt than the odds themselves that decided him. Reinhardt nodded and rose to his feet. 'Ten minutes,' he said. 'I'll see you downstairs. And, sir?' Freilinger paused at the door. 'Thank you.'

Reinhardt took a moment to wash his face, make his ablutions, and thought back to the way this had all started, just like this, just three days ago. A knock at the door in the early morning. News that turned your life on its head. He was not the same man now. He felt calmer, more centreed, more at peace with himself than he had felt in a long while. For all he seemed to have dug himself a hole, he felt he could now see further than he could for a long time, and for all that the days had seemed to draw themselves out interminably, he felt events now accelerating past the point where he could control them, even if he had wanted to.

He packed a few things in a rucksack – a change of clothes, his toiletry bag, then the file. He slipped Carolin's picture from its frame and folded it into his tunic pocket, noting the wear and tear on his uniform, the whisper of threads at the end of the embroidered eagle. Looking around the room, he saw nothing else to take, and, if he was honest, his chances of coming back were slim.

Downstairs, Freilinger was waiting next to a *kübelwagen* that had been kitted out for a mission. A spare tyre with a rope coiled around it was fixed to the front deck, shovels and cans of water were strapped to the sides, and a pair of MP 40s were racked behind the front seats. Claussen stood arranging supplies on the rear bench. Reinhardt walked up to him, then offered his hand. Claussen took it.

'Sergeant,' Reinhardt said. 'I am… happy that you are coming.' Claussen just nodded, handed over a helmet with a set of goggles attached, and put his rucksack into the car.

Freilinger handed over a sheaf of fuel coupons. 'Which way will you go?'

'The eastern road, through Rogatica. It's a bit less travelled than the southern route. It'll be quicker.'

Freilinger nodded. 'I'll try to put it about subtly that you took the road south through Trnovo, then.' He seemed to hesitate, then extended his hand. 'Good luck, Reinhardt.' He thought a moment, his lips tight. 'I am sorry we didn't trust you sooner with what we knew and suspected.'

Reinhardt took his hand, remembering the conversation with Meissner. 'Sir. When did it begin for you?'

'Resistance?' Reinhardt nodded. Freilinger held his eyes. 'Kragujevac,' he said, simply, and nothing more was needed. Freilinger gripped Reinhardt's hand hard, and then he was gone.

As they drove out of the barracks, the sky was still dark and dotted with stars, but the tops of the hills on either side of the valley were silky with the coming dawn. Turning right at Vijećnica, they drove up past the old stone span of the Goat Bridge – for centuries the point that marked the beginning of the long, long road to Constantinople – climbing up and around the rocky flanks of the mountains that channelled the river into the city, into the rising sun, until up ahead they saw a sandbagged checkpoint at the crossing where the road forked. Straight on and up, to Bare and Stambulčić, or left, deeper into the mountains, towards Rogatica in its valley, towards Goražde and Foča on the banks of the Drina, towards the far-flung slopes of Mount Sutješka, where Operation Schwarz was now under way.

Various signs were posted at the checkpoint, including the by now standard one for Berlin (1,030 kilometres, apparently) and one for vehicles to stop and check in. A Feldgendarme corporal put down his cup of coffee next to the barrel of the heavy machine gun covering the road and saluted Reinhardt, casting a bleary eye over the vehicle.

'Corporal. How are things ahead?' asked Reinhardt, lifting the goggles.

The Feldgendarme indicated a status board leaning against the sandbags. 'Latest is the road's clear as far as Rogatica. You'll have to check in there for conditions farther on. Your destination?'

'Foča.' He proffered his movement orders at the Feldgendarme, who glanced at them before handing them back.

'Safe trip, sir.'

Reinhardt nodded and took a deep breath, lowering the goggles back down. He shared a quick glance with Claussen, then squared his shoulders and looked ahead. Claussen hauled the wheel left and started down the road. The Feldgendarme watched them go until, flickering through the trees, the car vanished over a rise and the sound of its engine faded away into the still air of the mountains.

Part Three

33

THURSDAY

As they left the checkpoint behind, the road switchbacked up Mount Romanja, which lay athwart their route east, snaking through lands that had once been well inhabited, and past houses, alone or in hamlets, built of wood and dressed stone. Most were empty, and many were destroyed, walls collapsed in rubble and skewed timbers blackened and burned, gardens and fields overgrown and abandoned. These lands had been farmed and worked mainly by Serbs until the Ustaše came, and most of the people had been slaughtered, rounded up in camps, or driven off into the arms of either the Partisans or the Četniks. Signs of life were few. A spiral of smoke from a chimney, a handful of goats that twitched their heads nervously as the car went by, washing hanging from a line.

They rose higher up the rounded flanks of the mountain, the countryside flattening into view to their left. As always, when he saw it from the heights, Reinhardt found something about the Bosnian forest that registered on a level below that of rational conception. It spread out beneath and around them, a canopy of varied greens and shifting forms, rising and falling with the land hidden beneath it, and the earth was lobed by the frayed sweep and curve of hills, fissured sometimes by flanks of exposed rock like the bleached karstic bones of the land.

The road swung across the rounded summit, through a forest sunk in gloom, the trees flowing against the blue sky that streamed overhead through a tracery of branches. They drove past mountain meadows across which marched the matchsticks of broken fences made to keep in livestock long gone. Big houses, like chalets or ranches, stood abandoned and gutted. When they emerged from the forest, at a point where the road swung down the other side of Romanja, they stopped for a break and to have something to eat.

Claussen had brought a flask of coffee and some bread and sausage, and Reinhardt walked to the edge of the road, sipping from a mug, and looked down across the country below them. The road wound away across flatlands to where a range of mountains broached the haze around their foothills, summits seeming to hang in the air like the brushstrokes of a painter. Standing there, he felt happy or, at least, resigned to a course of action. Perhaps they were the same thing, he mused, as he took the Williamson from his pocket, rolling it over in his hand and watching the play of light across the inscription. In any case, happiness did not mean conversation. Neither he nor Claussen had exchanged more than a couple of words since they left, but there was a comfort in that silence that he was loath to break for the sake of mere speech.

They did need to talk, though. Finishing his coffee and lighting cigarettes for them both, Reinhardt spread a map on the hood of the *kübelwagen*. The wind lifted one edge, and he weighed it down with the watch. 'Have you ever driven down to Foča? No? Two possible roads there from Sarajevo. South, through Trnovo, Dobro Polje, then east to Miljevina. Or east, then south through Rogatica and Goražde. That's the road we're on. It's a fairly straight run through Rogatica' – he pointed to the map southeast of their position – 'to Goražde' – farther south still – 'and then along the Drina to Foča. Schwarz is aimed at the Partisans, here,' he said, his finger circling the map south of Foča, over Mount Sutješka. 'But this is where we might have trouble. Brod.' He pointed to a section on the map where the Drina, flowing north, made a sharp turn east towards Foča. Brod was where the southern and eastern roads met. A crossroads. If word of them had gone out, it would find them at Brod. 'I don't know of any way around it...' He trailed off, looking at the map. 'Nothing for it but to get there as fast as we can and then... play it by ear, I suppose,' he finished, tossing the cigarette butt away, picking up the Williamson.

'A favour, sir?' Claussen motioned at the watch. 'What's the story with that? Never seen you with it before.'

Reinhardt ran his fingers over the inscription, giving himself time to surmount the reluctance within to talk of it. Only Brauer and Meissner knew the story. And poor old Isidor Rosen, but if anyone deserved to hear it now, it was Claussen. 'It was that same battle in 1918 I got the Cross. That British redoubt. We fought a game of cat-and-mouse with the Tommies through the trenches for three days. I killed their officer, but not before he gave me this,' he said, pointing at his knee, 'and ended my war. Before he died, he gave me the watch and... asked me to give it back to his father if I survived the war.' He paused, remembering suddenly, vividly, the viscous slide of mud, the latrine stench, the spatter of men across the bottom of the trenches. 'I put it down to things a dying man says. But then the war ended and what he said stayed with me. I wrote to his father. We met. Spoke of his son. I offered him back the watch, but he said to keep it.' Which he had, the watch taking on a significance that, after all this time, even Reinhardt himself was not sure of anymore. Only that it reminded him of a chance meeting of kindred spirits, a short space of time when he could be something other than the creature he was turning into, and because that Englishman was the last man he killed in that war, and that was worth remembering.

He weighed it in his hand, hesitating, then pulled the file from his backpack. 'This is what it's about. The evidence against Verhein.' He explained the case, outlining what they knew and suspected, Claussen's eyes moving from the file, to him, and back.

'You can't leave that lying around,' Claussen said when Reinhardt had finished. He took a crowbar from the tool kit and levered the spare tyre away from its rim. 'Under here,' he said, voice strained. Reinhardt pushed and shoved the file under the tyre, against the inner tube. When it was done, they shared a blank look, a shared complicity that needed no words.

They set off again, descending steeply down the side of the mountain until the road emerged onto the flats, and Claussen opened the throttle and put the car on the road that arrowed straight across a wide, empty prairie, where the light undulated over a wash of grass runnelled winter pale and spring green. Gradually the foothills ahead emerged out of the haze, and the flats ended, the road sliding its way down into a deep canyon, down to where Rogatica nestled in its valley. The road took them past a destroyed hamlet, past an Orthodox church with its steeple blown off, the remains of its walls skirted in rubble, and through scarred neighbourhoods that showed the signs of much fighting, until they found the German headquarters.

A Feldgendarmerie officer informed Reinhardt that the road to Goražde was backed up with traffic, and movement was slow around the bridge over the Praća. As they drove slowly back out, the town seemed sunk under a slough of decay and abandonment. Bullet holes pocked the walls; many houses were destroyed, and more burned out. Charcoal scrawls on some of the walls showed crosses, Catholic and Orthodox. Once, a Star of David on a house where the doors and windows gaped open. What few people he saw seemed stooped over, whatever their age, their eyes elsewhere. There were Serbs among them, mostly old women in black headscarves and black dresses who walked with a bandy-legged shuffle. Reinhardt could feel the fear in the town. As in the lands around Sarajevo, Rogatica's Serbs had mostly been deported, massacred, or fled to the hills.

Leaving Rogatica, the road wound through a gorge between high cliffs of blunt rock. It was cold, the sun shut out by the height of the rock walls. A wind blew down the steep cut in the mountains, bringing with it a dark, damp chill that seemed to push them on their way until, at length, the mountains pulled apart and the vista suddenly opened out. The light changed, as if a gauze had been snatched away, and they drove along the lathered shores of a river, the Prača rushing east out of the mountains, a froth of water that foamed and streamed away to the east towards Višegrad. The sun shone brightly on the brilliant green of the water, and on the other side thickly forested hills rose straight from the river. A military bridge spanned the Prača, the river backing and curling around its pillars, and that was their road south.

An Italian convoy was stopped in front of the bridge, heavy trucks with their engines off and their drivers idling around the vehicles. 'Road down to Goražde's too narrow, sir,' said a Feldgendarme, saluting Reinhardt as he asked what was going on. 'Medical convoy's coming up from Goražde, so they've got priority. Won't be long now, I would think.'

'Time for a break,' said Reinhardt, walking back to Claussen. He stretched as Claussen began checking the car. Huddled around the spire of a mosque was a hamlet tucked up against the sides of the cliff that faced out over the water. A small herd of goats picked at the grass on the steep shoulders of the road. An old lady had a small fire going, pots hanging over and in the flames. Reinhardt sorted through the supplies on the backseat.

'Do we have any coffee?'

'Pack on the floor,' replied Claussen, checking the *kübelwagen*'s tyres, a Mokri clamped in the corner of his mouth. 'You want one?'

'Not for me, sir, thank you.'

Reinhardt found coffee and sugar and walked up to the lady. She backed away from him, staring up at him from the stoop in her back. He offered the tins to her. 'Coffee? Can you make me some coffee?'

By dint of gesture and a few words, he seemed to make her understand, and she fetched a small metal pot and began to make the coffee in the traditional way he had come to appreciate. She handed it to him in a chipped mug, and he lit a cigarette as he stood by her fire, staring around him. This was a truly beautiful spot, with the river, the plunge of the mountains. A man could be happy here, raising a family.

Something caught his eye on the far shore, and he stared at it a moment, his eyes squinting around a curl of smoke from his cigarette, before realizing it was a burned-out house. Where there was one, there were usually more, and his eyes found them eventually, in their ones and twos, scattered across the face of the mountain. Someone had gone to quite some trouble to burn those people out, the houses standing blackened and empty, like skulls.

Skulls got him thinking of Stolić, and of Verhein. He knew he had no real plan, no real idea of how to approach these two, or where to find them. He had movement orders as far as Foča, and he had Thallberg's letter, which he knew he had to be careful about using. He also had to assume Becker would soon realise he was gone from Sarajevo, if not already, and the word would be going out to the Feldgendarmerie. Any checkpoint at any time might stop and detain him. Which of them was the priority? Stolić was SS. Strictly speaking, as an army officer Reinhardt had no authority to question him at all. He was, however, Verhein's liaison, so maybe the best thing would be to start with Verhein, and then request permission to question Stolić. Thinking about Stolić had him thinking about that knife. The knife was one of the keys, he knew, but he still could not quite factor it into how the murders had played out that Saturday night.

Movement on the other side of the bridge became a convoy of trucks with red crosses on their sides. Over the bridge they came, passing in front of him on their way to Rogatica. There was movement all along the stopped vehicles, the creak of metal and stamp of doors, and engines coughed into life with gusts of black exhaust.

Reinhardt drank the last of his coffee and picked up his tins. Pausing, he looked among the old lady's possessions and saw two empty little pots. He emptied half his coffee and half his sugar into each of them. The lady looked at the pots, then at him, and her face opened up, as if something within wished to get out. Her eyes stared up at him from deep within their sockets, but then there was a blast of noise, the Feldgendarmerie blowing their whistles, engines revving, and whatever it was, was gone. Her face closed up and in, the wrinkles on her face drawing tight, like the threads of a net, and the light in her eyes fell back and down, closing around whatever words might have bridged that sudden small space between them. Claussen had the engine running as Reinhardt climbed back into the car, and as it pulled away he looked up at her, lonely by her fire, a little pot in each hand.

34

The convoy of trucks rumbled over the bridge, the *kübelwagen* at its tail, and after about an hour of driving they came down into Goražde through small villages where most of the houses were burned. The city was spread out along both banks of the Drina, connected by a pair of bridges, and long rectangular fields ran up from the banks of the river and into the bluffs of the hills, minarets poking up above the town's red roofs.

Although the streets reminded him of the old Ottoman city in Sarajevo with their cobbles and whitewashed houses, the town was choked with refugees. They were mostly farmers, it seemed, Muslims by their dress, and they stank of fear and the rich, heavy earth they farmed. Men and women bred to a tough life, but with desperation and fatigue etched into the leathered grime of their faces. In their slope-shouldered stance, gnarled hands listless by their sides, he saw a resigned incomprehension to the vagaries their lives had become, and he was reminded of that porter in Sarajevo bent double under his load. He wondered again what such people thought – could think – of events such as these that cut straight across the steady furrows of their lives, uprooting them from the mute certainties and traditions of their fathers, and their fathers before them.

They drifted slowly past the dull gaze of the refugees, past the Italian garrison, following the tactical signs to the German headquarters in a hotel just next to the first of the town's bridges.

'That doesn't look too good,' Claussen said, as he parked and leaned forward, putting his weight on the steering wheel.

Parked in front of the hotel were an Italian staff car and a car with Ustaše plates. An Italian stood at parade rest next to his car, with an Ustaša slouching against the front bumper of his. As he stepped out of the *kübelwagen*, Reinhardt could feel the tension between them. The Italian straightened and saluted him; the Ustaša barely moved.

'Bit of a risk, isn't it, sir?' Claussen asked.

Reinhardt nodded, his hands feeling clammy. 'Don't see how we can avoid it. We need to know what's ahead.'

Exchanging salutes with a sentry, he paused in the entrance, listening to the buzz of conversations, the ringing of phones. Inside was a hum of activity, and Reinhardt could feel the edge in the air that proximity to action sometimes brought on. He knocked on a door marked OPERATIONS. Inside, several soldiers sat at desks working on telephones and a harassed-looking lieutenant stood as he came in.

'Sir?'

'I'm on my way down to Foča, Lieutenant, and I wanted to know the conditions of the roads between here and there.'

The lieutenant pointed to a tactical map and was about to speak when a burst of shouting from somewhere in the hotel stopped him. A couple of the soldiers on the phones looked up, and one exchanged a knowing glance with the lieutenant. No one explained, however, and Reinhardt did not ask for details. 'The road down to Foča is still considered safe for single-vehicle traffic. We have not had any confirmed Partisan activity on it for several weeks now, but don't use it after dark. It's just past midday, so you should be in Foča in about an hour if you leave now.'

There was more shouting and a thump of feet. Reinhardt looked up at the room's ceiling, raising his eyebrows.

'Just our Italian allies having a bit of a tantrum, sir.'

'About?'

'The Ustaše, I would imagine, sir, it usually is.'

Closing the operations room door, he heard a clatter on the stairs and someone shouting again. Two Italians came down, one a colonel no less, followed by a German captain. The colonel was visibly furious, his knuckles stretched white against the hat clenched in his fist, which he slammed against his thigh to emphasise his words.

'Barbarians!' he seethed, his German thick with an Italian accent. 'Absolute *barbarians!*'

The captain caught sight of Reinhardt and frowned but kept his attention on the Italian. 'I am sorry, sir,' he said, with an air of having repeated the same thing several times already. 'There is little I can do about it. Please, I advise you to take your complaint to divisional headquarters.'

'My *complaint*?' roared the Italian. He looked up past the German at two Ustaše coming down the stairs in their black uniforms. The colonel shook his fist up at them. 'They are *your* allies,' he bellowed. '*Yours!* Control them. Do *something.*' One of the Ustaše paused on the stairs, his mouth stretched in a sneer of a smile, and the vitriol in his reply was evident. The Italian went red, let loose a strangled expletive, erupted in a stream of Italian, and made to climb back up the stairs, but the captain got in his way, his arms up; the other Italian spoke urgently into the colonel's ear, and he allowed himself to be pulled away, still roaring in fury.

The Ustaše laughed and came downstairs, screwing on their caps. The German officer stood in the doorway until the Italians had left. The Ustaše seemed not to care, sniggering among themselves. One of them turned and saw him, and Reinhardt recognised him as the one who had been at Stolić's table back at the Ragusa. Ljubčić, Freilinger said his name was. Then the captain was gesturing them out, and Reinhardt did not know if the Ustaša had recognised him. They gave the captain a mocking salute and were gone, laughing and nudging each other.

'You are… ?' the captain asked as the Ustaše drove away, people cowering to either side of the car as it cut through the crowded streets.

'Reinhardt, Abwehr,' he said, shaking hands with the officer.

'Seigler,' sighed the captain as he removed his cap and ran a hand through thinning hair.

'What was all that about?'

Seigler shook his head. 'The Italians claim the Ustaše have been… that they destroyed a village south of here and massacred everyone in it. The village was once Serbian, until they were all… killed. Then Muslims moved into it after they were displaced by Četniks.' He sighed again. 'He's probably right.'

'He *is* right,' said Reinhardt, looking out at the slow shuffle of refugees.

'What?'

'They are our allies.'

Seigler shrugged. 'Yes. Well, we usually can control the… worst… of it with them, but with the operation, everything's committed to that and they are pretty much free to…' He trailed off. 'Although now the colonel's saying it's the SS encouraging the Ustaše.'

Reinhardt swallowed slowly, keeping his eyes as uninterested as possible. 'SS? In this area?'

'Liaison unit. Arrived about a day ago. I think they're down near Foča. Maybe Kalinovik.' The captain's eyes drifted away.

'Town's full,' said Reinhardt.

Seigler nodded. 'They started coming in two days ago. There's been fighting up along the approaches to Čajniče,' he said, motioning behind and across the river where the hills swelled up into the distance. He frowned. 'Is there something I can help you with?'

Reinhardt shook his head. 'Just updated route information to Foča. Your operations people have already helped me.'

'Good. Well, drive carefully.'

Reinhardt stood there a moment after Seigler left. The hotel was near the river, and there was a sandbank out in the flow, a smooth teardrop shape, white sand shining in the sun. Children were playing on it, seemingly oblivious to the choked tenor of the streets, and their laughter drifted faintly across the rush of the river as it purred along over its rocky bed. He felt very afraid, and very cold. An SS unit could mean anything, but it almost certainly meant Stolić, and if, as it seemed, he was in a killing mood, Reinhardt had no idea how he would approach him, nor what the presence of that Ustaša might mean. He told Claussen what he had learned. The sergeant swigged from a canteen, screwing his eyes shut as he lifted his face to the light and wiped the back of his mouth with a blocky fist.

'Change of plan?'

Reinhardt shook his head. 'Let's get going. We should be able to make Foča in an hour, maybe less.'

The drive to Foča was uneventful but particularly beautiful. The Drina flowed in broad, languid sweeps and bends to the left, now bottle green, now turquoise, now a lather of foam where it ran shallow over its stony bed, rocks lying like mosaics. The land along the river was good, the rich alluvial soil ripe for crops, the banks dotted with small hamlets and settlements, but the signs of war were everywhere. Many of the villages were empty or destroyed, fields and crops unkempt and uncared for, and on the far bank, smoke ribboned up from burning houses. The fighting along the Drina had been bitter and internecine since the war first came here in 1941, with Četniks massacring Muslims, Ustaše massacring Serbs, and the land suffering under the succession of German, Italian, Croat, and Partisan armies.

The road was busier, mostly German traffic coming up from Foča, but they passed a bus trailing a plume of filthy exhaust, horse carts, and men, women, and children on foot. More refugees, haunted and hunched under what little they had, herded and pressed to the side of the road by soldiers in Croatian Army uniforms.

Despite the thickening traffic, they made good time to Foča, the road crossing over an iron bridge with sheet metal flooring that clanked and clattered under the car's wheels. The town was much narrower and darker than Goražde, and like Rogatica showed the signs of fighting: bullet holes in walls, the heaped remnants of destroyed houses like rotted teeth in the lines of streets. As for the townspeople, it seemed most of them were gone, and the place had an empty, haunted feel despite the troops who thronged through it – German and Croat mostly. They passed a group of Četniks gathered on the steps of a dilapidated building that looked like it had once been something official, a shambles of shaggy ponies and rickety carts, and men with thick beards and long hair that splayed out from under rectangular caps and who watched them go by with sullen expressions, distrust writ large across their heavy features.

They followed the tactical signs to the local headquarters building. While Claussen went in search of fuel, Reinhardt searched through the scrum of activity inside, finally cornering a harassed operations lieutenant who pointed at a map to a location west of Foča. '121st were at Brod last night. They were supposed to advance on Predelj today,' he continued, tapping the map farther south. 'Last information is their reconnaissance battalion is stalled somewhere here,' he said, pointing to the long, twisting route that led south from Brod towards Šćepan Polje, on the Montenegrin border. If you're looking for them, they're around there.'

'How's the operation going?'

'Well, I think. Early days. Some pretty stiff fighting over by Čajniče. Lots of confirmed kills. That's all I can tell you for now,' he finished, as he turned to answer a telephone.

Reinhardt stared at the map a moment, feeling a sudden wash of nerves as he contemplated how close he suddenly was. Reinhardt felt someone behind him and turned to see Claussen standing in the doorway, his face drawn tight.

35

'I think we have trouble, sir,' he said quietly. There was a window with a view onto the street. 'There.' Following his finger, Reinhardt saw a Feldgendarmerie unit parked, two motorcycles with sidecars. There was one man standing by the machines, his uniform dirty and lined with white dust. 'They came down the Kalinovik road about five minutes ago,' said Claussen. 'Don't know if they're after us, but I got the strong sense they were in a hurry. They went into the Feldgendarmerie post right after they arrived,' he continued. He paused, as if waiting for Reinhardt to say something, but nothing was forthcoming. 'Where to, sir?' he asked.

'The 121st was in Brod,' Reinhardt said after a moment. 'West of here, bit less than half an hour's drive if we're lucky.'

'I don't think we should take any chances,' said Claussen, panning his eyes across the street. 'There's a parking lot around the back. I can meet you there. I doubt they're looking for me.'

Stepping out into the back of the building, Reinhardt passed through a crowded parking area, trucks and cars and troop carriers in serried rows. There was a wall and fence of dry-looking wood topped with a twist of barbed wire along the length of the parking area where it ran along a lane around the back of the headquarters. He made himself walk easily past the vehicles, skirting a platoon of soldiers as they boarded trucks under the hoarse instructions of a sergeant. He lit a cigarette as he came up to the sentry at the back gate, just as Claussen pulled up in the lane. Reinhardt saluted the sentry as he went past, ignoring him but feeling himself tense up as he waited for a challenge, but none came.

Claussen pulled away gently, bumping the car over the rutted lane past dishevelled houses that seemed to sag under the weight of unkempt roofs. The place reeked of despondency, the whole town seeming to be holding its breath, as if in expectation of more violence than it had already suffered. After a few minutes' driving, they found the tarred road that ran through the centre of town, with the Drina a long stone's throw to their right. 'Left, now,' said Reinhardt, unfolding a map, 'then find somewhere to pull over.'

The houses petered out into a jumble of scrubland, and Claussen pulled over in front of a house with a gaping hole in its second floor. The two of them looked at Reinhardt's map. 'The 121st is somewhere along this road, leading south from Brod,' Reinhardt said. 'To get there we'll need to get through the crossroads at Brod, and there's bound to be controls there. If those Feldgendarmerie came down the road from Miljevina,' he said, his finger tracing the road that headed south from Sarajevo and then swung east and ran through Trnovo to Foča, 'and if they're looking for us, then chances are the controls may have been reinforced.' He paused, running his eyes over and over the map, looking for a way, any way, to get through Brod. If Thallberg had been with them, he might have known a way, or he would probably just have taken them through any control, trusting in the authority of the GFP.

'I've got no bright ideas, sir,' said Claussen. 'I don't know this country at all, but' – he paused, looking back over his shoulder – 'that platoon is coming up behind us. We might tag along with them. Safety in numbers.' The trucks clanked past, open-topped and filled with soldiers, some of whom glanced over at them incuriously, and Reinhardt nodded at Claussen.

The sergeant accelerated the *kübelwagen* after them, keeping a short way back as the road wound along the steep sides of the hills along the south bank of the Drina. Ahead, one of the soldiers flicked his cigarette butt out into the road, where it bounced and sparked. Reinhardt followed it as it rolled to the side of the road and saw movement out of the corner of his eye behind them. Shifting in his seat to look back down the road, he saw a flash of grey through the trees.

'Trouble?' asked Claussen, as he straightened in his seat.

'I think those motorcycles are behind us.'

Claussen glanced into the *kübelwagen*'s wing mirrors. Reinhardt could hear them after a moment, the high pitch of their engines getting louder and louder. 'It's those two, sure enough,' said Claussen, tightly. He shifted the car to the side of the road and waved them by. They went past in a surge of noise and dust, the rider of each sidecar holding on to a mounted machine gun. The second one seemed to pause, just a moment, the passenger's eyes lost behind his goggles as he looked at them. Reinhardt went cold, a chill erupting all over him as he forced himself to remain still, and then the motorcycles were onto the road ahead of them. Reinhardt's breath came short and high as he waited for them to stop, to pull them over, but they caught up to the trucks, weaved around them, and were gone.

Claussen puffed out a breath and exchanged a wry look with him. Reinhardt laughed, an explosive release of tension, and Claussen laughed back. The sergeant shook his head. 'Like geese before Christmas, the pair of us,' he snorted. Ahead and below them, a cluster of buildings stood inside a tight bend in the Drina, the river flowing up from the south and swinging sharply to the east. A road wound out of a steep-sided valley ahead of them and split, one fork continuing south on the far bank of the river, another crossing the Drina over a stone bridge. From here, they could see that the crossroads was busy, vehicles backed up on all three of its forks.

'Not out of the woods yet, seems like,' muttered Claussen as he followed the trucks down into the town, which, apart from the military traffic through it, seemed abandoned.

'Listen, Claussen, if it goes bad, you say you knew nothing.

Understood? You were just following my orders to drive me here.'

Claussen did not look back at him. 'Let's cross that bridge when we come to it, shall we, sir?' he said, as he braked behind the last truck. They moved forward slowly, the soldiers in the truck in front engrossed in a card game, and Reinhardt's nervousness grew as they crawled through the town and then over the bridge. They could see the checkpoint up ahead on the far side: sandbagged machine gun emplacements, a half-track, a tent with a radio mast. 'Here they come,' said Claussen, softly. A Feldgendarme walked up to the cab of the truck in front, said something to the driver, then waved it on. The truck pulled away, following the others as they went south. Reinhardt saw what he took to be one of the two motorcycles with its crew parked by the tent as the Feldgendarme waved them up, standing in front of a block of concrete placed in the road at the end of the bridge.

'Papers.' The Feldgendarme's eyes were hard and focused under the brim of his helmet. He checked their documents, then handed them back. 'Very well, proceed.'

Claussen pulled away, then paused as a convoy began passing in front of them. A space opened up between a truck and a pair of Kettenkrad half-tracks, and at a nod from Reinhardt, Claussen slipped the *kübelwagen* into the convoy. Reinhardt craned his neck to look in the mirror but saw no one at the checkpoint paying any attention to them, and then it was gone. He breathed out and exchanged a look with Claussen. The sergeant shrugged, no words needing to be said, the release of tension almost palpable.

The road ran almost due south here, clinging to the steep western bank of the Drina, the river flowing up from Montenegro down a narrow gorge thick with trees. The tarred road petered out soon after Brod, becoming a dirt track the engineers had resurfaced and reinforced in places. The trucks lifted plumes of white dust into the air, and Reinhardt and Claussen were soon covered in it until the sergeant was able to overtake them, and then the road was open to them, unrolling before them like a ribbon in twists and turns around the sides of the gorge. It was midafternoon, now, and very hot.

Reinhardt had no idea how far they would have to drive to find the 121st. If the unit was still in Predelj, it was about a dozen kilometres or so south of Brod, but on these roads that could take well over an hour. Thinking about it, he saw the first signs of fighting. A pair of burned-out trucks, a swath of forest that looked like it had been shelled, and farther on a chunk of earth gouged from the embankment that looked like it had been mined. As the road swung around the flank of the gorge, he saw, far off over the humped back of a ridge, plumes of smoke rising up into the sky and a spotter plane, a Storch, scribing tight circles over the hills. It swooped up, and moments later it seemed there was a shiver in the air, studs of light along the underside of the smoke as an artillery barrage came down. Seconds later came a ripple of noise, the crackle of explosions.

Claussen snaked around a big crater, and there was more wreckage by the roadside. Down in the trees above the river the back end of a half-track poked up from a cradle of bent and burned trees. Houses appeared, ones, twos, a ruined hamlet that still smoked, and then there, in the road, a Feldgendarmerie motorcycle with a trooper hunched over the foreshortened barrel of a machine gun. A second Feldgendarme stood in the road. As Claussen braked hard, Reinhardt spotted two more behind the cover of a low wall. He watched the Feldgendarme walk up to them. The man's MP 40 was held in both hands, not exactly aiming at them, but not turned away either. He looked at them expressionlessly, eyes tracking from one to the other.

'Pull the car over there.'

'What is the problem, Sergeant?' asked Reinhardt, putting an emphasis on the man's rank and holding his eyes. He was scared, again. From his breast pocket, he took Thallberg's paper naming him a GFP auxiliary.

'No problem. Sir. Over there, please.'

'Better.'

Claussen drove slowly to the side of the road and parked by the Feldgendarme behind the wall, the machine gunner on the sidecar following them all the way. 'Out of the car,' one of them snapped.

'What the hell is going on?' demanded Reinhardt, rising up in his seat.

There was a metallic rattle as the Feldgendarmes levelled their MP 40s at them. 'Out. Now.' Reinhardt and Claussen exchanged glances and stepped out of the car. 'Hands up.'

'I am with the GFP, Sergeant.'

'Shut up. And get your hands up.' The sergeant took the paper, gave the order to disarm them, and then at gunpoint ordered them up a narrow track towards a house. Farther up the path, across an open patch of ground, was another cluster of houses, with men lined up in front of it who had the hunch-shouldered look of prisoners, but that was neither here nor there as the Feldgendarmes pushed them inside, and face to face with Becker.

36

'Well, well, look what the cat brought in.' Becker smiled as he said it, but there was a tightness to his jaw, to his eyes, that belied his levity. He glanced at the paper as the sergeant handed it to him. 'Wait outside,' he said to the Feldgendarmes. There was a surge of light as the door opened and closed, and Reinhardt saw that Becker was holding a pistol against his leg. He smiled again. 'Quite a merry chase you've led us on, Gregor.'

'Well, if I'd known you wanted to play, Major, I'd have made a bit more of an effort for you,' said Reinhardt, forcing a levity into his voice that he did not feel.

Becker's eyes flicked to Claussen, and his brow creased slightly, as if trying to remember if he had ever met the sergeant. 'Who is this?'

'My driver.'

Becker flushed, as he always did when Reinhardt did not address him by rank. 'You. Wait outside with the other Feldgendarmes.'

Claussen did not move, and Becker's flush deepened. 'Wait outside, Sergeant,' said Reinhardt, after a moment. 'I'll call you if I need you.'

'Very good, sir,' said Claussen.

Becker smiled as the door closed. 'You have a habit of backing the wrong horse, Gregor. And you've done it again.'

'Which horse would that be?'

'A highly placed one. One that you should never have started to piss off. One that you know something about, and I want to know it, too.'

'You're not making sense, Becker,' said Reinhardt, dismissively, allowing his eyes to roam away from the major. There was not much, just a couple of rickety-looking chairs, a battered table with a tin water bottle on it, and a stack of chopped wood piled next to a blackened iron stove. The scent of earth and wood smoke mixed and merged in the humid atmosphere in the house.

'Look, I'm going to put this away,' Becker said, making a show of holstering his pistol. He took his glasses off, holding the frames in his two hands, facing to his left with his head up. 'You were right, the other day at police headquarters. I am looking for my ticket out of here. I've got a good one, but I think I see a better one with you, and what I reckon you've got.'

'Sense, Becker,' snapped Reinhardt, using the tone he used to use when he was Becker's superior in Kripo. 'Make sense. Start naming names. Or this is all so much hot air.'

'Names are dangerous, Gregor,' Becker snapped back. 'You know that.' Becker bit his lip, and Reinhardt could see the perspiration that lined his hair on either side of his parting. 'Look, I can tell you this much. Someone asked me to help them. Someone you don't say no to.'

'I never knew what to think when you opened your mouth, Becker. I still don't. So stop pissing around the pot. I'll give you a name, Becker. General Paul Verhein. How's that?'

'That's not a bad name, and he's part of it but not all of it.' Becker twisted his glasses in his hands, his stance shifting to his right, looking down. 'So this someone offered to help me in return. They didn't need much. They needed Lieutenant Krause found, and they needed whatever they thought he had. That's all.'

'And for that, you impeded an investigation into the murder of a German officer.'

'Oh, get off your high horse, Gregor, for fuck's sake,' Becker snapped. 'Yes, I *impeded* your investigation. So bloody what? You should never have had it in the first place.'

'And then what?'

'Then what?' Becker paused, as if he were about to say something else and thought better of it. 'Then things began getting out of hand. I couldn't find Krause, then there was the film, then you got in on the act and began making waves. Making people uncomfortable.' His stance shifted again.

'Tell me about Thallberg. And try to keep still, will you?'

Becker's mouth made an O of surprise. 'Keep… ?'

'Forget it. Thallberg.'

Becker shrugged. 'That wasn't supposed to happen like that.'

'Well, it did.'

'He came to me last night, accused me of… well, accused me of what I'd been doing, I suppose,' he said, nonchalantly, the old Becker starting to reemerge. 'Tempers flared, and he let slip that this was much bigger than covering up how some tart of a journalist met a sticky end. I told the people I was working for, and they told me to get what Thallberg knew. By any means.'

'You killed him.'

'I tried to make him a deal, but he was having none of it. Things… got out of hand. He didn't say much, actually. I got more out of his corporal. Like Hendel being SD, maybe Krause too, and actually after Verhein as well. What're the odds, eh?!' Becker giggled, suddenly. 'You can imagine my position, Gregor. Trying to get Verhein out of a sticky patch was my ticket out of here. Actually being able to get him into an even stickier patch might even be better for me. What's an honest cop to do?!' He giggled again, an edge to his hilarity like rust on a blade. 'I don't know exactly what Hendel and Krause had on Verhein, but I think you do, and I want to know what it is.'

'How did this "someone" know to ask you for your help?'

Becker shook his head, a little grin on his face, and he turned again. 'No. You don't get to know tha –'

'I said keep still. Still want to play silly games with the

names? You were out at Ilidža the night Vukić was killed. Trying to calm Stolić down.' Becker maintained his grin, but it went tight at the edges. 'An officer with a history of violence. You were last seen out there with him. And Vukić turns up dead shortly afterwards.'

Becker swallowed, moved his mouth a few times. 'That's good, Reinhardt. Very good. But you can't pin her murder on me.' He shook his head. 'No. You have something I need. A file, on Verhein, I believe. I'll trade for it. They'll kill you for it.'

'If I had such a file, you would be the last person I would give it to,' Reinhardt replied, with a confidence he was not sure he felt. It was so hot in the house. He picked up the water bottle, keeping Becker in his line of sight as he swigged from it.

'Help yourself,' murmured Becker.

'I didn't say I was trying to pin her murder on you. Hendel's, perhaps… A bit of a stretch, but I could probably do it.' His turn to grin now.

'You might,' Becker said after a moment. 'How about this, though? As much as you think you've got me over a barrel, I *know* I've got you over one. Disobeying orders. Consorting with the enemy. Interfering with a Feldgendarmerie investigation. Oh,' he said, looking down at the paper, 'and I'll want to talk to you about the deaths of Captain Hans Thallberg and Corporal Jürgen Beike.'

'Not interested.'

Becker held his eyes as he calmly tore the paper in two, then again. 'Still want to play silly buggers, Gregor?'

'Still not interested,' said Reinhardt, forcing a smirk as he held Becker's gaze.

'What exactly do you hope to achieve, here?' Becker's tone seemed honestly intrigued. 'You're trying to bring down a general. People like him don't sit still waiting for someone like you to prick them on the arse. Nor do the people around them. They'll swat you aside, especially at a time like this. Normally,' he grinned, 'I'd stand aside and enjoy that, but if you go down, I end up with a losing hand. Rather, I end up with a winning hand – I get that either way – but marginally less good,' he giggled.

Something in what Becker was saying sparked something in Reinhardt's mind. Something similar to what he and Thallberg had talked about. 'You keep saying "someone", referring to "they". You're not hiding Verhein from me. So he's not the one you're dealing with. Is he?' Becker's grin went tight again, and Reinhardt knew he had hit a nerve, and he had to keep hitting it. 'What do you have on them? Or what do they have on you? What happened in Ilidža that night? How did they bring you into this? Who is it, Becker?'

'You're fishing again, Gregor.'

'Ilidža,' repeated Reinhardt.

Becker turned to his right, lowering his head as he put his glasses back on. He drew his pistol, and although Reinhardt's breath hitched a second, Becker only held it down by his leg. 'I can wait a little longer for you to see sense. In the meantime, someone wants a quiet word with you. He may be able to help you see the relative merits of your position.' He gestured with the pistol. 'Outside.'

Reinhardt backed through the door, blinking in the bright daylight. Becker followed him through, and Reinhardt could see the strain he was under. His hair was soaked with sweat, and he opened his mouth to breathe, panting like a dog. Casting his eyes around quickly, Reinhardt could see no sign of Claussen, and he dared not ask about him in case he put him in more danger.

'Take Captain Reinhardt,' Becker said to his Feldgendarmes, nodding over to the other houses. 'Someone wants to talk to him.' One of the guards smiled. 'And when Captain Reinhardt is done, bring him back here.'

37

They ordered him up a rutted earthen track towards the cluster of houses Reinhardt had seen earlier. A couple of vehicles were parked outside them, one of them a Horch staff car with open sides. As Reinhardt came closer, he could see the SS plates and decals identifying them as belonging to 7th Prinz Eugen. He had not realised he had slowed until the guard who had smiled poked him in the back with the muzzle of his MP 40. More cars were parked in the trees, black-suited soldiers lounging around them. Ustaše, and one of them was Ljubčić. He looked back at Reinhardt, his eyes glittering.

Two SS troopers stood guard over a group of prisoners lined up outside a house. Some of the prisoners were obviously soldiers – Partisans – but others just seemed to be peasants. Farther on, an army truck was parked with a squad of soldiers standing around it, most of them smoking with their heads down and their hands in their pockets, and unless Reinhardt was very mistaken they were not happy with what was going on. Something caught his eye on the Horch's front seat. A tube, white with red caps, fetched up against the angle of the seat and its back.

There was a scream from inside the house. Long, drawn out, the choking sounds of a creature in agony. Then nothing. A sigh went through the prisoners, and the soldiers around the truck seemed to huddle closer together. The door to the house banged open and two more SS dragged a body outside and dumped it on the ground. At least two other bodies already lay there, but Reinhardt could not be sure because following the two SS out, a long, bloodied blade in his fist, was Standartenführer Mladen Stolić. He had a blank expression on his face, but his eyes were wide and staring over a smear of blood across one cheek, like the war paint of a red Indian. He saw Reinhardt and smiled. His teeth were very yellow in the gash of his mouth.

'I could get to like this liaison work,' leered Stolić. He was wearing a black shirt with his sleeves rolled up. His hands and forearms and the front of his shirt were bloodied and gored, and he carried the knife – the Bowie – in one fist, red to the hilt. He washed it in a rain bucket, wiping it clean and dry with a ragged cloth, breathing quick and light. There was a light in his eyes, the whites visible all around. Reinhardt could see the signs of his addiction clearly now, and wondered that he had not spotted them before.

'Let's talk, you and I,' Stolić said. 'Why don't we go inside? After you.' His hand trembled slightly, the blade quivering.

Reinhardt looked at the darkened doorway, at Stolić and his two SS, standing immobile and dough-faced. 'After you.'

'I insist,' grinned Stolić.

Reinhardt knew, somehow, he had to win this, this small test of wills. 'Make an old man happy.'

The Standartenführer chuckled again. He told his two men to wait outside, then stepped into the house, the rough boards of the floor creaking underfoot. Stolić made a grand gesture, a sort of cross between a genuflection and a bow, his arm spread wide, inviting Reinhardt in. 'Beauty before age, eh?' he smirked.

'In the trenches, we always used to say, "Shit before paper".'

Stolić stiffened, then turned, shutting the door. The corner of his eye twitched as he smiled. 'You're very funny, Reinhardt.'

'I've been told that, you know.'

Stolić blinked, his smile fading away. 'You've been asking questions again, haven't you?' He held the big knife by the pommel, twirling it back and forth between the tips of his fingers. 'Telling tales out of school. Old man,' he said, with a lazy sneer.

A long flash of light went up the Bowie as he spun it back, then forth. The blade had a curl at the end, the last part of the top edge curving sharply down to the point, and Reinhardt remembered that pathology report, the strange shape of the wounds on Vukić's body. Stolić stepped closer to Reinhardt. 'I often wonder what you old timers're made of,' he said. He tapped the tip of his blade on Reinhardt's Iron Cross. *Tick tick tick.* 'What would you have to do these days to get one of these?' *Tick tick.* 'A bit more than floundering around in the mud. No?' *Tick.* The blade paused, that wickedly curved point resting on the medal. Stolić pushed slightly, then harder. Reinhardt let himself be pushed to the side, then back. Stolić's eyes widened, brightened, vanished behind a slow blink. 'I mean, really, how hard could it have been?'

Reinhardt breathed long and slow, feeling a flush of anger creeping up his back, and that light-headedness that presaged something reckless. 'A bit harder than putting on a black uniform and pretending it makes you German.'

Stolić's face tightened. 'Don't piss me off any more than you've done already, Reinhardt.'

'Heaven forbid.'

The light in Stolić's eyes hardened, then lightened. 'What've you got there in your pocket? Not fiddling with yourself, are you?!'

Reinhardt had not realised he was holding the Williamson, and held it up. Stolić stepped closer and peered at the inscription on the casing. 'What does it say?'

Reinhardt did not have to read it. He knew the words by heart. By feel. 'It says, "*To Lieutenant Terence Blackwell-Gough, 5th Somerset Rifles, from his father, Michael Blackwell-Gough. November 1917*".' He realised as he spoke them that he rarely said them out loud. They took on a different rhythm and weight, he realised. He looked at the old watch, as if seeing it anew.

'I didn't know you spoke any English.'

Reinhardt shrugged noncommittally. 'A few words.'

'Tell me its story.'

'Why?'

Stolić grinned. 'Something to pass the time. Break the ice. 'Cause I'm asking nicely. Take your pick.'

Reinhardt shook his head. 'I took it off a dead Englishman. That's all you need to know.'

'The only Englishmen I ever met in Spain weren't worth all that much. Most of them finished up on the end of this,' Stolić drawled, sloughing through Reinhardt's memory, his eyes focusing on the tip of his knife.

'Most Englishmen I came up against would have snapped you in two without thinking about it.' Stolić put the Bowie's point back on Reinhardt's Iron Cross, pushed. It slipped, caught up against the medal's edge. 'What is with you and the knife?'

Stolić smiled at it. 'Part of an Ustaša's holy triptych, Reinhardt. "Knife, revolver, bomb." The most effective and suitable means to an end. You know, we took our oaths in front of a crucifix, a knife, and a revolver.'

'Except now you're SS. And you're still playing with boys' toys like knives?' Stolić pushed hard again on the Cross, but this time Reinhardt took a quick step back, let Stolić's weight pull him forward. 'And what is it with you and medals? You want one?'

The Standartenführer's face went white, then red. 'Tell me, Reinhardt, have you actually *killed* anyone in this war? Or have you spent it behind your desk while others did it for you?'

'I'm sure my body count's not as high as yours, but most of the ones I killed could shoot back.'

Stolić snorted. 'Why have them shoot back? An unfair fight's a fair fight by me.' He flipped the knife, caught it by the handle. He grinned, yellow teeth like filthy nails. 'It's like a drug. All this.'

'And I did my killing with a clear head.'

'What?'

'How long have you been addicted to Pervitin?'

'*What?*'

'You're addicted to Pervitin, Stolić. Addicted to speed. I saw the pills in your car. I can see the signs of addiction all over you.'

'Wha… ?'

'It takes more than popping pills and butchering unarmed men to make you a brave man, Stolić.'

Stolić's face creased into a snarl. 'I don't need any fucking pills to make me –'

'You take them because you're weak, Stolić. Because they make you feel better about yourself. About missing out on all the action in Russia. About not being more like Grbić,' said Reinhardt, remembering the name of that Croatian Army colonel Stolić seemed to despise so.

'*Grbić?* What do you –'

'Did you kill Marija Vukić?'

A flush crept up Stolić's neck, the planes of his cheeks going red. 'You arrogant little shit,' he hissed. 'You accuse me… ?'

Reinhardt felt cold and focused, but a part of him gibbered at the risks he was taking. He pushed that part away, the weak part, the part that had cowered in the corner of Meissner's house all those years ago, the part that had run away from his life as it was then instead of trying, however futilely, to make it right. He forced himself to smile at Stolić and then found that it felt right, and he did not have to force it after all. 'Vukić was really something.' Stolić's face went blank. 'She'd have got an Iron Cross if she were a man. That drove you mad, didn't it?'

Stolić made a sound, as if he were gagging. 'You don't –'

'She was more of a man than you'll ever be,' Reinhardt slashed across Stolić's words.

Stolić hefted the knife, holding it out in front of him in his right hand. 'I don't care what Becker said,' he muttered, seeming to talk to himself. 'I'm going to cut you up, you miserable turd.' He stopped, frowned. Reinhardt drew his baton and extended it. Stolić sniggered. 'What the fuck is that? A magic wa –' Reinhardt flicked the baton at Stolić's fist. The tip flexed and slashed into Stolić's knife hand. He squalled in surprise and pain, and the knife flashed and clanged to the floor. Reinhardt whipped the baton up and slashed it down into the junction of Stolić's neck and shoulder. The Standartenführer slumped to his knees with another cry.

'You piece of *shit*,' Reinhardt snarled, hoarsely, as he smashed the baton into Stolić's upper arm. 'I ate people like you' – he struck him again – 'for fucking' – he struck him again, across the ribs – '*breakfast*' – again, across the thighs, the knees – 'in the trenches.' The rage encompassed him, filled him. He was ice all through. Stolić rolled into a ball on the floor, his breath rasping. Reinhardt stood over him, the baton raised in his quivering fist. 'You *prick*!' he rasped. 'You think I got this Iron Cross by being a fucking *choirboy*?!' He beat Stolić again across the back of his thighs.

Stolić whimpered, raised his arms over his head. '*Stop*, please. No more.'

As fast as it came, the anger flowed out of him. He felt it recede, from his fingers, up through his arms. He blinked once, twice, and it was gone. He pulled Stolić's arm down from where he had wrapped it around his head. Stolić cried out, turned his head down into the ground. Reinhardt grabbed his ear and twisted, turning his head back up towards him. Stolić's eyes were wild and rolled back like those of a cornered animal, and his breath gusted up, fetid and sour. Reinhardt lifted his fist up, the baton held high. Stolić fastened his eyes on it as if it were some kind of salvation.

'Don't look at that, look at me. At *me*, you shit,' he hissed. Stolić rolled his eyes on him. 'Did you kill Marija Vukić?'

Stolić shook his head. 'No. No, I don't...' His eyes turned back to the baton.

'At *me*, Stolić. Look at me. That's right. You don't what?'

'I don't know...'

'What?!'

'*I don't know if it was me.*'

'What do you mean, Stolić?'

'I don't... blood. There was...' He trailed off, his eyes folding away. Reinhardt struck him across the side of his thigh, above his knee, on his hip, his ankle. Stolić shuddered with pain, curling up tighter.

'There's *always* blood. Who killed her?'

'I don't know.'

'I don't believe you.' He hit him again on the knee. 'I know you were there that night. Tell me about it.'

'Wha... ?' Reinhardt raised the baton, and Stolić's eyes fastened onto it. '*Yes*, yes! All right. Yes, I was there.'

'*Where*, Stolić?'

'The hotel. At the hotel. But I didn't kill her. I didn't. Please. Tell me I didn't.'

'Was it Becker?'

'I don't know. *Please.*'

'What did you see that night? What did you *see*?'

'There was... I saw Becker. We were talking. Outside the hotel. Then... my room. I don't remember. I don't *remember*.'

'*Think*, Stolić!'

'There was someone. I saw someone. I think...'

'Who, Stolić?' The Standartenführer's head dropped, away from the baton, and he seemed to go limp. Whatever fear or tension held him together drained out of him, and he folded against the floor. 'Was it Verhein? *Stolić!*' Reinhardt felt for his pulse. It was there, faint but rapid. He stood up, blinked, and suddenly realised the position he had put himself in. He collapsed the baton, putting it back in his pocket, looking down at an SS Standartenführer lying unconscious on the floor.

It was quiet and he did not know how long he stood there, but the creak of the door and a sudden intake of breath made him turn. One of Stolić's SS stood there, mouth agape. He seemed to remember himself, fumbling at his rifle and screaming over his shoulder. Reinhardt stood away from Stolić, hands wide at his side. The other SS erupted briefly into the doorway and then left.

'Are kneeling and staying still,' yelled the first SS, a Croatian accent thickening his German. 'Are staying *still!* Are not *moving!*' He called to Stolić once, twice, his eyes darting from the Standartenführer to Reinhardt. He knelt there, hands at his sides, and wondered how the hell he was going to get out of this.

38

He heard voices outside, and Becker stepped inside with a drawn pistol, followed by the two SS. A tight smile stretched across his face but did not meet his eyes. 'Oh, Reinhardt. Reinhardt, my God, but aren't you in the shit?'

Reinhardt forced a smile. 'The questioning got a bit out of hand.'

Becker nodded tightly, his cheeks flushed against the pallor of his face. 'Get him out of here,' he said to the two SS, pointing at Stolić. He pushed the door shut behind them as they dragged him out. He waited an instant, listening, then turned to Reinhardt. 'So?'

'So what, Becker?'

'Did he confess?'

Reinhardt smiled. 'What kind of an idiot do you take me for?'

Becker's mouth moved. 'What've you done, then?' he hissed.

'What you wanted, no?' Becker's eyes narrowed. 'You wanted this. Either for him to kill me, or me to kill him. What was the plan? That before killing me he would get me to confess about the file? Or that before me killing him he would confess to murdering Vukić?'

'Reinhardt –'

'Was I supposed to be grateful to you for delivering him to me? Was that it? And then I'd tell you about the file? Is that it?'

'He *was* your killer, Reinhardt, you arse.'

'I admit he was perfect.'

'He *is* perfect! He even has the knife!'

'How would you know that?'

Becker went still, white, said nothing.

'The knife's a big part of it. The Bowie, left in Stolić's hotel room. All covered in blood. Except I spoke to the maid. There was blood on the knife. But nowhere else. Not on his hands. Not on his uniform. Not in the bathroom. He's been torturing prisoners here, and he's covered in it. Vukić was stabbed twenty times, and he was spotless?'

'He's a killer, Reinhardt.'

'But not mine. His knife killed her. He didn't. You just wanted me to think that. You and whoever you're working with. How did you know about the knife?' Becker's jaw clenched, and he said nothing. 'This can't go on, Becker. Who is it?'

There was a commotion outside. 'I can't keep the Ustaše away,' said Becker, looking over his shoulder. 'Ljubčić will go berserk. I can only help you if you help me.' There was a fury of voices, the sound of blows. 'For God's sake, Reinhardt.'

Reinhardt shook his head. Becker's face twisted, warped, and he stood back with the pistol aimed at Reinhardt's head as the door crashed open and Ljubčić thrust his way in. Three of the Ustaše grabbed Reinhardt, slamming him up against the wall. 'No more playing around, Reinhardt,' Becker snarled, his eyes wide. 'You give me what I want, and I let you live.'

Reinhardt had to think his way out of this one, think around his fear. Becker could not stay here forever. He was too exposed and taking too many risks. He could not hope to control the Ustaše, but looking into Becker's eyes, he could see that any pretence had been dropped. There was no more acting or posing here. Becker was desperate. 'I don't have anything to give you.'

'You're lying. You're *lying!*' screamed Becker. He seemed to check himself, took a lurching step over to Reinhardt, and put the pistol to his head. The Ustaše seemed to tighten, leaning their weight into him. *'Give me what I want!'*

Reinhardt looked at him, up past the pistol, up the shortened length of Becker's arm. He felt calm, suddenly. 'No.'

'I'll kill you, Reinhardt, I swear I will,' snarled Becker, but there was a twist to his voice, a hitch like that of a sulky child. 'Don't think I won't.' Reinhardt said nothing. 'Don't look at me like that. Don't fucking look at me like *that*!' Becker hit Reinhardt across the mouth with his pistol. Reinhardt's head exploded in pain at the blow, and he fell sideways, the Ustaše hauling him back up. He felt a blow to his ribs, then his stomach, and his knees gave way.

The Ustaše's feet slithered and shifted as they fought his weight. They let him fall to the floor, twisting his arms up behind him, and one of them knelt on his back. Reinhardt writhed and heaved against the weight of him and the burn of frustration he felt. Becker ground his face into the floor, and he choked and coughed at the blood and dust that filled his mouth. He could not breathe. 'Fucking stubborn son of a bitch! *Tell me*, Reinhardt,' grated Becker, grinding the pistol into the back of his neck. Reinhardt groaned under his weight, turning his head away from the pistol. He felt a hand grabbing at his collar, and he was hauled back and up, where he slumped forward on his hands and knees. Becker's hand wormed into his hair and yanked his head back, and the pistol went back against his forehead. 'Just fucking *tell* me.'

'You can't do anything to me I haven't thought of doing myself,' slurred Reinhardt, swallowing against the scum of blood in his mouth. All those nights he had lain alone in his bed, alone with his memories and regrets, letting it all spiral down into the gunmetal circle of a pistol's muzzle. 'A thousand times I've put a gun to my own head and been too weak to finish it. So finish it for me, Becker.' He leaned forward against the pistol. 'Do it.'

'You think that's the worst I can do. It's not. I can do worse.' Reinhardt said nothing. 'I'll do it,' panted Becker. 'I'll let them do it.'

'I know you will,' Reinhardt replied. He looked at Becker, who looked at the Ustaše and nodded. Reinhardt was yanked back to his feet. Two of them held his arms as Ljubčić put a hand on his shoulder and looked him in the eyes, like he was measuring him. He had those eyes, like the priest's, blank and shiny atop the pasty pale slump of his cheeks. Whatever was there, whatever looked out on the world, it was different. As if it moved sideways from reality. He raised his other hand, and he held Stolić's knife. He put it close beneath Reinhardt's eye, twisted it, the light smearing down its bloodied length. Ljubčić smiled, stepped back, switched the knife to his other hand and slammed his fist into Reinhardt's stomach once, twice. As Reinhardt's head came down over the blows, the Ustaša punched up. Reinhardt's head pitched back, then down. He felt another blow, then a harsh mutter of words. What little breath there was burst from him as he was flung to the ground. He coughed on the dust, then felt a stab of pain in his hand. He was stretched on the floor, held down by the two Ustaše, Ljubčić's foot on his left wrist. Their eyes met, and then Ljubčić dug the point of the Bowie under Reinhardt's fingernail. Reinhardt screamed, tried to pull away, heaved his head around, scraping his cheeks raw on the boards. The pain stopped. He caught his breath. It started again, the same finger, the knife sliding and probing, and he felt himself slipping away into unconsciousness…

… and sliding over the top of a trench into a British redoubt. Peering around a corner and seeing a file of Tommies slipping round-shouldered through the smoke with bayonets on the end of their snub-nosed rifles. Striking a grenade and tossing it around the bend. An explosion, agonised cries, charging on across a splintered ruin of wood and flesh, his Bergmann blazing away until it was empty, his feet sliding on muddy duckboards, hurdling khaki-clad bodies, reloading, tossing more grenades down dugouts and around every corner. On and on, not stopping. He crashed into an Englishman who flung him against the trench wall and hacked a sharpened spade into his knee. He fired the Bergmann into him as he collapsed, leaving the

Tommy quivering around the sodden ruin of his belly. They fell together, lying broken beside each other, the Englishman with a big watch gripped against his bloodied mouth, whispering, 'Father, Father, it hurts.' Reinhardt dragged his eyes from the mangled gash of his knee, looked up and around for help and saw them there. Brothers, twins perhaps, standing small and lost in each other's arms at the end of the trench. He saw them, and they him, and he had but to reach out to them and he could take them, take them away from here. He knew it, they knew it, he saw himself doing it – he felt himself doing it – but then the boys were gone, taken away. The moment was past, a fading outline of possibilities…

… He felt a sting of smoke and came to himself, those two memories clashing apart, his heart pumping what felt like ice. Ljubčić had his fingers in Reinhardt's hair, wrenching his head back, but he was not looking at him.

The men in the room were frozen, heads cocked as if they listened to something. Ljubčić was following something with his eyes, sliding over to the window. There was a suggestion of movement, a ripple of light through the slats of the walls. The Ustaša hauled his pistol out, snapping something at his men. He smashed a pane of glass and fired out. Two others grabbed their rifles and fired through the walls. The din was incredible, the silence deafening when they ceased fire. There was a thump from outside, the sound of something choking.

'What's going on?' hissed Becker. The Ustaša ignored him, peering out, straining for sound. 'What? *What?!*'

'Partisans,' snapped Ljubčić without looking around.

'*Here?!* How is that *possible*?'

There was a shatter of gunfire from outside, and the walls seemed to blow inward, the house filling with splinters and stabs of light. Two of the Ustaše twitched backwards and fell, the others hunched down and away from the shredding tear of the bullets.

The gunfire stopped. The inside of the house was a craze of smoke and dust, webbed by the cones of light from the holes. There was a voice from outside. The Ustaše whispered frantically among themselves as two of them hauled Reinhardt to his feet again. The voice came again, a note of finality to it. Ljubčić yelled back, then put his pistol on the floor. His men did the same, the Ustaše motioning at Becker furiously. '*Down!* Pistol *down!*'

Becker rocked his pistol to the tips of his fingers, then let it drop. Slipping slowly, he followed it to the floor, and Reinhardt saw the spreading red stains along his thigh and groin. He slumped into the angle of wall and floor and gave a keening groan as he slid sideways, his hands clutching at his wounds.

None of the others spared him a moment's glance as the door crashed open and a pair of men stepped inside. They looked rugged and solid, their eyes and rifles scanning around the room, one dressed like a farmer, the second in an old Royal Yugoslav Army uniform patched at the knees and elbows. One of them called something over his shoulder. A third man dressed in unmarked German combat fatigues and a pair of binoculars hanging on his chest stepped into the room. He had a hard face, all planes and angles beneath a short, thick beard, flinty eyes that fastened on Becker, on Reinhardt, the Ustaše holding him up, and they seemed to quail from him like dogs from a wolf.

The Partisan stared at Ljubčić, and their gaze seemed to strike sparks. Something visceral, unforgiving. Like two forces of nature, neither with any concept of pity for the other. The Partisan looked past him to the Ustaše holding Reinhardt. Moving smoothly, unhurried, he drew a pistol and, aiming past Ljubčić, shot the two of them in the head. Reinhardt gasped at the spatter of brain and blood that slapped across his face. His legs shook, then folded, and he slumped back against the wall as the two Ustaše collapsed like empty sacks.

Ljubčić went very still, but all the lines of his lumped body screamed outrage. The Partisan locked eyes with him again.

The hate seemed to resonate between them, shimmering, like a mirage. The Partisan stepped back and snapped something at the Ustaša, who put his hands atop his head and walked out, head high, the two Partisans following him out.

The Partisan shifted that stony gaze onto Becker, who shrank against the wall, hands up and out. 'Don't. Please.' He pocketed Becker's pistol, glanced at his wounds expressionlessly, then walked over to Reinhardt. There was a finality in how he turned his back on him that left Becker blinking after him in confused awareness that his wounds were fatal.

The Partisan watched impassively as Reinhardt slid heavily to the floor and let his head hang down between his knees. His breath caught, hinging on a sob. He had no idea if this was the end, but it felt like it.

'We have met, you and I,' said the Partisan.

Reinhardt looked up, narrowed his eyes. A memory sparked to life. 'Goran?' The man nodded. 'Begović's driver.'

'When I have to be. Drink this,' he said.

Reinhardt took the canteen Goran offered, rinsed his mouth and spat, the water all bloody where it splashed on the floorboards, and then drank. He poured some into a cupped hand and wiped his face as best he could. He worked his mouth, running his tongue over his teeth. 'Thank you.'

'You are welcome. So, Captain Reinhardt. Is this where your Ilidža investigation has led you?'

Reinhardt shrugged, twisting his mouth as he rinsed and spat again. 'It would seem so.'

'You seem to have many friends, Captain.' He stared at the bodies in the room. 'I've never met a man so lucky.' Becker shifted where he lay, his eyes gleaming wetly. The floor under him was sodden with his blood, and his face was very pale.

'You forget the Partisans.'

Goran gave a tight smile. 'Some of them, for sure.'

'Not you?' Reinhardt put a hand on the floor and pushed himself upright. He leaned against the wall, straightening up against the pain in his stomach and ribs. His fist quivered as he closed his fingers around what Ljubčić had done to his hand.

'I cannot tell what you are, Captain. That worries me.'

'Dr Begović seems to trust me.'

'Muamer is a good man,' replied Goran. 'Sometimes too good for his own good…'

'Lucky he has you to watch over him. Is he here?'

'No,' said Goran, shortly.

There was a sudden air of decisiveness about him, and Reinhardt was afraid again. 'Why did you shoot them?' he asked, pointing at the two Ustaše. He felt overwhelmingly the need to keep Goran talking, and it was the first thing that came into his head.

'They deserved it.'

'Ljubčić does not?'

'Ljubčić will be dealt with differently.'

'What about me?'

'What about you?' Goran's eyes gave nothing away.

'Am I your prisoner?'

'We are a raiding party, Captain. I have no time for prisoners.' Just a few words, but the weight behind them was inexorable, and Reinhardt found he had nothing to say. Goran looked at him. 'Where are you going?'

'I'm looking for the German 121st Division.'

'I believe they're south of here. In Predelj.'

'You could just let me go. Let me continue.' The words felt weak, and feeble.

'I don't think so, Captain.'

'Begović trusts me enough to let me know he is Senka,' Reinhardt blurted.

Goran's eyes narrowed. 'He told you that?'

'Yes,' Reinhardt lied. 'The Shadow. There's no one the Gestapo want more.' It was a desperate throw of the dice, just something he had guessed from things Begović had said, but it was all he had.

'Why would he do that?'

'Why…' Reinhardt repeated, then paused. He felt the ground

teeter under him, his guts tighten as if in expectation of a fall. All of a sudden, he realised he could see more than those two proverbial steps ahead, but the path was not clearer for it. He stood on perilous ground. Untrodden. Very few of the steps that might lead him out of this would avoid betrayal. It lay here, suddenly, all around him, and there was the sense that he had to choose his way carefully, as there would be no path back. 'He and I… we see some things the same way.'

Goran took a long, slow breath, his eyes not leaving Reinhardt. 'I must think about this,' he said, finally. 'But first, I have something I must attend to. You will wait, and we will talk again.' He turned and left, a shift of movement at the door as a Partisan stood guard.

Reinhardt felt adrift, just that cold feeling in the pit of his belly anchoring him in place, a reptilian awareness of danger he was not yet out of. The dust settled in the room, spiralling and sparkling down through the lattice of light from the bullet holes, and he began to feel the outlines of an understanding of something he had heretofore only felt unconsciously. He forced himself to calm, to consider what he felt taking shape.

There was a fork here in his path, he realised. One path led onward. One path ended here. He could go on, try to follow his investigation, do it in the way that would let him remain true to himself, and maybe serve the wider cause Meissner had shown him. Or he could shrink back, turn away. If he went forward with what he felt taking shape, what would it cost him? What accommodation would he have to make? Betrayal was never to be taken lightly, but would that accommodation be any worse than the dozens – some mundane, some not – he had had to make over the last few years?

There was a low moan from Becker. Reinhardt knelt next to him. There was nothing he could do for him, but even if there were, would he do it? This realisation terrified him. He had never been in such a position before. Becker was an obstacle to him. He realised now that to make work what was taking shape in his mind, at least two men had to die. The chances were that both of them would, here, today. He remembered what he said to Begović, that everything good that had happened in his life had happened despite him. It was happening again.

'Becker, can you hear me?'

The Feldgendarme's mouth moved, his lips blue in the pallor of his face. '*Thirsty,*' he whispered.

'You're dying, Becker. I can't help you. But you can help me. Can you do that? Can you tell me who is behind this?'

'*Yes,*' Becker whispered.

'Tell me.'

'*Yes.*' Just a thread. His eyes quivered open, wet, slack, searching for Reinhardt, finding him. '*The knife. It was the knife.*'

'What about the knife, Becker?'

'*Caught him. Putting... it... back. Red...*'

'Caught who?'

'*... red-handed. Caught him...*'

'Who, Becker? Tell me.'

Becker's head lurched. His eyes cleared. '*You?*' He stared up. '*I could... tell you. But... I won't.*' Then the focus in his gaze bled away and, amazingly, at the edge of his life, he laughed, a stuttering high in his throat. '*If you... could see... your face. Gregor... the crow... Always...*' His eyes turned up, and he was gone.

Reinhardt paused there, staring down at him. He tried to care, but there was nothing. Not even any sense of triumph at having outlasted Becker, he who was the master manipulator, always managing to find the right angle to any situation.

He poured water over his hands again, scrubbing his face and smearing his hands dry on his uniform, painfully flexing his fingers, still not wanting to look. He paused, searching around the tangle of bodies, spotting the Bowie where it had been dropped, shoving it point down between the floorboards. Standing, he put his heel on the pommel and pushed. He strained, his knee twitching. He pushed harder, but the knife only bent against the floorboards. He gritted his teeth in anger, then reached down and flung it skittering away across the floor. The guard shouted, peering at him nervously as Reinhardt walked to the door. The guard stood to one side, distrust writ large across his broad features. Reinhardt stepped carefully outside and looked around the clearing. The surviving Ustaše and SS were lined up in front of what clearly were firing squads. A small group of German soldiers, mostly Feldgendarmerie – Claussen among them – made up a separate group huddled under the guns of a circle of Partisans, and there was a hush in the clearing, a clear focus of attention.

Stolić and Ljubčić were kneeling in front of a tree from which dangled two nooses while a Partisan read something from a piece of paper. Stolić looked dazed, Ljubčić contemptuous, and he had eyes only for Goran even as the Partisan commander gave the order to put the ropes around their necks and made them stand. There was a pause, and then Partisans hauled on the ropes. The two men arched up, then jerked like puppets, legs flailing as they fought to breathe. A hideous wet croaking slipped past the swell of their tongues, a macabre counterpoint to the gentle rustle of the tree's branches. The bodies bumped and snapped off each other, and with their popping eyes and contorted faces it was as if they played some childish game.

It seemed to take them a long time to die, but after they stilled two men jerked down on the bodies to make sure. Reinhardt looked up at Stolić. He had fouled himself as he died, and the stench was awful, but Reinhardt only saw him as an absence, the second man who needed to die. He realised Goran was standing next to him, looking at him.

'You object to our justice?'

Reinhardt swallowed hard. 'Is that what it was?'

'They were condemned by a people's court a long time ago for crimes against the citizens of Yugoslavia. This was their sentence, and it was more justice than they deserved or ever gave.' He turned and looked back at the bodies as he spoke.

'What was it between you and Ljubčić?'

Goran looked back at him, at the bodies where they hung

like carcasses. 'You noticed?' His mouth twisted. 'We grew up together. Then he became *that*. An Ustaša. Obsessed with a world that had no room for those not like him, and a future that never will be.'

'And what of them?' Reinhardt indicated the other Ustaše and SS. 'What of them?' The Germans. 'And me?'

'What about you, Captain?'

'Dr Begović was helping me. He believed doing that was helping you. Your cause.' Goran said nothing, and Reinhardt felt as if he scrabbled across a pane of glass.

'Muamer is a good comrade. One of the best. If he believed that...' The Partisan shook his head. 'He believes that whatever it is you are doing, it is causing confusion in your ranks.' He looked around the clearing. 'And I must admit I have seen many things, but never a German soldier being tortured by a collection of Ustaše, Feldgendarmerie, and SS. So he may have a point. I need more than that, though.' He turned those flinty eyes back on Reinhardt. 'He believes you are a member of the German resistance.'

'I am,' said Reinhardt, and he felt the truth of it as he said it. It settled around him, through him, and it felt right.

'Somehow, I have my doubts.'

'I cannot prove it to you. But we do fight the same fight, if in different ways.' He could see Goran still hesitating. 'You have nothing to lose,' Reinhardt continued. 'You can send me on my way and hope I will do and act as Dr Begović thinks. Or you may keep me here. Either way, I am no threat to you or your men. But my way – Begović's way – I am... I am in your enemy's camp.' He swallowed around the word he should have said. *Ally* was the word, but he could not bring himself to say it. Not yet.

Someone called from the forest, and Goran waved a hand in acknowledgment, never taking his eyes off Reinhardt, as if he could hear the word Reinhardt could not say. He had never in his life, Reinhardt realised, been the focus of such attention. Just like that moment in his dream, Goran's eyes were pivots around which his life might turn, or they were nails from which it would hang.

'Very well. You may go.'

'Please, I need him,' said Reinhardt, pointing at Claussen, needing to make Goran turn and look somewhere else, if just for a moment, so he could escape the pressure of his gaze. 'He is one of us.'

Goran sighed, then nodded. He called something to the guards, who pulled Claussen out of the group, pushing him over to where Reinhardt stood. Reinhardt watched the faces of the others, saw the hope in their eyes that faded as only one of them was culled from their number, and he turned away from the voiceless expression of their need.

'Go, now,' said Goran. Across the clearing, Partisans were filtering back into the forest, save for those guarding the prisoners.

Claussen said nothing as he walked next to Reinhardt, a huge bruise darkening the side of his head, an ugly, red welt. Two Partisans escorted them back to the road, to where the *kübelwagen* was parked behind the ruined wall, still loaded. A dead Feldgendarme lay there, flies already crawling over a wound in his neck. The Partisans melted back into the trees, and they were alone. Behind them, suddenly, came a rattle of gunfire, then, after a moment, the crack of single shots. The two of them looked at each other.

'You look…' said Claussen, trailing off.

'You should see the other chap,' mumbled Reinhardt, thickly. He searched through the packs, finding the first-aid kit. He poured sulfanilamide over his fingers then bandaged them, wrapping three fingers together. He flexed them, wincing at the pain, and looked at Claussen.

'I don't know what you said, or did… but, thank you,' said Claussen.

'Let's get going, Sergeant,' replied Reinhardt, hoping a measure of formality would give him time to consider what had just happened.

39

Reinhardt unclipped the MP 40s and brought them in front, looking at the forest now with new eyes. They moved steadily south, and Reinhardt found his mind caught between what had happened to him at that village and what might happen to him ahead. He knew he ought to feel something – a fear that official sanction might catch up with him, and a fear of what he had committed himself to. Stolić and Becker had to have been acting outside their authority, though, and there was no proof Reinhardt had ever been there. When he realised that, he breathed easier. For the rest of it, the implications of that fork in the road he had just taken, he put it aside.

The road wound on down the gorge, undulating above the Drina as it flowed torpidly north. They came up on the tail end of a convoy and stayed there, pulling their goggles down and wrapping scarves around their mouths to breathe through the dust. The miles fell away and they began to pass through lines of soldiers and trucks drawn up by the side of the road. There was an air of expectation that was palpable. Reinhardt could see it in the faces of the men around him, the imminence of action. The convoy slowed, lurching to the side under the directions of a pair of Feldgendarmes. Reinhardt's breath caught at the sight of them, but they simply made to pass by, banging on the *kübelwagen*'s hood to pull over and park.

Up ahead, Reinhardt could see a pair of half-tracks with tall radio antennae, and a staff car. He figured they had to be controlling movements and might know of Verhein's whereabouts. Telling Claussen to wait, he stepped out and straightened his uniform. Reinhardt felt somewhat self-conscious as he walked past the waiting troops, remembering how it used to feel before an attack and, here, feeling only a distant echo of it. 'Afternoon,' he said to a captain, who nodded back, not moving from where he leaned against a truck, his eyes taking Reinhardt in from his bandaged hand to his face. He looked tough and competent, the red slash of the Winter Campaign medal bright against his tunic. Shifting his MP 40 on its straps, Reinhardt lit an Atikah, then offered one to the captain.

'Reinhardt, Abwehr,' he said, lighting the captain's cigarette.

'Tiel,' the officer replied, nodding his thanks, drawing deeply. '121st.' He looked Reinhardt up and down. 'Had some trouble?'

'Been in worse. Mind telling me what's going on?'

'We're going up that hill any minute now,' Tiel said, motioning backwards with his head. A rutted track headed steeply into dense woods. There were soldiers on the track, beginning to make their way uphill. 'Partisan brigade up there, somewhere. We dislodged them yesterday, and they're trying to move northwest.'

Up where the path began to merge into the trees, it looked like there was something of a commotion, a vague sense of shifting forms. 'Is there something going on up there?'

'General's inspecting the boys.' He gave a glimmer of a smile. 'Like he always does,' as if anticipating a question Reinhardt might ask.

Reinhardt gave a tight smile and hoped it did not show. 'My lucky day.'

'You want the general?'

Reinhardt nodded. He felt Tiel's eyes harder on him, suddenly, as if Verhein were something to be protected. 'Actually, I want his IIIa,' he said.

'Intelligence?'

'Colonel Gärtner,' said Reinhardt.

It seemed to satisfy the captain. Tiel nodded towards the half-tracks. 'Over there.'

'Wouldn't mind introducing me, would you? A friendly face'd go a long way to getting me some attention.'

'Of course,' Tiel answered. Together they walked over to one of the half-tracks. The captain put his head inside, then extended an arm as Reinhardt joined him, pulling him into conversation with a colonel who was standing hunched over a fold-down map table in the vehicle's load bed.

'Fine,' the colonel was saying. 'Just a few minutes. Your men ready, Captain? You're up next.'

'Ready, yes, sir. And here he is.' Tiel nodded, then stepped away.

Colonel Gärtner's attention was fixed on a radio technician sitting just beyond him. 'What do you want, Captain?'

'I would ideally like to speak with the general, sir,' replied Reinhardt.

'The general. Really?' said Gärtner, with a faintly disbelieving drawl, looking at his map. He looked up, frowning at the state Reinhardt was in. 'Bloody hell, man, what happened to you?'

'It's nothing, sir, thank you.'

'Nothing?'

'The general, sir?'

'About what?'

'All due respect, sir, that is business best discussed with the general.'

'I'm his IIIa, Captain. You're Abwehr. We're both in intelligence. If it's something affecting the division, you'd better tell me now.'

'No, sir. Nothing affecting the division.'

'Very well,' said the colonel, his attention going back to his maps. 'I suppose you can wait, but no promises.'

'Thank you, sir.'

'And try and clean yourself up, would you?'

Reinhardt felt alone, all of a sudden, flicking his finished cigarette into the bushes. His hand stole into his pocket, fingers running over the Williamson and its inscription. He calmed down a little, becoming aware of movement and activity around him. He saw Tiel heading up into the woods with his men spread out in a line on either side of him. Officers were clustered around Gärtner's half-track, and then the colonel stepped down out of the vehicle, talking to an officer with his back to Reinhardt. He had a bald patch on the back of his head, rather like a tonsure. Gärtner spotted Reinhardt over the other officer's shoulder and said something. The other officer turned.

It was Ascher. He looked at Reinhardt, and his eyes went wide, then flat. He turned back to Gärtner, the line of his shoulders stark with his anger. Gärtner's face creased in incomprehension as he listened, and then he straightened, looking accusingly at Reinhardt, then back at Ascher. He shook his head, backing away. 'No, no,' Reinhardt heard him say. 'He's your problem now, Clemens. You deal with him.'

Ascher walked over to Reinhardt, his jaw clenched, and then looked around, as if searching for someone. '*You?*' Reinhardt had the presence of mind to come to attention. Not that he was surprised to see Ascher. It was the man's tone, the way his eyes kept searching behind Reinhardt, then focused on his injuries. He was aware of danger, as if a chasm had opened up right before him. 'What the *hell* are you doing here?' His eyes strayed away again, as if he could not help himself.

'I beg your pardon, sir. I'm here to speak with General Verhein.'

'About *what*?'

Reinhardt paused. He had no idea of this man. No idea what made him tick. He only knew he had been one of the officers who had complained to Freilinger about Reinhardt's behaviour that afternoon in the mess. 'I'm sure you must know, sir. It's about the investigation.'

'What?'

He took a risk. 'About that woman.'

Ascher's nose wrinkled. 'Woman?'

He was buying time, Reinhardt could feel it. 'Vukić.'

'*Her?!* You were supposed to have dropped this, Captain. As I recall, your superior was given specific instructions.'

'Yes, sir,' Reinhardt said, retreating behind a façade of dumb obedience.

'And… ?'

'Rescinded, sir,' lied Reinhardt. 'I was ordered to proceed.'

'You cannot be serious, Captain. You wish to persist with this here? *Now?*'

'If I must, sir,' replied Reinhardt.

'This is *ridiculous*, do you hear? We're about to go into action and this is the moment you choose to come asking your questions about that woman?'

'I would not say it's a moment I choose…'

'Don't be *impertinent*, man!' snarled Ascher.

'Impertinence?' came a deep voice behind him. 'You know what I always say about impertinence, Clemens.' Reinhardt turned and snapped to attention. Standing there, tall and broad-chested, shock of white hair like a biblical patriarch's, was General Paul Verhein. He had glittering brown eyes, round and open under bushy white brows, framed and creased in a fine web of wrinkles like laugh lines. He wore a simple uniform, sleeves rolled up over his thick forearms, only his red collar flashes and epaulettes showing his rank. He appraised Reinhardt openly, his eyes flickering over his Iron Cross, his hand, back up to his face. Verhein's Knight's Cross hung at his neck, and the Winter Campaign ribbon cut across the front of his tunic next to the black-and-silver badge of the Pour le Mérite. A gold close-combat clasp was fixed to his left breast. Somewhat incongruously, hanging at his side, he carried a Russian PPSh submachine gun, its wooden stock burnished to a rich shine.

'Yes, General,' replied Ascher, a slight air of suffering in his voice. 'I know what you say about impertinence.'

'Is he scolding you, Captain?' grinned Verhein, still looking at Reinhardt. 'He's like a mother hen, always pecking around.' Ascher's mouth tightened in a strained smile, as if this were a long-running joke. 'Would you know, Captain, about impertinence?'

'I might hazard a guess, sir.'

'But you would feel impertinent doing so... ?' Verhein laughed. 'I believe an impertinent officer will always look beyond the obvious, and more often than not will arrive at a pertinent answer. Impertinence is a quality I value highly, Captain... ?

'Reinhardt, sir.'

'Are you an impertinent officer, Reinhardt?'

'I believe I have been called that, or something similar, at times.'

Verhein laughed again, an open, honest laugh, and Reinhardt found himself smiling back. 'Of course you are, Captain, else you wouldn't be here, would you? I know who you are, and I know why you're here, Reinhardt.' Verhein's words wiped the smile from his face. The general's eyes flicked to Ascher. 'I had a fairly good idea you'd be turning up. Didn't I, Clemens?' The colonel said nothing, his face blank. 'I've a feel for men like you, Reinhardt. Ex-copper, aren't you?'

'Yes, sir.'

'Coppers can be stubborn sons of bitches. Never give up if they feel they're in the right. Right?'

'General, if I may, there is not time for this,' said Ascher.

'I think there may well be, Clemens,' replied Verhein, not taking his eyes off Reinhardt. 'I think there may have to be...' He trailed off. 'I will talk to you, Reinhardt, but not right now. I've got to get my boys into action. My car's up there. You can wait for me. Will you wait for me?'

'Yes, sir,' said Reinhardt, somewhat taken aback by this man, by his presence, his style. He had met him only a few minutes ago, and he already liked him.

'Good man,' exclaimed Verhein, clapping him on the

shoulder, then striding off. Officers and men gathered around him as he walked over to the tree line. Faces turned to him, wreathed in smiles, his arms reaching out, bursts of laughter.

40

'You've got some nerve, Reinhardt.' Ascher was pale with his anger, the fury coming off him in waves, like something palpable.

'The general said to wait for him by his car, sir. With your permission?' He saluted and about-faced, walking past the half-tracks towards an open-sided Horch, feeling Ascher's eyes on him the whole way. Reinhardt stepped onto the road, looking back down the line of vehicles, and gave a surreptitious wave to Claussen, the sergeant acknowledging him with a raise of his hand off the steering wheel.

The Horch's hood was up, someone working on the engine. Reinhardt froze, suddenly. That smell, that acrid stink. A soldier stepped out from the front of the car, head down, wiping his hands on an oily rag. He looked up, and Reinhardt clenched his jaw to keep the surprise and, if he was honest, the fear off his face. The soldier had dark, slanted Mongol eyes resting on top of his heavy cheeks, and a cap of thick, black hair. His limbs were short and stocky, his torso thick and round. There was a cigarette like a rolled piece of cardboard in the corner of his mouth, thick as a thumb. Reinhardt felt he might have hidden his recognition, but it was clear the soldier knew who he was as he too froze in place.

'Didn't they teach you to salute when you joined up?' Reinhardt snapped, saying the first thing that came into his head, trying to break the silence before things became too obvious. The soldier came to attention, saluting. Reinhardt returned it, then turned his back on him, ignoring him, feeling as he did it that it was one of the hardest things he had ever done, like exposing his throat for an enemy's knife. He looked back up the line of vehicles and saw Ascher talking to a pair of soldiers, one small, one large, then begin walking towards him. There was something familiar about them, but he could not place it, could not think, not with that Mongol behind him, and the reek of his papirosa, remembering Frau Hofler and her little dog from what seemed like a lifetime ago.

Ascher seemed to erupt in front of him, his eyes flat. 'So just what are you planning on doing, Captain?'

'I'm hopeful General Verhein will be able to help me with my inquiries into the death of Marija Vukić.'

Ascher shook his head slightly. 'That's what you want, not what you're planning. What you're planning is proving the general had anything to do with that woman. You're going to try to blame him for her death.' Reinhardt shook his head, tried to speak, but it was clear Ascher was not listening. 'And what you'll end up doing is not only sullying the name of a fine soldier, you will impair the operational effectiveness of this unit. I cannot allow that.'

'The general seemed willing enough.'

'The general is always willing. That, if you will permit the remark, is part of his problem. It is my job to ensure that his willingness does not do him more harm than good.' There was a thud behind him. Reinhardt risked a glance back and saw that the Mongol had shut the Horch's hood and was staring at him. Turning back, he saw that the two soldiers Ascher had been talking to had appeared. Reinhardt suddenly remembered where he had seen them. At the Feldgendarmerie station in Ilidža. And driving past the café where he had sat reading Verhein's file. The big one had his hand on the strap of his rifle where it hung from his shoulder. His hand was bandaged, Reinhardt noticed. Looking down, he saw the smaller one's hands were too.

He was surrounded, he realised, by killers. Or those who had participated in its cover-up. He looked at each of them, taking a small step back as he did so. 'Don't move, Reinhardt. And keep your hands away from that gun,' said Ascher. A wash of sour air was all the warning Reinhardt had as the Mongol stepped in close behind him and stripped the MP 40 away, and Reinhardt had not even heard or felt him move.

'Ah, there you all are! Good! Good!' Verhein came bustling around the corner of the half-track, and the effect was like a bighearted child charging into a flock of pigeons. Reinhardt felt the Mongol jerk back and away. The two soldiers, Little and Large, flowed to the side, and the colonel started like a little boy caught in the act. If Verhein noticed any of it, he gave no sign. 'Car fixed, Mamagedov?'

'Is all fixed, sir. Good all like new,' the Mongol replied, his German thick with a Russian accent.

Verhein tossed his PPSh into the Horch and looked at Ascher. 'Demmler's and Tiel's boys are moving. I need to get around to Ubben's. Come on. Everyone in. Ascher. Reinhardt. No, I'll drive, Mamagedov. I said *I'll* drive, stop *fussing.*' He crunched his weight into the driver's seat. 'He's a real fusspot. Absolute devil in battle, but an old woman out of it. Aren't you, Mamagedov? Worse than Ascher.' The Asian grinned like a child. 'He's a Kalmyk, from the Caucasus. Just turned up one day and wouldn't go home. Reinhardt, sit in the front with me.' The other two climbed in the back. Little and Large had vanished.

Verhein gunned the Horch's engine, and the car took off with a spray of earth and dirt. Reinhardt lurched against the car's movement and shifted in his seat. Glancing backwards, he saw Ascher and Mamagedov staring at him like cats at a mouse hole.

'You've been in the wars a bit, Reinhardt, have you?'

'General?'

Verhein pointed at his mouth. 'Someone's had a go at you? Unless you tripped in the bath?'

'It's nothing, sir. Trouble with some Feldgendarmerie on the way down.' Reinhardt felt the back of his neck tensing, as if feeling the burn of Ascher's gaze. 'You should see the other chap.'

Verhein guffawed as he sounded the horn. A file of soldiers stopped and waved as they went past, and the general slowed, leaned out, and slapped a couple of them on the helmet. 'Good luck, boys. Though with a face like Schaar's there, you'll have the Reds running for their mothers' cracks 'n' wishing they'd never been *born!*' Laughter followed them as the general accelerated again. Glancing back at the soldiers as they passed, Reinhardt saw them smile, saw them lighten, just a little, and he saw the sour, pinched expression on Ascher's face as he stared at the back of Verhein's head.

'So tell me, Reinhardt, what do you know about Schwarz?'

'Only what they tell us, sir.'

'Well, I'll tell you a bit more. *Hey*, Martinek, how's that leg?'

'Fine, sir,' came the reply from a soldier as they sped by.

'Schwarz, Reinhardt, will destroy the Partisans. There's over 117,000 of our lads in this, and we don't reckon there's more'n about 20,000 of the Reds. Now's the time to finish 'em if ever there was.' He hauled the Horch around a corner, stones and gravel spinning off to the left and down the slope to the river. A file of soldiers leaped to one side as they sped by, the general waving to them. 'You know why we're in a bit of a rush, do you?'

'I've an idea, sir.'

'Course you do, Reinhardt, you're Abwehr. It's not a secret the Italians are in a bit of trouble. The Allies look like they'll be landing there any time and any Italian worth his salt will want to be home for that, not here.' He braked the car as they squeezed past a pair of trucks unloading soldiers. '*Ihgen!* Bloody hell, man, why the long face? It's not my *funeral*, you know!'

Laughter followed them as Verhein drove on. 'So we've got to try to put an end to the Partisans while we've still got the Italians here with us. But it's not just them. We've got to figure that sooner or later, the Allies are going to come through here themselves. So we need this place secure.' Driving past more soldiers, all of them waving, and calling out 'Good luck' as they drove by. Verhein waved back. 'You don't need *luck*, lads. It's the *Partisans* need the *luck*!' He put both hands back on the wheel, smiling ahead. 'They're good lads, all of 'em. The best. And it's the best job, leading them like this in the field. Wouldn't you say, Reinhardt?'

'Haven't really had the experience you've had, sir.'

'Nonsense, man! That's a 1914 Cross you're wearing there. You must've led men.'

'I did, sir.'

'And?' Verhein turned the car off the road and up a narrow, rutted track that hauled and bumped its way up the side of the hill.

'Well, it was more something that needed to be done, rather than anything I enjoyed doing, sir.'

Verhein laughed. 'I guess that's where we differ, you and I, Reinhardt. I love it out here. In charge of men. Leading them. There's no feeling like it. Nothing.' He cast a glance at Reinhardt as he drove. 'Why would I want to give that up?'

'I'm sure I don't know, sir.'

'No?' Verhein smiled at him, and there was something conspiratorial in it, Reinhardt thought. 'Short answer is I don't want to give it up. I don't want to be anywhere else than here. And speaking of here... Mamagedov, get the bottle ready.'

Verhein braked the car in a burst of dust, took a bottle of champagne from Mamagedov, and jumped out of the car towards a group of soldiers gathered around a half-track in a clearing in the forest. Reinhardt watched as they gathered around him, and he handed the bottle to a soldier who went bright red as Verhein enfolded him in a bear hug. The banter flew, jokes were cracked, hands shaken and shoulders slapped, and over it all that shock of white hair. Despite himself, Reinhardt was drawn to him, to that kind of camaraderie, although God knew he did not want to be, and he could not afford to be. He had known men like Verhein in the first war.

Charismatic. Energetic. Liable to leave a slew of bodies in their wake. The last thing he needed was to get distracted by how he felt, or how he thought he ought to feel.

He glanced backwards, seeing that twist to Ascher's face as he watched the general. The colonel looked at him, balefully, then back to the general. 'Thank God this will be over soon,' Ascher muttered.

Reinhardt twisted in his chair. 'The operation?'

'No. *This.*'

'Piening's wife just had twins,' announced Verhein. 'Boys. If you can't celebrate that, what can you celebrate, eh?!' He revved the engine, slewing the Horch around in front of the soldiers, who cheered him on his way. 'Where were we, then?' said Verhein, as he settled the Horch back on the track. The light that fell through the trees overhead flickered and flashed across them. 'Leading from the front. I don't know any other way to do it. Certainly not from behind a desk, which is where some want to send me. Including some – eh, Clemens? – who ought to know better.'

'Yes, General,' said Ascher. 'I have only your best interests at heart.'

'"My best interests", it's what he always says,' snorted Verhein, leaning over to Reinhardt as if to draw him into this particular relationship. Reinhardt glanced around as Verhein said that, catching again that sour look on Ascher's face as the light streamed over it. Like an exasperated housewife, thought Reinhardt. 'As if I'd be a damned bit of use pushing paper around, farting around in offices and poncing around in dress uniforms.'

'General,' interrupted Ascher. 'You know that your transfer to headquarters has been ordered by the highest authorities…'

'I don't give a damn.'

'… who must therefore see some quality that you can bring to high command…'

'I don't give a damn.'

'… and I must object, sir, to your discussing this in front of people not familiar to you…'

'I don't *fucking* give a fucking *damn!*' roared Verhein, without taking his eyes off the road. Reinhardt felt a flush of embarrassment for Ascher. That image of a housewife came again. Long-suffering, overlooked… 'Over my dead body… Good luck to you, too, soldier!… Over my dead bloody body will they drag me off to bloody Berlin. What do you think, Reinhardt? Is there anything – *anything* – to compare to combat?' The car hurtled around a corner, more troops scattering left and right into the trees along the track. 'The sights. The sounds. The smells. That exhilaration. Is there anything like it?'

'There's nothing like it, sir,' replied Reinhardt, desperately uncomfortable, like a child faced with the reality of the sourness of its parents' relationship. 'But I wouldn't say it's the best thing that ever happened to me.'

'Each to his own, Reinhardt. Eh, Clemens?'

'Subject to higher exigencies,' sighed the colonel.

'Higher powers?'

'Exactly, sir.'

'You and your bloody philosophy, Clemens. Bad enough you have to meddle in politics, but there's entirely too much of that popish mumbo jumbo in you still. And Christ knows I've done my best to thrash it out of you. Did you ever meet Marija Vukić, Reinhardt?'

Reinhardt looked askance at him, taken aback by the sudden shifts of conversation. 'Once, sir.'

'And? What did you think?'

'She was… quite something.'

'She bloody well was. God's own handful. The sexiest, most passionate, most infuriating creature there ever was. Never a dull moment with her around. Was there, Clemens?' he asked, peering into the rearview mirror.

'Never, sir,' rasped the colonel.

'Saint and sinner all wrapped up in one delectable package. By Christ, she could stand you on your head. Make you see black when it was white. Day when it was night.'

'General, if I may?'

'You may not, Clemens.'

'Are you trying to tell me something, General?' asked Reinhardt.

Ascher jerked forward from the back. 'What the general's trying to say...'

'What the *general* is saying,' snapped Verhein, whipping his head around to stare back at Ascher, 'is that what happened to her is the last thing I wanted.' He braked the Horch outside a wooden-walled house that stood at the edge of a clearing, with the hill pushing up beyond it. A canvas awning hung along one side, overshadowing a trestle table with a radio and other equipment on it. Trucks and cars were parked around the clearing, a field kitchen was dispensing coffee, and a battery of heavy mortars were set up on the far side. The place had the feel of a forward headquarters.

Verhein stayed at the wheel, both hands on it, staring forward as if at nothing. Reinhardt looked at him, forcing himself to ignore Ascher and Mamagedov behind him. His heart hammered that he was suddenly, apparently, so close to the end. 'But something did happen to her,' he prompted, quietly.

Verhein seemed to slump in on himself. 'I know,' he said, softly.

'What happened?'

Verhein seemed to revive himself. 'I lost it, Reinhardt. What else?'

'Sir...' began Ascher, again.

Verhein lifted a hand. 'Leave it, Clemens, please,' he said. All the fire seemed to have gone out of him.

'I will *not*! Mamagedov, take the captain under arrest and –'

Verhein hunched around in his seat as the Kalmyk began to draw his pistol. 'Disregard that, Mamagedov. Think of it as confession, Clemens,' he said, swinging his gaze onto the colonel. 'God knows, I've confessed enough to you over the years, no?' He began picking up his equipment and looked at Reinhardt, gesturing at Ascher with his head. 'You know we sometimes call him Father Superior? Half the time, I think he ought to have stayed a chaplain.' He stepped out of the car, looking back at Ascher. The colonel was white-faced, his chin bunched tight at the end of his jaw. 'Would've made things a bit easier, sometimes. This time, I'm not confessing to you, Ascher. But maybe the penance won't be what you fear it will be. Now,' he said, 'Reinhardt and I will have a talk. I need you to check in with Oelker and get an update.' He looked up the hill at a sudden crackle of gunfire, then at Reinhardt, frowning. 'You coming or not?'

41

Reinhardt had gone cold, as if he had been doused. A piece of the truth had suddenly flared and bloomed here, and the pattern of the case as he understood it had shifted. Reinhardt knew his confusion was showing, but he could not help it, and he saw something sparkle in Ascher's eyes. A part of the truth was here, right here among them. Reinhardt could feel it, feel the way into that explanation that was bunched tight and only needed the right tug on it to unravel, but the way was fading, the shape of the case slumping back into the dull glow of its embers.

Reinhardt followed Verhein under the awning. An aide-de-camp offered the general a clipboard covered in signals, which he glanced at cursorily before telling him he did not want to be disturbed. He went inside the little house, dropped his PPSh and the signals on a table, then walked to a window, just an empty frame of splintered wood. The sound of gunfire came again, staccato bursts, the dull crump of explosions. He put his hands in the small of his back and stretched, sighing, then turned to Reinhardt, the light washing over his mane of white hair. 'You know, in a way, I'm glad you came. It's been… difficult.' He stared at Reinhardt, waiting as if for a reaction. Reinhardt could see that, but he was still feeling his way cautiously around the new shape of the investigation.

'Sir, why don't you just tell me what happened?' he managed after a moment.

'You know I met her in Russia?' Reinhardt nodded. 'We quarrelled there. Over... an incident. It's not important.'

'It may be, sir,' interrupted Reinhardt, thinking of that collective farm at Yagodnyy, the Sonderkommando, the Jews, the Red Army. He held back, though, wanting to see what Verhein would say.

'It was an operational issue,' said Verhein after a moment, turning and walking slowly to a trestle table and leaning his weight back against it. 'She travelled with my division a while, but she would head off on her own from time to time. She was in the propaganda companies, you know? So, once, she went out with a Sonderkommando and my unit passed through its operational area, and I found her –' He paused, suddenly and obviously upset. His mouth twisted, and he looked down and away. 'I found her torturing someone. A Jew. A woman. In front of her children. I knew she had strong feelings about Jews. She had strong feelings about a lot of things. And I knew she sometimes... expressed... well, it went beyond words. I knew of one incident with captured Red Army soldiers. I had heard of others. I didn't believe it. Not really. But I saw it with my own eyes.'

His own had fallen away, gone somewhere else, to that wet field at Yagodnyy. 'You could almost say it drove me quite mad. I wanted nothing more to do with her. We fought, and I sent her away. She was furious, incandescent with rage. She swore I would regret it, but when I came here, she contacted me. We met, and we agreed to let bygones be bygones. I had no wish for a relationship with her, although God knows I was still attracted to her. We met once or twice for drinks. That was it. Then she asked me to her house the night the conference for Schwarz ended...'

'Go on.'

'Marija was in a strange mood. Very hyperactive. She was very aroused. And, God help me, she was arousing. We had sex. It was... quite something. Then she kept talking about Russia, about what she'd seen there. She kept talking about Jews. What she had seen done to them. And then – she seemed unable to help herself, like a child who knows a secret she ought not to – she revealed to me she understood everything. She told me I was finished, that people in Berlin knew everything. I did not know what she was talking about, she had me so confused, but it was clear her mind was not quite all there. She began to scrape at herself, at her arms, her shoulders, at her… at her sex. She said she was dirty, unclean, that I made her that way.

'I began to feel afraid, but I still did not know what she was talking about. Then she laughed, and said my sister would pay the same price as me. Only she would pay it first. At that… I felt enraged and… panicked. I demanded she tell me what she was talking about. She only laughed harder, taunted me further. I struck her. She laughed, told me I hit like an old woman. I hit her again. And again. And again. I could not stop myself.' Verhein drew in a long, slow breath, and his gaze reeled itself back in from wherever it had been. He turned and looked at Reinhardt. 'And then… nothing. Just coming to my senses standing over her.'

Reinhardt drew in his own breath. 'Then what did you do?'

'Then?' Verhein shifted on the table. 'Then I left. For the front. First thing on Sunday morning.'

Reinhardt knew there was an untruth in what the general had just said. It was his old policeman's instinct. The suspect answering a question with a question. The hesitation. The shift in position. 'She was dead?' Verhein nodded. 'You knew this how?'

'I have… beaten men to death, Captain. I know how it looks. How it *feels*.'

'You were sure you had killed her?'

Verhein nodded, his eyes narrowing now. 'I was.'

'You are sure you beat her to death?'

Verhein shifted, his big hands gripping the edge of the trestle. 'Captain,' he growled. 'If this is a game… ?'

'It was Colonel Ascher who told you, wasn't it? Confirmed it.'

'Yes,' said Verhein, after a moment.

'You sent him back. To clean things up. To make sure you

had killed her.' The air felt thick to Reinhardt, so thick he could hardly breathe.

'He said she was dead,' Verhein said, finally. 'That I had killed her.'

'That you beat her to death.'

'*Yes!*'

'Marija Vukić was stabbed to death, sir.'

'*Enough.*'

Both Reinhardt and Verhein jerked around at the sound of the voice. Ascher was standing at the entrance, a pistol aimed at Reinhardt. Mamagedov stepped out from behind him, sidling over to stand behind Reinhardt, his stink filling Reinhardt's nose. The trestle table creaked as Verhein shifted his bulk off it. 'Is this true?' The pistol snapped around at him before slipping back onto Reinhardt. The angles of Ascher's face were pale, drawn tight, and the tendons of his hand were stretched taut around the pistol's grip.

'It's true, sir,' said Reinhardt, locking eyes with the colonel. 'Marija Vukić liked to film herself with her lovers. There's a film of you and her. It shows you beating her, but not killing her. The colonel has been searching for it ever since he found out about it.'

'Clemens, is this true?'

Ascher looked back at the general, and Reinhardt could see the stress he was under. Verhein's influence was strong; the words were damming up in the colonel's mouth, but he somehow swallowed them back, his chin butting forward.

'The colonel has been working with a major in the Feldgendarmerie to find this film. They've been following me. Getting in my way. And last night they killed a fellow officer to get information about what I am doing.'

'Captain,' grated Ascher, shaking his head. 'You know nothing of what you are saying.'

'I know what you did, though,' countered Reinhardt. 'You thought you were just covering up for the general, but you ended up doing more than that. Vukić was a risk to him, and to you. She knew things that would ruin him and you. Guilt by association. It's a common enough theme in this Reich of ours. For someone like you who has hitched his wagon to someone like the general, it can be fatal.'

'Clemens,' hissed Verhein, taking a step forward. He stopped as a soldier appeared at the door. Ascher hid the pistol against his chest, but the soldier must have picked up on something of the atmosphere in the room, as he hesitated.

'Sir, combat action report from Captain Tiel.'

'Later, Sergeant.' The soldier hesitated again, then left.

'Clemens…' Verhein said, again.

'General,' snapped Ascher, spearing the air with the pistol. He was left-handed, noted Reinhardt. 'Just sit quietly, and this will soon be over.' Verhein's eyes went wide, but he subsided, and Reinhardt was again reminded of husband and wife. How many couples played out roles like this, he wondered? The position of strength switching according to circumstance? 'She was going to destroy you, sir. I couldn't let that happen.'

'What happened? Did she run her mouth off? Say things that horrified you?' Reinhardt forced a sneer into his voice. 'Did you panic at the sight of her in her underwear?'

Ascher flushed. 'She was uncontrollable. Like she usually was,' he said, speaking to the general. 'She attacked me. I had to defend myself.'

'By stabbing her nearly twenty times?' Verhein made a small noise in his throat and turned away. Ascher flushed again. 'Vukić was working with an SD officer, Lieutenant Hendel,' continued Reinhardt, focusing on the general. 'They were supposed to confront you together about evidence he had that could damn you, but she could not wait.'

'Quiet, Captain,' snapped Ascher.

'Hendel had a file of evidence against you. That Feldgendarmerie major was looking for it, as well as the film. I'm fairly sure the colonel knows about the file –'

'*Quiet*, Captain.'

'File?' asked Verhein.

'– but neither of them really knows what's in it. Only I do.

They just want to use it against you. The film was bad enough, but they could handle that, just about. The file, though, was something else.'

Ascher snarled something at Mamagedov as Reinhardt was talking, and the Kalmyk slammed the butt of his MP 40 into Reinhardt's kidneys. The world went red, and Reinhardt collapsed to his hands and knees. He looked up at the ring of faces around him and gasped as he went back onto his haunches. From outside, the distant thunder of gunfire rolled down over the clearing.

'The thing I couldn't figure, Colonel, is what Becker had on you. He had to have something. What was it? Dirt from the past?' He managed to duck his head just in time, taking Mamagedov's swipe across the back of his neck instead of across the ear. The blow still floored him, though.

'I'm guessing it's the knife. Stolić's knife.' Ascher's mouth went firm. 'You killed her with Stolić's knife.' Mamagedov kicked him in the thigh. 'You took it from him when he caused all that trouble in the bar. Then put it back in his room when you'd finished with it.' Mamagedov kicked him again, then stamped on his calf. 'Did Becker suggest you pin it on him? Or did you think that one up yourself?'

'Clemens, what is going on?' breathed Verhein. 'What is this about a file? A knife?'

'General, it's under control. You have nothing to worry about.'

'Oh I doubt that,' muttered Reinhardt from the floor. Mamagedov's kick flopped him onto his stomach, where he curled slowly into a ball. 'It's blackmail, sir,' wheezed Reinhardt. He raised an arm to fend off another kick and took the blow on the biceps. It knocked him over again. 'Vukić was going to blackmail you with what Hendel had. Ascher was blackmailing you with thinking you'd killed Vukić. Becker was blackmailing Ascher over the cover-up. But the file trumps everything.' Mamagedov's boot thudded into his back, and pain flared along his ribs. The Kalmyk had a kick like a mule, and this was the second beating he had taken in the last hour or so. He did not know how much more he could take, not this close to the end. He made himself small, raising a hand he did not have to force to shake. '*Please*. Make him stop.'

'Mamagedov, enough,' whispered Verhein, but it was at Ascher that Mamagedov looked for direction, and only after a moment did the colonel nod. The Kalmyk stood back, his heavy fists at his sides and his flat, round face blank. Reinhardt put one hand in the small of his back, wincing, and carefully as he could, drew his baton out, letting it lie up the inside of his palm and into his sleeve.

'Stand him up,' said Ascher.

Mamagedov hauled Reinhardt to his feet and kept him steady with a hand in his collar. His body ached from the blows, but he managed to look at Verhein. 'There is a file on you, which Major Becker is after, and as he and Colonel Ascher have been working together, I see no reason to doubt that he,' he said, jerking his thumb at Ascher, 'is after it too. It's his ticket out of here.'

'And here I was thinking you were about to start making sense,' erupted Ascher, furiously. He jerked his head at Mamagedov, and the Kalmyk rammed his boot into the back of Reinhardt's knee. It was the old injury, and there was an agonising wrench as it seemed to tear, and Reinhardt dropped with a cry. 'I've had enough of this. Mamagedov, go and find Geiger and Ullrich and see if they're finished.' The Kalmyk grunted and turned for the door. 'I've had them preparing the ground for you, so to speak. Just in case things turned out... well, turned out the way they have.'

'Just tell me one thing, Colonel,' said Reinhardt, tamping down on the pain and desperation he felt. 'What was it between you and Becker?'

Ascher chewed his lower lip, glancing at Verhein. 'He was there when I brought the knife back. He was putting Stolić to bed. He agreed to cover things up, help out, in return for... unspecified favours that he would call in when it suited him.'

'So he caught you with the knife. There was nothing more? Nothing to do with an altar boy in Zagreb… ? Or… one in Munich, in 1937?' Ascher paled, and his eyes narrowed, and he shook his head, but from the surreptitious swallow he made, and the slight twitch from Verhein, somehow Reinhardt knew he was not far from something. He could not help but smile at Ascher. 'You were had. Becker had you over a barrel.'

42

Ascher flushed, but never responded. The light from the
door blacked out as Mamagedov walked backwards
into the room. There was a blur of movement, the thud
of a blow landing; Mamagedov staggered, one hand held to his
head. Claussen slid quickly inside, shutting the door and sliding
along the wall, covering the room with an MP 40. Seeing his
chance, Reinhardt flicked the baton out and slashed it into the
side of Mamagedov's knee, then back across the other. He fell
to one side and, lunging forward, Reinhardt whipped the
baton's tip across Mamagedov's shins, seeing his broad face
dimple up as he hissed with pain.

'*Stop it!*' barked Ascher, his pistol aimed at Reinhardt but his
eyes fixed on Claussen. '*You*. What do you think you're *doing*?'

Claussen's eyes ran hard around the room. 'If he's your man
down there, sir, you tell him to keep still, now.'

'Damn your impudence, man,' snarled the colonel.

Claussen glanced at Reinhardt. 'You all right, sir?' Reinhardt
nodded, then struggled to rise to one knee, then to his feet.
'Let's just all of us relax, shall we?' murmured Claussen. 'You
especially, big man,' he said, nudging Mamagedov's head with
his boot.

'Mamagedov, keep still,' ordered Ascher. 'You. Drop that
stick.'

There was a tense silence in the room. Faintly, now, came the
sound of fighting from somewhere on the hill. The three of

them stared at each other, Reinhardt at Ascher, Ascher at Claussen, and Claussen back at the colonel. Someone cleared his throat, and they all jumped. 'Will someone please tell me what the hell is going on?' demanded Verhein. The general seemed frozen to the spot. Whatever authority he normally exercised, he had none here.

'What's going on, General, is you've been betrayed by your chief of staff, here –'

'That's a bloody lie!'

'– and you're a marked man. You're in a bad situation. You look good for Vukić's murder, even though you didn't do it. He did it,' he said, pointing at Ascher.

'I told you, I did it for you,' said Ascher, his eyes flashing at the general.

'Then he killed Hendel...'

'That was Mamagedov,' blurted Ascher. Mamagedov shifted where he lay, his flat gaze fastening on the colonel.

'... and then you wept and prayed on your knees in a church,' finished Reinhardt, looking at the colonel. 'You prayed for forgiveness for what you'd done.' He held Ascher's gaze, looking past the foreshortened barrel of the pistol, seeing him flush and glance at the general.

'It was for you, sir. You deserve better. You deserve better than this... this *shithole!*'

'Sir, someone in Berlin wants your head,' said Reinhardt, 'and it doesn't matter to him whether you stuck the knife in Vukić or not. Hendel was working for him and had been following you since Russia. This someone's been watching you, General. Since Chenecourt, July 1940.' Verhein sucked in a sharp breath. Ascher's eyes flicked between them, and he knew he was missing something. 'There's an SD Standartenführer called Varnhorst who has had it in for you ever since that day in France. You know the one. He thinks he's found a pattern in your life. One involving –'

'Yes, Captain,' interrupted Verhein. His face was very white, the line of his jaw etched sharp. From outside came a fresh burst of firing, seemingly closer, the dull thump of explosions and the roll of machine guns.

There was movement outside the door, the squawk of the radio, the light sliced as men moved around outside. The same sergeant knocked at the door. '*Out!* And stay out!' Ascher shouted over his shoulder. The soldier paused, then left. The colonel kicked the door shut and turned back to face them. 'What?' he demanded. '*What?!* Tell me.'

'You've been backing the wrong horse, Colonel,' said Reinhardt. He took a deep breath. He had to end this. He had to break this link between the two of them. The general had not moved, and maybe, thought Reinhardt, he had miscalculated by mentioning that French village. Maybe Verhein now saw him as someone to be got rid of as well. 'This man you admire and loathe equally, this man you have protected despite himself – despite yourself – is not who you think he is.' He paused, as Verhein's eyes had come up, his head as well, his whole bearlike frame straightening.

'That file is the proof, all the proof that could be found…' He paused. There was a pleading in Verhein's eyes, a dumb supplication like that of an animal caught in an agony it could not conceive of ending and was thus eternal. Reinhardt could not imagine what it was like for a man like him. A warrior, the son of one people forced to partake in the butchery of another. A man who gloried, it seemed, in the martial arts, and who ended up flailing against the forces that made him what he was, trying to find a way out, enacting what small acts of rebellion he could. He took a deep breath. 'All the proof that could be found that General Paul Verhein is a member of the German resistance. Committed to the overthrow of the Führer and the Reich.' The words felt like acid as they twisted across his tongue. Lies, but leavened with just enough of the truth to hide it. Just words, but enough to galvanise someone into action, to break the back of this confrontation and end it.

'The *what?*' exclaimed Ascher. On the floor, Mamagedov had gone very still, rising slowly up on one elbow.

'The resistance,' repeated Reinhardt, staring straight at Verhein. He saw the light in the general's eyes change, the animal patience fading away, replaced with something more calculating.

'General. *General!*' Verhein's head swung slowly to Ascher. 'Is this true? It can't be true?'

'It's true,' said Reinhardt. The atmosphere in the room was charged, as it sometimes was in a police cell during an interrogation, just before the suspect broke. Unconsciously, he straightened, ignoring the pain in his knee and back. He focused on Ascher, his tone turning resonant, commanding. 'What better way to disguise his activities than as a brilliant commander? What better way to worm his way into higher confidences than bringing his tactical prowess to the strategic level?' He put a lash in his voice, taking a small step towards Ascher. The man was once a chaplain. A man of the book. Old Testament, surely. 'It so nearly worked. And you would have helped him. In covering for him, you would have allowed such a snake as him into the bosom of our people. Such a sin that would have been, Colonel.'

'No…' whispered Ascher.

'They will think you knew. Both of you,' Reinhardt said, bringing Mamagedov into it too. The Kalmyk glared up at him from the floor.

'No,' Ascher whispered again, shaking his head.

'You think the Gestapo will believe that when they start pulling your fingernails out?' sneered Reinhardt. 'Kick in the doors of your family? Put Mamagedov up against a wall? Or hand him back to the Reds?'

'*NO!*' roared Mamagedov. He exploded suddenly into action. He twisted and spun on his backside, his feet slicing into Claussen's ankles. The sergeant fell backwards, and Mamagedov flung himself off the floor at him. The two men crashed together, feet thumping and scrabbling for purchase. Mamagedov clawed his hands across Claussen's face, fingers hooked. With the MP 40 caught between them, Claussen tossed his head from side to side, keeping his eyes away from Mamagedov's fingers. His own fists bunched knuckle-white around Mamagedov's ears, thumbs digging for his eyes. Mamagedov bellowed like a bull, butting his head forward into Claussen's face, twisting, ramming, dropping his hands and pounding his fists into the sergeant's ribs.

The pistol wavered in Ascher's hand, then turned towards the two struggling men. Reinhardt lunged through the pain of his knee and grabbed Ascher's gun hand, punching him on the jaw as hard as he could. The colonel careened backwards, stumbling and slipping into a heap in the corner. Turning, Reinhardt scooped up the baton, and whipped it at Mamagedov. The ball at the end of the baton took him in the back of the head. There was a sound like an egg cracking, and the Kalmyk sagged over Claussen.

A bullet splintered the wall by Reinhardt's head as Mamagedov slithered heavily to the floor. Ascher's second shot took Claussen high in the arm, knocking him sideways. He hissed in pain, his hand closing over the wound, blood welling between his fingers.

Urgent voices came from outside, and the wood rattled as someone knocked at the door. 'General? *General?!*'

Ascher motioned at Verhein to say something. 'It's fine,' Verhein called out, eyes on the colonel. 'Everything's under control. I'll be out in a minute.'

Ascher pushed himself up and took an unsteady step out of the corner. He looked at Verhein, drawing in a deep breath as if deciding something. 'He's right, you know. I want a way out of this. I deserve better after all the… the *mess* I've cleaned up. Always us volunteering. Always me organising. Never knowing if it'll be the last time. Well, I've had it. The crap you leave behind you. The drinking. The whoring. The fighting. The way you trample the rules. "Do what I *tell* you, not what I *do*"? And then coming to me. To sleep it off. To make things right. To ask for my help. To *confess* it? "Father Superior",' he sneered. 'You don't know the *fucking* half of it.'

Verhein shook his head, his gaze on the floor. 'Clemens…'

'You're just like her. You think the world revolves around you. You sent me back to her. To *her*. And I find her alive, when you said she was dead, and you *know* that all she had for me was scorn, and she was *screaming* at me that you were finished, that I was finished, and I had that knife, and I was going to make sure Stolić took the blame if anyone had to, so I stabbed her, and she fought me and I stabbed her again. And again.'

'Clemens…'

'I did what you should have done. I made sure of it.'

'Clemens, I.…'

'*NO!*' The pistol was now very much aimed at Verhein, and Ascher's eyes slavered like a zealot's. 'You think harsh words at night fade with the morning. One of your stock phrases, right? *Right?* And she was the same. All smiles one minute, and scorn the next. Well, that doesn't work. Not with me. Maybe with those sheep outside you call men, but not with me. I remember it all. All those offhand remarks. The backhanded compliments. The insults. All of it.'

Verhein looked bewildered, a bear brought to bay. He shook his head, the light passing over his white hair, and he still could not seem to meet Ascher's eyes. 'Clemens, what are you saying?'

'Either you take him away,' Reinhardt guessed, 'or he makes his own way out. That was the plan.' Ascher's eyes bored into his. 'But now I've ruined it. The hold he would have had over you is gone. You didn't kill her, General. He did.'

'Bastard,' whispered Ascher. He was looking at Reinhardt as he said it, but it was meant as much for Verhein.

The general stirred himself for the first time in what seemed a long while. He took a step towards Ascher. 'Clemens, we are who we are. I don't –'

'*NO!* I can't *take* it anymore,' Ascher screamed. 'I can't take it.' His face seemed to collapse inward on itself as the tears began to flow, and the pistol wobbled in his hand.

'Fine,' cooed Verhein. He took the final step, reaching out and putting his hand gently on the pistol. Ascher tried to pull back, but it was too late. Ascher's face creased in pain as his fist was twisted back. Verhein's other arm went around his neck, and he pulled him in close. The colonel bucked and shook, but his efforts availed him nothing against Verhein's strength. 'Shhh,' murmured Verhein, lowering his lips to the top of Ascher's head. Ascher gargled, went rigid in his panic. 'It's all over. It's finished.' His arm curled up under Ascher's chin and wrenched it back and around. Ascher's hoarse scream was cut off as his neck snapped and he collapsed bonelessly to the floor. Verhein stepped back with his arms raised out to the side, like a stage magician with his act. He stared at the body, and then his eyes searched the room, fastening on Reinhardt. They were like ice, and Reinhardt saw his death in them.

'I never could abide a man who weeps.' Verhein blinked once, twice, and the ice was gone.

43

Claussen let out a long sigh and slumped down the wall. His face was tight and pale as he gripped his arm. Verhein moved across the room to kneel next to him. 'Let me see that, soldier.' He peeled Claussen's fingers away from his wound, glancing at Reinhardt as he did. 'Thank you.'

'For what?'

Verhein unfolded the blade of a small pocketknife and began to hack away at Claussen's sleeve. 'For not revealing everything.' He pulled the sleeve down and over the wound, a puckered and bruised little hole that welled sluggishly with blood. He lifted Claussen's arm, peering underneath, and twisted his mouth. 'No exit wound, Sergeant. You're just going to have to grin and bear it.' There was more clatter from outside, firing, and the *whump whump* of mortars opening up. Verhein leaned over and pulled a field dressing from its pouch on Mamagedov's belt and began strapping it around Claussen's arm.

'I never would have,' said Reinhardt, as he applied pressure to the wound while Verhein strapped it up. 'A man's faith is his own.'

'And some men cannot escape the faith they are born into,' replied Verhein, eyes on the dressing. He tied it off and sat back. 'There! A four-star dressing if ever there was one.'

'Thank you, sir,' managed Claussen.

'Sit tight, Sergeant. You too, Captain.' He stepped outside into the increasing din. Reinhardt lit Atikahs for himself and

Claussen, then shuffled across the room, suddenly and overwhelmingly exhausted, all the aches and pains of the day clamouring for his attention. His knee, his fingers, his face. He ignored them as best he could, took a drink of water from a canteen on the table, and took the Williamson out. He held it gently between the fingers of both his hands, the inscription fading in and out as he turned it against the light. He put it away, noting again the state of his uniform. His fingers picked at the eagle's stitching, pulling away a few loose threads that he twitched to the floor, then turned and leaned back against the table.

'Well,' said Claussen, looking up at him from the floor, face shifting slightly behind a cloud of exhaled smoke. 'Looks like you did it.'

Reinhardt nodded. 'Wouldn't have been able to without you, Sergeant,' he said, toasting him with the canteen. He limped back across the room and handed it to Claussen, then went back to the window. He peered out, squinting around the smoke that spiralled up into his eyes. Smoke was rising to the west and Germans were falling back into the clearing. If the mortars were firing, it meant the Partisans had to be fairly close.

'What now, Captain?'

Reinhardt shook his head, still looking out the window, but before he could answer Verhein came back in, a sheaf of papers in one hand. Reinhardt shot a look at Claussen, seeing the sergeant staring fixedly back at him.

'I don't have much time, Captain,' Verhein said, coming over to him. He laid the papers on the table, looking out the window at a group of soldiers running over to the woods. 'How do we end this?'

'You didn't kill her, sir.'

'No.'

'You didn't order her death?'

'No.'

'Then my investigation is over, sir.'

Verhein looked steadily at him. 'And the rest of it… ?'

'I have no control over that file, sir. I found a copy of a case against you during my investigation. I won't be able to make it go away.'

'No,' whispered the general.

'Sir, if I may ask? What actually happened, that night? What did she say to you to make you react so?'

'She taunted me into admitting… into admitting the truth of my origins.'

'Can't you say it, sir? "Jew"?'

Verhein gave a tight, tired smile. 'When you have hid part of what you are so long, Captain… It was only when she brought my sister into it that I snapped. You see, my parents were Jewish. They were Volga Germans, and they had both known persecution, in Russia. They moved to Neustadt, in West Prussia, and then when those lands were lost after Versailles, to Bremen. My mother died when I was very young. I was raised by my father, and he only told us on his deathbed. My father… he said he did all he could to spare us what they had known. He gave us Christian names. Had us baptised. Never took us near a rabbi or a synagogue. Never circumcised me. And when he told us, well, it was too late. The Nazis were in power, and we were trapped.

'All I ever wanted,' he sighed, 'was to be a soldier. To defend my country and my people. Who I thought were my people…' He trailed off. 'God help me, but I love my life. I love soldiering. I have fought two wars for my country, Captain. Bled for it. Been humiliated for it. Been as angry as anyone at the betrayals of 1918. Only now I find I am not one of them. Of us. Of you. Why is that?'

Reinhardt shook his head. 'I don't have an answer, sir.'

'Of course not. My father, though, he knew it would always come down to what others thought I was, not who I thought I was, or what I had done. When the Nazis came, I knew he was right. I found Künzer, paid him a fortune, and he altered our records back in Neustadt. God knows how he managed. But I knew, those times in Russia, in France, when I acted the way I did, I was attracting attention to myself. But I could not help it. Can you understand?' he asked, looking at Reinhardt. 'I was raised to be "normal". To be Jewish was to be weak. To risk persecution. But when I saw what was happening, when I saw what the army – my army – was willing to overlook, and then to do...'

His eyes were far away. 'I could not look away. So I did what I could, when I could. I comforted myself that I was resisting, in my own way. But I was scared. And so *angry* at the way they just seemed to let themselves go. Never lifting a finger to defend themselves. I've seen columns of Jews walking to their deaths, and only a rifleman to escort them. What kind of people can do that? And what kind of person am I to turn away from it?' The agony in his voice was raw. 'Did the file say how they discovered my orig – that I am a Jew?'

'Künzer.' Verhein nodded his head, slowly. 'He was arrested and under interrogation mentioned you and so came to the attention of Varnhorst. He did his job well, though. Whatever Künzer did, they couldn't disprove it.'

'I thought that might be it. My sister wrote she had been questioned about the parish records...' He cocked his head at a new burst of firing, then looked at Reinhardt. 'My sister is all I have. I will do anything to protect her. The resistance knows that. I told them if they could guarantee her safety I would work with them.' He paused, then began to buckle on his equipment. 'But they couldn't. So I didn't. And now... they'll just use this. Put strings on me, make me dance like a puppet. Like Ascher would have. I don't see a way out, do you?'

'Sir?' replied Reinhardt.

'How do I make it through all this alive and unharmed? The truth will out. Those boys in Berlin won't give up, and if they get me, they get my sister. The resistance won't leave me alone. So what options do I have?'

Reinhardt shook his head, slowly. 'Not many, sir.'

'Not many,' repeated Verhein. 'I have one, though. I go out

on my own terms, in my own way. I go out as a soldier,' he said, the old Verhein beginning suddenly to seep into his words, his posture. 'And I make such a big bloody show of it they'll never see past it. They won't ever dare go after her. What do you think, eh?'

'I think it could work, sir.'

'Course it bloody well could. Because as well, I'm sick and bloody tired of hiding. I'm sick of living in the shadows and living a lie. Never knowing who might be watching and waiting. I'm sick at what my army has become, and I'm sick at the thought of this world we're creating. So I'm going to end it. My way.'

The sound of battle ratcheted up, and there was a different timbre to the gunfire now, a higher-pitched rattle of different ammunition. Verhein picked up his PPSh, checked the action, and – just for a moment – Reinhardt saw in the sideways glance he threw at them, and the way his hands shifted on the submachine gun, the temptation to do away with him and Claussen. What were they but problems to him? What easier way to solve two problems… ? He froze, went cold, even stiffened as if expecting a bullet, but the moment passed and Verhein hung the PPSh from his shoulder. 'What about you?'

'I'm in a bit of trouble, sir. I don't know if I can go back.'

'Always room for one more where I'm going, Captain.'

'Thank you, sir, but I don't think I'm quite ready to take your way.'

'Please yourself. In any case,' he said, indicating the sound of fighting outside, 'if that keeps up, you may not have to worry about making a choice.' He stood up straight, every inch the general, a boy's own hero, the Knight's Cross at his throat and the Blue Max proud on his chest. He looked at both of them. 'I suppose I ought to thank you, Captain. For bringing me to the point where I can't hide anymore.' Reinhardt's mouth worked, but nothing came out. Verhein held up his hand. 'No words. None needed. It's just the way things are.' He paused at the door. 'And you, Captain. Did you find what you were looking for?'

The question took Reinhardt by surprise. The day had swept him along, and he had not realised the full weight of what had happened to him. 'I don't know, to be honest, sir.' He glanced at Claussen, looking up at him. He thought of the two boys. 'I think I found a part of myself I thought I'd lost a long time ago.'

'I suppose that's all we can ask, in the end. Good luck to you, Captain.' He grinned devilishly, winked, and was gone.

Reinhardt limped after him to the door, looking out as Verhein stormed into a crowd of soldiers, pulling them after him like filings after a magnet. They spread out, charging up at the forest, gathering up those who had retreated out of it. A heavy machine gun on a half-track opened up, covering their charge. Fire from somewhere plucked at the line, men falling back and away. An explosion ripped through them, another, and there were few of them racing across the clearing through a haze of smoke and dust, Verhein's white hair shining at the forefront, and then they were gone into the trees.

Forms flickered and flashed in the tree line, the spark of gun flashes and the flare of explosions. Something hit the house, thudding into the wall and roof. Reinhardt backed into the room, scooping up Mamagedov's MP 40. 'We need to go, Sergeant.'

Claussen pushed himself up, shoving the hand of his wounded arm between two of the buttons on his tunic, hanging his MP 40 around his neck and holding it by its pistol grip. 'Where are we going to go, sir? Before, you sounded like you were looking at the end, but you just turned down a place at the general's side.'

'When we left Sarajevo, I didn't expect this to end anything other than badly. I thought the journey would be its own end. That nothing else after it mattered. I realise now I was wrong. Something's… changed. I have to go back.'

Claussen looked back at him levelly. 'Back to do what?'

Despite all they had been through, Reinhardt was not sure he could say it. He was not even sure himself what he was going to do, and it was only now that the implications of what had happened in that forest clearing, of the course he had set himself, were catching up. 'I can't… I can't pretend anymore, Sergeant. I can't pretend this is not my war, and just hope it passes me by.'

'What does that mean?'

'It means… I have a decision to make. And despite all we've been through – or maybe even because of it – the less you know about what I'm thinking, what I might be doing, the better.' Claussen's face twisted, and he made to speak, but Reinhardt held up a hand. 'Please, understand. It's not about trust. But if you know nothing, you can't say anything. If… you know…'

Claussen nodded, shifting the MP 40. 'Everyone talks.'

'Everyone talks.'

They paused at the door. 'Car's over there,' pointed Claussen, back across the clearing to where the track emerged from the forest. An explosion ripped through one of the mortar crews, strewing them about like skittles. A band of Partisans erupted from the forest, washing over the second mortar. More of them poured from the trees, men in uniforms of dun and brown, blanket rolls folded across their shoulders like Russians, flowing across the clearing.

Hopping and stumbling, Claussen and Reinhardt reached some cover behind a stack of chopped logs. They ducked their heads as the wood splintered from bullet strikes. A nearby grenade burst showered them with clods of earth. He fired a quick burst at the Partisans around the mortars, then crouched back down. 'Try to make for the trees by the car. Go. I'll cover you.'

Claussen surged up and ran, firing as he went, but with the MP 40 in one hand, most of the shots went wild and high. He reached cover, sliding down behind a big rock, and beckoned Reinhardt over. Firing a long burst himself, Reinhardt began his run, pushing himself through the tearing pain in his knee and flopping down next to the sergeant, his breath raw in his throat. *Don't stop*, he remembered. *Stop and you're dead.* 'Over to the car,' he panted.

'You first, this time.' Wincing, Claussen laid his wounded arm on top of his MP 40 and fired a long burst across the clearing. Stooping over, Reinhardt ran for the *kübelwagen*, crouching into cover next to it. Claussen made his run as Reinhardt opened up in turn, but dust kicked up around the sergeant's feet, there was a sudden burst of red, and he gave an agonised cry and fell. Spinning around, Reinhardt glimpsed dun-coloured shapes sliding through the trees behind him. He fired until the magazine clicked empty, then scuttled out and grabbed Claussen and pulled him into cover. The sergeant groaned as Reinhardt dragged him up against a tree, barely conscious, his legs in bloody tatters.

This had to be the end, Reinhardt realised, as he changed magazines, trying to look everywhere at once. The air was full of the stench and blast of war. Smoke gusted up around the clearing, explosions blooming orange that curled into black. '*Captain*,' whispered Claussen. He held a key out in a trembling hand.

Reinhardt grabbed it, then hauled Claussen over to the *kübelwagen*. Straining everything he had, he managed to get the sergeant into the passenger seat, where he collapsed in on himself, his body folding around the hard edges of the car. As Reinhardt limped around to the driver's side, a bullet clapped past his ears, then another. He saw a band of Partisans racing through the woods towards him. He leaned his elbows on the *kübelwagen*'s hood and fired. Bullets struck spurts of dust and blood high on one's shoulder; the others dropped into cover.

Reinhardt flung the MP 40 into the car and fumbled the key into the ignition. Hunched low, he floored the accelerator, spinning the *kübelwagen* in a tight circle and aiming it back down the track. There were stabs of flame and smoke from the forest, and the trees around him splintered and shattered as Partisans fired, bullets thudding metallically into the body of the *kübelwagen*.

An explosion in front of the car blinded him in a shower of dirt and earth. There was another one, right underneath, and the rear of the *kübelwagen* flared up into the air. It twisted around and crashed off the track with an eruption of splintered wood. Reinhardt felt a tremendous blow to his head as he was flung out across the hard ground. The car rolled onto its side, teetered as if undecided, then slumped onto its back. A wheel spun itself down, a length of ripped rubber flapping slower and slower on the car's chassis.

Groping blindly through the pain in his head, Reinhardt's hand closed around the Williamson and dragged it up to his mouth. Its metal shine dulled under the dusty heat of his breath, and from far away he remembered another place, hacked from the grudging earth.

Father, Father, it hurts.

Part Four

44

FRIDAY

Reinhardt's eyes fluttered open and he stared upward, confused by what he saw, until he realised it was the light shifting through the tracery of branches in the trees above him. His vision steadied and it all came back in a rush of memory, and with it the pain in his leg, and another in his head.

He was lying on a thick bed of grass, his knee heavily bandaged. Lifting his hand, he felt another around his head, lumped over his right ear, and he ached everywhere, his fingers throbbing heavily. Sounds began to filter in. He could hear an aircraft, somewhere, the sounds of men talking, and a steady murmur like the lap of water along its banks. Pushing himself up, he saw movement through the trees. Lines of men moving steadily through the dim light of the forest. Men dressed in uniforms from a half dozen armies, red-starred caps and blanket rolls, shouldered rifles. Partisans. Off to one side, a group of men knelt around something on the ground, their backs and shoulders all rounded and taut, and on the other side of him, he now saw, were more wounded, all Partisans, and the realisation began to sink in that he was a prisoner.

Reinhardt's eyes shifted upward as the noise of the aircraft suddenly increased. All around, the forest went still, the marching lines of Partisans melting into cover. There was a blur across the forest's canopy as the aircraft passed above. No one moved, and then came a ripping sound, like fabric tearing, as an artillery barrage tore overhead and somewhere, not so far away, came a long tremble of explosions. There was silence again, then a ripple of movement as the Partisans resumed their march.

One of the kneeling men stood up. He was wearing, of all things, what looked like a white sleeveless waistcoat, with thick coloured stripes around the deep V of its neck. He assumed a stern expression as he plucked a pipe from his mouth and spread his hands to either side.

'*Wiiiide*,' he said, and Reinhardt froze. The others laughed. Someone threw a pine cone. The man grinned, saw Reinhardt, and gestured at him with his pipe stem. The others straightened and looked around. One rose to his feet and walked over to him. He was a tall man, his face and arms deeply tanned, and his hair a wavy blond. He wore a khaki uniform with a major's insignia on the shoulders. The sleeves of his shirt were rolled up high past his elbows, and a big pistol with a lanyard in the butt was holstered on his left hip.

He was British.

He knelt on one knee next to Reinhardt, looking at him with clear hazel eyes. 'How are you feeling?'

Reinhardt swallowed against a thick, dry mouth and nodded. 'Thank you, I am well.'

The British officer nodded. 'Glad to hear it, although it's no thanks to me and my chaps.' His German was slow, quite heavily accented. 'Here's the doc that put you back together.' There was a rustle of grass, and Dr Begović knelt on Reinhardt's other side. 'Understand you two know each other?'

Reinhardt let out a long sigh, then smiled. It felt right to smile, but it felt heavy, as well, like another sign that whatever journey he had been on these past few days, it was over. 'We know each other. How are you, Doctor?'

'I'm well, Captain.' He smiled back. 'You have been out for the best part of a day. Your knee is quite bad. You won't be doing much with it for some time.'

'Doctor, I was with someone. A sergeant, who was wounded, but I don't see him.'

'Your sergeant is dead, Captain. Of his wounds.'

Reinhardt looked away, his mouth tight.

'Friend of yours, this sergeant?' asked the British officer. Reinhardt nodded. 'Sorry, we've not been properly introduced,' he continued, extending his hand. 'Major Brian Sanburne, Rifle Brigade.'

Reinhardt shook the proffered hand. 'Captain Gregor Reinhardt.'

He took Reinhardt's papers from a pocket. 'I know. Not often a captain of the Abwehr falls into our hands,' he said, with a twinkle in his eyes.

'Am I your prisoner, or theirs?' asked Reinhardt, motioning to Begović.

'Both, really,' said Sanburne. 'They found you, but they're not sure what to do with you.'

'There is some reluctance to take prisoners, as you might understand, Captain,' said Begović. Up here, in the mountains, he seemed subtly different to Reinhardt. Harder, more purposeful. Like a man in his element. 'Prisoners slow us down, and you have not exactly been particularly caring of those of us who have fallen into your hands.'

'Yes, well, no one's talking about abandoning you, or having you shot,' said Sanburne, wryly. 'At least not yet.'

'Captain, I personally am glad you are well, but your countrymen are making our lives very difficult. Major Sanburne has offered to take you off our hands for now, and that has been agreed to. I have many other duties to attend to, so…' He rose to his feet. 'I'll leave the two of you alone. Perhaps later, Captain.'

'Doctor, before you leave… Do you have news of that young man in Sarajevo?'

'Jelić? We have him.' Reinhardt felt a rush of relief. 'That was clever, using that drop-off to leave a message.'

'The days of the Shadow are over, then?' said Reinhardt, watching Begović carefully.

The doctor looked back at him, then grinned, a sparkle in his eyes. He nodded at Sanburne, then left, back to his wounded.

'So, Captain… we've a bit of time before we have to move on. I thought we'd have a chat? Something to drink? Tea?'

'Tea,' said Reinhardt.

'*Sarn't Major, two cups of that tea you made earlier, if you please,*' Sanburne called out in English. He turned back to Reinhardt. 'Been a bit of trouble getting the tea made. In the desert, we'd just pour petrol over a can of sand, and voilà, practically smokeless fire.'

'You were in North Africa?'

'Long-range desert group. Odds are we might almost have crossed paths a few times, eh?' Reinhardt took a tin mug of tea from a sergeant with the heavy features of a boxer. 'Cigarette?' asked the major, proffering a silver case. 'Turkish, here, or English…'

Reinhardt took a Woodbine, which Sanburne lit for him. 'What are you doing here, Major?' he asked, drawing the tobacco deep. He coughed, not used to such strong blends anymore.

'Liaison group. One of several.' Sanburne's eyes were steady on him as he lit his own cigarette. 'The Četniks are a dead loss. Not to mention practically German auxiliaries as well. We're putting our weight behind the Partisans. Official policy now.'

Reinhardt breathed out, nodded. 'We thought so.'

'You with that general?' Sanburne asked suddenly, mug held in two hands.

'What?'

'Begović told me you were after a general. One got himself killed yesterday. Chap by the name of Verhein. There was a devil of a fight, but his death threw your chaps off quite a bit and allowed a couple of Partisan brigades to break through. You had anything to do with that?'

'With the general?' Reinhardt nodded, thinking of Begović's bargain with him. *I help you, I help my people.* 'In a way, yes.'

'I'd like to hear about that a bit later. In the meantime…' He brushed a lock of hair off his forehead, and Reinhardt was struck by how, behind that tan, and the deep lines around his eyes, and his rank, the major was a young man. 'You've a decision to make.'

'Oh?' Reinhardt drew deeply on his cigarette.

'I'll be blunt, Captain. I'd like you to work for us.'

Reinhardt exhaled, narrowing his eyes around the smoke. 'What makes you think I'd do that?'

'Wild guess. A hunch. Something the good doctor might have let slip.'

'Such as?'

'Not being overly happy with your life.'

'It's a long way from not being happy with one's life to becoming a traitor.'

'Well, put it this way. It's us, or them,' he said, motioning to the Partisans. 'I can afford to be slowed down even less than them. I've a job to do that doesn't require me babysitting someone like you. So a yes gets you out to Alexandria, and a chance to make a difference in this war – I'm guessing a difference you've been wanting for quite some time – but a no sees you given back to them.'

Reinhardt was taken aback. 'That sounds less than gentlemanly, Major.'

Sanburne grinned, his eyes suddenly very hard. '"Gentlemanly",' he repeated. He stubbed his cigarette out on the ground. 'I have always wondered why the English and that epithet seem to go hand in hand. Put it this way, Captain, and forgive the bombast. We didn't build the biggest empire known to man by being gentlemen.'

'I see,' swallowed Reinhardt.

'And before you throw "blackmail" at me, it's not. If we weren't here, you'd be theirs anyway.'

Reinhardt was silent a long while, sipping from his tea. It was milky and sweet, the way the British seemed to like it. It felt good going down. 'There may be another way.' Sanburne raised his eyebrows. 'May I have a little time alone, Major? To think?'

Sanburne nodded. 'Not much, though. We'll be moving on come morning.' He took something else from his pocket. 'I think this is yours,' he said, handing over the little leather package Meissner had given him and holding up the Williamson. 'Must be a good story with this one. Perhaps you'll tell it to me, one day.' Reinhardt took it, a little too quickly, perhaps. Sanburne's eyes widened, but he said nothing.

'Thank you,' said Reinhardt.

'Until later, then.'

Reinhardt finished his cigarette and lay back, feeling light-headed. He thought about Claussen, about his steady presence from the very first minute of the case. There had been a sense of kinship there, towards the end. It did not seem right for Reinhardt to have reached something like an ending, only to have Claussen lost behind him.

He closed his eyes and must have slept, for he opened them with the light deeper. He managed to get himself to one knee, then to his feet. He wobbled as his knee throbbed in pain, putting out a hand to hold himself against a tree. A Partisan with a rifle stepped forward, snapped something. Reinhardt mimed walking with his fingers, gestured at the forest. Mollified, the Partisan quieted. Reinhardt took a tentative step, then another, his knee hurting but not unbearably so. He looked around, spotted where it seemed a little lighter, and pointed. The guard nodded.

He limped through the trees to where they thinned, the guard following quietly. A file of Partisans marched past, one of them still a boy with an oversized cap tilted back on his ears walking with a man who had to be his father. The boy talked quietly, excitedly; the father looked at Reinhardt as he went past, face broad and dark and his hands massive where they held the strap of his rifle.

Limping to just inside the tree line, Reinhardt saw that they were camped high on the side of a mountain, its flanks dropping away before him into a steep-sided bowl of a valley. It was late in the day, and far away to the west a milky sun was setting where the mountains lay knuckled across the bottom of the sky. The valley below was sunk in shadow, and he could see no sign of the Drina. He took off his jacket and sat down gingerly, flexing his fingers, back against a tree, and looked towards the setting sun, thinking, letting his mind drift where it would.

He remembered what he and Brauer had talked about all those months ago in Berlin. Had they burned away enough of themselves to survive this war that was not theirs? He knew now, as then, that he had not and that he never would. But he also knew now it *was* his war. It was just that he had been fighting it the wrong way. Head down, in the shadows, back bent, and every day a little more of himself sliding away to wherever the parts of yourself went when you lost them.

He remembered as well what he had told Begović at the safe house in Sarajevo – that the track of his life was a scar that hid what was and what might have been. Scars healed well if they healed quickly, he thought. Was this such a chance? To change the track of that scar, alter it, make it something different? Heal it? Cauterise it? What image was he looking for? The past was what it was, and what might have been, could have been – should have been – lay hidden, lost, obscured by its weight. The past could not be changed, but the future was different, and it was here, now. It always had been.

He thought of the people in his life whose opinion he might have sought. Meissner, Brauer, maybe even Freilinger, certainly Claussen. Dr Begović. His son, if he was alive. And Carolin, most especially. He unfolded her picture and held it in his hand, his thumb stroking that fall of her hair. Then he thought that all his life, he had waited on the good opinions of others and nearly always done what was expected of him, hoping it was the right thing. Often it was. Sometimes, it had not been. This time… this time, it felt right that there was no one to ask.

He shifted the tunic on his lap, his eyes switching back and forth between the eagle and swastika stitched onto the right breast, the Iron Cross on the left. Almost unconsciously, his fingers began to pick at the loose stitching along the eagle's wing again, working and worrying it. Something had happened to him these past few days. He had found himself again, and found a new side to men he thought he had known well. He had found respect in the ranks of his enemy, and danger from his own side. He had become aware of another way of fighting this war, the presence of a fork in the track of his life, and in that hut in the forest he had taken the first steps down that different path.

He knew now he had never lacked for choices; it was decisions that were missing. So often, he had been passive in the face of what needed to be done. Running that confrontation in the forest over and over in his mind, pinned to the certainty in Goran's eyes, he was afraid he still was. That he had only really decided when faced with the inevitable. It felt right, what he had decided, what he felt, but he could not help but ask himself – his old self-doubt surfacing – how genuine a feeling, a decision, was it?

He tried to imagine Alexandria, a place away from this war, of safety, and could not. All he could think about was Meissner, and Freilinger, and the others like them who fought a war of shadows. He thought of his functions in Sarajevo, the war of cogs and wheels and information and what a man might do within that system that could not be done from outside it.

His watch had stopped, and he wound it up slowly, thinking. It had come to him on his last day as a fighting man in the first war. Was it just chance, then, fortuitous circumstance, that it should come to him again on the last day of this war that he would choose not to keep on the way he had been going? The second hand slid into motion as he wound it, flicking around its little dial as if it, like him, sought a new north. One day, this war would be over, and there would be a reckoning. Every man would have to stand face to face with judgment of some kind, and often the hardest judgment came from the face you saw reflected back at you every day. A face you saw reflected everywhere, in mirrors and windows, in metal and water, sharp-edged or sunken, chopped or blurred. The splintered facets of yourself that stared back at you from a thousand pairs of eyes. A face you saw reflected within you.

The light slid from the sky, stars scattering themselves in its wake. There were no mirrors here, only the weight of mountain and sky and the image one held of oneself within. Somewhere behind him in the trees, a man began to sing. Others joined him in a refrain, soft clapping keeping time. The air smelled of wood smoke, and he breathed it in without flinching, without the image of those two boys grating at him. He paused, reflected on that, and then, face to face with the mountains, he made his decision. He smoothed down the stitching, stood and shrugged back into his jacket, medals and metal clinking dully, and limped back up into the trees.

Historical Note

Following the German conquest of the Kingdom of Yugoslavia in April 1941, Bosnia was ceded to their allies in the Independent State of Croatia (the NDH), ruled by Ante Pavelić's fascist Ustaše. Croatian rule in Bosnia was incompetent in the extreme but made infinitely worse by the Ustaše's widespread persecution and mass killings, often of astonishing savagery, of Serbs and Jews.

Such was the Ustaše's brutality that many Serbs took up arms with the Četniks, a Serbian nationalist and royalist resistance movement that conducted guerrilla warfare against the Axis occupying forces in those parts of Bosnia it regarded as Serb, but which itself committed numerous atrocities, mostly against Bosnian Muslim civilians. Muslims tried to navigate their own path, which, depending on context, involved a mixture of collaboration, resistance, or passive acceptance of their situation. Bosnia's Jews and Gypsies were all but exterminated.

Then, starting in 1941, Yugoslav Communists under the leadership of Josip Broz Tito organised their own multiethnic resistance, the Partisans, which fought with increasing effectiveness against both Axis and Četnik forces. So effective, in fact, that the Germans and Četniks began to make common cause against them. The result was a kaleidoscope of shifting front lines as Germans, Italians, Croatians, Ustaše, and Četniks fought the Partisans, often with almost medieval barbarity.

Unlike the exclusive and ultranationalist positions offered by the Ustaše and the Četniks, the Partisans offered one of a multiethnic postwar Yugoslavia united under Communism. By 1943, it was clear to the Allies that the Četniks were a lost cause, virtual German auxiliaries, and their support swung fully behind the Partisans with the dispatch of liaison officers and advisors and increasing supplies of munitions.

————

The very real rivalries that bedevilled interwar Yugoslavia only erupted into open conflict following the Axis invasion. Axis forces were not passive observers to the playing out of 'ancient Balkan hatreds' but were instead active participants. Bosnia was divided into German and Italian zones of influence, and the NDH's authority was severely limited where their interests were concerned. These interests were primarily economic, and their occupation policy was basically one of maximising the economic contribution of Yugoslavia to the Axis war effort at the least cost and by whatever means necessary. Its corollary was a total disregard for the needs and rights of the local population.

The Germans aided the Ustaše and, to a lesser extent, the Četniks, turning a blind eye to the extremes of their allies, or else were actively complicit. Rare were the voices raised in protest, and when they were it was invariably to protest the damage Ustaše extremes caused to German operations or the occupation policy, rather than any appeal to humanity. In addition to the support it gave its allies, the German Army itself committed widespread and numerous atrocities. These included mass shootings of civilians as reprisals and the summary execution of Partisan prisoners of war including, most notoriously, the execution of some two thousand wounded Partisans and medical personnel at the end of Operation Schwarz.

————

The German Army in World War II was, in many ways, a heterogeneous and polyglot formation. The soldiers of many nations fought for it, with it, and under it, and it was itself divided between regular army units and those belonging to the SS. In Bosnia, the Croatian Army was a virtual auxiliary formation, almost devoid of independence, although the Ustaše militias maintained a degree of operational autonomy.

————

There never was a 121st Jäger Division, nor did General Paul Verhein exist, although there were many men like him – half Jewish, referred to by the Nazis as *mischling* – who fought for the Germans and who only can really know the reasons why they did what they did. Operation Schwarz – what the Partisans called the Fifth Enemy Offensive or the Battle of Mount Sutješka – failed in its objective of destroying the Partisans, although it inflicted grievous casualties on them. After almost a month of fighting, the Partisans managed to break the German encirclement of their position, although they had to leave behind nearly all their wounded, who were all executed. The Partisans' breakout is commemorated by a massive sculpture and reliefs at the memorial complex in Tjentište, in southern Bosnia-Herzegovina, an area of spectacular natural beauty, but now sadly abandoned and run-down since the war in the 1990s.

————

This book is a work of fiction, albeit one set in a world which once existed. I have tried to be as accurate as I can to the places and events of those times. Any mistakes are just those, and the sole fault of the author, or have been made deliberately for the needs of the story.

In writing this, I am indebted to four works in particular:

Sarajevo: A Biography, by Robert Donia (Ann Arbor: University of Michigan Press, 2006).

Sarajevo, 1941–1945, Muslims, Christians and Jews in Hitler's Europe, by Emily Greble (Ithaca, NY: Cornell University Press, 2011).

Svjetlost Europe u Bosni I Herzegovini, by Ismet Huseinović and

Dzemaludin Babić (Sarajevo: Buybook, 2004).

War and Revolution in Yugoslavia, 1941–1945: Occupation and Collaboration, by Jozo Tomasević (Palo Alto, CA: Stanford University Press, 2002).

Reinhardt has come to the end of one part of his journey, but his journey is not yet done. Actions have consequences, and consequences must be endured. Reinhardt will march again.

Cast of Characters

IN THE GERMAN ARMY IN SARAJEVO

IN MILITARY INTELLIGENCE, THE ABWEHR

Captain Gregor Sebastian Reinhardt: counterintelligence officer, a former detective in the Berlin Kriminalpolizei (Kripo)

Major Ulrich Freilinger: chief of the Abwehr in Sarajevo

Lieutenant Stefan Hendel: internal army security

Sergeant Martin Claussen: a former policeman in Dusseldorf

Kruger, Maier, Vogts, Weninger: Abwehr officers

IN THE MILITARY POLICE, THE FELDGENDARMERIE

Major Becker: second in command of the garrison's Feldgendarmerie detachment, and a former Kripo detective

Captain Kessler: in charge of Feldgendarmerie traffic control

IN THE SARAJEVO GARRISON

Standartenführer Mladen Stolić: 7th SS Prinz Eugen

Lieutenant Colonel Johannes Lehmann: 1st Panzer divisional intelligence

Eichel, Faber, Kappel, Forster: colonels in the army

Captain Hans Thallberg: 118th Jäger Division, and officer in the Secret Field Police (Geheime Feldpolizei)

Captain Paul Oster: army medical corps

Lieutenant Peter Krause: movement supply officer, a friend of
  Hendel's

Tomas and Pieter: panzer officers

Corporal Jürgen Beike: assistant to Captain Thallberg

Corporal Gerd Hueber: transportation corps, a Serbo-Croat
  translator

ON THE FRONTLINES

General Paul Verhein: commanding 121st Jäger, on Mount
  Sutjeska

Colonel Clemens Ascher: his chief of staff

Gärtner, Jahn, Nadolski, and Oelker: Verhein's senior officers

Tiel, Demmler, and Ubben: captains in the 121st

Mamagedov: Verhein's driver, a Kalmyk, from the Caucasus

**Generals Eglseer, Grabenhofen, Kübler, Le Suire, Neidholt,
  Phleps, von Grabenhofen, and von Oberkamp**: officers
  commanding divisions in Bosnia.

IN THE CITY: ITS CITIZENRY AND POLICE FORCE

Marija Vukić: a journalist and filmmaker, an Ustaša

Vjeko Vukić: her father, a senior Ustaša, killed in the war

Suzana Vukić: her mother

Chief Inspector Putković: of the Sarajevo police, an Ustaša

Inspector Andro Padelin: of the Sarajevo police, an Ustaša,
  ordered to partner with Reinhardt

Dr Muamer Begović: a medical doctor, a consultant with the
  police

Bunda: of the Sarajevo police, an officer of imposing size

Goran, Karlo, Simo: men of the city

Colonel Tihomir Grbić: of the Domobranstvo, a decorated
  veteran soldier

Niko Ljubčić: an Ustaša officer in the Black Legion

Frau Hofler: an elderly Austrian, Marija's neighbour
Duško Jelić: Marija's sound engineer
Branko Tomić: Marija's cameraman, her oldest collaborator and friend of her father
Archbishop Šarić: a committed Ustaša
Father Petar: a priest at the church of St Joseph's
Alfred Ewald: receptionist at the Austria Hotel

AT THE RAGUSA CLUB

Robert Mavrić: the manager
Dietmar Stern: maître d'
Dragan: the barman
Anna and Florica: singers
Zoran Zigić: a waiter
Milan Topalović: Zoran's uncle, a Communist and suspected Partisan

ELSEWHERE AND ELSEWHEN...

Friedrich: Reinhardt's son, lost with the German Sixth Army at Stalingrad
Rudolf Brauer: Reinhardt's former partner in the Kripo and his oldest and closest friend
Colonel Tomas Meissner: Reinhardt's mentor, and regimental commander during WWI
Major Brian Sanburne: Rifle Brigade, a British liaison officer
Carolin: Reinhardt's wife, died of illness in 1938

Also available from No Exit Press...

The Pale House

A GREGOR REINHARDT NOVEL

As the Nazi war machine is pushed back across Europe, defeat has become inevitable. But there are those who seek to continue the fight beyond the battlefield.

German intelligence officer Captain Gregor Reinhardt has just been reassigned to the *Feldjaegerkorps* – a new branch of the military police with far-reaching powers. His position separates him from the friends and allies he has made in the last two years, including a circle of fellow dissenting Germans who formed a rough resistance cell against the Nazis. And he needs them now more than ever.

While retreating through Yugoslavia with the rest of the army, Reinhardt witnesses a massacre of civilians by the dreaded *Ustaše* – only to discover there is more to the incident than anyone believes. When five mutilated bodies turn up, Reinhardt knows the stakes are growing more important – and more dangerous.

As his investigation begins to draw the attention of those in power, Reinhardt's friends and associates are made to suffer. But as he desperately tries to uncover the truth, his own past with the *Ustaše* threatens his efforts. Because when it comes to death and betrayal, some people have long memories. And they remember Reinhardt all too well.

And now, Reinhardt will have to fight them once more.

978-1-84344-551-7 £8.99

About Us

In addition to No Exit Press, Oldcastle Books has a number of other imprints, including Pulp! The Classics, Kamera Books, Creative Essentials, Pocket Essentials and High Stakes Publishing > oldcastlebooks.co.uk

For more information about Crime Books go to > crimetime.co.uk

Check out the kamera film salon for independent, arthouse and world cinema > kamera.co.uk

For more information, media enquiries and review copies please contact
Harriet > harriet@oldcastlebooks.com